MARIGOLD

MARIGOLD

I have met monsters in stories,
but none as gentle as the ones inside me.

HEENA SINGHAL

First published by
Papertowns Publishers
72, Vishwanath Dham Colony,
Niwaru Road, Jhotwara,
Jaipur, 302012

Marigold

10 9 8 7 6 5 4 3 2 1

ISBN Print Book - 978-93-6185-844-4

Printed in India

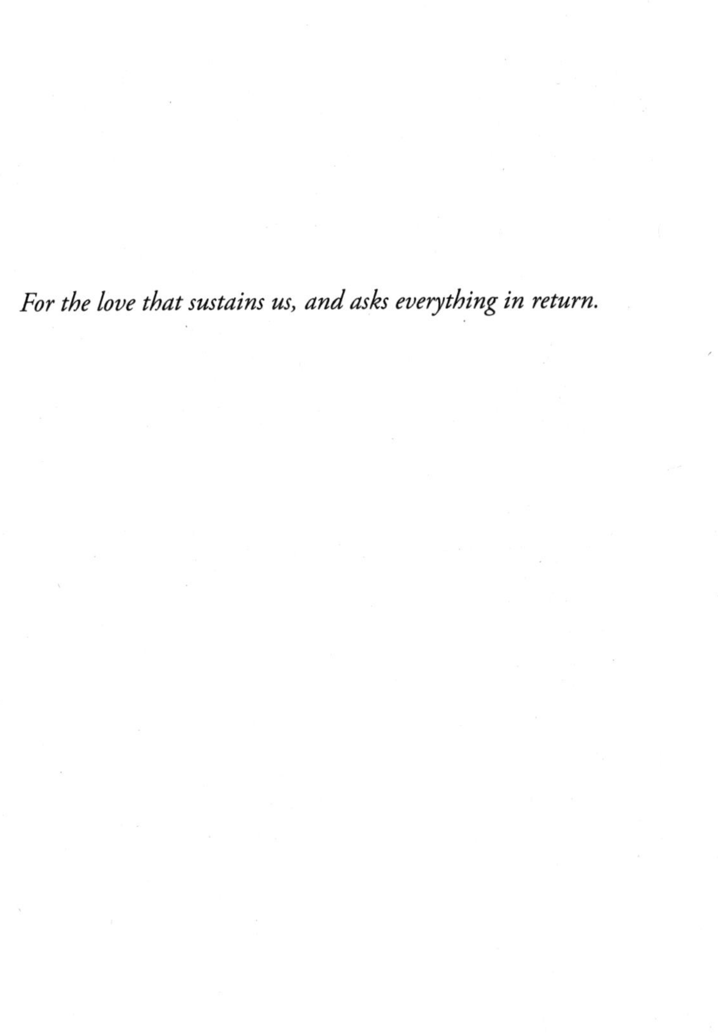

For the love that sustains us, and asks everything in return.

Preface

Some parts of us are formed before we ever learn how to name them. They stay with us quietly, shaping the way we love, the way we withdraw, and the way we move through the world. This book grows out of those early, unnamed places.

Parenthood sits at the heart of this story, but it does not belong only to parents. It belongs to anyone who has been a child—which is to say, all of us. I return often to one unsettling truth: the child is the father of the adult. What we become does not arrive suddenly with maturity; it is carried forward, shaped by who we were when we were small. Our fears, our tenderness, our silences, our longings—many of them were learned in rooms we barely remember.

When I began working on *Marigold*, I was circling a simple, frightening thought: *If you don't heal your traumas, they raise your children.* Over time, I understood that this sentence reaches beyond parenthood and into inheritance itself. We live with what was handed to us—sometimes gently, sometimes carelessly—and much of adulthood is an attempt to make sense of it. Once this awareness enters us, innocence is altered. We become more careful, sometimes more afraid, and often more uncertain. I still wonder if things were easier when we knew less—before love came with instructions, before every feeling demanded examination. That version of living, I suspect, is closed to us.

The stories in this book come from two places. Some were lived closely, without distance. Others were gathered through watching—through paying attention to people, to silences, to moments that lingered long after they passed. Over time, I learned that what we witness can shape us as deeply as what we endure.

Art became the way I learned to stay with these questions. It held my anger, softened my anxieties, and gave form to emotions that felt too large to carry. That is why art moves through this novel—not as ornament, but as breath. As memory, confession, and repair.

This book took shape during a crowded, uncertain season of life, divided between work, creativity, and the care of my young children. By the time it was finished, I was sitting beside my father while he recovered after an illness. Time had curved inward. Writing carried me between being a parent and being a child. I remembered how he once checked on me at night, quietly, without waking me, his care so gentle it almost disappeared. Now the roles had shifted, and it was my turn to reassure him—and myself. It revealed a long-held illusion: that our parents are unbreakable. Even as we make space for ourselves in the world as adults, another life continues beneath it—one in which we are still children, quietly longing for the protection of those who raised us.

I chose the name *Marigold* for its quiet poetry. It is an ordinary flower, seldom praised for its beauty, yet found everywhere—blooming where it can, for as long as it can. It does not demand ideal soil or gentle seasons; it simply endures. There is a grace in this persistence, in being necessary rather than admired. The marigold lives at thresholds—in rituals, in grief, in celebration—its presence assumed, its resilience unnamed. This novel carries its name for those lives that bloom without recognition, for the unnoticed strength of staying, and for the soft, stubborn act of continuing to grow.

Marigold stays close to me because it holds both sides of a shared human truth: what it feels like to be a child who is unseen—who feels too much, thinks too much, and senses that the world is not wide enough for the weight of their heart—and what it means to grow older carrying responsibilities that remain largely invisible.

It is offered to anyone who has stood at a threshold—unsure, hopeful, imperfect—and chosen to keep going; and to the child, past or present, who still wonders when the world first began to feel too small.

If you recognise yourself here, know that your tenderness has always been real, and that it belongs.

PART 1

Rome, 2018

The Shape of Memories

Chapter 1

Dostoevsky asked: How can you live and not have a story to tell?

So here, I'm going to tell you mine.

People prefix my name with the accessory of their choice. My dad once told me about the beauty of my name, or the flower I am named after: easily grown, adaptable to different soils and climatic conditions. Remarkably common but able to sustain a blooming life long after being cut from the source, unlike a reed flute that laments in perpetuity to be one with its origin.

But I don't resonate with any of these qualities. Except that I am common. For me, I am that part of Marigold which is not just one flower, but a myriad of flowers attached to a stem. I am layers and layers of petals in one.

In the country where my parents were born, I am a metaphor, a satire for giant noisy families consisting of many people.

Fancy education was not for me. But even though I had always grasped at straws for my grades at school, I am certain I have a cosmic connection with books. Unlike people, books don't tire me.

I can trust them and keep them forever with their tales intact, with all the intricacies. They don't call me Plumpy Mari or Crazy Mari behind my back. They don't call me anything at all. They simply stay—quietly, patiently—giving me a kind of power I never had with people: the power to read them, or to look away.

Today begins like any other, quiet and unremarkable, until the mirror reminds me of my mother. As I dress for work, I notice how the faint line on my forehead has begun to follow the exact curve of hers.

There are mornings when inheritance reveals itself not in stories, but in the soft geography of a face.

She lies beneath a wrinkled blanket, her face half-visible, still and calm like a millpond. Our likeness startles me—the same thick brows, the same dark, round eyes, the same skin the colour of warm cinnamon, catching gold whenever the sun slips through the curtains.

I watch her face resting on the pillow and feel a quick, tender urge to lean down, kiss her awake, and borrow comfort from the scent I once knew by heart.

But she fell asleep only at dawn after another long day at work, so I restrain myself. Instead, I line my eyes with kohl and mist my shirt with her old perfume—oatmeal and shea butter, a fragrance she guarded like treasure. My mother collected scents the way some people collect summers. My father, in his more patient years, would lecture her about the chemicals that drifted into the air, but she never cared; perfume, for her, was a small rebellion against the heaviness of the world.

But that was my father in a once-upon-a-time sort of way. I often wonder if the man he used to be still survives beneath the reeking cloak of whiskey he wears day and night.

In the kitchen, I draw the curtains and push open the window. A faint breath of rosemary and basil drifts in—plants Donna tended for years with quiet devotion. Now they droop at the edges, slowly surrendering, as if time has grown heavier even for them.

I check my watch—still an hour before I need to leave for work. A burst of energy rushes through my veins. I sort the vegetables in order of their freshness. Cauliflower, beets, and carrots are in category three: beginning to shrink. Potatoes and tomatoes in category two, and lettuce and eggplant appear as fresh as I feel.

I sit by the window and begin to peel carrots. I chop them into even rounds and deposit them in a large glass bowl. On the stove, I wait for the cumin seeds to flutter in the mustard oil and toss in grated ginger before I hurl in the carrots. As the sweet, steamy aroma snakes around me, I think of Donna. The sound of her humming still lingers, months after she has gone.

She would lift her chin to the heavens, 'My Nonna said you're never alone in the kitchen. There is a whole crew of wisdom passed down from the generations that accompany you.'

I stab a fork into a carrot to see if it is tender enough. 'Tender like you, dear Mari,' as she used to say.

I mop the floor after eight days of deferring this activity. I check the watch again and see that I still have twenty minutes, so I run a round of laundry in the washing machine and slip out into the yard with my book. It is my father's from his younger days. The pages have yellowed and thinned like old skin.

Anna Karenina.

My mother has always been drawn to her tragedy—far more than to her life.

Pressing my face to the pages, I breathe in the scent of time, dry and deep, like the lingering air of an old cellar. A sudden growl at my feet tears the silence. Fig stands there, panting, his tongue a pink ribbon of madness.

Fig, my dog.

Worry seeps in, not with a shout but like fog under a door—slow and inevitable. Then comes the weariness curling around my limbs. It's the kind of tired that isn't just in the bones but in the air, in the light, in the very idea of standing up. I sit still for a while, as if rising would unravel me.

I decide to stop at Paul's Coffee and Doughnut and force myself out the door. The air is thick with butter and cinnamon. It reminds me I haven't eaten. Cinnamon has followed me in strange ways: when I wouldn't stop sucking my fingers, my father pressed cinnamon sticks into my palms; when I turned seven, he bought me two T-shirts with cartoon rolls and the line, '*cinnamon is how I roll*'. I wore them like armour without knowing what they were meant to protect.

'Wacko!'

Kamal's voice cuts through the air, followed by the ragged laughter of his friends. My fingers tighten around the fabric of my maxi, twisting it as if wringing water from cloth. I quicken my pace. Passing the green-laced wall of his garden always feels like moving through a tightening throat, one that might swallow me whole. My breath thins. As a child, I steadied myself by imagining him sinking into the Tiber—him and his snarling boys—dragged under by their own noise. Perhaps I read crime novels too early.

My appetite dissolves entirely.

The ancient stones beneath my feet press steadily and patiently, worn by centuries of footsteps and stories. Halfway across the Ponte

Fabricio Bridge, I bite my lip and turn around. Fig is nowhere to be seen, vanished, like a lover's letter left on a porch.

I close my eyes and inhale the musty breath of the Tiber curling beneath me. *Breathe in, now breathe out,* just as Donna taught me.

Gaius is already here. His tall, sturdy physique stands out like a magnificent ship in the sea of excited tourists. His demeanour softens with love as he beholds the Theatre of Marcellus.

And like every time, as if he received a coded message through the wings of the breeze, he just knows of my arrival. He lifts an eyebrow. 'Mari, you look—' then squeezes his other eye in a way that sends a flutter straight to my bones.

I know what he thinks of me.

Shoving another jolt my way, he places his hand on my shoulder. I feel the warmth seep into my body, smoothing all my jagged thoughts. I follow his eyes, unaware that the ache I carried had already begun its telling.

I wonder how true all the names are that I am given: plumpy, tender, wacko, or just something only he calls me.

Beautiful.

Perhaps I am none. Or maybe I am everything.

I am Marigold.

I am layers and layers of petals in one.

Chapter 2

I glance down at Fig curled at my feet and let go of a breath I didn't know I'd been holding. I check my phone. I'm late.

'Mari,' Gaius slips his long, pale fingers across the back of my palm, lacing them gently with mine. My chest rises, almost involuntarily, stirred by his touch—soft as a dandelion, yet wild in a way that unsettles something deep within me.

I don't know if I even make sense. But in this moment, I feel both still and storming. Both tranquil and taut. Maybe I really am a little bit of *wacko.*

Gaius leads me to a broad silver-grey stone, and we sit side by side, facing the grand sweep of the theatre. Fig climbs into my lap. I wait a moment—then, unable to resist, I bury my fingers in his fur. The softness is undeniably real.

A tear begins to prick at the corner of my eye. I blink, 'I've made up my mind,' I say, my voice breaking as it rises from somewhere small and hidden. I don't look at Gaius. I look at Fig instead.

Gaius exhales; the sound comes out soft and weary. 'It's all part of mourning, Mari. It breaks you before it heals. Be kind to yourself, please. Give your heart some time to grieve.'

I close my eyes. I know all of that. Hemingway's quiet truth echoes in my mind: *The world breaks everyone, and afterwards, many are strong at the broken places. But those who will not break, it kills.*

But the tightness in my throat clenches like a fist. 'Three weeks and two days of grieving today,' I say, my voice small and hoarse.

Behind us, the theatre looms in dignified silence, its ancient stones catching the golden hush of Roman light, as if they have borne witness to heartbreak for centuries.

Gaius tosses a pebble into a quiet patch cleared of tourists. 'You know what she'd think of you?'

I turn to him, drawing in a large breath of air, 'We both know she wouldn't be the first one to think that.'

He clicks his tongue, the lines on his forehead revealing his years. He leans in, gently cupping my face between his large palms. The minty scent of his breath coils around me like a snake, slow and invasive. I inhale instinctively—distracted, disarmed—and for a moment, I forget everything.

'Mari, it happens to everyone—especially with the ones we love too much.' He plants a kiss on the side of my face, then murmurs, 'They like to linger a bit longer.'

I glance down at Fig curled in my lap. Still, as a tombstone.

'You know it's true, what they say about them,' Gaius adds, his lips twisting in the way he does when he begins to sense defeat—or something close to loss.

I grind my teeth, choking back the helplessness sprouting like rot beneath my thoughts. Gaius has never been so insistent, never this firm against one of my decisions. He has always been the one to draw a thought out of the shadows of my heart and hold it up to the light.

He knows me the way salt knows the ocean. The oyster, its pearl. Then why is he acting so strange about this?

He looks at me with a gaze as irate as it is imploring, 'One moment of sharing your life with them and you are never the same again.'

I remember how many times in the last few months my father has asked me to visit her, and the excuses I have given to refuse, because deep inside I always knew Gaius would not like it.

'She's also my aunt. Don't forget that she is…' I hesitate, trying with definite failure to convince him, '…family.'

Gaius scoffs. 'But you are not visiting the aunt in her. Are you?'

We fall silent after that. The kind of silence that doesn't settle—just hovers like dust in an abandoned room. After some time, Gaius stirs beside me. 'Do not fear the parts of you that tremble, Marigold. Even the strongest bridges shake in the wind,' he whispers.

I don't say anything. It's time for me to leave for the library.

My library. A pale old building tucked between a bakery that smells perpetually of burnt sugar and a tailor's shop where jazz music floats faintly through a cracked window. The sign over the door reads *Classici di Carta*, faded gold on wood, the colour of dried leaves given up too soon by the trees.

No one wanted the lone job. So it's mine alone. I rent out the books, keep the records, and stamp the cards. Every morning, I take pleasure in wiping down the worn spines of Austen and Alcott, Baldwin and Brontë—like I'm brushing sleep off their shoulders. Occasionally, I mop the floor with a vinegar solution that makes the place smell faintly of old apples.

I've never met the man—Mr. Ell—who owns the place. But he seems kind enough to have left all of this in my care. Sometimes, I think he knows I need it more than anyone else. That it's only in the pages that I can let my loneliness breathe.

I begin to walk away.

From the corner of my eye, I catch him still seated on the stone, his face twisted, his eyes searching for answers in the grassy ground stomped by the tourists. My decision wavers, and I bring myself to believe that maybe Gaius is right after all—until I feel the wet lick of Fig on my ankle. Again.

Walking along the cobbled street that measures my steps every day, my thoughts drift to Solo. It is odd to realise I don't even know her name. Maybe because I was never told. Aunt Solo had only ever been that to me—Aunt Solo.

I remember asking my mother once, a long time ago, as she combed my hair in the small pearl dressing mirror she brought with her from India. Her face was fresh as a daisy. Her eyes—the usual contrast—ever so distant and lonely.

It was because of Solo's stark resemblance to the Italian actress Sophia Loren. The same tint of yellow in her hazel eyes on a magnificent face, the same auburn hair. The same vivacious smile—the one that holds the potential to calm the wildest of storms.

Chapter 3

I place my bag beside Fig on the stone steps and extract the keys from my pocket. Throwing the glass door open, I watch Fig scoot inside. I close my eyes and absorb the aroma of ripened pages that hold in their wombs a thousand antiquated tales of love and loss, of romance and betrayal. I feel my worries dissolving, and for a fleeting moment, I am relieved Fig is here. I see him take his usual place near the ceramic planter beside my desk, and the sight warms my heart. I switch on the coffee machine and my day bubbles to life. I place my book on my desk and pull the string of the old table lamp, which spreads its light over the stories and characters around me.

I prefer to keep the lights in the library off until I have a visitor. Perhaps because I can see my own thoughts better in the darkness. When there is so much to see with the eyes, the imagination of the mind is blinded. Mom used to say when she read me nighttime stories, 'Close your eyes, Mari, and let your mind see. Imagine, my little flower.'

I think of Mom, my childhood, the soft tickle of her hair brushing against my face. Her whispery voice, as gentle as a butterfly's breath. *Imagination is the only weapon in the war against reality.*

It was always the same book I insisted on reading.

Alice in Wonderland.

The memory is so far lost in time that I doubt it was ever real. Was there really a time when Mom had time for me?

The screeching whistle of the coffee machine tears me from my reverie. But there is something else that grabs my attention. A strange sensation of something lurking in the darkness behind the corner-most bookshelf on my right, the one closest to the main door. I am certain I did not see the door flick open, so there is no chance I missed noticing a visitor enter the library. Besides, it's very early in the day to even have one. Most people pour in during the afternoon hours—young boys and girls working in clothing stores on their lunch break; fancy-looking girls in oversized T-shirts with props and a friend tagging along as a photographer. Bookstagrammers, as they call themselves.

I pause to observe the shadow flickering between the shelves. Alarm crawls into me as I hear the thud of a book dropping onto the hardwood floor. A rat, I tell myself unconvincingly. My heart pounds. Thud. Thud. Thud.

The footsteps are faint, as if disguised. I swallow, grab the iron scale from the pen holder, and proceed towards the source of the sound. I have never hurt an ant in my life. I can't kill anyone. I am not a murderer. I can't.

Something lands on my shoulder from behind. A hand.

I lose my grip on the scale, and it drops onto the rug soundlessly. Fig remains motionless—brave, like one is after death.

I sigh, relieved it's him, but my chest is still thick with panic. Beads of sweat line my face.

'Gaius.'

'There was something I wanted to say,' he looks into my eyes, a throbbing care melting in his gaze, and suddenly I feel the need to lean on him and cry.

'Go see your aunt if you must,' he presses his lips, drawing all his strength to agree to what he is offering. 'But don't tell her anything about me. Or she will—'

A warm smile lifts the corner of my lips. My heart feels so full it might burst apart.

'I won't.'

I turn around and pull the knob of the wooden cabinet to extract two coffee cups. 'I'm so happy you—'

I stop when I notice he is already gone. Without a sound. In an incredulous flash, as if he were never here at all.

I had always believed love was hard to find. Love like Elizabeth and Darcy, or Heathcliff and Catherine. A love so deep it seeps into your veins and bleeds through your being. So whole it hurts, like a boulder resting in your chest. But I've seen that love between my parents.

I've seen the torment and the calm it brings. The strange, wordless knowing that passes between them like wind through old trees.

But they never tell me how it began. Perhaps it's too sacred, or too painful to revisit. Still, I like to believe it started in a moment as spellbound, as irrevocable, as the one when I first met Gaius.

My eyes fall on Fig, and I bring my palm to my heart, which has begun to race again. It is all going to be alright now, I tell myself.

Time disappears as I begin to read the book I started two days ago. *A Room of One's Own* by Virginia Woolf. I trace the underlines as if I could find something I had missed earlier—a prophecy, perhaps.

There is a woman in the aisle behind me now. I didn't notice when she crept in. She hasn't spoken a word.

I watch my fingernails as they run along the lines written only for me.

You deserve a stable, private space—mental and physical—where you don't have to mask, perform, or explain your brain.

I read on, no longer sure where the world ends and the words begin.

Chapter 4

After a long, hesitant pause, I knock on the oak door, mystically lit in the pale golden glow typical of a Roman afternoon. It has always reminded me of the door in *The Secret Garden*—the kind that seems to breathe with the promise of secrets waiting just beyond its hinges.

Aunt Solo never had a doorbell.

'Either you've got friends, or you're a shrink,' Solo had said, propping a foot on the chair. When Mom frowned, she added with a shrug, 'Everyone who comes here has to book an appointment.'

Solo's job is to ask too many questions—the reason I haven't seen her despite Dad's insistent requests. I was ten then, puzzled as to why her visitors—pearls, tuxedos, perfect smiles—never looked sick. It was around that time Mom began seeing her too, because Lorenzo was apparently stressing her out.

'It's a grown-up thing,' Dad had said, and that was reason enough for me to lose interest. Grown-up things, as I understood them, only made you feel sick in the head—like drinking wine, knowing it was just rotten fruit, crushed underfoot.

It takes Solo a good fifteen minutes to answer the door after I knock. She is luxuriously frowning beneath her flawless skin. Beads of sweat—or water—sparkle on her smooth forehead. I look at her and marvel. She is the most beautiful woman I have ever seen.

'Now who should you be, young la—' Solo pauses her rant abruptly and draws her eyebrows together.

I lick my lips and shift my gaze to Fig, who quickly hides behind my legs, panting.

'Hi,' I clear my throat to smoothen the scratchiness of a voice unused for so long.

Solo squints, chimes the word like an old lullaby she has almost forgotten, 'Marigold!'

I nod weakly, as if frightened of being unveiled earlier than I had planned.

Solo tightens the knot of her bathrobe around her waist, screeches my name again, then grabs me in her ample embrace. A strong smell of cigarette frivolously covered in mint envelops me, and I am quickly reminded of the olden days—the days when Mom and Solo spent so much time together that Mom smelled of tobacco instead of her own buttery scent when she lay beside me to read at night.

I feel the coolness of droplets sliding from Solo's wet hair onto the fabric of my sleeves and wonder if she smoked in the shower. We stall in the lobby, just behind the main door. Solo throws her arms in the air, then observes me from head to toe. 'What an attractive woman you've grown into, in such a short period of time, Mari!'

I offer a polite nod, acknowledging Solo's comment and steadying the pounding in my chest.

There is no going back now.

CHAPTER 5

Solo's house is just as I remember. Faint Hindi music spills lazily into the air, seeping through the walls as if the house itself were humming. The lights are dim—just enough not to stumble. The floral chair, the table with its timer bell, and the leather couch are all in their familiar places. Between the living room and the kitchen, a tall bookshelf rises, books arranged by the shade of their covers, glass candles resting among them like forgotten prayers.

In gentle, conscious steps, I tail Solo towards the kitchen. I am startled as I register the nakedness.

Solo glances over the gas stove, 'I got rid of the table a few months ago. It was spreading toxicity in my thoughts, reminding me I have no friends, nor family, to sit around it anymore.'

She says it so casually, I have no time to gather pity.

I stare at the empty space between us, and memories surge like a flock of captive birds released into the sky.

The sweet tinkle of spoons against plates. The joy of just being together on an ordinary day. As a child, Mom never really looked sick, but now that I am older, I recognise the pain that had always settled beneath her dark eyes—even as she sat around a warm meal with the people she loved.

I clench my eyelids and jerk away the pain that comes with the memory: of having a family once; of seeing Mom more often than just a tiny glimpse through the chink of my weary eyelids in the middle of the night; and of Dad as a father who once told jokes, combed my hair, clicked my pictures as we sailed on the prettiest gondolas in Venice—the one who brought rainbow ice creams in cones and kissed Mom on her forehead when she went quiet for a little longer. He always brought her back into the moment somehow. It was his superpower. But that was a long time ago—not measured in days or months so much as in memory.

Solo stirs the thick red gravy in the pan with a wooden spatula. 'This needs me right now, or we'll have to order greasy pizza with eggplants again.'

With pursed lips, I nod. A small stretch of silence follows as Solo types a message on her phone. When she turns her attention back to me, her gaze is unblinking. I squeeze my fingers into my palms and clear my throat. I push aside the urge to flee, pulsing inside me, and summon the courage to speak, 'Would you please keep this to yourself, Auntie?'

Solo dips her finger into the pan. It comes out red—the colour of a beginning, as Mom used to say. Releasing a soft moan as she licks it off her finger, she announces, 'I haven't spoken to your father in a year, Mari.'

'I meant…' I wince at the hunger gnawing my insides—perhaps the craving to taste lost memories. 'I meant both of them. Don't tell this to Mom either,' I say, finally.

I see the colour drain from her face at the mention of Mom. Perhaps she still harbours hatred for the woman who was once her kindred spirit. Solo drops the spatula onto the slab without looking. It lands halfway, then tumbles to the floor. Tiny red droplets spatter the white marble and the pale oak drawers. Unconcerned by the abrupt mess, Solo stares at me, as if making a mental note to pour it on paper later. It is not bewilderment that drapes her eyes, I notice, but a keen, measuring observation.

'I know that you two are not friends anymore, but… I need to have your word before I—'

Solo turns off the stove, presses her hand on my arm, and leads me into the living room. She has always treated her clients seated across from her on the floral chair she calls her thinking chair. With me, she sits on the couch beside me. Perhaps, I think, because she doesn't yet know the purpose of my visit. Or maybe she does—because I see her pull out a new notepad from the bundle on the coffee table. She clicks open her pen, dates the page, and writes my name.

With her other hand, she holds the edges of her bathrobe together as they stray apart, revealing the sheen of her hairless thighs.

'I'll wait here,' I say, tearing my eyes away from her legs.

Solo rolls her tongue inside her mouth and shifts her gaze from me to the pen between her fingers. 'I'll be a moment then.'

Barely a minute later, I am emptying the contents of my bag in search of my wallet. It would be awkward to ask for Solo's fees at this point—but more awkward not to ask at all.

'So what is it that really brings you here, Marigold?' She sits on the thinking chair now. Holding my gaze, she begins to arrange the contents of my bag on the table between us, almost taking control of my belongings.

'My dog,' I glance at Fig, who has wrapped himself comfortably around my right leg, shifting his gaze between Solo and me. Fig has come here many times as a tiny pup.

'It's just a tiny piece, Mari,' Solo would sigh.

'No chocolates for Fig,' I'd say. Fig would try with all his might to unwrap the shiny packaging, then, piqued by failure, run in circles around the lobby.

Solo chimes, 'I still remember the first time my eyes met that fluffy miracle.' Her gaze lingers on Fig, who sinks further behind my legs, trying to vanish from her line of sight. 'And the story of how you two met? Pure serendipity!'

Then she scribbles something on the paper.

I swallow the tide rising within me. If only memories could be sifted—the good kept, the rest left to drift away like silt in water. But life isn't so kind; it makes you carry everything, the sweetness and the ruin alike. It was during one of those bleak stretches of time that Fig walked into my life, bringing with him a small, stubborn light.

I was seven.

Dad had gone to leave Mom inside the Art Building. It wasn't really an art building—I had known even then, because Donna sobbed every time she packed Mom's bags for her extended stays, complaining they wouldn't allow her to stay with her signora. I also knew there couldn't be uniforms at art buildings.

'It's our family's little secret, Mari,' Dad used to say on our way back home. And before I could question him, he would veer the car towards the ice-cream parlour or a bookstore—as if ice creams held all the answers for children. Books, however, I soon realised, did hold some answers. Escape from the questions, at least. Thankfully for Dad, there were plenty of both on our way home.

In time, I stopped asking. Maybe I sensed that the truth, when it came, would wound deeper than the wondering.

That afternoon, outside the Art Building, I sat upright on a tufa stone bench, reading a book in the small garden laced with towering cypresses. Knotted clouds kept the sunshine from breaking through.

I always carried my book on those *we-are-going-to-drop-Mom-at-the-art-building* trips—one book, always—because *Alice* soothed the pain of parting with Mom.

That was when I spotted a pup slumped in the grass just outside the staircase leading to the main door. He stared at the dreadfully tall grey building, waiting—just like me—with the stillness of a corpse.

Following my curiosity, I noticed a brass coin hanging from his neck, letters engraved on it spelling a name.

Fig.

When I perched beside him, he didn't stir, nor did he seem distracted. By the time Dad asked about his family, I knew our stories were the same.

The young man Fig was waiting for had been inside the Art Building for over two weeks. It was his first time there, and I knew too well the feeling of being unprepared for an absence. The first ones are always the hardest.

The owner of the Art Building, Matteo Diam, was a large man with red skin and small, kind eyes—like an elephant's. Dad had designed Matteo's house a few blocks from ours. His daughter, Sherry, always offered me chocolates and sometimes unsolicited company while I waited.

'Just this morning I told myself this little guy is too small to be on his own,' Matteo chirped. After that day, I carried Fig around like he was my baby, my little brother—tickling his soft belly and breathing in his sweet breath.

Pulled out of my reverie, I blink affectionately at Fig, only to register the barbarity of my situation when Solo asks, 'What about him?'

Her eyes study me carefully.

Fig shifts behind my shoes. I feel his fur brush against my ankles.

'He is right here,' I spread my feet apart, feeling the muscles in my stomach clench. My face flushes at the admission.

'And—' Solo pauses, pen hovering, waiting. Her gaze sharp, eyebrows lifted.

'He follows me everywhere,' My voice breaks, but I try to stay coherent. 'Even though—' I stop, refusing the glass of water Solo brings closer.

My gaze wanders—halts at the painting, the bookshelf, a square blotch on the wall where once hung a picture of Mom and Solo, clicked by Dad, pinching the tip of the Leaning Tower of Pisa. Mom's hair swayed in the breeze, a jasmine tucked behind her ear—her favourite scent in the world.

'Even though what?'

I bring my eyes back to Fig. My jaw tightens, but I force the words out, 'It's been three weeks and two days since I buried him.'

My heart pauses as I search Solo's face for judgment. Wacko. Mad. Stupid. Anything.

Nothing.

Solo isn't stunned. She has the stillness of golden wheat on a windless summer afternoon. A surprising relief seeps into my skin, and I wish Gaius were here to witness this.

But Gaius would never come here with me.

He never goes where he might be recognised.

Gaius is my little secret.

Only as much as I am his.

Chapter 6

After a long silence, Solo leans back in her chair. Her gaze remains fixed on the notepad.

'Marigold, how do you fill your days?'

My lips press into a thin line. My eyes fall to my hands. Instinctively, I curl them into fists—to hide the scars as much as to steady myself.

I didn't come here to talk about my routine. I just want a simple fix and to return to my life with Gaius.

'I, uh…' I stammer, clearing my throat under her watchful gaze. 'I work at a library. It rents used classics.'

I regret it immediately. No one knows about my job at the library. I told Matteo and Dad I was attending a writing workshop. But I don't ask her to keep it a secret. That would weaken my stance and add to her suspicion about the credibility of my thoughts.

Solo's eyes move over the exhibition of my belongings—the frayed hardcover with threads spilling from its spine; a leather wallet swollen with coins; a broken chain with a peridot and blue topaz pendant; a transparent pouch filled with book tabs, pencil shavings, highlighters, and sharpeners.

'All these years, watching you grow up among books, I thought you might turn into a writer—or a poet. Maybe even an artist like your mother.'

Our eyes meet. I look away. Solo's hands fly to her chest, her features softening, 'I don't mean to say a job at a bookstore is any less.'

'A library.'

'Yes. A library.'

I wet my lips, 'I'm happy working around books. It gives me time to do what I like. I'm also writing my own novel.'

'How is the business?' Solo jots something down. 'In your… library?'

I frown, 'Most people prefer new books nowadays. Traces of strangers—their scribbles, even their scents—escape them. They'll take a hundred pictures for Instagram, but when it comes to taking a book home, they buy a new one elsewhere.'

Solo scoffs, 'I hardly see how it makes a difference. Old or new, a book serves its purpose as long as it's readable.'

She flips through the pages, heavily marked in my handwriting.

'For me, a book does more than inform,' I say. 'It crawls into your soul and becomes part of you. Every fingertip, every eye that touches it alters the story. An old copy carries many hidden lives folded into the original text.'

'I think you're giving it too much thought. They're just books.'

'I think you're giving them too little.'

Solo smiles faintly at the book, as if a memory has surfaced.

'So… you're mostly on your own every day?'

'No. There's—' I freeze.

'Someone who keeps you company at the library?'

I picture Gaius. His soft smile. The grey threading through his black hair. An old copy of Homer in his hands.

'Fig,' I say. 'Like I told you—he follows me everywhere.'

'What about weekends?' Her voice is professional now.

'The library is open every day.'

Solo pauses.

'We'll need more time together, Marigold. But right now, I'm starving.'

I breathe out.

From over her shoulder, she adds, 'Perhaps my instincts knew I'd have company for dinner. I cooked more than I could eat in a day.'

The mention of food tightens my stomach. I smile—and then I remember.

I shove my things into my bag. Panic leads to my clumsy hands. Last week, Matteo had told me to hide the whisky in the guest room closet. Dad never goes there. But what if he did?

Two possibilities. One—he's tearing through the house, smashing everything in search of his bottles. Two—he's slumped at the kitchen table, muttering into his pocket dictionary between the broken notes of his old cassette player, the urge tightening around him like a snake. Eyes bloodshot. Hands trembling.

He will need you, Marigold.

When Solo returns with the tray, I am already at the door.

'Dad,' I say softly.

For the first time, shock flickers across her face.

'I need to be with him,' I whisper.

She doesn't protest. Only says, 'Please come back, Marigold.'

Outside, the air is heavy with roses. I glance at the tiny pots I painted with Dad—little huts and a mango tree behind them.

'I will.'

I walk away, leaving her alone with cutlery for two in a house emptied of life. Dusk paints Rome pale orange.

The colour of my name.

Marigold.

Chapter 7

It was a few months ago when a casket appeared on our doorstep. Its battered condition made it clear—it wasn't a present or a parcel. The sooty wooden box bore no mark of a sender. Someone had simply walked up, set it down, and left—without ringing the bell.

I was heading out to the library when I saw it. At first, I thought it was a prank. Inside were chipped hairbrushes, crumpled sketches, empty perfume bottles, broken hairclips—someone's discarded life.

It felt like vengeance packed in a box.

But then my eyes caught something that froze me. For a moment, I couldn't breathe.

A sketch, brushed in oils, its corners scorched and brittle—like a memory that has survived too long in the fire of love and life.

The one my mother lost a year ago, the night before her exhibition last September. The one she had carried from India, loved like a limb, sobbed into. It had grown porous with her—her breath, her tears, her ink—so alive it had almost become her.

It was the sketch that inspired her to paint her first portrait, she had told me. It was my dad she was trying to capture—the only portrait of him she had ever made by looking at him. All the others she painted through imagination, memory, and her idea of him.

I bring the paper to my face. It smells of old rooms and forgotten touch, of turpentine and ghosts. I feel my mother's hand caressing the shape on it.

A strange sense of familiarity mushrooms in my chest, as if it is not just paper but my mother between my fingers, preserved within the ink—like a pressed rose that still bears fragrance and a tale of its own. Mysterious. Delusive. Sorrowful. The mother I remember from the olden days.

I breathe in the last of the dust and lock the door behind me. On quiet feet, I cross the kitchen where Dad lies slumped in a chair—half awake, muttering in fragments; half asleep, too far gone to notice as I kiss him goodnight. His skin is warm against my lips, his breath heavy with whiskey. His eyes, as always, were moist.

In the lampshade's glow in Mom's room, I slip into the blanket with *Alice in Wonderland* gripped fast between my fingers. I close my eyes, and in lieu of sleep, memories—like a clan of hyenas in the middle of a forest—begin to cackle in my mind.

It was the first time Mom had taken me to Florence. The first time I heard Lorenzo's voice rise, sharp and foreign against the clatter of coffee cups and the hum of the trattoria. I couldn't follow the words, only the heat in them. Mom's face was tight with anger, her grip on my wrist so hard I thought it might leave bruises. Yet I liked it—being held as if I were something precious, too easily lost.

And then, at the train station back in Rome, the crowd pressed like a tide. Perfume, sweat, cigarette smoke, the echo of announcements ricocheting through the air. I felt my mother's hand slip away. In an instant, she was gone. I spun in the stream of strangers, searching for her red scarf, but the station blurred into reds and blues and greens and hurried faces. Minutes stretched into lifetimes, my satchel digging into my shoulder, the concrete cold beneath my shoes. I must have been eight.

I don't remember who found me first—Dad or Matteo. Only the relief of a hand pulling me back to shore.

That night, after Donna's lullaby faded and she thought I was asleep, Dad came into my room. He kissed my forehead; I smelled wine.

I was never taken to Mom's art gallery in Florence again.

Outside the window, there is a quietness to the night—the same one that gnaws at the house every evening after Dad's muttering ebbs and before I hear Mom's heels tapping on the floor. I wait with my book between my fingers. Sometime before dawn breaks, as I swing on the branches of oblivion, I hear a rattle at the door—or is it the window battling blind winds? I tighten my grip on Fig's soft fur. He moans. The birds in the tall pine trees have long sung their last lullabies.

Dreamily, I peek through heavy eyelids and watch the contours of Mom's pale skin in the cold moonlight. She slips beneath the sheet beside me. In my hazy sight, I watch her chest rise and fall.

'You're back,' I murmur, tangling my limbs with hers. I feel the soft brush of her oatmeal-and-shea-butter-scented hair on my face and the warmth of her skin against mine.

'Dream, my Marigold.'

And finally, beside the person I love most in the world, I find a few sweet hours of sleep in the darkness behind my eyes.

Chapter 8

'Why are there lines on your forehead?' Gaius says from across from me on a jagged wooden chair. The library is dimly lit, but I can see him clearly. He is scribbling on a piece of paper with curling corners—the kind that reminds me of royal messages from ancient times. I wonder where he finds such peculiar things in a city that sells everything wrapped in bright plastic.

'Mari?' he says again, now pouring all his attention on me.

I let out a long gasp, 'Two things.'

He sets down his pen and casts a calm glance in my direction. There has been a question lingering in his eyes since morning, but I would rather not mention my meeting with Solo unless he asks. If I say too much, Gaius might tell me not to see her again.

'Tell me the second one first,' he says.

'What?'

'The creases on your face.'

'Oh,' I whisper. 'There's a boy outside, staring at me like I'm teaching philosophy to a teapot.'

Gaius tilts his head, not turning fully, as though imagining the boy instead of looking.

'Perhaps he's waiting. Or planning on renting a book.'

'It's not the first time he's been here,' I tell him.

He shifts, almost turning, and instinctively, I reach for his hand.

'Don't,' My voice is a pleading whisper. 'I don't want him to know I'm talking about him. I'll watch him for a week and then think of what can be done.'

'Is he alone? What is he doing exactly?' He places his pen on the table.

I lift my eyes and glance towards the boy. 'Alone. Eyebrows raised, eyes wide—just staring.'

'And how does he look?'

'Pretty face. A little plump. A shadow where a moustache wants to be. A child halfway through the flight to becoming a man.'

Gaius chuckles, 'You ever think he might have a crush on you?'

I close my eyes and sigh, 'Gaius, please. He's a child. Think of his age.'

'Age,' he repeats, clearing his throat, mischief flickering in his eyes. 'Age has little to do with longing—or love.'

Heat rushes to my face. For a moment, the ground slips away, and I feel myself hovering—weightless, unanchored, foolishly light. *Love.* I repeat the word silently, storing it away for the hours when silence grows deep enough to hold it.

'It happens,' he continues. 'Boys often begin there—adoring someone older.'

I don't react. I can't. I think of a book I read once—a tender coming-of-age story about a teenage boy who falls for a young war widow one summer. *Summer of '42.* It still lies in my bedside drawer.

'Anyway—what's the second thing?' he asks, pulling me back.

I press my palm flat over the brittle page of the ancient book before me.

'The reason no one ever comes here,' I say, 'This book has lost a part of itself. No one wants what's unfinished. I'd rather read a whole story—or none at all.'

Gaius sets aside his half-scribbled paper and reaches for the book. His fingers graze mine—just briefly—but the warmth of his touch startles me. I inhale sharply, the sound small and foolish in the quiet room.

I lean back and watch his brow crease. Wisps of grey hair fall into his eyes as he squints, accentuating the wrinkles around them. Gaius is losing hair.

This moment feels so serene, I could sit here and adore him all my life, do nothing else, and still be happy. Gaius is more beautiful than any of my mother's paintings or any of the exotic tales lining the shelves. But he pays no attention to my fixated gaze. He runs his tongue over his lips and murmurs, more to himself than to me.

I watch him with wonder and desire. Books speak of people travelling—to northern lights, mountain treks, camping, diving—oblivious to the fact that real pleasures live in dim silences, in looking at a person who is all those places for you. I wonder if anything could be more rejuvenating than watching Gaius now, scribbling with his old-school fountain pen, his fingers creating a quiet symphony.

He lifts an eyebrow at my unwavering stare.

'What?'

Gaius holds up the paper he has written on, 'The part that was taken away—it's yours again.'

'Funny!' I snatch it and read aloud: *...any moment might be our last. Everything is more beautiful because we're doomed. You will never be lovelier than you are now. We will never be here again...*

'I'm so glad,' I say dryly.

'That your book has become whole again.'

My jaw tightens.

'I'm glad those lines were taken away. Why must all great love stories end in tragedy?' I say, resigned, almost heartbroken—as if they were all mine, 'Patroclus and Achilles. Romeo and Juliet. Cleopatra and Caesar.'

He purses his lips, 'Some people are born for quiet tragedies. You, Marigold, you were born for beautiful ones.'

I stare at the curves of his handwriting and crumple the note in my palm. I close the book and push it aside. It doesn't need those lines.

'Sometimes you freak me out,' I say.

He smiles, 'Then we're not very different.'

A small laugh escapes me.

'But how can you do that—memorise an entire poem?'

'Benefits of growing up without Instagram,' he says, pointing to my phone.

I laugh. I've started posting photographs of my library online—Bookstagram, as they call it. More people like my pictures than they ever liked the idea of me in person. I admit, I enjoy the validation of strangers.

'You talk like you were born in ancient Rome,' I tell him.

'Look at me,' Gaius gestures to the folds of his white tunic pooling over the denim on his thighs. 'Don't you think I was?'

I have to agree. No one dresses like Gaius. Instead of shirts, he wears loose, flowing tunics of linen and wool. Sometimes I recognise him at Mercallus by the laurel wreath crowning his head. Oddly, no one notices but me. No one stares at him the way they stare at me when we are together. Perhaps people are more interested in who accompanies a peculiar species than the species itself.

Gaius suddenly stills. His jaw tightens.

'It was really my mother,' he says. 'She was devoted to my education. Back then, it was expected of us to memorise vast amounts of literature. I had a very skilled tutor—trained in Egypt, proficient in Greek and Latin rhetoric.'

I study him. I hadn't given it much thought until now.

'That's some rich childhood,' I say.

'Rich?' he spits mockingly.

I understand his reaction. I know about his childhood. He grew up in a small house nestled between butcher shops in a lower-class neighbourhood that smelled of sausage, fresh bread, and Arabian perfumes—somewhere between the Viminal and Esquiline Hills. It still amazes me that his family managed servants to greet guests at the door.

'You were lucky your mother was so devoted,' I say softly.

'Lucky children don't lose their fathers at sixteen.'

Guilt presses my chest.

'Oh, Gaius. I'm sorry.'

He stares at the table for a long time. Just as I reach for his hand, my phone alarm shrieks.

Appointment with Solo.

Gaius looks at the phone. His lips part, then close again.

'So it's an everyday affair now,' he says, disappointment—and something close to fear—radiating from his face.

'Gaius,' I plead, 'Fig has to go.'

His features soften slightly, 'Is he here now?'

I scoff, relieved by the question. Two young girls nearby stare at me with confusion and fear, as if they've understood what Gaius asked.

I meet their gaze with a gentle nod, then lean towards Gaius, 'Right beside you.'

Suddenly, panic surges.

His eyes clamp shut. His face contorts. I call his name and reach for his shoulder, but he jerks away. His lips turn white. Sweat gleams on his skin like dew on plum leaves.

I hold him firmly as his body bucks. My voice shakes as I call for help, but the girls flee, faces scrunched, as if they've seen a ghost. Teenagers these days.

His skin is clammy. My beautiful Gaius. I cradle his head and stroke him gently. A song perches on my lips. I hum, tracing the contours of his face—his eyes, his nose, his mouth.

He opens his eyes and lets out a laboured smile. I breathe again.

'Are we doomed?' he whispers, fragile as a thread.

Something breaks open inside me. I press my forehead to his—whether I feel his breath or only my own rising heat, I can't tell.

'Never.'

Chapter 9

I stand at home with my fists tight at my sides, fingernails pressing crescents into my palms—marks that tell my story. I press my lips thin and try to block out the sounds crashing from the kitchen across the lobby. Dad is drinking again.

From the corner of my eye, I see Fig, patient as ever. I grit my teeth and look instead at the round wooden clock. I wheel all my attention to its faint tick-tock. Beneath it, I stare at the mammoth mural that covers almost the entire wall. It is the only painting of Mom that I could never find it in my heart to hate—perhaps because, unlike the canvases hung in strangers' homes, this one stayed, etched on our wall as it is in my heart.

A remarkable piece of art: a woman with the beauty of a plump rose after rain. Her aquiline nose and jutting chin point toward a man with broad, stone-sculpted shoulders perched on a gilded chair. His eyes hold the calm of a moonless ocean, yet he looks enraptured—mythically spellbound by what he sees.

As always, the painting deluges me. The air swallows all sound—the cacophony of glass shattering in the kitchen, Dad's wailing, even the tick-tock of the clock. I hold out a hand and trace the carved initials in the corner. Against my fingertips, the name feels as gritty as the rug beneath my feet.

Ira Lall, 1997.

I imagine Mom painting this years ago, her slender fingers delicately gripping the wooden brush. Perhaps, with her other hand, she was stroking me as I drew another breath in her womb. I imagine her larger-than-life eyes squinting as she watched colour seep into the lime plaster, becoming one with the wall. The familiar curl forming at the corner of her lips, as it always does when she pauses to think. I picture the three-line pearl strings lacing her neck.

I imagine.

It is all that I can do.

CHAPTER 10

I walk to Solo's house thinking of the words Gaius had written: *Any moment might be our last. Everything is more beautiful because we're doomed. You will never be lovelier than you are now. We will never be here again.*

I remind myself to keep Gaius a secret. Why am I terrified?

I don't want us to be doomed.

Maybe all of this is happening because I am seeing Solo against his wishes. I should never have come here in the first place.

'Marigold, how is your father?' Solo opens the door at exactly 12:30 p.m. With that kind of punctuality, perhaps she truly doesn't need a doorbell.

'The same,' I say casually, as if it were the most normal state a human being could exist in.

I watch Fig scoot inside and settle himself in the lobby, right beside the leg of the table where we are going to be seated for our conversation, which is now called a session. A *session.*

Solo brings two large ceramic mugs on a floral tea tray and places them on the table. A strong aroma of ginger fills the air. Instead of her floral chair across from me, she perches on the arm of the sofa beside me. I shift slightly, and then, with gentle strokes, she runs her fingers through my hair. I have long lost the feeling of this touch.

'So much time has passed,' she says. 'I think I should have seen you—at least you—in all this time.'

My stomach clenches at the intimacy of her gaze.

'You've got your father's dark eyes.' She isn't looking at me anymore; her gaze drifts beyond the boundaries of the room. 'Large. Captivating.'

With a small shake of her head, she returns, cups my face, and tilts it gently, 'And your mother's golden skin.'

I release a long-held breath as she finally moves away. Solo takes one of the mugs and settles into the floral chair. Her lipstick is glossy red—the same shade as the cup.

As she sips, a comfortable silence settles between us. She places a notepad with my name on her thighs and uncaps her pen.

'You're beautiful, Marigold,' she says again.

My eyes flicker to the table—the teacup waiting to be held, the alarm clock Solo hasn't turned on.

'Thank you, Aunt Solo, but…' I say, wetting my lips, awkward with compliments. How many people have ever called me beautiful, apart from Gaius, anyway?

'I'm no Cleopatra,' I add, then instantly regret the analogy. Perhaps I had spent too much time staring at the mural last night.

Solo tilts her head slightly, halting the cup at her lips as if filing the thought away. For a moment, I think I've offended her—but I haven't.

'Interesting how you mentioned her,' she says slowly, savouring the word, 'Cleopatra.'

She exhales and sets the cup down, fingers interlacing, 'Tell me everything you do—right from the moment you open your eyes.'

I glance around the room before answering, mechanically, 'It's an easy question. I wake up sometime before dawn.'

I don't tell her that I am awake most nights—thinking thoughts I don't remember the next day, or watching Mom surrender to exhaustion as she collapses beside me without a word.

I watch Solo scribble furiously on her notepad. When she stops, her eyes remain on the page.

'I know she has grown distant from all of us,' she says. 'But… how often do you really get to see your mom?'

'Most days she comes back around midnight, so tired that she drifts into sleep as quickly as she sinks into the blanket beside me. In the mornings, as I get ready for work, she's still asleep. She's been working very hard this past year—a big exhibition coming up, I believe.'

'Do you not wish to wake her up?' Solo asks.

'I distract myself from the temptation,' I say. I don't tell her that most days I do try—that Mom moans and squirms, sometimes half-dreaming, a softness blooming on her face as she registers me, but she almost never wakes.

'I clean and mop, water the plants. Saturday nights are for laundry. I come home by seven most days and cook dinner for three, pushing away the dread of knowing Mom will eat at the studio. Sometimes I check on Dad, but he's seldom himself. Then I do the dishes and sink into Mom's bed.'

Solo stares at me in disbelief.

'You haven't had any help all this time? I thought Donna went on a short break.'

I shake my head, swallowing embarrassment, trying to avoid the pity rising in her eyes. I hate pity more than disdain—more than the crude indifference I grew familiar with during my school years.

'I tried sending word to Donna through her brother. I used to have his number, but he never wants to talk. Tells me to fuck off every time I call.'

'Oh, I'm sorry, dear girl,' Solo says softly. 'But trust me—sometimes people aren't really mean when they say mean things.'

I scoff, 'People being mean is the last thing that bothers me.'

Solo shakes her cup and takes a final sip.

'They just don't realise they need help themselves.'

'You mean they don't know they're sick?'

'Yes. Because—'

'It's non-perceivable, the illness,' I finish. 'I know.'

I pick up the alarm clock and trace it with my fingers. It was Mom's gift to Solo when she was seeing her, just months after Florence. After I had begun to hate Lorenzo for shouting at Mom.

~

One evening, I was reading in my room when I heard a vase shatter.

'GET OUT,' Mom screeched at Lorenzo, who—as her curator—had come to understand why she had vandalised her own painting.

'The gallery approved it already.'

'It bore my name on it. Not the gallery's. And I wasn't happy with it.'

'Six galleries across Italy have banned us because of your pathetic whims. Do you even care about the business? Have you been drinking again? Where is your husband?'

'Get out.'

The door opened gently, then slammed shut, throwing the world into silence. I stayed on the staircase until I heard Mom move to the lobby, open the cabinet, and pour herself a drink.

Later that night, at dinner, Mom told Dad she could never paint just to sell a painting. She painted to survive. It was her way of breathing—of staying alive.

Eventually, the gallery agreed to delay the showcase so she could create new work.

Lorenzo brought a bouquet of lilies. He was careful not to infuriate her until the day of the showcase. That night, a month later, Mom was indisposed.

For four hours, she stayed in the bathroom. Dad kept telling me it was a health issue.

But I knew.

I knew even then.

Mom was sick in the head.

Chapter 11

Solo runs her tongue over her teeth, as if weighing an unpleasant thought. Perhaps she is thinking about Mom, too.

'I think Mom needs you more than any of us,' I say. 'She has consumed herself in work. She never speaks to us anymore. It's almost as if we are invisible to her. Most days, she spends the night in Florence.'

Solo smooths the edges of her satin dress over her knees and clears her throat.

'Marigold, I'll help your mother when she needs me. For now, let's talk about your predicament.'

Suddenly, a lump thickens in my throat. My goodbyes to Fig are nearing.

Solo softens, her eyes losing their guard for the briefest moment.

'There's no need to be nervous. We'll take this step by step.'

A sob spills from my mouth.

'Oh dear!' Solo fills a glass of water and offers a hug. I refuse both.

I think of the nights I wait for Mom beneath the blankets in her room. The warmth of Fig's fur carries a quiet reassurance—a feeling of not being alone. I crouch, wrap my arms around Fig, and settle him in my lap. On the nights Mom doesn't come home, he waits with me, awake, until the late hours, when he moans softly and then sinks into my arms.

'How soon will it be?' I ask.

'You mean how long until he disappears?' Solo's gaze drops to my lap, as if she, too, can conceive of Fig's presence.

I nod.

'Let me tell you something from my own experience,' she says. 'Sometimes, the more vivid the memories, the longer the claws of the grief that follows.' She almost smiles, the gesture brittle at the edges, 'Goodbyes are overrated. I think it's best to say them in time.'

My eyes flutter like the wings of a trapped moth, fighting tears.

'Marigold, there's something I need you to understand. I think starting medication soon may help you. I'm a therapist, but I have a friend who can help with the medication—and you can continue seeing me.'

'Medication?' I spit, stunned, deciding in a split second that coming to Solo was a mistake—and that Gaius had been right all along.

'I thought we were going to talk, and that would solve—' I pause, helpless. 'Do I suffer from the same ailment as Mom?'

'Marigold, first I need you to know that you are not the first person to…' Solo searches for the word. '…to experience something like this.'

My eyes widen, even though I already know the answer, 'You can see Fig?'

'No… no. That's not what I meant.' Her gaze holds me gently, 'You know you're not dreaming Fig.'

I scoff, 'I don't even remember when I last dreamed—or slept enough for a dream to creep in.'

Solo gestures with her long fingers, 'Sometimes there's a thin boundary between hallucinations, misperceptions, and illusions. People see things, hear things—some can even touch things that don't really exist.'

A small wave of relief washes over me—the comfort of not being alone. Solo continues, 'To the person experiencing them, though, these things feel very real.'

In my mind, everything clicks. I shake my head violently, lips pressed tight, holding back a sob.

'It's all because of those books I devour day and night,' I cry. 'All those books about expanding imagination and escaping the real world.'

Solo's gaze deepens.

'My dear, what you're experiencing,' she steadies her voice, 'is not imagination in the way it functions when you read a book. When you conjure ordinary images—say, a character—the images remain in your mind. They may be vivid or vague, but they aren't projected into external space the way they are in hallucinations, where you actively create and revise images at will.'

I realise I'm no longer breathing.

'In contrast,' she continues, 'you are helpless in the face of hallucinations. They are autonomous. They appear and disappear when *they* please, not when you do.'

A tear slips down my face.

Fig.

~

The next day

I am expecting Gaius when Solo arrives at the library. I switch on all the lights.

She wears glossy, unworn-looking heels and a beige suede belted dress that must be new. Her hair is pulled into a high ponytail, her eyes dark with thick kohl and mascara. Here, she looks like a goddess stepped out of a classical text.

I offer her the seat across from me—the one Gaius usually takes. She attempts a smile, then runs a finger along the table, blowing dust away before coughing softly.

'I meant to clean today,' I say, embarrassed.

She checks her gold watch, 'We mustn't be late.'

Gaius flashes through my mind. He was already wary of me seeing Solo; the thought of a psychiatrist terrifies me.

We drive to Solo's friend's clinic in Parioli. On the way, she tells me she once sought his help herself—to climb out of the swamp. In my agitation, I don't allow myself to consider a therapist needing help.

The doctor wears a tailored grey suit, immaculate, expensive-looking. He is clean-shaven, his hair cropped in a military cut. For a fleeting moment, I imagine Gaius dressed that way. Heat blooms in my stomach.

He asks whether I want Solo to wait outside. I say I'd feel better with her present. He shows her out anyway.

We talk about my routine. I describe my time with Fig in detail as he notes everything meticulously. Unlike Solo, his questions are short and precise. He does not linger over my answers. When he's finished, he calls Solo back in. They discuss pills—names I can't follow—then rise abruptly and exchange goodbyes.

Solo drops me off at the library at three. The sun is Roman-strong. I sink into the leather chair and close my eyes. Minutes pass—hours, perhaps.

The sound of turning pages wakes me.

Gaius sits across from me, holding a gilded copy of Homer's *Iliad*, his face resting in his palm, elbow propped on the table. Fig lies near his leg.

I sigh.

Everything is going to be all right, I tell myself.

CHAPTER 12

It is Sunday evening, a week later, and the news of a daytime robbery is still fresh and stifling. Three armed men entered an apartment where a widower lived alone with his two guinea pigs. Reporters say the poor old fellow—a retired college professor—was robbed even of his artworks, the Moroccan carpets, and the silver lampshades that ornamented his otherwise modest two-bedroom apartment.

He lives two blocks from Solo's street, and it is only natural to expect uniformed men stationed throughout the neighbourhood.

'You would be wise to avoid that side today,' Gaius says.

I exhale through my nostrils, teeth gritted.

'Mari?' He leans forward.

He takes my hand, and I become a snowflake melting on his fingertip. I catch the mint on his breath, the green shadow of his stubble. I wrench my eyes away, annoyed by the desire knocking inside me.

'Where have you been this whole week?' I ask.

His eyes flicker, and the urge to touch him threatens to drown me.

'I kept waiting and waiting—' I trail off, studying his face. Darkness pools beneath his eyes, singing testimony to sleepless nights. Suddenly, he seems older, as if he has aged considerably in the week I haven't seen him.

He stiffens his jaw and looks away. A flush creeps across my face. I draw a breath before speaking, my voice crackling.

'Gaius.'

He tightens his hold on my hand.

'Time is thinner without you, Marigold.'

Gaius has never been one to speak of feelings, much less name what lies between us. He is peculiar in every way—his methods, his silences, his sudden turns of thought. Perhaps that is what drew him to me when others chose to look away. People say I drift in conversation, that my mind slips elsewhere mid-sentence. Gaius never minds. Maybe because he, too, lives slightly apart from the world.

'Have you been examined?' I ask softly as his head comes to rest on my lap. It has been happening more often now—the fainting spells.

He catches my hand mid-stroke, 'They say there isn't enough blood reaching my brain.'

'Do you—' I hesitate. 'Do you want to come see Solo?'

'I cannot. And neither should you.' His voice tightens, 'Not today. Not anymore. I don't trust that woman near you. She could have helped your mother—but she didn't. And now look at her. She's drifted so far from you all.'

'It seems to be helping me,' I protest, twisting the fabric of my dress between my fingers.

'Are you not afraid of being lonely again?' he asks quietly. 'Why awaken things best left sleeping?'

Anger flares through me, sudden and sharp.

'I'm not imagining Fig,' I snap. 'You think I want this? I can't control what I see, Gaius. It's like living with a—' I search for the word, 'A ghost.'

Resignation settles over his face. His eyes close.

'Not all ghosts are dead. I hope you've been careful.'

'I told you,' I interrupt. 'I won't tell anyone about you. Not until you say I can.'

From the marble floor outside my room comes the scrape of a suitcase. Keys rattle—metal on metal—and soon the kitchen cabinets are opening and slamming shut one after another.

'Dad's here. You must leave,' I say, panic threading my voice.

Gaius remains unnervingly calm, as though at the click of a finger he could fade—blend into the room, disappear into one of Mom's paintings on the wall.

I rush into the kitchen. Dad is pacing around the island, clasping and unclasping his fists. His face is pallid.

It hurts to see how his body trembles constantly, how he seems far older than his years. He runs toward me when he sees me, grabs the table for support, and stutters, wiping sweat from his brow. His lips are ashen, as if they have never known water.

I uncap a bottle and hold it out. Words dry in my throat.

This is the man who took me to the Leaning Tower of Pisa and told me about the seven bells representing the seven musical notes. The man who sat me on his lap in a gondola and spoke of Roman refugees who founded Venice.

He drains the bottle in one long gulp.

'I'll do as you say,' he says, his voice trembling.

'Dad,' I sob, reaching for his damp face. 'You can do without it. I know it's hurting you and—'

There is a knock at the door.

Gaius flashes through my mind. He must not see me like this. But I asked him to leave.

Footsteps enter—perhaps Gaius left the door unlocked as he went. Then a cheery voice fills the house. Relief inflates my chest.

'What is my old rag up to?' Matteo says, bustling into the kitchen.

I breathe.

'What the fuck, asshole,' he mutters under his breath as he reaches Dad. He seats him, drops a pill into a glass of water. The fizz clouds the glass, filling the room with sound.

'Thank you for coming,' I whisper, shutting the cabinets gently.

Matteo cups my face.

'Let me take it from here,' he says softly, guiding me out of the kitchen.

From the lobby, I search for any trace of Gaius. Matteo follows my gaze and squints.

'Everything alright, princess? Is there someone else here?'

'Oh—no. Just… my… my friend,' I stammer, hating how foolish it sounds.

Matteo beams. He has often encouraged me to spend time with his daughter, Sherry, only a few years older than me, but capable of speaking my yearly quota of words in a day. She lived on cola and once dreamed of becoming a stand-up comedian before settling as a receptionist at Matteo's rehabilitation centre.

Yes—the same place where Mom created most of her paintings.

'You've got a friend at home?' Matteo immediately begins searching the living room for signs of this invisible presence. He stops at my bedroom door.

'Hello?' he calls, eyebrow raised.

Panic coils around me. Of course, Gaius has gone, I tell myself.

'I was saying,' I rush out, 'I need to go see a friend, now that you're here—'

'Oh yes, of course, dear girl. I'll take care of your old man.'

I grab my coat and wallet from the cabinet and head for the door, my heart still pounding.

Chapter 13

'Aunt Solo,' I call out, reluctantly stepping into her house. The silence has the quality of a child holding its breath in the woods. A thick aroma of cigarette smoke masks the fragrance of fresh roses adorning the living room therapy table. I place my bag beside the vase holding strands of baby's breath and weigh my choices—waiting here for Solo to appear, or intruding further into her house.

Minutes pass. Nothing stirs except the faint honking of vehicles outside on the road.

I make up my mind and push open the door to Solo's bedroom. It swings and hits the wall to its left with a thud.

'I'm sorry,' I say, flushed.

Solo doesn't seem to mind. She is sprawled on the floor. Tin boxes, pouches, watches, and jewels are scattered around her like maple leaves in autumn—beautiful, but severed and dry.

'It's alright, Marigold. I was expecting you.' She looks at me through thick lashes.

For the first time, it occurs to me how alone she has been. Mom once told me Solo had found love very early in life—a love so strong it was enviable. Was it unrequited? Or was she widowed young? Nevertheless, she carries herself with an authority that renders the absence of a husband almost invisible.

'I'm sorry I barged into your personal space like this,' I say, my voice faltering.

'Oh, Marigold,' Solo lets out a dry laugh. Wilted grief creases her forehead, 'Jewels are the last things I keep secret and safe.'

'My treasury consists of my memories,' she adds, lifting a leather-bound journal from the scattered pile.

She gestures for me to sit beside her. I do, and am ambushed by the freshness of her minty cologne. I remember this scent on Mom, back when she spent all her time here. Even after changing into her satin nighties, Solo's mint—mingled with tobacco—would cling to her.

Solo reaches for an old photo album.

'Look at you,' she says, pointing a glossy fingernail at a picture.

My eyes drift to her bracelet—South Sea pearls, her name etched into the beads. I haven't seen it on her wrist before, yet it feels familiar.

I am wearing a sleeveless frock printed with yellow tulips and green leaves. Solo wasn't ready for the photograph, food still stuffed into her mouth. Beside her, Mom smiles faintly—like sheepish sunlight at dusk. Light pours through the tall windows of Solo's living room, glinting off the pearls at her throat. Dad is not in the picture. He took it.

In my mind, I step into that day. The crisp aroma of spices swirling through the house. Mom and Solo, holding hands, giggling at Dad's miserable attempts at humour. He was never a funny man—never someone you'd notice in a group—always a quiet shadow in immaculately ironed shirts, even on picnics. Always sensible. Always talking about books.

Yet he could always coax light into Mom's face. He could—until he changed.

My lips curve faintly before I notice a drop gleaming on the photograph. Solo wipes her eye with the back of her palm and sniffs. Silence clamps down between us.

'What happened between the two of you?' I ask.

She bites her lower lip and shifts her gaze to the paper dolls on the shelf—ones I made with Dad in this very house.

'Something went wrong between you and Mom?' I add. Suddenly, I remember—Mom has the same bracelet, her initials etched into the pearls. She never wears it.

Solo looks at me. 'Nothing ever went wrong, Marigold.'

'Then why did she stop seeing you?' I trace a finger over Mom's face in the photo.

'I know you had an argument.'

Solo scoffs.

'Oh, that. I found out she wasn't taking the medication her doctors prescribed regularly.'

'Who told you that?' I ask.

She doesn't answer, but her eyes confirm it.

'Dad?' I say through clenched teeth, hating how distant I've grown from him.

Solo presses her palm to my thigh, 'He only meant well. Always.'

'Then why is he letting her rot now?' I snap. 'He never even bothers to see her anymore. He makes me so angry all the time—sometimes I just want to put an end to my—'

'Marigold,' Solo interrupts gently. 'Are you taking the medication the doctor gave you?'

I let out a bitter laugh at the deflection.

'Yes,' I lie.

I've only taken one of the three prescribed pills. I hate them. I hated them when Donna kept them by Mom's bed with a small vase of roses. I hated the way Mom cried at the sight of them. I hated how they became the axis of Dad's worry—how Donna and Dad forced them into Mom's mouth through tears and resistance. I hated watching Mom claw at his face, shaking him with the strength that revealed just how powerless she felt.

'And Fig?' Solo asks, breaking my reverie. 'Do you still see him?'

'Seldom,' I say, grief gripping me as though Fig's death is only now happening. 'He's becoming distant. Blurry.'

Solo takes my hands, but I jerk away. Rage bursts through my voice, startling even me.

'Why can't you set aside your issues and help Mom now?' I shout. My hands are trembling.

'I will,' Solo says calmly. 'I will help her find peace when she's ready to see me again. But first—you, Marigold.'

My expression softens.

'Will you see her once?' I plead. 'She's hardly home, but… You could stay the night. Or we could go to Florence—to her studio. Though she wouldn't like it. Lorenzo would be there. Maybe home is—'

'Marigold, listen,' Solo cups my face, pressing gently at my temples, grounding me.

'You can help your mother by giving her all the love you can—before it's too late.'

My words collapse in my mouth.

'Is Mom very sick?' I whisper, 'Is she dying?'

Grief pierces me. I drop my face into her palms and sob.

'Marigold,' she says firmly. 'You must take your medication on time.'

'Or what?' I snap hoarsely. 'I'll die? There isn't much I want to live for anyway.'

'When I asked about your routine,' Solo says quietly, 'I wanted to know whether there were friends filling your life.'

I wipe my face as she continues.

'No one understands better than I do how colour drains from life without friends.'

'You don't abandon your friends to die over a quarrel,' I say.

Solo exhales deeply.

'There was no quarrel. But yes—there were things I could have done differently a year ago. Then I went to India for a few months. Still, as I told you before, I can be there—for you.'

'I have friends,' I blurt out, defiant. 'I even have a boyfriend.'

A solemn shade crosses Solo's face.

'Oh,' she says, sounding both relieved and unconvinced. 'That's lovely.'

'Why didn't you tell me about him earlier? Where did you meet? Is he Indian, or—'

I inhale sharply. The air tastes like a promise freshly broken.

'He's Roman,' I say.

'Roman? From your school?'

'No. He's older.'

She rubs at her breastbone.

'How much older?'

'I know how this must look,' I say quickly. 'But what Gaius and I share is beyond—'

'Gaius,' Solo repeats the name softly, filing it away. 'Where did you meet him?'

'I told you what I could,' I say.

Chapter 14

I don't let go of his hand as I speak.

'The first time I saw you, you were like a dream.'

He leans closer, his lips brushing my forehead, 'That's all I am, isn't it?'

Before I can answer, the noise begins—shouts, gasps, the scrape of metal against stone. The street bends into chaos. Tourists crowd the pavement, cameras dangling from their necks. And then, cutting through the heat, comes a single horse—wild, untethered, its hooves cracking against the cobblestones, spraying dust like sparks.

'Anyone else? Or shall we call it a day?' A large man booms, playful, mocking.

'What a shame,' another jeers. 'This is the pride of Rome?'

And then—I hear it.

A voice from beside me.

My stomach drops. Gaius is already cutting through the crowd, which parts instinctively for him. His body is taut with resolve.

The man spits out a matchstick and laughs.

'And how much for this tall, salt-and-pepper man?'

'Tw—twelve euros,' a woman calls softly, her voice strangely delicate, like velvet torn at the edges.

Gaius fixes her with that gaze—sharp, deliberate, intoxicating.

'Make it fifty.'

She smiles then, coy and cruel in her red blouse, her lips painted the colour of sin. But she fades into the blur of faces, dissolves into the crowd, until only her voice lingers.

Fifty it is.

Cheers erupt as Gaius pulls off his shirt. The crowd whistles. His skin gleams in the late sun, his body cut like marble. When he swings himself onto the horse, it is with such ease, such poise, that he seems carved from myth.

I shrink into the corner. The crowd's electricity blinds me, yet beneath it I feel something lonelier than silence. One moment, he is theirs—an idol, a god—and the next, he is still mine, somewhere nearby, staring at the monument as though he were born from its stone.

What do they lose if something happens to him?

Nothing.

But me?

I lose everything.

I bury my face in my palms. Memory rises unbidden—the first time. It is always about the first time. How beginnings brand themselves into the world, etched into air and dust, refusing to fade.

It was less than a year ago. I had just turned nineteen that October. Mom hadn't come home for days, and the house had begun to sound hollow, like a shell echoing the sea. Dad barely spoke; the silence between us was too dense to breathe.

So I left. Still in my pyjamas, carrying *The Iliad* as though it were both shield and scripture. The morning smelled of espresso and rain. I walked without purpose until I reached the Colosseum—vast and mournful, its arches like open mouths remembering glory. I sat on this same bench and began to read.

Somewhere between Achilles' rage and Hector's farewell, my eyelids gave way. Sleep came like a surrender.

When I woke, the light had thinned to honey. My body was cold, and an unfamiliar rug had been draped over me. It was coarse, smelling faintly of smoke and pine. For a moment, I thought I was still dreaming. Then I saw him.

He stood by the fountain, watching ripples break against the marble lip. He didn't move when our eyes met, as though he had been waiting for me to wake—not to speak.

'Did you put this on me?' I asked.

His voice was even, distant, 'No. But I'm grateful someone did.'

The words were plain, yet something in the way he said them made me tremble. Perhaps it was the cold breeze.

'You sound like you've been here a while,' I said.

'Long enough to finish a thought and begin another.'

'And what was the thought?'

He studied me.

'That you read Homer the way one reads a letter from a lover—with too much feeling, and too little armour.'

I couldn't tell if he meant to provoke or protect me.

'You were watching me?'

'It was impossible not to.'

The air thickened. I sat up, clutching the book.

'Do you always speak to strangers like this?'

'It never feels that way,' he said. 'Strange, I mean. Not when something has already been written.'

His gaze lingered on mine, as if remembering rather than discovering me. The city dissolved—the chatter, the footsteps, even the wind.

I remember thinking, absurdly, that this was how Achilles must have looked at the horizon before the ships burned—certain and lost, all at once.

'Who are you?' I asked.

He smiled faintly, the kind that leaves no trace.

'Someone passing through.'

'Through what?'

'Through the same world you're trying to escape.'

There was no arrogance in his voice, only an unsettling calm—as though he saw too much and pitied the knowing.

'You speak as if you've known me before.'

He didn't deny it.

'There's a kind of grief one recognises, no matter where it hides.'

I looked away, tracing the frayed edges of the rug. The air had warmed; light spilled like glory over the ruins. He stepped closer, gravel shifting beneath his sandals, and I noticed his age—the deep lines, the quiet fatigue in his eyes. Something ancient lived in his stillness, something that made time feel irrelevant.

'Do you live here?' I asked.

'I arrive. I stay. And then I go.'

'That sounds lonely,' I laughed.

'It is,' he was close now. 'But there are moments that make it bearable.'

He looked at me, and for an instant, the ruins, the city, the centuries folded into that single gaze.

'And this?' I whispered, 'Is this one of those moments?'

He didn't answer. Instead, his eyes drifted to the book.

'You stopped where Achilles waits,' he said softly. 'Before he knows what the waiting will cost him.'

I turned the page, though the words had already vanished.

When I looked up again, he was walking away—the wind catching the edge of his tunic, the light swallowing him whole.

But the rug remained. And *The Iliad* lay open on my lap, a single petal caught between its pages—as though marking the beginning of something I did not yet understand.

Now he is here again—riding bareback through circling dust like a figure carved from sunlight and storm. The crowd swells, yet I see only his feet—sandals loosened, blood threading down his heels.

'Gaius…'

His name leaves my lips like a prayer. Or a wound.

He laughs—not with joy, but with possession. He belongs to this: dust, glory, the brief illusion of being untouchable. And yet, when his eyes find mine across the roar, the world collapses into stillness.

'You don't forsake a ship because its sails are torn,' he says quietly.

He throws the tunic over his shoulders, the fabric clinging to his back, streaked with sweat and light. My pulse pounds in my throat.

'You thought I'd fall?' His lips curve faintly. 'I'm an expert at horsemanship.'

Something in his tone unsettles me.

'There's something I never told you,' he says.

'Please—don't. Not now.'

'Before all this,' he continues, 'I tended temples.'

I let out a small, disbelieving laugh.

'You? A priest?'

He smiles, but his eyes drift elsewhere.

'For a time. I believed holiness was absence. Then I met you—and learned it is the ache that refuses to leave.'

The world contracts. The roar fades to a single heartbeat—his or mine, I can't tell.

'You don't believe me,' he murmurs, brushing a lock of hair from my cheek. His fingers smell faintly of earth and iron.

'I don't know what to believe,' I whisper.

'Then believe this.' His voice trembles now, low and certain. 'When I look at you, I see everything unfinished in me. Every sin that asked forgiveness. Every prayer that never reached the sky.'

He leans closer, breath warm against my temple.

'And when I look deeper,' he says, 'I see something else.'

'What?'

'The life that will come from me and return to you.' His voice is barely audible now. 'My child—waiting behind your eyes. A future breathing inside your gaze.'

I freeze. Air, sound, self—everything halts. The world stands ancient and new, like marble before the sculptor's strike.

Then he whispers my name—not as a word, but as a vow.

'Mari.

A son.

We will have a son.'

Chapter 15

How ironic. I was missing what, only weeks ago, I had so desperately wanted to be rid of. I think of Fig—his soft fur, the small moans he made as he licked the hollow beneath my chin. I miss his insistent presence, the quiet proof of another life breathing beside mine.

The sunlight wanes until the words on the page blur. I close the book and look around, inhaling the sweetness of orange blossoms drifting through the air.

Gaius is nowhere in sight.

I pick up my phone, dial his number, and hover over the green button. I'm not supposed to call him. Not now. Not ever. That's the price of loving him—loving him in the shadows, the way one reads forbidden poetry, careful not to be seen turning the page.

At home, I miss the fragrance that once greeted me through the kitchen—rosemary and garlic melting into cheese. I ache to see Donna. The envy I once felt for her has dissolved, forgotten, like steam lifting from a pot left on a low flame.

At one of Mom's exhibitions many years ago, Donna had lingered before a painting as though spellbound. Lorenzo later told Mom that the girl returned every day for a week, hoping to meet the artist. But Mom was never one to dwell on her work. Once a painting was finished and released, it belonged to the world, not to her. She almost seemed eager to be rid of her art—perhaps because it carried too much of herself.

That painting showed a man and a woman seated by a river, the moon rippling across its dark surface. Between them lay a supper of figs, bread, and wine, half-forgotten as their eyes held one another's. In the background, musicians played soft, haunting notes—rendered only in faint outlines and blurred strokes—yet their presence filled the canvas with sound. The figures weren't touching, but the space between them pulsed with something more intimate than touch itself.

Anyone with a taste for history could have guessed who they were—two rulers by the Nile, suspended between empire and desire. But for Mom, it was never about history alone. She once told me the river was the part of her she never showed anyone: deep, restless, carrying everything away. The supper, she said, stood for fragile peace—always on the brink of being overturned. And the music, music that did not truly belong to the scene, was her reminder that even in moments of intimacy, there were always witnesses. Always shadows.

Perhaps that was why she let go of her paintings so easily. They were too heavy with her secrets, too raw with her longing.

At Donna's quiet insistence—and with Lorenzo's persuasion—Mom finally agreed to meet her. What followed surprised her. Donna spoke of the paintings with an intensity no one else ever had, asking about colour, texture, brushwork, the emotion buried in each stroke. Only later did it make sense when Mom learned that Donna had been orphaned young. A history student who had dropped out, she was still drawn to stories—worlds within worlds.

They began meeting every weekend at a café near Mom's studio in Florence, their conversations wandering from Roman emperors to Indian dynasties. One afternoon, Donna asked if she could help at the studio. Mom hesitated, then agreed, telling herself the salary might nudge the girl back toward her studies.

What began there—Donna quietly observing the act of painting—slowly unfurled its wings. Mom never allowed anyone to touch her canvases, yet she trusted Donna to clean her brushes once a painting was finished. When Mom fell into her silences, her long withdrawals, Donna began visiting the house. She cooked. She cleaned. She coaxed Mom to take her medicines, sometimes reading her to sleep. At first, it was occasional. Then it was days. Then weeks. And somewhere along the way, without anyone quite noticing, Donna crossed from assistant to something far more essential—Mom's anchor. And, in time, my friend too.

But sometimes I wondered—if Donna hadn't been there, maybe it would have been me. Maybe I would have been the one caring for Mom. And maybe then, I would have had more of her for myself.

Now that Donna has vanished without a word, it isn't her betrayal that lingers in me, but the hollow ache of her absence.

'Mari,' Dad calls, his voice careful, as though testing its own steadiness.

He stands at the door. 'Your mother may not come home tonight,' he says. 'Would you like to spend some time with me?'

'I…' My words falter as something shifts in the air. The house smells different—faintly sharp, unfamiliar. Recognition lands like a quiet blow. How could I forget this scent?

'Dad, have you eaten?' I ask.

'Yes.' He glances away. 'I had a sandwich.'

'You ordered food?'

'Yes. I did.'

He looks around, searching for something to occupy his hands. 'How's your novel coming? Is the manuscript ready?'

'I'm still writing the end.'

'Are you looking for publishers? Lorenzo knows a few—I could speak to him.'

'I don't need his help,' I reply too quickly.

He nods once.

Pencils lie freshly sharpened on the table. Magazines spill across one side of the bed—the side where Mom used to sleep, when our lives still followed the rhythm of ordinary days. I leave to change, and when I return, he is already asleep, folded into himself.

I sit beside him, brushing a strand of hair from his forehead, remembering how he once did the same for me. The tenderness of the memory collides with something uneasy—the weight that now settles in this room.

As I reach to turn off the lamp, I notice a pile of papers: rough sketches of a dome, precise and lonely. Dad has been working again—after almost a year.

I gather the sheets to place them in the drawer of his unused study table. That's when I see it: an envelope, its corners curled, paper yellowed, the front marked with hurried Hindi scrawl. Old, yet new to me. A letter I have never seen before.

I leave it where it rests and walk back to my room.

The scent clings to my fingers.

Mint.

And cigarette.

Chapter 16

Dad is right. Mom does not come.

I think of Fig and feel the tears slide down, wetting the pillow, filling my ears before soaking into the fabric. I don't remember when sleep comes—if it comes at all.

In the morning, I don't cook or clean. I call Mom. Switched off. I don't take a picture of my book to upload on my Instagram story for my twelve hundred followers. I rush out, grabbing a few cashews and cookies from the jar on the table.

I think of stopping by the library, just in case Gaius is waiting for me, but I change my mind.

At 9:18 in the morning, I am at her door.

I see Solo's handbag on the couch. I slip my hand inside, searching for her phone. I turn the bag upside down and watch its contents spill onto the rug—one by one. A pen. Lipstick. Mascara. And then, finally, something weightless that drops my heart into my stomach.

Return tickets. Eurostar Italia. Rome to Florence. Florence to Rome.

'You went to my house, didn't you?' I say, my voice breaking. 'And when you couldn't find Mom, you ran to Florence to tell her about me—after denying my request to help her when I asked you. I can't believe I trusted you with my secret. Gaius was right.'

'Marigold—' Solo steps closer, the colour draining from her face. 'I last met your mother in September. The year before. I never saw her again. No one did—except you.'

I cry out, 'Because you all gave up on her so easily.'

'Marigold…' Her voice trembles. 'It's because your mother died that day.'

My heart slams against my ribs, furious and disbelieving—like an animal hurling itself against the bars of its cage.

Marigold…

Solo's voice trails off, the syllables dissolving between us.

It's a sign that you're healing.

I am healing.

Then why is everything blurring?

Only a voice remains.

Mom's voice.

'Close your eyes, Mari. Tell me—what colour do you see?'

I think of Mom's paintings.

Purple wisteria in the golden wash of afternoon light. A glass palette balanced between her fingers. The thin fabric of her gown. Her sleek legs beneath it. I marvel at her beauty as her curls fall against the skin of her shoulders.

I see yellow.

The thick pages between her fingers as she turns them, lingering over my father's handwriting tucked into the margins. Longing rising, unguarded.

I see blue.

The bruises she never explained.

And then—

I see the eyes in the face of the man in the mural.

Black.

Chapter 17

'Your mother died on September 25, 2017. Your hallucinations were keeping her alive—through memory,' Solo says, her voice low and steady. 'Did you ever wonder how she appeared only at night and never woke with you? How she ate, bathed, or spoke to you—or to your father? Why did she never call, or create new artworks, during the hours she supposedly spent at her studio in Florence?'

'I should have known.' My knees give way.

'Marigold, you are not well. You need help.'

I look up at her through the blur. 'Gaius warned me never to come to you. I should have known it wouldn't be just Fig you'd make me lose. A shrink like you would take more than that.'

Solo's face twitches, a shadow crossing her composure. 'Your mother had to go, Mari, so you could carry on. You still have your father. Now that you are healing, he will heal too.'

I clutch my head and weep, but even in my delirium, I am not shocked.

Perhaps because, secretly, I already knew.

Yes.

I always knew.

Solo moves closer and lowers herself to the floor. Her knees crack softly. She takes my hands in hers. They are warm, like a scarf just lifted from the neck.

'And then there is... Gaius,' she says carefully. 'How long have you been together—you and him?'

I grit my teeth. All I want is to collapse into his arms, to cry until language dissolves, to beg forgiveness for not listening. The answer rises from somewhere inside me, I no longer recognise.

'Long enough for love to take root,' I say. 'Too long to ever unlearn it.'

'Mari,' she says gently, 'Could I meet him? Perhaps we could go for a coffee—just the three of us. There's a lovely café near your library.'

I laugh, sharp-edged. 'That's what you did to Mom, isn't it?'

She holds her breath, then exhales slowly, 'How often do you see him?'

'Is that why she killed herself?' I snap. 'Because you made her believe she was crazy?'

I notice Solo's fists clenched at her sides. So she isn't as calm as she pretends.

'Marigold,' she leans closer and whispers, 'Why did he ask you to keep him a secret?'

I can't think anymore. I just want her to stop speaking.

'It's because—'

'Go on.'

'It's because Gaius is married.'

The colour rushes back to her face, 'Married? You mean—'

'To another woman,' I say.

Chapter 18

How does one learn to live without a mother?

Is it even possible?

I feel like a damaged boat—splintered, leaking—still drifting on a sea that refuses to end. There is no shore in sight, only the endless hum of waves demanding that I keep going.

Matteo has taken Dad for therapy at his centre. The house feels hollow.

I reach for my phone, my fingers trembling, and type into the search bar:

Ira Lall.

Dozens of articles bloom on the screen like poisonous flowers. Every word speaks of her life: *The Tragic Life of a Modern-Day Genius. The Brush That Never Spoke.*

Only one mentions her death: *The Mysterious Death of an Indian-Italian Artist.* But when I click on it, nothing loads. The page has been taken down.

I scroll through photographs—some stolen, some staged. In each, she looks as if she is in the middle of becoming someone else. Yet not one article tells me how she died. Only that on the evening of September 25, Ira Lall was found dead in her house in Rome. Survived by her daughter, Marigold, and her husband, the architect Nihal Sagg.

A thought circles me like a vulture refusing to land.

What if my mother was murdered?

Sleep deserts me. My body is drained, but my mind crackles awake, electric and merciless.

I climb the attic ladder. Mom kept everything she brought from India here—sketches, diaries, old canvases wrapped in brittle paper.

Paintings of flowers: bougainvillaea, lotus, flame lilies—dated as far back as 1993. On the back of each, her delicate handwriting: the place, the month, the year. Some are crude, almost hesitant, as though drawn by someone still learning how to see.

It strikes me—these are not the works of Ira Lall, the legend.

They are the desperate beginnings of Ira, the girl from New Delhi.

I am about to unroll the canvases when something stops me.

Then I see it.

A file, stamped across the front in bold black letters:

NEW DELHI

Inside are neatly typed pages. A manuscript.

No title.

No acknowledgements.

No name.

A chill moves through me.

It is her story.

I freeze. The world narrows to the sound of my own breath.

Was I meant to find this?

Was this her way of returning—of telling me everything she never could in life?

Perhaps she left her truth not in words spoken, but in words written.

And perhaps, in the only language I understand, she has finally begun to speak.

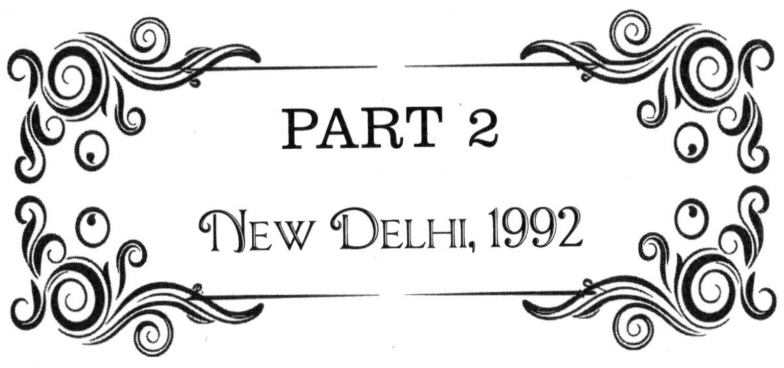

PART 2

New Delhi, 1992

The Silence That Raised Us

Chapter 1

Ira flattened the paper with her palm, sucked the back of the pencil, and sighed. She had prepared the easel earlier but found herself too distracted. Too angry to keep thinking about *him*.

Beside the nightstand, she let out a little frown at the sight of white roses.

An old memory stroked her. Amma was picking lice from her hair in the garden. Aarya, whose turn was next, drew circles in the air, watching the clouds as she lay on the sweet-smelling grass. It was an October evening. Amma's eyes had not yet learned the art of betrayal.

'White roses in autumn mean a girl is likely to become a young bride.'

Amma had become a widow at fifteen. But unlike other women bound by the same fate, she chose to live—fully, defiantly. She dressed beautifully, spoke her mind without hesitation, and carried herself with unrepentant grace. Naturally, few relatives wished to engage with her or her unsettling opinions. So, she devoted herself to raising her one son, Ira's father, Aryaveer, and to her flower garden—a place that always reciprocated her love.

Throwing the windows open, Ira inhaled the chilled air. It relaxed her for a while before it began to prick her skin. She was glad it wasn't autumn. Ira harboured a deep dislike for her life, and somehow believed marriage could only make it worse. She had seen how wearily marriages functioned—between her parents and their friends.

Amma never questioned whether Ira missed school. 'The real education is delivered in the lap of nature.'

Ira didn't need to bring to her notice the special reason for doing so today, and her parents were only expected to be back in the evening.

The young girl moved in a daze until she decided to wash up and stare at the blank sheet for forty minutes, a sharpened pencil clenched between her fingers. She cupped her face and muffled a scream or two, feeling beneath her fingertips the tiny bumps forming on her forehead—the ugly invitees of adolescence.

The evening slipped in too fast, and she dressed in a woollen maxi dress she had bought with Amma for today.

'Are they here?' she asked Shivani, who was arranging roses into the three silver vases of ascending height on the dining table—the ones Ira remembered buying with her mother from a flea market on a bleak evening in Mauritius. Their last holiday as a family. It was dark, the street almost empty, barring tired vendors and a few tourists. She had held tightly to the hem of her mother's dress on one side and Aarya's hand on the other.

'Any moment, Didi,' Shivani's voice carried a hopeful calm.

Ira shook her head and peeled the skin on her lips with her teeth, a habit she found hard to quit. 'Did you see the flowers we planted?'

'Yeah…the tiny buds already. That's marigold for you.' Shivani gestured for her to stop. 'Did you tell Nihal? He was so excited to see them bloom. Funny how he likes marigolds of all flowers.'

The ache of betrayal returned. She licked the faint blood on her lips and flopped onto the sofa. Once certain that no one was paying attention, she picked up the receiver and dialled the eight digits of his neighbour's landline number.

'Hello!'

'Hello—can you get Nihal to speak with me, please?'

'I haven't seen him in days.'

'Can you check once?'

The call dropped.

Gritting her teeth, she banged the receiver back onto its antique body. Patience is a weight the heart learns to carry slowly. The telephone survived, as did her irritation. It was from an auction of palatial items in England—a gift from her maternal grandfather at her parents' grand wedding, held at a fort in Jaipur. Most of what they owned—especially the expensive things—came from her mother's side of the family, including their residence in the most celebrated part of New Delhi. But it held little value for Ira today. Especially the telephone.

The doorbell blared, startling the cook, who was leafing through a magazine on the kitchen counter, admiring a photograph of Rekha in a man's suit. Ira rose, a faint smile grazing her cracked lips. The next moment, she froze.

It was all *four* of them.

'So you won't see us when your friend isn't here, is that it, Lalit?' Putting on her thick glasses, Amma chimed as she cornered the tall man. The hallway suddenly filled with chatter and activity.

'Forgive me, Amma,' Lalit removed his coat and handed it to Shivani, who placed it carefully on the coat stand. 'I had a good reason to come here two weeks ago, but managed to crash through the staircase... and my landline was not working for some reason. I couldn't even go to the court.'

Ira felt her throat throbbing; she could almost hear it like drumbeats in her ears. The gushing blood lent a fiery tone to her face and neck. Her father hugged her from behind, then placed a packet wrapped in blue paper in her palm, a book maybe, or another diary she could use to write letters.

'How is my Frida Kahlo?' Aryaveer asked.

But Ira was barely able to register a word.

Amma watched with painful eyes as Mandira planted a near-dead kiss on Ira's forehead—the daughter she hadn't seen in the last two weeks—before making her way to the staircase. Her large sunglasses cloaked her eyes.

'She has been a great help to me this past week,' Amma announced, pressing her granddaughter's palm reassuringly and trying with definite failure to compensate for her mother's distance. But Ira was not thinking about her mother, not just yet.

She looked everywhere but in the direction of Uncle Lalit, completely losing the little of what remained of the charm of meeting her parents after weeks of separation.

More of a friend than a brother-in-law to Ira's father, Lalit was a lawyer, nearly as successful and financially plump as Ira's family. Growing up in a modest neighbourhood and going to the same school, the two had always been friendly, but fair to say they bonded mostly over the grief that befell the Lall family three years ago.

'The family would have been doomed, if not for Lalit,' Amma had once told Ira. Ira didn't tell Amma that she felt the family was doomed anyway.

'Won't you show me your flowers?' Lalit's eyes were fixed on Ira.

She felt hot in the weight of his gaze. 'They are not flowers, yet.'

Aryaveer squinted.

'I met her at the nursery. She was with a...' Lalit pretended to remember what he hadn't forgotten all this while. 'With a boy, must be a classmate...or was he a senior?'

'It was Nihal,' Ira snapped, her cheeks burning.

'During school hours,' Lalit added.

Amma's mouth twisted when Aryaveer's voice took on a coarse quality, 'Ira, did you miss school?' Aryaveer's voice hardened, 'I'll speak with Nihal.'

Lalit guffawed, immediately diffusing the fire he had put on in the first place, 'It must have been the school picnic, there were several other students.'

Ira nodded weakly, acknowledging the fragile intimacy of the new secret she was now sharing with Uncle Lalit. It wasn't their first secret. The girls were toddlers when Aryaveer stayed for months in Vishakhapatnam, designing a shopping centre. Lalit would accompany Mandira for the vaccinations of the girls, secretly slipping a chocolate bar into their pockets for being nice. The girls giggled and obeyed. On their way back, he would then insist that Mandira take them for lunch because they had been *cooperative*.

'What's all the commotion?' Sujata's exaggeratedly cheery voice soared before her eyes fell on Ira, 'Oh my darling little girl!'

Ira had never been more delighted at the sight of her aunt, who emerged through the powder room, setting her sprawling hair with her wet palm. Her lips, the usual brown like dark chocolate, made her teeth appear even whiter. Sujata was Mandira's first cousin, a dentist and a fancy one at that. Her clients wore pearls and came in imported cars.

Ira felt the gentle touch of Sujata's lips on her face. She had always been warm, both literally and metaphorically. 'I can't believe you're thirteen already,' she placed her hands on the solitaire strung on her throat, portraying disbelief in a manner only grown-ups are capable of. 'When I was thirteen, my father had begun imagining his grandchildren.'

Ira noticed the strain in her laughter. She always did, like a layer she had painted underneath a landscape only she knows about.

~

A comforting aroma of garlic settled around the dining room. Authentic Indian curries and breads decorated in ornate silverware were served in silence while Mandira remained in her room, still wearing her sunglasses, staring at the only remaining family photograph in the house. It was hypocritically funny because Mandira decided to remove all the photos from the house but kept the one at the closest proximity. On her bedside table lay a small photograph of four broad smiles that looked like an animated dream from another lifetime. The thing about grief is, no matter how new, it always feels ancient.

A small plum cake with crushed walnuts that Sujata had ritually baked was cut and served alongside the dinner as if to save time, igniting the trivial conversations about the school's management, Sujata's dental practice and the upcoming conference in New York where she was speaking about the importance of early orthodontic intervention. Amma's roses and infantile vegetables in the garden were intricately discussed. A few times, between the mouthfuls, Amma asked random things like the weather and the people of Spain. 'Are they big like the Americans? And tall? Do they eat pasta for breakfast and dinner?'

'Not at all, Ma,' Aryaveer said, chewing, then getting back to eating in silence.

Outside, the evening yielded to the gloomy quietude of night typical of winters. Ira barely followed as her father filled the air with his experiences with Spanish cuisine on the insistence of Sujata. It was the whiskey doing the talking now, Ira knew.

'They call their starters *hors d'oeuvres*. My client called them, 'horse divorce'.'

Everyone laughed, except Ira. She didn't find it funny because she thought she would have probably spoken the same way had she not been told otherwise.

Sometime later, Mandira appeared, dragging her steps as if each step weighed a ton, her eyes dull and heavy. Like always, her sorrow filled the room, leaving little space for anyone else. She placed an unpacked box of sable brushes beside Ira's plate, much like a nurse assembles a box of pills for the patient she had been tied to for her entire life. Aryaveer took on the animated quality like he always does after a few drinks. He explained how the brushes are considered the pinnacle of brush making.

'The hair is sourced from the Siberian weasels, incredibly fine and springy. You'll see. We were told it can hold a remarkable amount of paint.' He looked at Lalit reassuringly, 'So I asked him to give us two sets.'

'Two?' Lalit licked the back of his spoon, praising his wife's baking skills with his eyes briefly.

'Yes...Mandira wanted to take it for Fiza as well.'

'The girl keeps her head in the newspapers, I doubt she will have any use of a paint brush.' Amma wiped the curd from around her mouth with the back of her palm because why should she waste a napkin when she will eventually wash her hands after the meal. 'And that reminds me to tell you I'd earlier sent meal boxes to the orphanage, samosas and bread pakodas.'

'I'm in my room,' Mandira announced, as if the most challenging part of her stage performance was over. No one pressed her to stay. Custard, with caramelised sugar and pomegranate, was served and polished in a mournful silence.

While the sweetness melted on her tongue, Ira felt a sharp, piercing feeling encroaching on her heart, almost numbing to her senses. A grief that she had been effortfully putting away from her thoughts surfaced. When Sujata's gentle query about the girl from the orphanage, Fiza, met Lalit's explanation, Ira's mind, fogged by sorrow, was already struggling to grasp the words. And once again, settling amidst them, seen and unseen by the naked eye like the particles of dust, was...

Aarya.

'Do you know who died three years ago?' Ira said to the empty side of her bed.

'Me. It wasn't you—it was me. A part of me died with you. Not the part you knew, but the part I was yet to become. The one I am now.

If you were to see the mother she has become, you would know.

You are still alive, while I am gone—forgotten, like a white canvas painted over.

And for that, I will never forgive you.'

Chapter 2

'You look like you haven't slept,' Nihal said, his voice a low rumble. Ira stared at the sketch in her hand.

'I didn't know mansions have mice too.' He tried to smile, but it felt forced.

'Some things aren't funny.'

She was wearing the white sweater Amma had knitted for Aarya and herself, with an *I* embroidered on the chest.

A wave of guilt washed over Nihal. 'You know…' he said quietly, 'I've been looking forward to seeing you all week.'

'Oh, have you?'

'I'm sorry,' he said, his eyes warm. 'I really am.'

'Yeah, well,' she muttered, turning away. Her gaze fixed on the drawing of a French balcony pinned to the wall in front of her. Peonies, Amma had always said, symbolised romance. Ira just liked the way the colours bled into each other, the shades of pink, like a bruise.

Cupping his face, he drew a deep breath and extracted a box from his school bag. He placed it on her lap. In a sudden, childish gesture, she flung it at the window. The box burst open on impact. Whipped cream streaked the glass, spilled down the lace curtains, and pooled on the wooden floorboards.

'What are you doing?' his voice, only as sharp as it was apologetic.

She looked at him with a strange, furious energy that suddenly softened, 'You… you're hurt?'

He touched his forehead, wincing, but it wasn't the pain. 'It was… an accident,' he mumbled, turning away.

'Tell me.' She straightened.

'Your birthday,' he asked instead. 'How was it?'

She knew it was a bargain. So she began, watching him rise to clean the mess of the whipped cream with a rag, 'A regular birthday. A cake, white roses...portent of my early marriage, apparently.' She rolled her eyes. 'And, of course, the imported gifts—a set of paintbrushes from my mother and a diary from Papa,' the words tumbled out like a torrent of pent-up emotions. 'Your turn?'

'A lawyer came home,' Nihal said in a low voice. 'To get Ma to sign my father's licence.'

'Licence?'

'Yeah, to marry again.'

'And she said no?'

'She... she wouldn't say yes...' The stitches on his forehead seemed to pulse with every word he spoke. 'Then things got a bit out of hand.'

Ira felt a surge of anger. 'The lawyer... did he hurt you? We can speak to Uncle Lalit. He is also a...'

'No, no,' he said quickly. 'It was really an accident. It had nothing to do with the man. He was only doing his job.'

Nihal thought about the large man's words that echoed in his ears long after he'd left his house. He didn't tell Ira how the anger built inside him, consumed him like embers beneath the ash. He didn't tell her about the sudden, violent impulse that sent his head crashing against the looking glass in the bathroom. 'I slipped,' he told his mother when he came out after dressing himself and cleaning the blood stains from the off-white floor tiles.

Nevertheless, Ira believed him.

Nihal then pulled another package from his bag. The paper crinkled between his fingers. She tore it open, and inside, rolled in the tissue paper, was a paintbrush. The handle, worn smooth in years.

'It's beautiful,' her voice caught in her throat.

'Found it at a pawn shop,' he said, 'The owner said it belonged to an Englishman. Here, look... a marking.'

The inscription was a tiny, poignant story. 'To Stella, with love from George, 1930,' she read aloud. 'Poor Stella.'

Nihal was now examining the hair with his thumb. His lips curled, 'Maybe George was an ass, or maybe he spent a good night with Amelia...or Bella.'

Ira smiled. And it was enough for him to remember how.

'So… tell me about school,' she asked.

Nihal's smile was an amused one, 'Don't tell me you've been absent for a week?'

'You know me!' Ira's eyes danced with mischief.

'I know both you and who your father is,' Nihal teased, then began to tell her all. She listened intently as he described the upcoming birthday party of one of the famous boys from his class, where he was invited for the first time. This was the new project he had been given by the principal himself, after his article on the world's most astonishing monuments was published in the national daily. He went on to tell her about the school's annual day theatre auditions and the country chosen this year. *Italy*, he told her. And then, carefully placing this piece of information towards the end, he told her about the new girl in class 10th who had taken the entire senior wing by storm.

'I don't know what the project is about, but I'm the only one in the entire 11th grade to participate. I'll be representing the school, can you believe it? Me?' Pride radiated in his eyes.

Ira sank into the couch beside him, her laughter still lingering. 'Why is everyone always so pleased with you?' she teased.

Nihal smirked. 'A girl was furious with me just last week.'

'I missed you,' she said, lightly punching his cheek.

He winced. 'Ow! My tooth! You're dangerous, you know that?'

She grinned, settling a cushion on her lap and folding her hands over it. 'So tell me—new admission in the middle of the session? Must be from an important family.'

He yawned. 'Aren't all of you from important families here?'

'Yeah, but she must be *something*,' Ira said, lowering her voice. 'To cause that storm you were talking about.'

His expression turned thoughtful, a flicker of something unreadable crossing his face. Ira caught the hesitation in his lips and tilted her head. 'Is she now?'

'I can't say for myself,' he said after a pause. 'Barely even saw her.'

~

Grief teaches you to speak to emptiness as if it were listening. *Nihal finally showed up.* Ira spoke to the empty side of her bed again. *I know he had hurt himself. I wonder if he gets to know such things about me without asking.*

She closed her eyes, but the words swirled in her head. The room suddenly felt small and airless.

When Ira was deep into sleep, she often felt Aarya's hand on her belly—warm and light. She felt her leg tangled with her sister's. Sometimes she warmed in that moment of cold darkness. Sometimes, she woke up scared. Every night, she reached for a ghost and found herself instead.

Chapter 3

Manicured hedges framed the tall entrance to Saksham's house. Nihal walked hesitantly through the lawn with pruned trees, already regretting his decision to come here. To his left were sheds—perhaps staff quarters—and to his right, a stone patio with a lit fountain. At a glance, he could make out two figures on the bench. The boy, whom Nihal could not identify, waved his hand. Nihal returned the gesture.

The three marble steps opened into a passage with papered floral walls and countless tall statues. Nihal felt a gaze on the back of his neck. He turned, and the sight stopped him — a girl with short hair and skin that caught the light like water, smiling as if she'd been waiting all along. Unsure, he returned the smile.

'You won the inter-state debate last month, right?' The girl squinted her eyes, observing him diligently now, as if to find something she had lost in his features.

With pursed lips and wavering eyes that kept dropping at the marble floor, Nihal nodded slightly. Suddenly, he realised she was the new admission but seemed like an entirely new person, not the one he remembered looking at briefly in school. She was wearing high heels, a black blouse and fitted jeans that sat just below her navel.

'I'm Sharan's sister, Sonam. Your junior by one class.'

A hesitant smile flickered on his lips. From the other side of the door, the merry cheers floated.

'My brother and Saksham often talk about you.'

Nihal held the copper handle to push it when he flinched as he felt her palm over his. Her fingers were warm, and she smelled of cocoa and bonfire. And maybe alcohol. He wasn't sure.

'Why do you look so scared?' Her gaze danced in amusement.

He cleared his throat, 'Nothing like it.'

Inside, the place brimmed with expensive-looking boys and girls, all of whom he had seen in school sometime or another. He remembered the lines from the novel he had been reading in the bus on his way here about an extravagant night and thought how strangely the words had come alive. The ballroom shimmered with a kaleidoscope of light, the chandeliers casting a dazzling glow upon the throng of elegantly dressed guests. Music swelled from the orchestra, a lively waltz sweeping the room in a dizzying whirl.

They were seated around a large glass table, on which lay an empty green bottle. 'Truth or Dare,' they sang in chorus. Saksham pulled Nihal by the rim of this shirt. 'Beer man, right?'

Nihal cleared his throat, 'I'm good. I don't drink.'

He had a faint idea about a few boys from his class who indulged, but he was astonished to realise how common it was among them and how different their world looked from his own.

'Guys, guys, he is Nihal. The boy is good at *everything*. He is… like a brother,' Saksham announced wide-eyed.

The crowd was utterly absorbed in the cacophony of clinking glasses, the rustling of popcorn bags, and the hushed whispers of anticipation as the bottle spun. Oblivious to the solitary figure standing slightly apart, even though he really was good at everything. Nihal's eyes darted across the room and caught Sonam again. This time, he offered a faint smile to which she quietly pronounced his name in a manner of telling herself loudly.

He sank into the sofa. Sonam sat beside him. Yes—she reeked of alcohol.

'Do you want to go out of here?' Her breath was warm in his ear.

'Here is good, I think.'

'It's a stupid game. No one tells the truth.'

His eyes fell on her wristwatch. Gold strap with red dial.

Sonam scoffed, 'But take it anyway. If you pick dare, they'll ask you to kiss a stupid girl from around here.'

Nihal looked at her, bewildered. What exactly was he thinking when he decided to come here? And just then, she rested her head on his shoulder, her lips grazing the edge of his ear. A shiver ran through him; he stiffened, but he didn't move her away.

'Have you ever kissed a girl on the mouth?'

Before he could answer, Saksham declared, 'Nihal! Take truth, brother. It's your first time.'

Nihal didn't know he was in the game.

'I told you,' Sonam whispered from the side. 'He'll take the truth,' she chimed.

Truth. Truth. Truth… the crowd joined in.

'Are you riding the freak because her father owns the school?' Someone from the side where the boys were seated asked, and everyone joined in the laughter.

Placing his glass on the rug, Saksham rose to his feet. 'Hey, don't be mean, guys.'

He patted Nihal's shoulder, 'You don't have to answer that, brother?'

'It's alright. Really.' Nihal looked around the room. He flattened his shirt and noticed the severed belt loop on his jeans.

'Her name is Ira,' Nihal announced, feeling a gentle squeeze of Saksham's hand on his shoulder. 'And it would be nice if you'd call her by her name, even in school.' Nihal swallowed, feeling confident and nervous at the same time. His heart was exploding with a feeling he couldn't identify. 'And Ira and I are good friends.'

He sat back, sighed to calm his quickened heartbeat and checked the time on Sonam's watch. 8.15 p.m.

'How close?' Sonam whispered.

He looked at her; she didn't need an answer and was already clicking her fingers over her yawning mouth. In front of them, a boy rose to kiss the girl sitting next to him. Nihal had seen her at the dance practice in the school auditorium a few times. The girl closed her eyes, and the kiss was over before it began.

Chips and mini burgers were brought in a trolley by a uniformed man who did not smile. Another carried a tray of soda and water. A few more boys and girls kissed. A peck on the lips, both parties reddening, grinning ear to ear as they tasted the stolen, early blooms of sweet youth. Youth, yet to be scarred by adulthood.

'Do you want me to kiss you?' Sonam's hand brushed the back of Nihal's palm. He quickly pulled away. A faint amusement flickered across her face.

'I...' He breathed, 'I'm leaving here soon...my mother is waiting.'

The crowd cheered, and the bottle pointed towards Sonam. Sharan threw his hands in frustration. Sonam looked at Nihal, who deliberately drifted his gaze to something in the distance. A piano beneath a large oil painting of Saksham with both his parents. It reminded him briefly of Ira and the warm feeling she always brings, which further accentuated his regret for coming here amidst these privileged teenagers. What do they know about the night spent in the groan of a sewing machine, trying to sleep, but the sleep wouldn't come because the stomach was hungry. Have they ever seen a high-headed stranger insult their mother while she remained silent for a few hundred rupees, and later unfurl all her fury on her son, who was too young to understand that it gave her a sense of relief and renewal and temporarily cleansed her pent-up feelings?

If they had, they would know what real truth and real dare look like.

Truth or dare.

'Truth.' Sharan said in place of his sister. 'She'll take the truth.'

Sonam shrugged her shoulders. Rolling her eyes, she exhaled a heavy, tired breath.

'If you'd chosen dare,' A girl with a heavy puff on her hair spoke between the sips of an amber liquid from her glass, 'What would you have liked us to tell you to do?'

Nihal felt something freeze inside him. He looked at Sharan, and even though he hadn't done anything wrong, a feeling akin to fear gripped him. He wanted to be invisible.

Sonam laughed dryly, passed her glance between Nihal and the small-faced girl, then halted her eyes on her brother, who was visibly annoyed. 'I would have liked you to tell me to pop ten sleeping pills in my mouth than to kiss any boy present here.'

The boys hooted, laughed and exchanged coded words before going back to the game. The moment Sonam took her place next to Nihal, he rose and told Saksham solemnly that he must be with his mother now. After a quick, tight hug and a pat on the back, Nihal charged towards the door.

'I need some fresh air,' Sonam tagged along, inviting herself out with Nihal.

'Back there, I lied.' She burped and apologised in the hallway.

'About the pills?'

'About the boys.'

'Oh.'

They were now in the garden. The sweet scent of jasmine was strong in the crisp evening breeze. The trees stood around them like witnesses, tall and watching. 'I would have happily kissed you.'

Nihal diverted his gaze again, but could feel his ears reddening as if on fire. Only this time, she held his hand in hers. Her grip was tight, like a fearful child in a public place.

'You should go back inside. It's too cold, and you are...' his gaze chanced on the delicate fabric of her top before catching the sight of the main gate.

'I grew up in the mountains...' Sonam spat.

Nihal tried to loosen his hand from her grip, but she wouldn't let him. Then suddenly, she freed him, but not his eyes.

Nihal sucked a breath, 'Should I... drop you home? I don't have a car, but we can get an auto rickshaw.'

'No, no.' Sonam was struggling to balance on her feet, so she put some of her weight on his right shoulder. 'You know what they call you when they see you on the stage.'

'I do.'

'Pet Pauper.'

Nihal laughed, but something inside him had begun to prick.

'Five years...and you'll beat them all in the face. You are...not like any of them.'

It pleased him to hear it, the five-year part. Sonam came closer and kissed his face on the side of his ear.

'And you're also very beautiful,' she whispered between heavy breaths.

It was a blur. One moment, her hand was in his; the next, it was gone, along with a curt, '*goodbye forever*' as she rapidly retreated to the stone bench.

Nihal closed his palms in a fist and considered staying a little longer, but then decided otherwise. He felt awkward when the guard saluted him. When the heavy iron gate screeched closed behind him, and he was finally on the other side—the rough, edgy side where people hustle to survive real life, the side he fitted into and felt home—Nihal found himself running back.

'Forgot something, sir?' The guard who had settled comfortably back in his glass cabin appeared swiftly.

Nihal pushed the door open and ran towards the patio where Sonam's silhouette was even darker against the night. She was hunched over on the bench, her face buried in her knees. Her hair was whipping in the wind. A panic ran through Nihal as he hurried towards her.

He held her face and straightened her. She was pale. 'Let me go,' she mumbled in broken words.

'Wake up,' Nihal shook her, and a bottle that read *diclofenac* dropped from her palm on the grass. He had seen this bottle at the shop and knew what it could do. It was hard for him to think. Instinctively, he opened her mouth and stuck his index finger to check. She bit him hard.

A low, painful screech left his mouth.

Sonam's mouth was dry, so he scraped the pills out with his fingers. In this moment, she heaped on the grass beneath him. Once he was sure there were no more pills in her mouth, he screamed for help.

Saksham was the first one to materialise from inside. He looked terrified. Two girls, completely dressed in white, hand in hand, followed him calmly.

'We need to call the ambulance,' Nihal said, rising to his feet.

A girl went back immediately and reappeared with Sharan and another boy—slightly older—who held his head in his palms. He was too far for Nihal to register, but he saw how tall he was. Six feet at least.

'Told you she is an attention-seeking bitch,' the tall boy declared to everyone.

Nihal felt a speck of rage run inside him, but he knew better. 'Someone call for an ambulance, please. She is...'

He felt Sonam's hand wrap around his shoulders from behind.

'I'm fine. Nihal. Can you take me home? Please…'

'There should be no need. Mom's going to be furious. You are not leaving here. Not unless you look sober.' Sharan grabbed Sonam by her elbow and led her inside, almost dragging her in the process. The two girls giggled and followed.

Saksham looked at Nihal and sighed. For a while, the two stood without a word. And then Saksham patted him goodbye, 'No one should know this, I hope you understand, brother.'

Nihal kept his word.

Chapter 4

'How was your day?' Prajakta released a long yawn. She dug her fingers into her temples with a force that seemed to hurt her.

Nihal glanced at the pile of clothes on the table and walked to stand behind her. Pulling up the sleeves of his sweater, he began to knead the muscles on her shoulders.

'Nothing special. Another day with the old man,' he lied, throwing a quick glance in the direction of the kitchen. The lights were turned off.

Prajakta closed her eyes. 'How many more days does the chemist need you for?'

Nihal ran his fingers through her hair in a rhythmic motion. 'A few.'

For over a week, he was filling in for a helping staff member for a chemist after school, a few streets further from his house. The old man spat when he spoke and never covered his mouth. He liked to rant about politicians turning the country into some sort of America, commented on every customer after they left, and kept magazines full of naked women in his drawer, which he flipped through during lunch. He kept forgetting where he left his glasses and often screamed at the boys for working too slowly or for stealing coins. If he were not paying Nihal three hundred rupees a week, he would never have liked to be near such a filthy man.

Nihal worked his way upwards, tracing the contours of his mother's skull, trying to ease the tightness that had gripped her like a vice.

Prajakta moaned, 'Can you drop the blouses at Lipi's house tomorrow on your way to school?'

He nodded, watching her lean into his touch, her body slowly relaxing. He noticed the silver strands multiplying in her hair, a reminder of how much time had passed since he saw her vibrant and young. For a fleeting moment, Nihal remembered the family photo at Saksham's house. How his mother laughed heartily, showcasing her perfect white teeth. A gold necklace almost entirely covering her bosom over a silk saree. His father's hand snaking around his wife's waist. The photograph exuded the air of opulence but also something else. A sense of wholeness.

He tiptoed into the kitchen, rinsed rice and moong dal, then stepped out onto the balcony with *Anna Karenina*. A bitter smile crossed his lips at the opening line: *Happy families are all alike; every unhappy family is unhappy in its own way.* After half an hour, he filled the pressure cooker with water, dropped in the soaked grains, and added salt and turmeric. He made a mental note to buy coriander and cumin on his way back from school tomorrow.

After dinner, which Prajakta barely touched, she cleared the kitchen while Nihal readied the room for the night. He brushed threads from the sofa, pushed the sewing machine behind the curtain that divided their room from the narrow lobby and mopped the floor.

The traces of moments spent between these walls coughed to life. A pang of something akin to longing, but also a dull ache of resignation, settled in his chest once again. He remembered the easy comfort they once shared as a family.

Grief does not stay with people alone; it seeps into walls that hold voices, into floors worn smooth by footsteps, and into the creases of bedsheets. Cupboards, no matter how fiercely emptied, cling to what remains—the scent of fabric in the wood, a scrawl of handwriting on the laminate, or some forgotten scrap—a handkerchief too trivial to be carried away.

'How is your tooth?' Prajakta appeared on the balcony with two cups of tea. He closed the book and placed it at the back of his chair.

'Better now,' he lied.

'Did you talk to Ira?'

'Ma, it's alright, I said.' He didn't meet her eyes. 'I've got homework now. You should sleep.'

Prajakta stifled a yawn. 'Yes, right.' She glanced at his book. 'I'll leave the hemming for morning.' She rubbed her neck, the sleeve slipping back to reveal a hole at the elbow of her sweater. He watched her with an almost-smile crossing his face; life had its quiet ways of making jokes.

Prajakta stitched clothes for the women in the neighbourhood. Buttons, hooks, the occasional even simple embroidery—all at prices kept lower than the fancy boutique owned by a rude-mannered lady down the street. There were whispers that she lived with her lover and not her husband.

In the beginning, Prajakta's fingers were always pricked and wrapped in white tape. Long hours at the machine left her with headaches and stiff knees. The fatigue, however, helped her lull the grief, and she eventually adapted to the tak-tak-tak rhythm of the machine, becoming an almost hypnotic counterpoint to the hum of the silent lives of the mother and son.

The women were mostly satisfied, but complaints always came—a seam out of place, a fit that didn't flatter. 'I should have gone to the boutique,' they'd sigh. Prajakta would respond with a small discount, unwilling to lose even a single customer when her sewing was the only thread holding the house afloat. From his corner, Nihal listened, wishing he could find a way to bring money.

'Oh, did she like your present?' She picked up her cup from the grill. It was an old one. Chipped and cracked china from the time she peeled peas, listened to the radio, and could afford a long afternoon siesta.

'I'm hoping she does.' His voice came tired. Or irritated.

'You know Dr Sujata is her family friend?'

'I will not ask for a favour, Ma.'

'It's not a favour. We will pay.'

'I have taken an appointment at the government hospital for this Friday.'

Prajakta gritted her teeth, looking away, her eyes beginning to tear. She emptied her tea in one long gulp.

Nihal watched as his mother fell silent. The rage that once burned in her eyes had faded. She looked older now, far older than the years that had passed. Once her thick black hair had fallen in a neat braid down her back, she barely lifted a comb. Grief, he thought, showed itself as age—most clearly on a mother.

Nihal closed his eyes and pressed them with three fingers, willing away the headache.

'Switch off the bulb when you come inside.' Prajakta rose and shuffled back to the room.

Nihal stared at the man crumpled on the pavement, a stray dog curled beside him. For a moment, he wondered if Ira had touched the brush he'd bought her. Then the thought swiftly slid to the new girl. Sonam. Her question: *Have you ever kissed a girl on the mouth?* Their question: *Are you riding the freak because her father owns the school?*

Then the aftermath—the pills scattered like seeds, her pupils blown wide, the panic when he held her limp in his arms.

He looked at the bite mark on his finger. Still red.

And then—another memory made its way. Older, sharper. From a time when he was still a boy.

Ma's scream. *I'll go away and never come back.*

His fingers shivering, but the paper was held tightly. A letter. He had chased her, barely able to see through the tears.

Her voice behind the slammed door: *You're just like your father. Thankless. A punishment. I wonder why he didn't take you with him forever.*

The hinge had caught his little finger when she shut the door on him. Blood bloomed on the floor. Not red. Maroon, like one of Ira's painted roses. *Sorry, Ma. Sorry.*

How he had shivered. A boy, not yet eight.

A tear burned its way down his cheek. He wiped it fast.

Father. No. He wouldn't think of him. He hated him. That's what he told everyone. Especially Ma. He hated him.

If only it were so easy to hate someone you love so deeply.

And that is why sometimes, late at night, he'd still unfold the letters—the ones he had written but never knew where to send.

The tea on the railing had gone cold. He looked at the novel on his lap: a woman with roses pressed to her breast, pearls circling the white skin on her throat. An ornament. Or a strangulation.

Beneath the roses, was she crying too?

Anna Karenina.

Chapter 5

Ira pushed her lunchbox closer to Nihal as he relished the cumin rice. She liked to watch him eat, as though it fed something in her she hadn't named. 'Amma was asking after you. What's keeping you busy?'

'My project mostly… but I'll come soon,' he said through a mouthful. 'The bookstore needs a hand.'

Nihal always walked Ira home after school—him drifting to the discount shelf, her lingering among pens and notebooks. With time, it had become their little ritual.

'You'll lie about your age?' Ira asked.

'You hardly get anything with just the truth.'

Ira took a long breath. She looked around. Her eyes caught the poster of the country of the year on the wall outside. A woman on a stone bench. Colosseum in the background.

'Is your project on the monument done?' She asked.

'Hmm?'

Ira repeated herself, and he told her he was yet to begin. She had noted how he was distracted lately. Even in this moment, his eyes flitted between the tables where the other boys from his class sat.

'So that means you are no longer with the stupid chemist?'

He shook his head, missing her question but smiling at someone on the table behind Ira's back.

She frowned, 'Do you want to go sit with them?'

'What?'

'Nothing.' She dropped her spoon in the lunchbox and pushed it further towards him. 'Are you embarrassed to sit with me now?' Ira's voice was sharp, her words clipped. 'After your little socialising spree with those *cool* people from your class? I know what they do at those parties.'

Nihal was about to say something when Sharan came charging toward him. Sharan's eyes slid right past Ira, as if she were invisible. She didn't mind—she was almost glad. Pulling a notepad from her lunch bag, she pretended to study her still-life sketches of flowers by the window, her face calm though something in her chest had tightened.

'The other day…' He paused, 'I didn't know you two knew each other from before.' Sharan's fingers tapped the table in sync as he spoke. Ira noticed they were grey at the tips. Perhaps he played guitar, sketched or smoked.

'I met your sister for the first time,' Nihal said, rising and pushing his chair back. 'Still, I'd have done the same for anyone in her place.' He cast a quick glance at Ira. She didn't look up, but he could tell—by the stillness in her shoulders—that she was listening to every word.

'Did she…did she tell you why?' Sharan's tone was now low. His fingers coiled in a fist that still lay on the table. He smoked; Ira just knew.

'Pop the whole bottle of painkillers?' Nihal said with a strange flash of sarcasm, which made Ira pause. Her eyes, however, remained on the notepad in her hands. A sketch of a banyan tree. Ira remembered sketching it years ago, when Amma had told her how, like marriage, the banyan strangles its host tree—erasing its existence, even as it thrives for years and years.

Sharan only nodded, unruffled. Nihal felt pity, sharp and sudden, for the girl who had to call this boy her brother.

'Is she alright? I haven't seen her since.'

'Oh yeah, she's fine. Gone home for a few weeks.'

'Home?'

'The freak isn't my sister, not real, I mean. Her mom and my mom are sisters. But I tell you, she is a nutcase, stay away from her, bro.'

Nihal's lack of reaction forced him to cut his wry laugh.

Sharan patted Nihal's shoulder and joined his friends back on the table where they huddled over a stack of cassette tapes. The bell blared. Chairs were swiftly scraped back, voices rose, and the canteen dissolved into a rush of bodies spilling toward the door.

'You were saying?' Nihal sat back.

'It doesn't matter now.' She shoved the lunchbox and the notepad into her bag and walked off. If she stayed, she would have cried. No way she was to do that in sight of Sharan. The boy who had called her a crazy bitch for not running with him on Sports Day.

Nihal glanced around the barren canteen. He wiped the spoon clean with his handkerchief and slipped it into his pocket.

It doesn't matter now.

Those words had carried him through M.L. International School, a place of polished shoes and crisp uniforms. He repeated them to himself on the long walk he had taken back to his classroom. And then somehow, his mind circled back to the question from the boys earlier.

Are you riding the freak because her father owns the school?

~

The Recital Day, 1989

The birthday girls, dressed in lavender overalls, were playing Atlas in the back seat of their father's Mercedes. It was a rainy July afternoon—not the kind that causes chaos, but one that carries the sweet smell of wet earth and lifts almost everyone's mood. Anyone's but the boy who trudged down the flooded streets with gaping holes in his overused shoes. The car's radio crackled with the voice of the commentator describing India's ongoing tour in the Caribbean.

The car stopped, but the sisters, age ten, took little notice or barely cared to ask why their father stepped out without an umbrella in his glossy black suit. They didn't notice when a boy in a drenched school uniform, which looked like a faded version of theirs, sat in the front seat. 'France', Aarya shrieked, taking a bite of Snickers.

1…2….3….4…

'Don't you try to distract me,' Ira snapped.

'You're taking too long. Papa, isn't she?' Aarya whined. The aroma of peanuts from her chocolate was dancing in the closed car.

'Estonia,' the boy mumbled, seeking permission with his eyes from the man who had let him in, mindful of his drenched uniform against the pale carpets.

The sisters giggled, ending the game as though it belonged only to them. Soon they were chattering about the dresses they would wear that evening. Their parents had spoken of a surprise awaiting them. Both knew the secret: their mother was to make her debut as a pianist in a grand theatrical musical.

Their father asked the boy, 'Which grade do you study in, son?'

'It doesn't matter.' The boy immediately regretted his curt tone. 'I'm sorry to be rude to you, sir. What I meant was that I might not be able to continue my education in this school.'

'Is that so?' Aryaveer's eyes were on the road.

The girls at the back were now silent. Aarya stopped chewing as the two listened carefully.

'I was admitted because of my merit, but my father has…' The boy fell silent.

'What happened to your father?'

'I cannot afford the fees anymore and… the scholarship only begins in class 11.'

'I see,' Aryaveer said, glancing at his daughters with a quiet warmth in his eyes. 'I'm too involved in something very important today. Do you see my little women here? It's their birthday. And a very special day for their mother, but why don't you meet me in the principal's office tomorrow morning? At 9?'

The girls glanced at each other and stayed quiet until the boy was let out at the red light, insisting his house was just around the corner. The rain had eased. But as the car pulled away, they caught him in the back window—disappearing not into a lane of homes, but through the door of a bookshop.

'What are you going to do with him, Papa?' Aarya asked.

'He is smart. And he can't be wasted.'

The girls grinned, catching the warmth in his voice.

'But now let's plan our evening. So, who is ready?'

A collective chant, 'Me!'

And the three drove cheerfully, singing their mother's favourite song. The song, which, when she sang, put each of them in a place of pure joy and calm. A song she would never sing after this day.

That evening, the sisters twirled in matching frocks. Ribbons fluttering in their hair. The night arrived generously, lived up to the promise of its melody and opulence, but marked itself in a colour that altered the course of their lives.

The colour settles between the rose petals in the night.

Black.

At 11.08 pm, it was still her birthday, their birthday, when Aarya died.

Ira had lost her sister.

And her mother.

Chapter 6

Grief turns people into robots. They eat, bathe, shop, and even smile at jokes. They go through the motions, ticking off tasks like loving a child or making love to a spouse, with the same detached rhythm.

Mandira hadn't always lived this way.

Once, Mandira flared with life. The first to rise, she lived with a kind of hunger—for beauty, for music, for movement. She lived for the extravagance: plunging necklines, designer handbags, evenings at the theatre, and dinner reservations. Heads turned when she walked into a room, and she knew it.

The soft strains of her piano would float up from the drawing room every morning, rousing the girls and Aryaveer from sleep. Her music set the rhythm of their day. The scent of pancakes followed soon after, always her favourite—smothered in strawberry syrup and layered with mangoes and sliced bananas.

She loved pottering around the house, tending to small joys. No vase was ever left empty. Roses, petunias, daisies, sunflowers—each room was a garden. Though she had grown up in a home staffed with maids and cooks, Mandira found quiet pleasure in doing things herself. She cooked for the family at least twice a week, reorganised the girls' avalanche of hair clips and dresses, and on some afternoons, traded the piano for colouring books and board games on the rug in the lobby.

When Aarya died, Mandira died, too—at least the mother Ira had once known. The mother who smiled in her pearl mirror had begun to move through life like a guest in her own home. She no longer noticed if the servants left wilting flowers in her bedroom. Her coffee sat untouched until it went cold; then she drank it in one quick gulp. She stopped calling her friends over for tea and stopped going out. She no longer appeared when Aryaveer's friends visited, so eventually, he stopped inviting them at all.

The house felt like a hotel now, and its residents became the strangers who shared the same address. Ira had begun to give up hope like the residents of the sea, but Aryaveer hadn't. He still took his wife along on business trips, where she spent her days in hotel bars or lounges, sipping whiskey, vodka, and whatever numbed the ache best. By the time he returned, she was usually already in bed—or in the bath. They made love in silence, bodies touching without souls meeting. Then the next day would unfold in the same way.

It was in the heavy warmth of a hamam in Istanbul that Mandira suddenly remembered the girl. A child, no older than six, dressed in tatters, trembling by the roadside amidst the screech of tyres and shards of glass. The world had tilted sideways. Mandira hadn't screamed or moved. Shock had wrapped itself around her like a second skin.

And yet, even in that frozen moment, she had seen her, just for a second. Through the cracked windscreen—those wide, haunted eyes staring back at her. Eyes that seemed to know.

In the weeks that followed, Mandira often woke in the middle of the night, the girl's gaze burning into her dreams. As if, through some terrible magic, the little girl had passed her pain onto Mandira—or maybe absorbed Mandira's own. It was three years ago that Mandira made her decision. She would work with children like Fiza.

Slowly, the alcohol retreated as she threw herself into her newly sprouted purpose. She met with the NGOs, spoke to journalists, and visited orphanages across the country. Eventually, Mandira began to wear her pearls and smile again. Soft, practised smiles that appeared in photos, in newspaper articles and on glossy fundraiser brochures. But never at home.

What no one saw—not even Aryaveer—was that in mothering the country's orphans, she had turned her face away from her own child.

Chapter 7

Mandira had sent a postcard from Milan.

Ira could observe a drawn line on paper and tell how the pen was held between fingers, how the ink skated on the paper. She could tell how the curves in the letters were formed. It had been written by her father. Why he still tried, she never understood, but it irritated her.

She dug the tip of a pencil into the bed of her palm until it hurt, so all her sensations were lost. She hated the pain that came afterwards when she was leafing through the photo albums from her mother's drawers. She hated it more when she found a file named Fiza Ahmed beside the table lamp. Inside, there were medical records, grade-wise mark sheets and passport-size photographs of this mysterious girl.

Had her mother replaced Aarya with her?

The new session had begun, and Ira was now in class 10. Nihal, in class 12—the school's senior-most—had convinced the stationery owner to let him work two hours, thrice a week, for five hundred rupees. He unpacked deliveries, stocked shelves, and sometimes wrote letters for the elderly who stopped by. Payment for the letters was rare—more often it was a blessing, a pat on the back, a kind word: *Your mother raised you well.*

Sometimes, it pulled him back to the letters he had written. And then, the rage they sparked in his mother.

In hindsight, he knew it was inevitable. A broken heart cannot hold anything, let alone love. Perhaps those letters were only an excuse to lock him in, to strike him with a scale. Perhaps he reminded her too much of his father—or the man his father had once been.

When his father left years ago, Prajakta withdrew herself. She didn't shower or cook for days. He watched her from afar, like a toddler watching a wildfire take his yard, knowing it would come for him, too. He learned to wash and iron his uniform before bed, where he often went hungry. The library books he borrowed became his lullabies. Enid Blyton, Ruskin Bond, and the Hardy Boys. The school librarian was amazed at his hunger for literature.

As for the hunger in his stomach, Ira must have understood right when she befriended him, because she began to bring lunch for two. Aarya would have done it too, she knew. She brought him packets of dry food to carry home. Home, where in the evenings, his mother told him she wanted to kill herself but couldn't—because she still had a burden to carry. A burden to live this horrid life for the sake of her ugly son.

Nihal wasn't ugly—only, he was as beautiful as his father.

Once, his mother tripped over a dictionary left on the floor and hurled it at Nihal's face. The hard corner struck his eyelid, leaving it purple and swollen for weeks. Her own face burned crimson with rage.

'I got into a fight,' he told Ira the next day at school.

During those months, when the abandonment was still raw, or so it seemed even after years, Nihal often wrote letters to his father, sitting in the same bookstore after school, sometimes in Ira's room while she sketched or painted. Homework, he'd tell her. He would find new words from the pocket dictionary, hoping to intrigue his father's curiosity. But he didn't know where to send these letters, so he kept them safe under the mattress of his side of the bed.

~

Ira had skipped school all of last week. She watched the days pass by like an exhausted tourist staring at ships on the waterfront. Sometimes, she sketched and painted her random thoughts. No reference image. She just closed her eyes and let her mind see. Kabir, her art teacher, had even complimented her and said her strokes reminded him of Shergill's early works.

She ate at odd hours, slept when exhaustion dragged her under, and did everything to avoid the world outside.

One evening, she filled the tub with scalding water, sank into it, and watched her skin wrinkle like a bird's hatchling. Afterwards, she cried without a clear reason. Was it for her mother, lost somewhere in Turkey, haggling over lamps and rugs with her father and his rich clients? Was it for the absence of Aarya? Or was it for Nihal—always occupied with his debating society, some idiotic project, and that godforsaken bookstore job? He was always doing things. The last time she met him was in the canteen.

But he did come after a week, carrying Aparajita seeds for Amma as a gesture. He recounted a tooth extraction at a cheap clinic where walls were filled with Michael Jackson's posters. Why couldn't he have gone to Sujata Aunty instead? Ira guessed it was his fear of Lalit Uncle. They, too, had once feared him, Aarya and herself, until he started bringing them Barbies with long hair and an array of imported colours.

That evening, they lounged in the drawing room, sipping Amma's impossibly sweet rose and honey tea. Ira caught Nihal's eyes drifting to the piano after he was done checking out the cassette player Aaryaveer had brought. The piano stood like a long-unused ebony monument, catching the day's dying light, reflecting a melancholic glow. It still looked, Ira thought, like the magnificent woman her mother had once been with pearls around her neck.

'I'm the finalist for the Debate,' he announced.

Ira tried to show how least she cared. She didn't ask for the details like she usually did. The school, the topic. It all seemed so peripheral.

But he told her, of course. He was speaking in favour of Globalisation. *Whatever that means*, Ira thought. Nihal plopped back on the sofa, took a long, exaggerated breath, and closed his eyes.

'This house is so silent,' Nihal mused after a while. He said it was a stark contrast to his own. 'The women are all over the place, getting out and into clothes, not even caring about the man present in the same room.'

'Are you really complaining?' Ira's lips lifted in a quiet, private smile, a subtle acknowledgement of his discomfort.

'God no, Ira,' he sighed. 'They are my mother's age, more than that, and so irritating.'

She looked at him properly, thinking. But what she really thought was how he managed to always look so adorable, even as he yawned. 'Do they never bring their daughters your age?'

He didn't smile. 'Never noticed,' Nihal closed his eyes. His palms folded on the back of his head.

The silence returned, settling between the two like a heavy shroud.

Ira thought of the house now, and of Aarya. How it once brimmed with laughter. She remembered the powdered women who poured in every Saturday for tea and biscuits. And the evenings with fine-looking guests, stemmed glasses in hands, gathering around their mother as she played the piano like some goddess at the centre. She could still see her in the three-stringed pearls and the velvet gown that accentuated her long neck. How vibrant she looked, and how happy.

'This wasn't always like this,' she mused.

He looked at her, feeling sorry he brought it up, 'I know.'

Nihal closed his eyes again, but Ira was looking at him with curiosity now, 'How was the party, Nihal?'

'What party?' He began and then suddenly remembered, 'Oh! It was good.'

Ira stared at the blank space for a while, conjuring up the words, 'You didn't tell me about her.' She could feel the heat rushing to her face and neck.

'I just felt it was wise not to talk about her personal stuff. About her moment of vulnerability.'

She felt small and beaten. Why does he always have an answer? And why was it always difficult to blame him for anything?

'It was wise of you,' she said, 'But now that I know, can I ask why she did it?'

'I don't know.' He yawned.

'You'd rather not tell.'

He looked at her, 'I really don't know.'

She inhaled and said what she hated to admit, 'So…they are your friends now?'

'You mean Sharan?'

'Yes…and,' Ira didn't want to speak her name, 'Her.'

'I guess Sharan is the same, only a bit grateful if I can hazard a guess. But knowing him, he will soon grow past the gratefulness. And as I said about her, I haven't seen her since.'

Ira's fingers traced the frill of the cushion cover, twisting it nervously, 'Do you want to see her?'

'Why would I want to *see* her?'

She sensed a flicker of irritation in his voice. 'Hmm,' she breathed heavily, throwing the cushion on the bed. 'Do you know why I didn't run with Sharan in the race last year?'

'I think I know.'

She nodded, the memory of his words, his arrogant sneer, flooding back. Sharan had called her the flat-chested bitch, and Ira believed it was a valid reason to abandon him on the sports day, which would lead to his disqualification from the event as they were running as a team in the ballet race.

The two sat next to each other for a long time, not saying a word, not moving. Nihal may even have taken a quick nap in the luxurious silence as the afternoon sun poured in through the window. Slowly, her head leaned against the back of the sofa. 'But I like this,' she murmured, rubbing her fingers on the spot where she had hurt herself on her palm.

'What?' His whisper was soft as a child's breath. He tilted his face to look at her. His eyes half closed.

'This silence.'

Nihal caught her eye supportively. She blinked a faint smile that flickered in her eyes when she looked at him. He smiled too, a slow, gentle curve on his lips dissolving all his exhaustion, his adolescent worries. And in that moment, amidst the lingering scent of dust and forgotten memories, a strange sense of peace settled over her. Over them.

Chapter 8

Nihal was leafing through his pocket dictionary in the school bus when his eyes spotted her. It was too late to look away. He knew she had joined the school a week ago. A few times, he had seen her in the canteen with Sharan and his other friends, but he averted his eyes to avoid any possibility of conversation. Perhaps it was Ira. Something she'd said. Or maybe it was just him. He felt… different around other people. With Ira, it was fine. But with the others, it was like his whole life, the bits he didn't want anyone to see, got bigger. Like he was under a microscope and all his wounds were on display. He also felt small. Like everyone could see how… not much he had.

He kept looking at his notes, trying to pretend he was doing something, and then his eyes caught her again. She was sitting a few rows behind him. Only this time, he couldn't look away quickly enough.

Sonam walked up to him, 'Hey!'

'Hi.'

'Are you ignoring me?' She dusted the seat with a flowery handkerchief and sat beside him.

'Why would I do that?'

'Reverse psychology?' Sonam laughed, revealing her white, symmetrical teeth.

Nihal dropped his eyes to his thighs.

'Hey! I'm just messing with you.' She snatched his dictionary and closed it in her hand, 'You are already winning this debate. Leave the preparation to the likes of us. Now tell me, where do you spend your time after school?'

He looked at her in confusion.

'What do you listen to? Who are your friends? Are you a Mario guy or a Contra man?'

Nihal offered a quiet, almost shy smile, looking away. 'I am a simple boy.'

'Ok?'

'I don't fit into that world…your world, I mean. I'm sure you had a good reason to do what you did the other day, but it was terrible to see you like that. I'm just glad you are alright now. I hope.'

Sonam smiled, tightly, the kind of smile only people with maturity are capable of smiling. 'To tell you a secret, I don't fit into this world myself.' She took a deep breath, 'The problem was…I kept trying. My father wanted me to go to the best school for higher education. And he had harboured this fascination with Delhi since his own school days. I just agreed to come here because this is what he would have wanted… if he were to live.'

'Oh…I'm sorry. I had no...'

'Both my parents are dead, actually. And it's alright; it's been long…' Sonam inhaled deeply. 'But I'm sure they would both have wanted me to study here. Delhi is their birthplace.'

'And you? What did you want?'

'Initially, I was thrilled because my boyfriend lived here.' Sonam pressed her lips together.

'Oh.'

'But as soon as I came here, we broke up. Guess some relationships best bloom in the distance. Anyway, I want to be home so bad. In Manali, with my Grandfather.'

'I assume he was…your boyfriend was the reason for you to?'

'No, no…I just wasn't thinking through, I guess, and I had too much to drink…for the first time.' Sonam looked around to check if anyone was in the proximity to hear them. Everyone around had their heads sunk in the notes they had brought with them for the competition.

'I was not so heartbroken—only angry.'

'On your boyfriend?'

'The other day, at the party, he tried to you know…typical. I slapped him…then he told me I was too homely for him. A small-town girl.'

'You did good.'

'I'm not suicidal or depressed, you know, I was just…' She rummaged for a word in her mind.

'Drunk. You told me,' Nihal said, warmed in her company now.

'Sharan hates that I'm here. Perhaps because my accomplishments highlight his failures. Anyway, I am just waiting for the finals next year and will leave this city for good. I want to be with my Naana, can't just survive on letters alone.'

When Sonam went back to reading the stapled papers she had brought along, Nihal found himself imagining the bond that must have tied Sonam and her father once, the love that brought her here against her own wish. Did he also read to her once back home in the evening when she was little?

Did he promise to never leave?

Memory has a way of surfacing when least expected. It was a week before Diwali when Prajakta noticed the uneven surface of the mattress. Under it, a bundle of handwritten letters. All of them were addressed to *Dada*. She read a few but was hardly able to comprehend the meaning of most words. Nihal spoke to his father in English, a language alien to his mother.

Prajakta cried, wiped her own tears and kept the bundle back where she had found it. When Nihal came back from school, she told him she wished he had never been born. He was God's way of punishing her for what she had done.

'Nothing would happen, your father said, and I was so naïve I trusted him. I was just a schoolgirl. A schoolgirl. And like a needy call girl, I let him.'

Nihal didn't know, at age nine, what a *call girl* meant.

But he had a dictionary.

CHAPTER 9

Nihal stood at the centre of the stage, clutching the first prize for the debate. When the jury asked about his ambition, he said he wanted to be an architect.

Which building fascinated him the most?

His answer was immediate: Neuschwanstein Castle in Bavaria. And so, under the soft Delhi morning sun, in the manicured lawns of an elite school, the boy with soiled shoes spoke with quiet conviction about King Ludwig and his dreamlike obsession with larger-than-life castles.

'Told you, you'd win,' Sonam said when she saw him near the gate after school. Nihal offered a perfunctory smile.

'I was going to fetch some biscuits to fuel my late nights with geography. Want to come along for tea? It's a small shop, but the tea is heart-warming—and I guess the bookstore is off?'

'My mom is waiting. And I have to make a few deliveries for her today.'

'Sure. I was just… taking my chance,' Sonam said. 'She must be so proud of you—your mom.'

Nihal shook his head and pressed his lips together, the same way he would two hours later on the crowded DTC bus. Only this time, his eyes glistened, and he made no effort to wipe them. There was a strange kind of freedom that exists only among strangers—a cocoon in which one can be more oneself than in the company of friends or family.

He must have been in Class Four or Five.

It was a hot summer day, the kind where the ceiling fan pushes hot air across the room. He had returned home after giving an exam, his white shirt sticking to his back. On the kitchen shelf, a tall glass of lemonade sat sweating. Prajakta slid it toward him, her eyes tired but also soft with curiosity.

'How was the paper?' she asked.

He took a gulp before answering, then admitted with a small frown, 'I made a silly mistake.'

'I could've got it all right if not for this stupid mistake,' he bragged, lifting the glass, the cool beads of moisture clinging to his palm.

Then came the crash—splinters across the kitchen floor, lemonade spilling and snaking between shards, rushing outward as if trying to escape the walls themselves.

Before he could breathe, his cheek seared, hot as iron. He was only eight, repeating one line over and over, unable to understand the burn that outlasted the sting.

'I'm sorry, Ma. I'm sorry. I'm sorry.'

He begged, not so much for forgiveness as for safety.

For love. For his father to return.

Nihal had always been at the top of his class.

That was his certainty, his anchor.

And that's why he knew he would win this, too.

Because Nihal always won.

~

Ira had managed three days of school in the last two weeks, which was… a good record, she supposed. However, she was visiting Nihal religiously at the bookstore. When she was not helping him with dusting or stacking the books on the racks, she lounged on the couch with some illustrated book on her lap. From the books she purchased, she had learned and practised Monet's water lilies and Van Gogh's sunflowers. Today, in her hands, it was *The Strange Library* by Haruki Murakami, and the illustrations were too scary to look at, so she closed the book. She rested her eyes on Nihal in the distance.

She had noticed, in these past few weeks, how people developed a fondness for him. They'd pick up a book, any book, and he'd have something to say about it. They would come again and chat with him for quite some time before choosing another book. The bookstore owner said one cool, rainy day, as they were having tea and biscuits on the shopfront, that he liked Nihal's driven personality and the way he connected effortlessly with people. It was strange because she had always believed him to be reticent except with herself.

Perhaps, he was changing. Or maybe, she hadn't known all his layers yet. Especially the one he revealed around books.

'Are you really able to memorise all these names?' Ira was glancing at the first page of Nihal's novel resting on the table. He was writing numbers in a small diary, copying from the screen of the calculator held together with a tape.

She fixed herself on the edge of the table.

'I make something like a chart...'

It was taped with the bookmark, he told her.

'Smart! Tell me…what happens to this one,' Ira pointed to the word—Levin.

Nihal had made a small star in red next to the word.

'The guy is always working on his farm, trying to figure out life… I think…you know, I really think I'm like him.'

Ira raised a brow.

'Always thinking, planning. He tries to learn everything he can. Knowledge is power, right? And power is money. That's what your father also says.'

'So, our Levin is rich, is he?'

'Levin isn't exactly rolling in cash, but he's got land, he's got ideas. He's trying to build something. That's inspiring. All those other rich people, like the ones in school, they just inherited everything. That's not how I want it. I don't want anything handed to me. Not that there's anyone to hand it to me, but you know what I mean. I want to earn it, not like Vronsky.'

'Vronsky!' Ira repeated, raising her eyebrows. 'I like how it sounds, Vronsky,' she tasted the word on her lips.

'That's also how he is…handsome, charming, rich. Sounds like a dream, right? He chases after Anna, knowing she is married. So…' Nihal pushes the pen aside and rubs his palms. Ira noticed the excitement in his eyes as he spoke, 'Vronsky gets caught up in this whole dramatic affair with a married woman… and for what? Sure, he gets the beautiful lady for a while, but it all falls apart. He ends up just as lost as he started. That's a lesson, I think. Looks aren't everything. Charm is not all there is. And love…my friend… is a tragedy. You need substance. You need a purpose. Money, most of all.'

Ira asked him about Anna, intrigued as she checked the cover again. She liked the painted roses, saved the image in her memory.

Nihal made a thoughtful face. 'Anna is complicated. Beautiful, of course, passionate, but trapped. She throws everything away for love, which, I guess, is romantic in a way. But it's also kind of reckless. She doesn't think about the consequences. She's…'

'In love?' Ira's eyes didn't blink.

'Impulsive.'

'She sounds like someone I could be.'

Nihal laughed, 'I hope not. Anyway, I'm the opposite. I can't afford to be impulsive.' He paused for a while, 'So yeah, that's *Anna Karenina for you*. You've read it with me in ten minutes.'

Ira purchased another copy of Anna Karenina. Something about the cover—or Anna herself—had intrigued her enough to make art inspired by her story.

Chapter 10

At home, the next morning, Amma was telling Shivani about Aryaveer's construction project in Pune when she saw Ira climbing up the stairs. Amma knew that walk.

Half an hour later, Shivani carried a pot with steaming chamomile tea. Ira found it hard to stand because of her crumbling stomach, so Kabir went back and brought some art magazines for her to look through. Together, they discussed the works of the world's famous artists.

With the little attention she could garner within the pain, Ira listened, 'Some say he fell in love with a woman he once saw at the temple and began to paint her voraciously in his paintings that followed.' Kabir was talking about the 19th-century artist, Raja Ravi Varma.

'While it is believed that Sugandha Bai was a fictional character.'

Ira laughed to herself.

'Why are you laughing?'

'I don't understand why someone would paint a fictional character. Just looking at real people makes me sick. I'd never waste my colours on imagining them.'

Kabir turned the page for her. Three women stood in a forest. One of them—with the quiet magnetism of a main character—rested a hand on her friend's back while, with the other, she drew a thorn from her bare foot. Kabir's eyes lingered on the text written beneath the picture.

'The lover. She is waiting for her lover,' Ira said thoughtfully.

Kabir shook his head, 'Did you see how the lover, though absent from the frame, forms a pivotal point of reference in the scene. How he is consuming the entire artwork. That's world-building with your brush.'

Ira's eyes remained on the page. She saw the image of a man emerging from the eyes of this woman who looked behind her, beyond the frame. She isn't happy or sad, but simply waiting, even as her body is pierced by a thorn.

'They say people love art and its unique form, maybe colours, but what truly holds their attention is the narrative it conveys, the memory it rekindles in *them*,' Kabir said, still looking at the page.

She let out a soft laugh, 'Most of my paintings are nonsensical, I think, especially in comparison to these.'

'Your art does tell wonderful stories, Ira. Stories of hope,' Kabir told her.

Ira folded her arms and squinted her eyes, 'Come to think of it, what do you paint? Can I see some of your artworks?'

Kabir had always refused to reveal his own work. But this time, he pulled a book from his bag and handed it to his young student. There were portraits of a woman in different postures and locations. In some of them, she was naked but wore only a ring on her finger. On closer inspection, Ira noticed it was not really a ring but a band of twigs.

'For me, my art is both a comfort and torment. It reminds me of what I lack and what I seek,' Kabir mused.

'I don't think my art has a story at all.'

He took the book and closed it on the table, closing any scope of conversation around his sketches, 'You should try portraits if you like these.'

'I'll never be able to do *fictional figures*.' Ira threw another brief glance at the page.

Kabir took a long breath before he spoke, 'Art is like a drifting cloud, Ira — chase it, and you'll never quite know where it will carry you.'

In the bathroom later, she pressed her stomach with both her palms and thought she heard her belly crunching. *Tides of womanhood*, Amma calls them. Ira looked at her face in the mirror. How would she appear if she were a portrait on the canvas? What colour would she use? Perhaps in muted ochres and pale blues—the colours of restraint, of someone trying to hold herself together.

Aarya would have looked the same — the pointy nose, the long, serious face, and the darkest shade of eyes. She noticed how her body was slightly different each time she looked at herself. Rounder, but only a bit. Ira leaned closer and, for the first time, really saw the very dark specks of brown in her own eyes. Her stomach crumbled again, but this time she did not flinch. She was studying her reflection the way an artist studies a reference image — not with vanity, but with the quiet awe of discovery. And then, like a sudden brushstroke across a blank page, a memory, fierce and strong like a flood, washed over her.

She remembered her first time with a smile that carried with it a strange sense of intimacy, a feeling she could neither name nor acknowledge. Not yet.

Nihal had to collect a few lace samples from a shop in Old Delhi for his mother. He had brought Ira along after convincing Amma he would take care of her in the crowd. Amma never said no to him. Never.

It was the first day of June. Hot like coal. The market was dense with noise, colour, and the heat of too many bodies pressed together. Laces in every imaginable design hung in heaps, overwhelming to look at, impossible to choose from. The two young friends retreated into a smaller shop, hoping for fewer options.

That was when Ira felt it—the first pangs. She had no words, no prior warning, only the cold terror of something horrid happening to her body. And she was right. In the dim ladies' room of a jewellery shop, she saw it for herself.

'I need to go home. Now,' she whispered to Nihal, eyes nervous, beads of sweat collecting on her forehead.

'But we just came,' he said absently, still scanning the hoardings as they wove through the perspiring, chatty crowd.

'We can come back later,' her voice thinned, strained with both anguish and pain. She pressed her hands against her abdomen.

'And spend another fifty rupees on the auto rickshaw?' he muttered.

'You stay. I'm leaving.' She turned sharply, but his hand caught her elbow. His voice was quiet now.

'Are you not well, Ira?' He looked at her. Her tears answered before she could.

'Sit down,' he said, urgent yet gentle, as though he already knew by the way she held herself. 'I'll be back. Wait here.'

She sat with a storm in her belly, shame burning her eyes. Minutes stretched like hours until Nihal reappeared, clutching a brown paper bag. His brows were furrowed over eyes rinsed in concern.

'Here. Now it's for you to figure out how to use it. Ask one of the ladies inside. And don't worry.'

She snatched the packet of sanitary napkins from his hand and fled back to the ladies' room. Alone, she stood for a long while, praying silently that her pair of black pants would conceal her secret.

On the auto ride home, they sat side by side in silence. The whooshing wind against their faces filled the emptiness where words did not go.

At home, Amma's face softened into a weary smile, the kind that carried both welcome and worry in equal measure. Her eyes lingered a moment too long on Ira before she asked Nihal to come inside.

'I'll be a minute,' he said, vanishing into the kitchen, calling back, *'I smell garlic.'*

Ira clambered up the staircase, clutching her rebellious insides, and sank into her bed.

When he appeared again, she was crumpled like a discarded bedsheet. The cramps ground through her abdomen, twisting her intestines like blades. She missed her mother—and despite everything—wished she were here, even in her cold, distant way.

Nihal's voice was low when he called her name. *Ira.* He placed something on the bed beside her. Too weak to look, she only felt the warmth spreading toward her.

'You could use this for a few days.' He slid the hot water bag closer. *Days?* She thought with horror before she pressed her palm on it. The heat seeped in, dissolving her exhaustion like salt in boiling water. He had even brought a towel to soften it against her skin.

Soon, the pain receded to a tolerable discomfort.

Covering her face with her palms, she closed her eyes. In the darkness, her mother's face returned. Before despair swallowed her, she opened them. Nihal was watching her—head propped on one hand, his eyes soft and searching. A pillow lay between them. She managed a small smile as gratitude flooded her chest.

For all that was missing in her life, she still had him.

'Feeling better?' His gaze flicked to her midriff, gentle, reassuring.

She nodded faintly.

'You'll be fine sooner than you know. This bag—it'll work better than anything else. And Amma surely has some tea for this situation here. Talk to her, alright.'

The silence between felt to Ira like varnish over an old painting, preserving what lay beneath but clouding it, too

'How many girls have you soothed before?' she asked at last, half-teasing, half-dreading the answer.

'I have a mother,' he whispered solemnly.

A sharp, bitter laugh slipped from her as she thought briefly of her own mother. 'I'm happy she has you.'

He waited a while, then said quietly, 'I am all she has,' and the words hung in the air, final and aching.

The memory left her with a longing. Ira stared at herself for a little longer in the bathroom. It had been a year ago, but it still felt like yesterday. A lump rose in her throat.

That night, after priming a square canvas with a yellow wash, Ira wrote on the back of it.

In truth, dear Aarya, he is all I have, too.

CHAPTER 11

Ira listened, a trace of irritation in her eyes, as Nihal spoke about his educational trip to Jaipur and the exchange program he was leaving for the next day. Then, as if to remind her of his importance, he mentioned the exhibition on monuments next week—just a day after his return.

'What are you going to wear to the exhibition?' Ira's eyes traced the delicate curve of the petal on her canvas as she moved a flat brush. She had tried and failed to recreate Monet's water lilies from the magazine Kabir left for her. The colours were too bright, the water a flat, unmoving turquoise instead of the murky, reflective depth of the master's pond.

'I've managed a suit from Saksham.' Nihal's gaze lingered on the way the sunlight caught the gold of the paintbrush. It was the one he had brought her.

'I hope not with *those* shoes of yours,' she said.

'I have my father's shoes—they fit me now.'

He stopped at his own words, tasting the irony and the quiet poison they carried. As a boy, Nihal had longed to be like his father—the way he stood tall, the way he slicked back his hair with his fingers. His father had always been gentle with him, listening with rare patience, telling small stories from his day. Nihal still remembered the strength of those broad shoulders, how he once sat atop them in the park and believed no place in the world could be higher, safer, or grander than that.

When his father returned from duty, his mother would still be in the kitchen. Before he even changed out of his uniform, he would put on his cassette player and sit with Nihal to read to him. A good father,

Nihal thought then. Fundamentally, as he once believed, the only reason to hate him was what he did to his mother, with another woman. But then, he had also abandoned him like a bruised fruit left to rot, never once checking back.

'Lost?' Ira clicked her fingers. Her nails were coated in pink acrylic.

Nihal circled his eyes in sync with Ira's fingers as if a silent communication was passing between them. He wondered how her brain worked. Did she paint before in her mind or just freed herself on canvas? After a while, he checked the time on the clock behind him. 'Now, hurry up and come with me,' he said.

She was wearing a cotton halter top that revealed the smooth line of her shoulders and wide pants that swayed with her movements. As he dragged her past the easel, the knot in her once yellow apron that was tied loosely around her waist snagged on the edge of the wooden plank with a soft, ripping sound.

Nihal tsked playfully, moving closer.

The scent of his sandalwood soap filled her nostrils. '*Did he always smell this nice?*' she thought. 'Can't you help?' Ira said.

Nihal turned her around, his hands briefly resting on her waist. The smile suddenly ebbed and brought a strange feeling into him. The light touch was a surprise. He reached for the ribbon, but in his haste, he confused the ribbon of her apron with that of her shirt. He tugged in one motion.

Ira gasped, a small, almost breathless sound. Laughing, she instinctively clutched at her chest as her blouse gaped open from the back. 'You idiot, you pulled open my top!'

Nihal's eyes flickered on her for a fleeting moment, taking in her delicate silhouette partially revealed beneath the thin cotton. An awkward but brief silence followed until he broke the ice.

'You wear a bra?' His voice was a low, teasing murmur.

Ira frowned, a blush creeping up her neck. 'Why wouldn't I?'

'Oh! I thought girls started wearing it once they're grown-ups …' he trailed off, his gaze lingering on her now and then.

'Are you saying I'm still a child?' she challenged, her eyes sparkling with a mixture of amusement and something else…something warmer.

'I never said that,' he replied in a husky voice.

Ira, feeling a sudden surge of playful boldness, draped her hands behind her back, pretending to loosen her blouse further.

'Wait. What?' Nihal's eyes widened, and he instinctively covered them with his hand. Ira noticed how his ears had turned red. And how she was enjoying this strange conversation until she gasped in terror.

'Uncle!' Her eyes widened at the large figure that filled the doorway. She turned towards the closet, her right hand still clutching the knots of her top behind her neck.

'Now don't bluff me, Ira Lall …' Nihal said, still unsure if he should uncover his eyes. 'I was just joking, alright. I already knew you wore one… but you shouldn't wear a black one under a white school shirt.'

'What are you doing here?' Lalit's voice boomed, striking the walls and then coming back.

Nihal straightened, stiffening like a startled deer. 'I… I just came by. I wanted her to see something I made…for a school…competition.'

'A gentleman your age should know better than to barge into a girl's bedroom and talk filth,' Lalit blared, his stare hard and piercing. He looked pointedly at Nihal, then shifted his attention to Ira, who had reappeared, now cloaked in a black cape with white and beige fringes on the edges.

'Your father is in the Police. Am I right?' Lalit's voice, now smooth as polished mahogany, carried an undercurrent that prickled the fine hair on Nihal's neck. It was a statement, not a question, delivered with the quiet authority of a man accustomed to being obeyed.

Nihal felt his throat was suddenly dry. He swallowed and managed a nod, exchanging a fleeting, tormented glance with Ira. He felt the weight of Lalit's gaze, a judgment that seemed to dissect him.

'I happen to know his senior very closely,' Lalit added, the words hanging in the air like a veiled threat.

'I'm sorry, sir. I…didn't mean…' Nihal stammered, the bravado he'd felt moments before dissolving like mist in the morning sun.

'It's not entirely your fault,' Lalit's tone was deceptively gentle now, but only as insulting. 'I have met him, your father, a few times.'

Nihal inhaled sharply, his gaze fixed on Lalit's shoes. They gleamed like a rock washed by the sea for years, reflecting the ornate chandelier above in a distorted, miniature dance of light. He wondered how they maintained such a flawless shine, a trivial thought that offered a fleeting distraction from the knot tightening in his stomach.

'He has taken a new wife, I've heard. Or is she just his…' Lalit paused, his eyes sharp and assessing, boring into Nihal, 'An apple does not fall far from the tree, does it?'

Ira watched, her heart like a trapped bird fluttering against her ribs. She yearned to meet Nihal's gaze, to offer him a silent reassurance, but he seemed frozen, caught in the amber of Lalit's cruel words. He closed his eyes briefly, and Ira saw on his face a flicker of pain, raw and unguarded. She was the only person he ever spoke to, if at all he did, about his father.

'We do not use this language with the ladies…not in respectable families,' Lalit's voice was a delicate blade of steel.

Nihal mumbled an apology, again, but the words drowned in the charged silence of the room. He couldn't bring himself to look at Ira as his own heart thrummed with anger, and something else. Shame. Lalit gestured towards the door with a dismissive flick of his wrist. Nihal walked out, feeling like an intruder, an unwanted presence in their carefully curated world.

The older man moved slowly around the room, as if trying to decipher the lingering residue of the teenagers' interaction. He paused at the easel, his gaze lingering on Ira's unfinished canvas, then sank onto the plush couch, one leg draped casually over the other. 'Ira, my dear,' he began, patting the soft upholstery beside him, 'Come, sit here.'

He took her hands in his. She obeyed with hesitation and felt that his touch was surprisingly warm and firm, a stark contrast to the chill in his eyes. He drew a long, measured breath, and Ira knew, from the subtle shift in his posture, the almost imperceptible hardening of his jaw, that he was about to say something she had never heard from anyone before. 'I know you very well, darling. But with your mother away, and in her delicate condition, someone must teach you to draw boundaries that every young woman your age must. Boys…' He closed his eyes briefly as if thinking, 'these young men… are not to be trusted, especially at this impressionable age.'

'It's not how you think of him, Uncle,' Ira protested, instinctively pulling her hands away from his grasp.

'If something untoward happens,' Lalit continued, 'it is always the girl whose life is tormented. Irrevocably.'

'He is a nice boy. You can ask Papa,' Ira insisted weakly.

'Your father is already burdened with so much. Let him be free from this worry.'

'It's not what you think, Uncle,' her voice rising like a prayer spoken in a dark tunnel.

'Do you know about his mother? What everyone whispers about?'

'But it's his father. He is the one who...'

'The world only remembers what the woman did, not the man she did it with,' Lalit announced with finality. He glanced pointedly towards the staircase where Nihal had retreated, then looked back at Ira as she nervously brushed a stray strand of hair from her face. 'A young girl is a growing flower, Ira. Once plucked before its time, it withers. No one claims it.' He looked at Ira's hands, stained with her failed attempts on canvas. 'Look at you, already blemished.'

Ira sucked her breath. She felt her belly disappear in rage.

Later, Amma told her about the Colosseum Nihal had built—a monument where men fought beasts for the entertainment of the *privileged.*

CHAPTER 12

'Do you have an older sibling we can call?' The woman's gaze was intense, her face a blur in the dim light. The smell of antiseptic drifted in through the corridor.

Ira narrowed her eyes. 'I'm sorry, Miss,' she murmured.

'I'm your new sports teacher. No one's answering the landline at your home. Do you have a sibling in another class?'

Minutes later, the door swung open. Nihal burst into the room, his hair wind-tossed and his face drawn tight with worry. He crossed the space in swift strides and took her injured hand into his.

She saw the concern in his eyes: quiet but urgent. The teacher stood nearby, arms folded. Another student followed, carrying Ira's hastily packed school bag, which still had a corner of her scarf caught in the zipper.

'Are you okay?' Nihal's voice barely masked his panic.

Ira winced at the pain.

Just an hour ago, the afternoon sun had painted long golden shadows across the playground. The girls were practising a pyramid routine, their limbs weaving in and out of formation like petals folding and unfolding. On the far end, the boys played cricket.

Nihal was batting when Ira jogged up to him, smiling. She had come to check if he's back from Jaipur—and to wish him good luck for the exhibition. The truth was, she wanted to make sure he was alright—her only reason to come to school after a week.

Saksham smiled faintly at her, and just as she began to return the gesture, another boy grinned and called out, 'Our boy's riding on two wheels! Got himself a little harem, huh?' He slapped his friend's shoulder.

Ira didn't know them. They were just abstract faces from Nihal's class.

'I'll talk to you on our way back. Now go, okay?' Nihal caught her from the side. His tone was sharp.

He looked at the boys, irritated and patiently watched her retreat.

The memory of their last time in her room swirled so heavily in her head that she didn't see the boy running toward her until it was too late. The collision sent her stumbling, and the sharp pain that followed told something terrible had happened: something within her had broken. A bone.

~

In the school van, she leaned against the window. Sunlight dappled across her face like the wings of a butterfly. 'What's a harem?' she asked.

'I don't know,' Nihal said, avoiding her eyes as he squinted against the bright light.

'You won't tell.'

'It's when a man has multiple partners.'

'Multiple?'

'More than one.'

She turned to face him. 'No, I mean—who were your friends talking about? One is me, I assume. Who's the other?'

'They're not my friends, alright.'

'They were referring to Sonam?' Her voice was soft, but there was a sting to it.

He nodded once. Just then, a jolt in the van caused Ira to clutch her hand, her face contorting. 'Ouch.'

'I'm here. It's okay,' Nihal said, his hand instinctively moving to hers.

'You have your exhibition today,' she murmured.

'Don't worry about it. Ms Sethi will take care of it.'

At home, Amma was still bent over the garden beds when Ira and Nihal walked through the iron gates. The scent of wet earth danced in the air, mingled with jasmine and spices floating from the kitchen window. When Amma saw the plastered hand, she dropped the spade with a hollow clang.

'What in the name of God…' She walked holding her knee.

'She broke her arm,' Nihal said calmly, slinging off his backpack.

Amma's forehead creased.

'I got into a fight with a nasty new girl at school. Her name is Sonam,' Ira quipped, smirking.

Nihal gave her a look.

'Okay, okay,' Ira said with a mischievous smile.

Amma went back to her roses with a shake of her head after a long trail of anxious enquiries that Nihal calmed, and the two walked to the porch, where he knelt to remove her shoes, handling her foot with such delicate care as if she were made of glass.

'You do like her, don't you?' She was watching him closely.

'Do you have nothing else to talk about?' He folded her socks neatly and placed them back inside.

'Is that a yes?'

He stood, brushing dust off his knees. 'I have no reason to *not* like her.'

She patted the space beside her. He took a seat. 'Do you like her the way you like me?' The question stunned her as she asked it.

He wrapped an arm gently around her shoulder. 'If there's one thing, I'm truly grateful for in this life, it's you.'

'But that's not an answer.'

'I love you, and you know that.'

'In what way do you love me?'

He thought a moment. 'In the way Amma loves her roses.'

At that very second, outside, Amma snipped a plump red bloom. The rose slipped from her hand and landed softly on the grass. Both burst into laughter.

Shivani arrived soon after, explaining that the temple visit was cancelled. Nihal told Amma to continue with their plan and that he'd stay with Ira until they returned.

'Lunch is ready. Have anything you find in the pantry,' Shivani announced over her shoulder.

As the evening arrived, they moved out to the garden. The sky was blushed in lavender and orange. Ira made a mental note of the colours to use later. The breeze was cool and fragrant when she breathed in gently.

'Are you hungry?' he asked.

'I'll die rather than consume Shivani's morbid okra.'

'You want to see my culinary magic?'

'Is there anything you can't do?'

He let out a close-lipped smile, 'Find myself a real job.'

Ira let out a tired sigh, 'You're sixteen.'

'My mom had me at sixteen,' he said with a shrug.

Ira tilted her head. 'What are you going to cook?'

'Nothing fancy. Wheat pancakes and…'

'Tea, of course.' She filled his sentence. Tea, for Nihal, was a solution for every problem in the world, if only for a while. He looked at her, a trace of warmth crossing his face.

'I'll come with you,' she said and followed him inside. He paused briefly in her father's study, plucking a copy of *Living Spaces*, then moved into the kitchen. Ira switched on the hanging light, and a golden pool spilled over the counter, softening the edges of the space.

She watched him as he worked the batter with effortless ease, each movement measured, almost ritualistic. The sweet scent of jaggery and ghee curled through the air. As he spread the paste in gentle, circular motions, the kitchen, as well as Ira, seemed to hold its breath, suspended in a quiet warmth the house was not used to.

They ate the pancakes side by side, knees touching beneath the counter. Later, Nihal rolled up his sleeves and insisted on fixing the leaky tap when he noticed it. Tools clinked on the granite as he worked, and she just sat there looking at him like a devout, adoring a deity in the temple, asking nothing but being grateful. She didn't realise when she began to draw him somewhere in her mind.

Ira knew of one thing: she would come back to this moment again.

That night, Ira spoke to the canvas—not with a brush, not with a knife, but with her fingers. The acrylic itched and burned along the small cuts on her cuticles, tiny wounds she didn't remember making with her teeth. *There was something I felt as I watched him today. The way he spread the batter on the pan.*

The softness of his movements, the focus in his eyes. It was like he was creating art. A masterpiece. I saw the way the light caught the sheen on his forehead, the pale line of the scar. A detail about him I had almost forgotten.

She spread the paint in slow, circular motions with the pad of her index finger. She was so close to the canvas that her breath mingled with the pungent acrylic.

She laughed suddenly, startling even herself. *He wasn't the boy you'd remember—shivering, soaked, as Papa pulled him into the car—nor the lanky teenager who spent countless afternoons in this very room with me after you were gone. He is different now. Taller. So much taller. Almost brushing the pendant lights above the kitchen island—the ones we used to call Monster's Straws.*

Ira rubbed at her teary eyes as the paint stung them. Some of the colour stayed under her skin, a wedge of pink smeared just beneath her lashes. *Aarya... do you think something is wrong with me?*

Chapter 13

In the bookstore, Nihal had just pulled out a book for himself when Sonam entered. She was wearing a purple kurti that clung to her skin. Her lips were glossy when she spoke, 'Poor luck you had to miss the opportunity.'

It took him a while to relate to the exhibition she was referring to. Nihal was disqualified for not presenting his model of the colosseum that he had built over several nights on the terrace.

'It'll come again.' He meant it.

Sonam waved his optimism with a hand, 'Where were you, though?'

'I was with Ira. She got hurt.'

Sonam didn't ask how, but she did ask if Ira was alright. Nihal told her she was.

'Are you auditioning for the play?' She asked, eyeing the books on the shelf.

'I'm not sure,' he said.

She brought her eyes back to him, 'I'm playing Calpurnia.'

Nihal looked at her, a genuine warmth in his expression, 'That's awesome. It's really interesting. The life of Julius Caesar.'

'I've been learning about him in the practice. You should come sometime.' Sonam read the title Nihal was leafing through now. *The poetics of space.*

'What is it about?' She asked.

'It's not something I'd usually read.'

'And that is?'

'Fiction,' he said.

Sonam raised an eyebrow, a faint smile playing on her lips, 'You don't really appear to me like a fictional person.'

'That's judgmental!'

'Sorry! You seem more of a philosophical kind of reader.'

'This one's philosophy.'

'Of?'

Nihal's eyes gleamed with a faint smile, the way they always do when he is talking about a book, 'It talks about how our lived experiences are intertwined with the spaces we inhabit, the attic, kitchen, and living room. The house becomes a metaphor in the sense that every nook and corner evokes a certain kind of emotion in us.'

'An attic would always remind me of a memory, a buried past maybe. A kitchen of my mother when she was alive. What about you?'

Every part of Nihal's house reminded him of the family they used to be—his father—but he didn't say this. Sonam reached for a stack of books on the table, aligning their edges until they were perfect. Nihal watched her with curiosity. 'So...what are your plans for the future?'

She brushed an invisible layer of dust from the shelf beside her and set the last book of the series exactly in line with the others. 'I just know that I want to help people.'

'Help like a doctor?' He said.

'I'm not sure, maybe, but I want to do something for the people who are lost in life, so they don't end up...' She searched for a suitable word.

'Doing what you did back then?' He finished it for her.

Sonam let out a hesitant laugh. She had a beautiful set of teeth, he noticed. 'Yeah. Ironical, I know. What about you?' She asked.

'I want to be rich.'

Sonam didn't smile this time. 'That's your aim in life?'

He tugged at the corner of his mouth, 'Well... yes. Isn't it everyone's?'

Sonam laughed softly, shaking her head, 'Ambition suits you, I see.'

'No...that's my need.'

She acquired a solemn tone now, 'You think only being rich will make you happy?'

'I think I wouldn't mind being sad with a bottle of expensive whiskey.'

Sonam stared at him for a while, 'But you mind being happy in a humble home?'

He sighed and made an entry of his own name in the register and followed Sonam out. They walked side by side along the quiet road, the soft glow of streetlights pooling on the pavement. The shadows of buildings stretched long across the asphalt. Nihal was careful that his hand didn't brush against hers.

'Are you free this weekend?' she asked, glancing at him.

'Depends—for what?'

'A small job. And you'll be paid,' she said.

'If I'm paid, count me in. By the way, are you alright now… with all that mess?'

Sonam crossed her arms, raising her shoulders, and let a faint, wry curve touch her lips. 'I will be, I guess.'

'You have to save a lot of them, right?' His smile was warm.

'I know it's too late to say this, but I'm glad you saved me the other day.' She pressed her lips together in a quiet confession.

They stopped at the corner where the road split. 'Your place isn't between them, doing what they do… It's time you help yourself first.'

'I'll remember this.'

She watched him disappear down the road, his figure swallowed by the soft glow of the streetlights. The quiet hum of the traffic and the gentle rustle of leaves followed him, leaving her alone with his lingering warmth and the weight of what he had said.

Chapter 14

The plaster on her hand irritated Ira now. 'But why would she want to meet me?' Ira said, frowning a little.

Nihal's visits, after the bookstore closed, were becoming a fixture, a predictable rhythm in her evenings. And with each visit, Sonam's presence grew, an invisible third party. The library, he'd say, was where they met in school, during the break, and then he'd launch into these little vignettes: Sonam's preference for lavender candles, her itch for order and neatness, the detail about her dead parents being teachers in Manali. It was like he was building a case, presenting her, piece by piece. Ira, meanwhile, couldn't ignore the sudden, almost suspicious, surge in Nihal's interest in Roman history. He was devouring books about emperors and senators, and she knew, of course, it was tied to Sonam's role in the school play. He was learning about Calpurnia, not directly, but the world around her, the context. It was almost calculated, she thought. Like he was trying to assemble a personality that would fit beside hers, a personality that would make him more attractive when she spoke about her role at the school theatre.

'She says she hasn't been able to connect with any girl in school and would love to make friends with the best one.'

'But I don't want any more friends.'

'You don't technically have any friends...and you aren't as boring as you think.'

'I never said I'm boring and I have you.'

Nihal's features fell. 'You know what, let it be. I'll tell her no.'

'Tell her I'm the girl his brother calls flat-chested bitch.'

Nihal felt mentally exhausted to tell her that Sharan was not Sonam's brother, not real. He somehow felt he messed it up, while he really wanted the two of them to be friends. Perhaps because he sensed he couldn't be with any one of them if not both. It was all too confusing.

He bit his lower lip with his teeth. 'I'll see you tomorrow.' He grabbed his backpack suddenly.

Ira studied him, his annoyance, and felt a kind of bliss in being the reason behind it. No one has ever been able to penetrate their friendship. The whole beauty of their friendship was in its exclusivity. The fact that they had no one else except each other. But Sonam, as much as Ira bittered to think of even her name, was able to very smoothly enter this sacred sanctuary that the two had built over the years.

Later in the evening, on their way back from the stationery shop where she stuffed herself with colours she already had, graphite pencils and a large scale for gridding, Ira stopped outside the bookstore.

'Nihal wouldn't be here at this hour,' Shivani said, holding her hand. She had already missed a part of her favourite show on Doordarshan.

Ira told her to wait outside and walked into the bookstore, not to meet Nihal for a change but to get herself an illustrated book on Roman history.

Julius Caesar and Cleopatra.

Chapter 15

'Now you're doing something your age,' Amma had said.

Ira brushed her hair and slid into a fresh tunic. She was expecting two of the girls from her class for a group project on rainwater harvesting, which needed her participation, even from home.

But they were coming in the evening, so Ira went out in the garden to sketch a face. A face that belonged to Nihal. The sharp nose, pointed chin, and the scar. But also a face that belonged in history. Roman history. Kabir had told her about how an artist must inhabit the person he wants to create with his hands.

Just then, a girl, almost Ira's age, was removed from the car's backseat with the help of Shivani.

'She's running a high fever.' Ira heard her mother say.

'I have set the guest room for her,' Shivani informed Mandira, who waved her off, 'No, she'll stay with me.'

Shivani caught Ira's eyes, both confused. Only Ira's were also burning. In rage or hurt, she couldn't say.

Next to Mandira's bedroom, where she tended to this sick, mysterious girl, Ira spent all her time in her father's study, where the new computer was placed. There were two computers Aryaveer had brought home, one for himself and another for the orphanage where Mandira now spent most of her day when she was not on her travels.

Moni showed up sharp on time and exuded a strong scent of coconut oil. She had meticulously divided the role of each person in the project. Ira shook her head robotically as she was allocated her job of making all the diagrams. The third girl was given the task of just attending the meetings, if she wanted to.

As Moni had expected, Latisha showed up two hours late with exhaustion painted all over her makeup. The apology Moni was expecting never came. Instead, a boy appeared, certainly not from their school. He had a full-grown man-beard and stood almost six feet.

'I need to pee,' Latisha announced with a yawn.

'I've never seen you around school?' The boy declared, as if talking to himself. Ira noticed how his skin shone like a snake's belly. She felt her throat tighten as she registered that he was talking to her.

A coy smile spread across his lips. Ira held on to the urge to touch hers to check if they were as chipped and dry as she had imagined.

',' he said, smiling kindly. Instinctively, Ira flattened her hair. 'But I'd rather you call me Chan like everyone else.'

In the meagre moments that followed, they stood there, Chan and Ira, blatantly staring at each other until Shivani brought back Latisha with a despicable expression on her face. 'Your friend is nauseous. I'll get her lemon water.'

When they left, Moni with her younger brother, who had a similar slick scalp and Latisha with Chan on his motorcycle, Shivani emphasised the fact that they were specifically the kind of wayward juveniles she should be wary of in school. 'The oily-haired girl was fine,' Shivani clarified.

Quite the contrary, Chan stayed in Ira's mind like a lingering melody, melting in every moment of the rest of her day. Maybe it was the way he looked at her or just the sheer beauty of him.

Towards the evening, Amma was stirring tulsi leaves in boiling water—the kitchen fragrant with something medicinal and oddly reassuring. It reminded Ira of the stranger in her mother's bedroom.

She knew her only from the periphery—and hated her already. *Fiza Ahmed.*

Ira dipped a finger into the pickle jar, licked it clean, and wiped her hand on her pants.

'Your mother thinks it may be typhoid,' Amma said, without looking up — as though she had heard the question forming in Ira's mind.

Ira frowned. 'Then why can't she go to the hospital?'

Amma paused mid-stir, her eyes fixed on the steam. Ira knew she wasn't thinking of the question, but of the right *shape* for the answer.

'My dear,' she began, 'It is hurtful, I know. But it isn't what you think. That girl hasn't taken anyone's place—not Aarya's, not yours.'

Ira's throat tightened. She blinked, but the tears slipped down anyway.

'Your mother,' Amma continued softly, 'feels a sort of duty towards Fiza. The kind that weighs heavier than love, and rewards no one.'

'Why?' Ira whispered.

Amma exhaled slowly, as though releasing years. 'Because guilt,' she said, 'is a guest that never leaves once invited.'

'I still want to know,' Ira said, her voice trembling.

'Patience, Ira,' Amma said, turning off the flame. 'Life reveals itself like tea — drink it too soon, and it burns your tongue.'

She set the pot aside. The conversation was over—because Amma had said so, and when she did, even the air knew to fall silent.

~

Chandan accompanied Latisha for the next five days. While Ira was quick to agree, Latisha somehow convinced Moni, too, to let him stay. Shivani's curiosity was settled when the trio told her he was Latisha's tutor, who was helping with the project.

Tired of explaining to be precise with labelling in their diagrams, or writing in basic handwriting, not cursive, Moni was more than happy to do most of the work herself.

Latisha, Chan and Ira often slipped in the garden where Ira watched the two young lovers smoke with slight pleasure and temptation. When Latisha buried her mouth on Chandan's ear randomly between the conversation, Ira looked away. Except one time when Chandan caught her eye. He didn't blink. Ira swallowed.

'I didn't know you were this loaded?' Latisha was lying on the grass, staring at the blue sky.

Ira didn't know how to respond to that. Chandan, who lay flat himself next to Latisha, sprang to his feet. 'How about a house tour?'

Following Ira, he rolled his eyes. He told her about the restaurants and clubs he ran with his father in Delhi and Bombay.

Latisha pulled a cigarette pack from Chan's pocket and announced she couldn't walk in heels anymore. She turned back to the garden.

Ira thought of offering her shoes, but didn't know how. She'd never been good with words around people.

'Do you play?' Chan had laced his fingers on the piano.

'My mom,' Ira didn't look at the piano but at her own fingers instead, 'She used to play.'

Chan showed little interest in seeing her father's study but was mesmerised by the DVD set, a wall-to-ceiling cassette case, and the speakers attached to the computer. 'Tech freak, is he, your father?'

'He is hardly ever home to use any of these,' Ira led him through the staircase to show the rooms upstairs.

Midway, in the lobby, he stalled, dumfounded. He pointed to the paintings resting on the easels, along with the unfinished piece she was currently working on. She had yet to define the background, but the man on the canvas was complete. Her first attempt at a portrait.

Ira felt a warmth spread across her face.

Ira curved her lips in a faint, embarrassed grin, 'I don't think I'm any good.'

'This is the best painting I've ever seen outside the museums. I only know this name. Van Gogh. We went to a museum where he had his posters all over in Zurich.'

'Did you like his paintings?'

'I don't really remember them. Only his name and the story that he chopped off one of his ears.'

Ira pressed her lips. It was so unfair for anyone to remember an artist from his tragedy alone. If she were to become an artist, she would hate to be remembered for anything other than what she created, not the pain that was used as a fuel to create them.

Chan placed his hand casually around her shoulder, 'An artist, aren't you?' He marvelled at her recent attempt at portraits.

Everything felt so strange and miraculous, and new. In his presence, Ira felt like she had just been born into this world yesterday.

~

She was still thinking about Chandan in the evening when Nihal showed up after his overtime at the bookstore.

'What are you doing?' He seated himself next to Amma, pushing his hair back on his forehead with the back of his palm.

'Ageing.' Amma fitted her fake tooth in her mouth and smiled softly, a lifetime of mischief and wisdom in that curve.

He laughed briefly.

'A wicked thing, age. Goes up and never comes down,' she said and asked him about his mother. Nihal had mentioned Prajakta's frequent headaches to Amma, and she had meticulously picked and dried chamomiles and lavender for her in the shade for the tea. 'There's never an ache nature can't cure.' She had said, 'Except, of course, a heartache.'

Nihal smiled, then asked permission to use Aryaveer's computer for the final reading of the essay he had written on *'The Magician Called World Wide Web.'*

'Yes, please go ahead and use that thing for whatever it is used for,' Amma said. It had taken her months to get used to the ring of the telephone; the computer, she decided, was a far more dangerous creature.

'A machine that could do the thinking. I hope to die before the day comes when people start to use it for thinking,' she had said.

Meanwhile, Ira brought out her own petty chores and soon began to draw grid lines on another white sheet. Amma and Shivani spoke about the new gardener, the growing crowd in Vrindavan and then again about computers.

'The day is not far when people will use this stupid telephone to stay in touch but forget how it feels to be touched,' Amma told Shivani dryly.

Ira laughed, but then her eyes met Fiza at the door. She was wearing a plain salwar Kamiz in grey and carried a few magazines in her right hand.

'I think I missed a joke,' Fiza said, hesitantly trying to make herself comfortable.

Nihal was smiling triumphantly when he appeared, making it evident that his essay was finally complete.

'Ah, we were talking about a bird called World Wide Web,' Amma told Fiza, asking her to take a seat.

Fiza radiated at the warmth, 'Isn't it amazing? You could instantly find information on any topic imaginable.'

'People would just sit around staring at screens all day,' Amma said.

'On the contrary, I feel it could bring people together, connect us with friends and family who live far away. Imagine writing a letter to someone in America and sending it in an instant,' Fiza said.

'Utter nonsense. How can such a thing even be possible?' Amma crinkled her nose.

Nihal looked at Fiza, and a gentle smile curved her lips. 'They say it will use electricity to send messages through the air! Like a giant telegraph, but invisible,' she explained, sitting upright in her position across Ira.

Shivani rolled her eyes and helped Amma to her room. 'Too good to be true, I'd say.'

Fiza was now articulating with her hands, 'Imagine a doctor in London being able to instantly consult with a specialist in India to save a life.'

'I had written an essay more against it than in favour,' Nihal ruminated, clearly amused and beguiled by the confidence of this young girl he had met for the first time. 'But now I think it may be a risk worth taking.'

Fiza's eyes were bright with anticipation, 'It is the future.'

'I guess, but I suppose we'll have to wait. I'll just stick to the books until then.' Nihal let a small, warm smile form, inviting her further into conversation, 'I'm sure you read a lot of books? Don't you?'

'I don't get my hands on many books at the orphanage. But I read newspapers,' Fiza said.

'That's doing you good,' Nihal said.

Ira had glued her eyes to her paper throughout the conversation. Finally, she spoke, eyes still on the grid lines she had drawn, 'Do you have a fever again?'

Fiza was confused, like the rest of them. 'I just stopped by for a while to see Mandira Mam. Have not seen her for a while. I thought I'd... check on her.'

'I'm surprised you don't know she is in Turkey, and too bad there is no world web yet so you could connect with her in an instant,' Ira said with casual bitterness.

An awkward look was passed between Nihal and Fiza. Ira's eyes remained on the pencils she was shaving with a blade now.

'When is Madam coming back?'

'You can call her mom if you like to, she won't mind, I'm sure,' Ira added.

Fiza looked around awkwardly, 'Thank you. With everything that she is doing for us at the orphanage, we believe she is more than our God.'

Ira scoffed, 'Your God is coming back next week. I believe you'd be the first one she'd want to see.'

Fiza nodded to Nihal. She rose and said a gentle goodbye to Amma in her room, touching her feet. Amma blessed her quietly.

'You were rude to her,' Nihal said to Ira after a while.

'I wasn't,' Ira spat flatly, beginning to draw a pupil on the paper. 'Or maybe I was. Maybe I wanted to be just that: rude.'

Nihal looked at her as if reading a message on her face. He waited there for a while. 'Actually, it's…it's alright, you know.'

'It's alright? I was rude or that I wanted to be rude?' Ira asked, putting her pencil on the table and paying attention now.

'Both things,' Nihal said.

Ira pressed her eyelids, 'I hate her.'

'I know,' Nihal said.

'Is it so hard to see what she is doing with her? My mother? One day she is grieving, and the next day she is all motherly with this girl.'

'Maybe that's her way of recovery.' Nihal was thinking out loud, 'Like yours is art.'

'Why this particular girl? She isn't the first person in the orphanage to catch a fever. I know she is bright, but I'm sure she isn't the only one to read newspapers and talk about the World Wide Web in the orphanage.'

Nihal blew air through his mouth, 'That's got me thinking myself.'

'And why doesn't anyone else see this as strange? Not even Amma.' Ira looked at him as if he would have the answer.

'Have you ever spoken to Mr Lall about it?'

'Like he has ever listened to anything against his wife. All he ever wants to do is to make her happy as if she were the only one who had suffered a loss.'

Nihal heaved a heavy sigh. 'Sometimes people feel their grief is somehow superior and, in this superiority, they forget about all the others who are grieving too.'

'Are you talking about *my mother* or yours?'

He looked at her knowingly and smiled.

Chapter 16

Sonam paid the conductor for two tickets, dropping the change back into her sling bag without counting.

'Where are we going?' Nihal asked.

'You'll see,' she told him.

The bus rattled through narrow lanes lined with peeling walls and laundry hanging from rusted balconies. When they got down, Nihal noticed the building she led him to had no signboard, not even a gate—just the sounds of life spilling from inside: children's chatter, the scrape of metal vessels, a woman's laughter echoing through the corridor.

'You have to help with Maths,' Sonam said. 'I assumed you'd be good with numbers like everything else.'

'Ah, wait—you said I'll be paid.'

'Yes.'

'I will be?' He asked.

Sonam smiled, 'Not as much as your bookstore job, but yes.'

Ten minutes later, Nihal was teaching trigonometry to a girl almost his age and fractions to two younger ones who grinned at every third word he spoke. The room smelled faintly of chalk, paper and something else. Cooked lentils. Sonam disappeared into what looked like a kitchen, following a kind-eyed woman with a tribal tattoo curling along her neck. When she returned nearly an hour later, everyone was sitting on a rug in a small room, empty plates in front of them. Soon, they were served lentil soup and a toast.

'You see her?' Sonam nodded toward the girl in the corner, sitting beside the one learning trigonometry. 'That one there, the one who was stitching earlier—she's been brought here from the brothel. Rescued, you could say. Best not to ask how she ended up there.'

A toddler waddled up to Nihal. He gave a soft, friendly smile and bent toward her. 'Hey, what's your name?'

'Dua,' Sonam said softly. 'But she cannot speak.'

'Oh.'

'She doesn't really know what she's missing.' Sonam fished out a candy wrapped in glittery foil and handed it to the child. 'The day her parents found out, they sent her here.'

Nihal looked at Sonam—part astonishment, part admiration.

When Sonam said her goodbyes, Nihal thanked the tattooed lady for the meal and promised the girls he'd come back soon.

In the bus, the air grew cooler, tinged with dust and the smell of frying snacks from the roadside. Sonam turned to him, 'I've never asked if you have any siblings.'

'Just me,' Nihal said quickly. He told her about Prajakta and her small sewing business, but nothing about his father. Talking about him always felt like opening the door to a stable full of wild horses—once they escaped, it was impossible to gather them again.

'So that's where you get it from?' she asked.

'What?'

'Your eye for detail,' she said.

He offered a faint, tender smile, carrying both admiration and melancholy. 'My mother's work started more as a necessity than a passion. That's all she could think of then—to raise both of us. I don't think she enjoys it.'

Sonam leaned forward just a little, a soft light in her eyes. 'Thank you for telling me.'

He made a small sound—half hum, half sigh—as he looked out the window. The light outside had turned amber, washing the road in gold.

'I come here every Sunday,' Sonam said after a pause.

'And what do you teach?'

She laughed softly. 'Oh, I'm no good at math or history. I just talk.'

'I bet you're good at that,' he said.

'I've come to believe I am—at least with them.' She smiled.

'I like talking to you, too.' Nihal surprised himself at his admission.

The bus hit a bump; Sonam steadied herself and then, almost without thought, rested her head on his shoulder. For a moment, he wanted to reach for her hand.

'Can I ask you something?' His voice was low, careful.

'Go on,' she murmured, not lifting her head.

'What happened to your parents?'

Sonam was quiet for a while. 'I was thirteen when we found out my mother had a tumour. She died five months after the diagnosis. It wasn't the pain that broke her—it was knowing she wouldn't live long enough. She loved life, you know. Waited for each day the way sunflowers do for the sun. Even that morning, she believed in some miracle. She never lost hope, even at the very end.'

Nihal listened, his eyes on the road ahead. 'How did you take it?'

'I think I get it from her—the hope, the delusion. That no matter how ugly, it will all be beautiful towards the end.'

'The delusion of the deprived,' Nihal said quietly. 'I think I read that in a book.'

Sonam cleared her throat and wiped the corners of her eyes with her fingertips. Then she smiled—a fragile, luminous smile that made her look older than she was, as if she'd already lived several lives.

'And your father?' Nihal asked softly.

'Metaphorically, he died with her, but we cremated him a month later. People laugh at this, but I believe one can die of heartbreak. Some love stories are that consuming.'

The bus grew silent except for the steady hum of its engine. Then Sonam reached for his hand.

'Can I ask you something?' she said.

Nihal already knew what it would be. He looked ahead, the city lights blurring into streaks outside the window.

'Another time,' he said.

Chapter 17

'It's all about the lights. You have to observe how the light falls on the objects. Then you can go about the highlights, shadows, midtones and reflections.'

Ira sat silently, absorbing the techniques Kabir was teaching in her portrait lessons. She had just begun drawing on a sheet when he held her hand. 'Don't draw a complete line.'

He adjusted the pencil between his thumb and index finger and began with a lighter grip, 'Use shading or changes in tone to suggest edges and forms. See, like this.'

Ira held the paper in her hands and looked at the face on it.

'Do you know what the most challenging part of an artist's life is?' Kabir asked, sharpening the remaining pencils with a blade. He grimaced at the sight of their chewed backs.

'Being judged?' Ira said.

'I wasn't thinking that?' He couldn't help but smile.

'The other day, you said that the paintings tell a story. If my paintings are really my story, I'd rather keep them a secret.'

He looked at the ceiling briefly as if to gather his thoughts, 'The beauty of art is that whoever looks at it finds their own story in it, instead of yours. They don't see you in the canvas but really themselves. Like in a mirror.'

'What was the challenging part you were talking about?' Ira asked.

Kabir chortled, 'earning a living, I was saying. Do you know that even Van Gogh was troubled by his financial dependence on his brother? All that fame and money only came after his death.'

'If I were to become an artist, I wouldn't want to worry about selling but creating.'

Kabir nodded with his lips pursed.

Ira narrowed her eyes, 'And you think it's because my father is rich?'

'No, because you would still be a woman. It's never a compulsion for them to make money because there will always be someone earning for them. A husband or a father.'

'I doubt I'd ever have a husband, but anyway, it's so unfair right… for the men?'

'So it is,' Kabir said. 'But it's not just men or painters, Plath was a poet. Do you know how she died?'

Ira didn't know who she was.

Kabir told her, 'She turned on the gas oven to poison herself. She was in the period of intense creative productivity leading up to her death.'

'So it is about *all* of them? Are you saying that?' Ira asked solemnly.

'People like to romanticise the idea of 'tortured artists', and I believe there may be some truth in it. Artists possess heightened sensitivity, so to say they feel more deeply…' Kabir was absently leafing through a magazine, '…lending themselves more vulnerable. They are…' He rummaged for a word, '…unconventional. While some studies have suggested the higher prevalence of mood disorders among artists and writers, romanticising creativity and mental illness is dangerous. It can discourage them from seeking help, making them believe their suffering is good, even *necessary* for creating great art.'

'Maybe it *is* good. The suffering…but…I wouldn't want to be remembered by the tragedy alone,' Ira said. She turned to face him, 'You are an artist. Do you think you are more productive when happy? Or sad?'

Kabir's eyes fell on his fingers, thinking, 'I don't remember the last time I was… happy.

Ira was quiet then. The last time *she* was happy, she thought, was when she was chasing Aarya on the beach. Her mother was blurry but beautiful in her lemon-yellow bikini in the distance. The air was damp and tasted of salt. Then there was the day of Mom's first piano recital. The warmth of Aarya's body as she slept over her shoulder. The sense of calm that only comes when you are sleeping, entwined with a loved one. A sister.

She sat in the remainder of the class, not following as Kabir explained about capturing the highlights in the iris, which gives life to the eyes on the canvas. Ira had tears in her own eyes. How much could she see across the blur of memories?

Kabir didn't ask for the special lemongrass and honey tea before he left the house that evening. On his way back in the bus, where he always took the last seat near the window, he closed his eyes and rested his head on the back of his seat. He was engaged to Aarti. They were high school sweethearts. 'What am I going to do without you?' Aarti would tell him when he corrected her figures on the large A3 sheet, basking in her earthy fragrance. They had both studied art in college, but while Kabir struggled to make his name in the field, Aarti's family was deluged with men making good money and promising a comfortable life for their daughter. She looked ordinary, but there was beauty to her ordinariness. On her insistence, Kabir was allowed a year's time to prove himself better than the offers Aarti was getting, but the least he could manage in the little time was a few home art classes to students who lived under the crystal chandeliers in the mansions as large as his unfulfilled dreams.

Now what was left of Aarti in Kabir's life was her name tattooed conspicuously on the underside of his right arm and a thought, 'How was she now doing? without him?'

Chapter 18

'This is just my first,' Ira explained like an accused, tossing her gaze between Nihal and the art in his hand.

Nihal was looking at her first proper attempt at a portrait. She had made a Roman figure—perhaps a noble or a soldier—that seemed quite hurriedly done except the eyes that seemed to possess a photorealistic accuracy and resembled his own. For a moment, the eyes held Nihal in the deep sadness that they possessed. He didn't like the overall feeling it stirred within him.

Ira was confused, 'You don't like this?'

'No,' Nihal said, 'I don't.'

Ira didn't expect it would hurt so much, his opinion of her art. She folded the paper, irritated. She didn't tell him she was trying to paint him. 'And who are you to judge me?'

'I'm not judging you, just being honest.'

'I don't… understand you anymore.' She began to clean the already clean oil bottles with a washcloth.

Irritation flared as she felt the sticky wetness of one of the leaking bottles on her fingers. With a frustrated grunt, she hurled it into the trash. The glass crashed and splintered on the metal base. The orange oil rushed out, swirling like a snake. 'You love it when she fills you with the details about Julius Caesar's life and hate it when I try to paint him.'

Nihal scoffed, 'Now, where did Caesar come from?'

'Oh right, he is your and your girlfriend's private muse?' Ira said.

'Wait, is this why you've got the book about him?' Nihal's eyes were wide.

'I didn't know books were reserved for the higher species. The intellectual ones who'd run the world one day. Make money and raise children, and read about us in the newspapers over tea in your busy mornings. *The miserable artists who took their own lives.*' She closed her fist so tight it hurt her.

Nihal's expression was one of confusion when the doorbell rang, and Moni showed up with a large smile that wilted as she absorbed the tension in the air. It was her birthday, and she had brought a purple metal box of Cadbury chocolates. It was the last day of their project. Nihal took one and left.

Latisha came late but without her boyfriend. She excused herself five minutes later and spent the rest of the time in the washroom smoking cigarettes that she carried in her pencil pouch.

The girls left two hours later, and Ira was called to the table.

'God knows this girl survives on water alone.' Amma frowned, adjusting her thick glasses.

Ira felt so tired she could barely move her limbs. She felt like her body was going to explode, dropping into tiny pieces around the room like confetti. When Shivani brought in sambar and rice, she could not look at the steaming bowls. All she wanted was to lie in her bed and stare at the ceiling.

To think of nothing.

~

Chan showed up the next morning, right after Amma and Shivani had left for the temple. Ira didn't ask the reason for the breakup.

The week that followed, Ira painted her nails and glossed her lips before she left home alongside Amma as she left for the temple. She met him beneath the Mango tree on the side of the park where the grass was drier, and the stray dogs slept for long hours. It was thrilling, keeping a secret. Although when Nihal talked about Sonam, she fought the urge to boast about her new company, but somehow her alliance with Chan felt something to be kept hidden, even from Aarya.

Chan spoke of his travels across the country. Sneaking out at night, riding to Ladakh on a borrowed motorcycle, stealing money from his father's pocket for his first cigarette. Ira said only a little, but listened with still devotion, as if living his stories second-hand.

When he talked about the girls who kissed him or sneaked him into their rooms, something inside her tightened. A knot she hadn't known existed. And yet, in the same breath, something loosened.

When he asked about her family, she mentioned her parents. But not Aarya.

Exactly nine days later, while on their own morning walk on the tracks near the small lake filled with ducks, Sujata and Lalit saw her. Chan had his hand over hers. The morning meetings stalled, but the touch of hands continued: in the garden at the golden hour when Amma and Shivani napped, in the tea shop next to the bookstore after Nihal's shift got over. And once in her father's study when there was no one home.

'There is something that I have only felt like doing with you,' Chan said as he held her against the bookshelf.

Ira felt the heat rush in her body. She smelled tobacco on his breath. It was nice.

'Know what it is?' He pushed a strand of hair behind her ear.

Heat rushed to her face.

'It's being honest,' Chan said, 'I don't feel like lying to you.'

Ira didn't know how to answer this. It was all so new. So exciting. So forbidden that she felt numb.

Chan's gaze grew distant, 'When I failed at school, I cried the whole night for the embarrassment that waited. Sumit told me it was cool to fail, but by crying about it, I was going to be a source of laughter. He told me to own it, be proud of it, laugh about it. He was right. The boys at school thought I was cool, that I didn't worry about grades and pleasing teachers like the rest of them. And then I started living like that, pretending all the time like wearing a mask. Becoming someone they all wanted to be like but couldn't.' Chan paused. Then spoke again, 'I could never make it through high school. By the time I should have passed school, I was frequenting sex workers in Old Delhi. Already a chain smoker. I drank every weekend, and my parents had given up on me.'

Ira saw the gleam in his eyes. He didn't flinch. 'But the worst part is… I was not pretending any more. I had become him. The cool guy.'

'How many—' Ira felt her breath inflating her chest against him, 'How many girls you have…' she asked.

Chan laughed ruefully, 'More than I could ever keep track of.'

'Have you loved any of them?' Ira really wanted to know.

Chan glanced at her with warmth, 'You think love would knock on the doors of a guy like me? Who would love me?'

'There is one love for everyone, that is what I know,' Ira said.

His laugh sounded like a strained cough, 'You know I could do anything with you, and something about your eyes tells me that you would let me. But I don't want to.'

Ira's breathing fell. His hands on her shoulders were warm and tight. She could feel all his fingers digging in her skin. 'You don't want to?' She whispered.

He let her free. Pushed his hair back with his palm and exhaled loudly. Facing the bookshelf, he spoke, closing his eyes, 'Not just yet.'

Chapter 19

'Mr. Ghosh was telling me he saw you with someone at the park. And then again at the tea stall. A tall guy, he said. It was him, right?' Nihal had seen Ira speaking to Chandan when he came to see her after school.

'Wait, he's your classmate's boyfriend — the jeweller's daughter,' Nihal said, frowning as he searched his memory, trying to place where he'd seen him before.

'They broke up,' Ira's voice was delightful as she ate chips from a packet. 'Hey Sonam!' She waved behind Nihal's back.

Sonam appeared with a large plastic bag in her hand, loaded with what seemed like clothes. In a tone only as sincere as not to sound irate, Nihal said, 'How do you know him?'

'Relax, we are just… friends,' Ira blinked at Sonam, leaving her confused as she spoke in an articulated way unlike herself. 'Like you and Sonam.'

Sonam raised her eyebrows, 'Who are we talking about? This special friend?'

Ira licked the salt from the corner of her lips and wiped her palms on the side of her skirt. 'Chandan!' she called out, her voice carrying across the air.

Heads turned. Chandan walked toward them, pulling off his helmet with one hand and tucking it under his arm with the ease of someone used to being watched.

Ira spoke with forced politeness, gesturing too much as she introduced Chan to Nihal and Sonam. Nihal barely nodded but kept his eyes on the boy he was still trying to recognise. When Chan greeted Sonam, she looked away.

Before Nihal could make sense of what was happening, Ira was already beside Chan. She swung a leg over the back of his motorcycle, smoothed her skirt beneath her thighs, and held on. The engine roared to life.

'Shall we go?' Sonam asked after the motorcycle was swallowed by the traffic.

Nihal sighed, then looked at her. 'You don't really have to do this, you know.'

Sonam didn't answer him; she didn't even look at him, just kept walking beside him, refusing him when he asked to carry the bag.

'Not everything is about you,' she said.

~

'This is the first time he's brought a friend home,' Prajakta said, half an hour later, stretching the measuring tape across Sonam's shoulders. The fan whirred lazily above them, stirring the smell of talcum powder and freshly ironed clothes. Prajakta worked her way down to measure Sonam's chest. Nihal lowered his eyes and walked toward the kitchen to put water to boil.

'I thought he only spoke to Ira,' Prajakta added politely.

Sonam removed her school belt and let Prajakta wrap the tape around her waist. 'She's a lovely girl,' Sonam said softly.

'Poor child, had to endure so much at such a young age.' Prajakta made a note in the small diary she kept tucked inside the cloth pouch at her side. 'There's no cure for loneliness.'

Sonam drew in a long breath. 'I'm glad they have each other—Nihal and Ira.' She loosened the tie around her neck but didn't take it off. The late afternoon light fell through the window grille, scattering honey-coloured patterns on the floor. Outside, a vendor's bicycle bell rang, followed by his singsong cry for onions and potatoes.

'Yeah, these two are tight. Tell each other everything,' Prajakta said, now spreading out fabrics on the low wooden table. Sonam noticed the faint pencil scribbles on its edge—maybe Nihal's, from when he was younger.

Sonam picked up a glittered maroon Lycra. On her palm, it felt rough like sandpaper. From the kitchen came the whistle of the pressure cooker, followed by the soft clang of a spoon hitting steel.

'My neighbours tease me,' Prajakta laughed. 'They say your son has already chosen your daughter-in-law… as if the two could ever be a match!' Her expression soured briefly before she looked away.

Sonam shifted slightly in her seat. Somewhere outside, a child's laughter drifted from the lane, and the house fell quiet again, filled only with the slow hum of the fan.

'I'm not saying I don't like the girl. Oh, she is wonderful. A pure heart… but a girl raised in gentle hands can barely sustain the burn of the sun. I'm not saying my boy is a bad egg.' Prajakta's gaze turned distant. 'Youth is passionate, my dear… but it always wears off—the passion, and the youth both. And when novelty draws thin, love often seeks shelter… comfort.' She paused, her voice softening, 'Sometimes in another's arms.'

Nihal had been listening from the kitchen. His temper flared as he appeared, carrying three cups of tea on a faded plastic tray. 'Ma, stop it.'

Prajakta exchanged a confused look with Sonam, her lips twisting into a friendly smile. Sonam noticed a single loose thread hanging from the hem of her blouse.

'Did I miss something?' Prajakta muttered to no one in particular, folding the remaining fabrics on her lap. Sonam reached over and refolded them properly after Prajakta placed them on the table.

Nihal held out a cup for Sonam. She drank it in one go—the tea scalding her tongue—and gestured that it was perfect.

'It's Ira I'm asking about. I miss seeing the child these days.' Prajakta took a small sip of tea and ran her tongue over her dry lips.

Nihal rose to gather the leftover fabrics and stacked them neatly into a plastic bag, which he placed in the corner, near the curtain. 'She isn't a child anymore,' he said quietly, almost to himself.

He then sat on the mat and emptied the contents of his school bag onto the floor, and began to organise a compass, a tattered notebook, and a few loose coins. As the two women continued to talk about necklines and sleeve ruffles, he heard them select buttons from an old aluminium Cadbury's box. His father had given him that box years ago on his fifth birthday, along with a red bicycle. He had also bought a cassette tape for himself, which he probably took with him.

After half an hour, Nihal turned to Sonam, 'It's getting dark.'

Sonam glanced at her wristwatch, surprised at how the time had slipped away. She rose to her feet and hugged Prajakta. 'There's no hurry, aunty. Take your time with it. I'm very excited to see how it turns out.'

'Anything would look lovely on a face like yours,' Prajakta said warmly, hugging her back. Then she handed her a folded scarf, 'It's your first time here. This is for you.' It was made from a leftover fabric from a customer who didn't want it back.

Outside, Nihal was already waiting on the pavement, counting coins in his palm. They began walking toward the bus stop side by side. The street was dusky and soft, the smell of frying pakoras drifting from nearby homes.

'Are you jealous?' Sonam asked suddenly.

He frowned. 'No. Why? Why would I be jealous?' He didn't look at her — his eyes were fixed on the setting sun, its dull light glinting off his forehead.

'I don't know,' she said. 'I just felt like asking.'

A man on a motorcycle slowed as he passed, muttering something under his breath. Sonam looked away. Nihal glared after the man, his jaw tight.

'You two are closer than I thought,' Sonam said after a while, trying to touch his hand as they crossed the road. Nihal didn't know what to say, so he stayed quiet.

At the bus stop, they sat on a stone bench beside a woman with greying hair. She was eating a vegetable patty wrapped in an old newspaper.

'Aunty was telling me about her parents… and her sister,' Sonam began, carefully watching Nihal's features. His expression was drawn, his lips twisting the same way his mother's did. 'Must have been tough on her,' she said.

'She knows how to deal with tough,' Nihal said flatly, checking his watch. 'She's never needed anyone's pity.'

Sonam noticed that the woman beside them had paused her eating and was listening. 'I'm not pitying her,' she said, her tone measured.

'Your bus is here,' Nihal said, rising.

Sonam reached out and held his arm, urging him to stay seated. She exhaled slowly, steadying herself. 'You know,' she began softly, 'she would have felt the same way after you and I… but she accepted it very gracefully.'

'Accepted what?' he snapped. The patty woman stiffened and looked away, pretending not to hear. 'You and I? It's not like we're getting married.'

'And neither is she,' Sonam said sharply.

The bus screeched to a halt, stirring a swirl of dust in front of them. The woman boarded it, still glancing at them through the window once she'd found her seat.

Nihal's voice rose slightly, 'I'm not one of those girls from the orphanage you feel you have to rescue.'

The bus pulled away, the dust hanging between them like an unfinished sentence.

Sonam inhaled deeply. 'I'll go from here. Or Sharan might see us. I'll take an auto rickshaw.'

Nihal shook his head and turned away. He didn't look back when she called goodbye. She stood still and watched until his figure disappeared behind the line of Ashoka trees.

Chapter 20

'I made plates full of these for your father when he was a child. He polished them all in two days and then held his tummy for the next two,' Amma mused, a warm smile stretching her wrinkled lips.

Ira kneaded the laddos in her palm, the ghee leaving behind on her skin. They were making them for Sujata. It was her birthday, and Amma thought it was a good way to return the favour of her baking every year for Ira.

A knock came at the half-open door.

'Lalit son, come in!' Amma called.

Lalit entered with his usual polished ease, a faint perfume trailing behind him. He leaned lightly against the doorframe, surveying the scene with mild amusement.

'Teaching your granddaughter the way to a man's heart already?'

Amma laughed, 'Lalit, the only heart I teach her to navigate is her own. As for the men… they can learn to keep up, if they possibly can.'

'Ahh, how I missed your wit, Amma,' Lalit laughed. 'Anyway, I was on my way to the airport. Thought I'd see you both since you two ladies live alone.'

'Lucky for you that my wit doesn't travel through airports—or we'd be responsible for your missed flight…and we, *ladies,* have each other,' Amma said, smiling. 'Why not stay for your wife's birthday today? You could go tomorrow.'

Lalit let out a soft chuckle. 'Tomorrow? No, I think she'll appreciate my greatest gift today… a little peace and quiet, free of me.'

He turned around, then back again. 'And oh, Ira, say hello to your new friend from the park. I hope this one keeps up better than that pauper.'

Amma closed her eyes, a small shiver of irritation running through her, but she stayed silent until he left. Ira glanced at her, hands trembling slightly.

Amma's eyes were on her own hands. 'Curiosity is a youth's privilege, Ira. Just remember one thing—one's boundaries are never optional, even when exploring the world.' Her voice was calm.

'Why does he try to act like my parent? It's not my problem that he doesn't have any children of his own,' Ira protested.

Amma laughed softly, the sound warm but edged with knowing amusement. Ira looked at her, eyes pointed. 'And why don't they, do you wonder?'

Amma lined the laddos in neat circular rows on the plate. 'Not every marriage is as simple as it seems from the outside, my dear,' she said, adjusting her spectacles. 'Sometimes it's far wiser to mind our own business—and leave the grown-ups to their performances.'

She wiped her hands with the towel and rose gently. 'Shivani, cover these and send them to Sujata's house.'

Ira watched her grandmother walk away, her thoughts drifting and folding over themselves like paper boats in a stagnant pond. Amma's words lingered, pressing gently against the edges of her mind. Wasn't everyone performing in some way, she wondered—even herself? Holding it all together on the surface while, beneath, everything felt as if it were dissolving into water.

Chapter 21

Nihal had started bringing work from the bookshop to school. He would sit in the library in the recess or free periods and make accounts, or a list of things to be ordered. Sometimes Sonam smiled at him through the window when she passed through the corridor.

One Wednesday morning, he was listing the names of colleges for architectural courses in Bombay and Calcutta when Sonam showed up. He could tell she was wearing makeup on her eyes. She sat next to him. 'Hey, you.'

Unlike the way she expected, Nihal curved his lips in a warm, easy grin as he looked at her. 'You were right the other day.'

Sonam squeezed her eyes; the expression made her look incredibly beautiful, he thought. 'In treating you like one of the girls?'

'In saying what you said and…I'm sorry I acted like a total jerk,' Nihal said.

'It's alright.' Her smile was warm.

'You were right about accepting with grace…' Nihal said.

The librarian walked past them. Sonam pretended to check the contents of the list of previous issuers of a book in her hand. There were none except another teacher who taught music.

'Listen, I know how you must feel. It happens in close friendships when a third person…'

Nihal cut her mid-sentence, 'It isn't about a third person, it's about that particular boy...I think I have seen him before. I don't like the way he…I don't know. The way he looks.'

Sonam shifted in her seat. 'Maybe we can warn Ira. I trust she is a very mature girl who would do the right thing.'

'Ira is not like other girls,' Nihal sighed.

'I don't mean to offend you,' Sonam said.

'Listen, I know what you're trying to say…she is…' Nihal pressed his lips together, thinking.

More than a person, Ira was a *feeling* to him. And like most feelings, she was difficult to describe. He tried, unsure, 'Sometimes she does things that she knows will hurt her eventually. She is very different in a way I cannot—'

Sonam began before he finished, 'and you think you have this responsibility to protect her.' Her voice was laced with something similar to irritation now.

'I don't protect her. Just…' he looked at Sonam but distantly.

'You know my Nana, he had never let me sleep alone in a room by myself till the time I was home because I had nightmares as a child. But one fine day, he decided to send me here. I think about how he must have convinced himself to trust that I would do fine by myself. Without him checking on me.'

Nihal gave a tight-lipped smile, 'I get what you're trying to say.'

'I'm just trying to say we are here with her. To warn her, support her and take care of her.'

Nihal shook his head violently, 'Do they really pay you for talking to the girls?' A smile finally reached his eyes before his lips.

'They offer to. The lady who now manages the affairs of the NGO is keen to pay all the volunteers, but I don't take it. Although I've heard she is very rich,' Sonam said.

'Then why not take it?'

'It's not what you think. I go there not for them but myself. It really is the best time of the week for me. Talking to those girls. It gives me a new perspective. I learn to be so grateful, and whatever my anxieties are, they look so small and insignificant. I am an orphan myself, but I still had a family in my nana and my aunt here in Delhi.'

'You know what…' Nihal said, 'You should really be an emotional instructor…if there is some job like that.'

Sonam looked at him, 'Thank you. Now can you smile?'

Gradually, and mostly with the help of Sonam, Nihal opened up to Chandan. The two were not friendly but cordial, in the sense that Nihal could stand his company without wanting to wreck his face. Weeks slipped in this new rhythm of the fours—catching the latest Hindi release at Chanakya, huddling in the dark balcony seats with samosas from the lobby; wandering Connaught Place on Saturday evenings, where Sonam and Ira darted in and out of record shops, arguing over which cassette to buy; stopping at Nirula's for Hot Chocolate Fudge or just to sit by the window and watch people pass by. On quieter evenings after the bookshop hours, they drove down to India Gate, piling out of Chandan's car to eat roasted corn and ice-cream cones, the monument glowing pale against the evening sky. Still, something about Ira being with Chandan was hard to swallow. Nihal never confessed this to Sonam or Ira, and refused to dwell on it when he was alone —until one day when it became inescapable.

It was late October. Delhi evenings carried a faint crispness but not yet the bite of winter. Neon lights buzzed over the colonnades, mixing with the honks of cars and the occasional blast of a Kishore Kumar track from passing auto rickshaws. The city was restless—half old-world, half hungry for its new malls, imported perfumes, and bootleg music tapes. Nihal had walked down to Ira's house, thinking about his father. It was convenient to think of him when he was not around his mother. Will he ever see him again?

Ira was wearing a dress. Not just any dress, but her mother's. It placed her somewhere between the girl Nihal had befriended years ago and the woman she was now becoming. For a moment, he didn't know where to place his eyes—on the memory of her, or the startling strangeness of his changed friend.

'How do I look?' excitement beamed in her eyes. It was all so new for her—for them—this way of standing before the world, being connected so suddenly. And seen.

'You look… weird,' Nihal said, his gaze catching on the blades of her shoulders, then flinching away.

'I'll take a while. Do you want to wait in the study?' she asked, her voice a little higher than usual, as though the dress had changed not just how she looked but how she spoke.

'I'm good here,' Nihal said, dropping onto the edge of her bed. The quilt was silk, embroidered with tiny paisleys, but the surface was scattered with pencils, an open sketchbook, and a Walkman tangled in its own wires.

After three minutes, he began knocking on the closet door. 'Are you writing a novel in there?'

'Shaving my legs,' Ira called back from the other side.

'Put something else on. A shirt and jeans, maybe,' he said.

'Or a blanket?' her restrained voice floated.

He sighed, flopping back on her bed, staring at the ceiling where glow-in-the-dark stars still clung. He was certain they were from the time when Aarya was alive. Though he never asked. 'I'm downstairs,' he muttered half-heartedly, but never moved.

When she finally came out, she had changed into another dress. Again, one of her mother's. A deeper blue silk, sleeveless, with a neckline that startled him. The hem floated above her knees, swaying as she stepped forward. Behind her, the closet yawned open, and it was nothing like the orderly picture he had expected: clothes spilling from hangers, a half-toppled shoe rack, an easel squeezed in awkwardly with a canvas still streaked in drying paint. A red scarf hung from the easel like a flag of surrender.

He looked at her as she walked past him, breathed in the new scent of her—oatmeal and shea butter. And strangely, he found himself wondering how she would have worn the dress—was there a zipper hidden along the back, or had she simply slipped it over her head? The thought carried him further than it should have, but he let it. He noticed the absence of her usual cotton undershirt, replaced by something lighter, more secretive—the kind of underthing his mother once mentioned when fitting blouses for her clients. The knowledge unsettled him, filling him with a curiosity so sharp it felt wrong.

A nearly shameful urge rose in him—to undo the dress just so he could know. The thought startled him, and more so because it had never come with Sonam, though it might have made more sense with her. With Ira, it was different, dangerously different, and Nihal couldn't shake the feeling that the novels he was devouring had begun to seep into his mind, rearranging his thoughts and desires until he could no longer trust them.

'What's with that face?' She asked at the door, switching off the light.

'Nothing… what… what have you done to your eyes?'

'It's called make-up,' she said.

He inhaled noisily, as if forcing himself back into the moment, shoving aside the storm of thoughts pressing against him. Maybe he would deal with them later. He followed her through the staircase.

'What now?' Ira asked him in the car.

'Why all this trouble?' His voice was soft so that Ira's driver would not hear him.

Ira huffed, then pushed a coy smile, teasing him. 'I didn't know these troubles were reserved for your girlfriend alone?'

'I tell this to her as well.'

'And does she listen to you?' She said.

'Ira… It's not the same with her. She's… different.'

'And I had always believed I was different,' her eyes were fixed on his, sharp and curious, daring him to stumble.

'It's a part of her personality,' Nihal murmured. 'She isn't putting on makeup for anyone else.'

'And who do you think I'm doing it for?' She asked.

Nihal sighed, looking out through the window, 'Forget it.'

Outside, the evening lay quiet, streaked with the long golden glow of streetlamps. A lone scooter hummed past their car, its faint engine sound drifting.

The two remained quiet for a while, but only on the outside. Heat rushed to Ira's cheeks, sudden and fierce. Her eyes stung before she could blink away the tears threatening to spill, and for a moment, he felt a sharp, helpless ache—an ache that had nothing to do with the dress or the makeup, and everything to do with her presence, so near and yet somehow more distant than ever.

'Hey,' Nihal said softly after a while, moving closer, a careful urgency in his tone. 'I'm sorry. It's just… You don't look like my artist-Ira. You are all neat and clean with no colours spilling on you. No funky smell of oil paints.'

She nudged him, looking away, finger brushing at her eyes. 'You ruined my eyeliner.'

He lifted his hand, brushing the corner of her eye gently with his fingertip. 'You don't need this,' he whispered, calm, steady, yet heavy with something he couldn't name.

'Right,' she said, 'but I'll put it. Makes me feel like someone new.'

He tilted his head, eyes soft, holding her hand lightly. 'So you are.'

For a long, suspended heartbeat, the car seemed to hold them both in a fragile, unspoken understanding—the quiet brush of silk against skin, the faint hum of the autumn evening, the faded whispers of bougainvillaea leaves. All of it folding them into a moment that was delicate, intimate, and achingly real.

Chandan had kept the best seat for the four of them near the performers. The food was as bland as it was expensive. Nihal was happy that the proximity of their table to the sitar artists rendered it impossible to have any conversation at the table. Throughout the dinner, his eyes found Ira's, and he smiled at her as if seeing her for the first time.

His thoughts kept circling back to the moments they had spent just before coming here. It was all too confusing, and he had yet to comprehend that some moments in life are better felt than understood.

Chapter 22

Ira smiled faintly as Nihal stopped before a painting. Somewhere in the corridor, a group of schoolchildren moved in a wave, their teacher clapping loudly to keep them in line.

'A typical boy, aren't you?' she teased, noticing his lingering gaze.

The marble floors gleamed, though faint streaks of water stains lingered where the janitor's mop hadn't dried fully. Kabir had dragged them to the art gallery after school. Nihal had agreed, curious and grateful for the sudden payoff from the bookstore owner.

The canvas before them read: *Self Portrait as a Tahitian* by Amrita Sher-Gil.

The figure stared out with a defiant boldness. A white cloth clung around the woman's hips, her abdomen slightly rounded, her breasts full, arms crossed in a quiet rebellion. Her brown skin glowed with firmness, and her eyes seemed to challenge anyone who looked too long.

'I'm trying to figure out the shadow around her,' Nihal said, as though to himself.

'Oh.' Ira tilted her head, impressed despite herself. 'It's said to represent her mental state—part of her bipolar personality.' She glanced at Kabir.

Kabir shook his head, brushing his hair back with a palm. 'Others say it's the aura of the painters who influenced her—Gauguin and Van Gogh. That shadow is her wrestling for her own space in the world.'

He pointed toward the artist's red lips, 'This has a symbolism here—semiotics of desire. A longing that women carried quietly in India during her time. Repression, pressed into colour.'

'She must have lived a rich, successful life,' Nihal murmured, ready to drift to the next painting.

Kabir's smile turned rueful. 'She moved to Lahore in '41, planning her first solo show. But she fell ill and died before the opening. She was just twenty-eight.'

The words clung to the air. Ira recalled the conversation she had with Kabir about the stigma of tortured artists. She didn't like the feeling the memory stirred in her. She shifted her eyes towards another canvas, one that arrested her completely—*Julius Caesar and Cleopatra.* The lovers looked at each other with a hunger that unsettled her. The art was both erotic and mysterious, done in impressionist style with heavy textures towards the four corners with a palette knife.

The painter himself was nearby, an Iranian man with long pink hair falling like a lion's mane over his face. His bell-bottoms brushed the marble as he spoke animatedly with Kabir. Ira stayed rooted, transfixed by Cleopatra's gaze.

After a while, Nihal returned to her side.

'Do you like her?' Ira asked, eyes still on the canvas.

'Cleopatra?'

'Sonam.'

He blinked, caught off guard. 'I think ......yes. And you? Do you like Chandan?'

'I don't know,' Ira said flatly. 'Real life isn't as romantic as fiction,' she said, meeting his eyes.

'This is not fiction,' Nihal looked at the painting.

Kabir reappeared, handing them paper cups of tea on a plastic tray. The tea smelled of ginger and cardamom, warm but not hot. 'Caesar was married already,' he said. 'But in Rome, it was acceptable to have partners other than one's wife. He even had a statue of Cleopatra placed in a temple.'

Nihal gulped his tea in one breath, crushed the cup in his palm. He looked around for a dustbin, but found none. 'I hate people who aren't loyal,' Nihal said.

'People don't choose to fall in love,' Ira murmured. 'If their heart betrays them, what can they do?'

'A marriage is a commitment,' Nihal's tone was serious, like he was in a debate on the stage, 'To your partner. To your children.'

Ira felt heat rising under her collar, 'Marriage doesn't guarantee love. Nor commitment.'

'But then nothing flows freely,' Nihal pushed the cup into the side pocket of his bag. 'Everything takes effort. Even love.'

'So what then? Pretend? Stay? Even when your heart is somewhere else?' Ira asked.

Nihal scoffed, 'Life isn't about whims of the heart. Families don't survive that way, Ira.'

She leaned in, lowering her voice, 'So what would you do if your wife told you she loved someone else?'

'I'll kill her,' Nihal said. He looked at Ira, whose eyes were solemn. He laughed briefly, 'I don't think I'll ever take a wife.'

Something in his tone silenced her. It told her she should not press further.

Just then, a tall man with a black hat on his long grey hair waved to Kabir from across the hall. Kabir excused himself, setting his cup on the ledge before striding off to greet the acquaintance. His voice faded into polite conversation, leaving Ira and Nihal alone among the muted canvases.

Nihal stared in the distance, thinking, as if something long sealed demanded release. Ira did not know he was speaking to her until he finished his sentence, 'You know my dad left his people to marry my mother back then? And then he started fucking another woman right after I was born.'

The words landed like stones on Ira's chest. Sudden and painfully heavy. 'You think your mother knew?' She asked.

Nihal's jaw clenched. 'I think she was waiting for him to grow past this woman. She thought her *love* would bring him back. But then came another woman, then another.'

'Then you agree? Pretending is the worst thing.' Ira tried to find something in his eyes. Couldn't.

'What's the other option? Keep hopping? Betrayal after betrayal. Breaking children along the way?' His voice trembled. 'I just wish my father hadn't fallen out of love with the woman he ruined in her childhood. She was just fifteen!' His eyes blurred.

Ira's throat tightened. She had no answers, only a dull certainty that love couldn't be taught or untaught like a habit.

Somewhere behind them, the guard coughed. A pigeon flapped lazily near the high window. Life in the museum went on: children laughed, the fans clicked, and outside on Janpath, a rickshaw bell rang. But Ira stood there, watching a boy too young for such sorrow, and too old to set it down. Perhaps, she thought, this is why they had always fitted together.

Two broken pieces, making a whole.

CHAPTER 23

The house was asleep, but Ira's room pulsed with the glow of the desk lamp. She bent over the paper, pencil in hand, sketching the faint outline of Cleopatra's eyes. The gaze had haunted her since the museum.

So he likes Sonam. She laughs. And yet, my dear sister, I don't feel as intimate with Chandan as I do with Nihal, even when he is yawning by my side, stealing foxnuts from my lap and saying nothing. To think of it, the silence with him brings me greater pleasure, the kind that breathes between words. If you know what I mean, Aarya.

She pressed harder on the pencil, shading Caesar's jaw now, then smudged the line with her finger until the face blurred and her finger soaked the grey of the lead.

The other day, he asked whom I wanted to please with the eyeliner and the dress. Her hand faltered, then carved Cleopatra's mouth in a single stroke.

It was him. Always him. Strange, I know, but I know it for sure—like mother's fingers on the keyboard. I want to be beautiful for him. As beautiful as the light that passes through the leaves.

She paused, staring at the two figures half-born on the paper, a man and a woman, in love, their eyes locked, their longing unfinished.

There is no greater intimacy than this, Aarya—the intimacy of being understood, even in the silence.

Her pencil dropped, and the room deepened into stillness, but her chest was alight, as if she had confessed something too large for words and too faint for the lines on the paper.

The street dogs howled into the night, their cries threading through the thin walls of the house. The bed was too warm and the sheet too coarse when Nihal woke past midnight. The conversation at the museum still fidgeted inside him, like a stitch pulled too tight. He reached for his mother but found her side of the bed empty.

He found her sprawled across the sofa in the lobby, her body slack. He rushed towards her quickly, but then saw the photographs that had littered the cushions, spewed carelessly on the bare floor like dried autumn leaves the tree no longer needs.

Nihal looked at his mother, the stillness around her. The calm. She didn't look like the woman with a tired gaze and a persistent headache. Stray strands of her hair curled damply at her temples. The dress she wore was unfamiliar—tight across her chest and stomach, a strap fallen loose at the shoulder, revealing her bosom almost entirely. The sight made him pause uncomfortably; it was a dress that did not belong here and yet belonged somewhere he could not name.

'Ma?' He whispered, not touching so as not to cause her a shock.

She did not stir. He gently came closer and covered her body with a duvet. Then he saw the glass. He coaxed it from her other hand as carefully as one might lift a bird from a trap. A few amber dregs swirled at the bottom. At her feet, a bottle leaned against the leg of the sofa. Nihal tucked it back into the centre-table box, and there he found it. His father's beloved cassette player she had been hiding all along.

Then the photographs drew him in. Kneeling, he gathered them with the same caution he had once seen his mother take with fragile seams, as if they might split open in his hands.

His mother wore the very same dress in the photo, only there it was stitched to her body like a second skin. In another, his father had a thin moustache shadowing his lip. His features, disturbingly like the ones that look back at him in the bathroom mirror he once cracked in rage. His father had bent into her neck, his hands closing around her as though he feared she might dissolve like a flame. Prajakta was smiling, open and shy at once, her curls thick, her face lit with a joy Nihal had never known in his mother.

Another frame, the third one he picked, caught them mid-laugh. Lips pressed, their faces blurred with motion, unguarded in a way that felt so free. And then the last—both presumably naked beneath a blanket, a Kashmiri window behind them spilling white with snow.

Her head tipped back against his father's chest, eyes closed, body slack with trust, his arms encircling her as if the whole world was theirs to lock away.

Nihal's throat tightened. With careful hands, he scattered the photographs back into their careless order. They were the secrets too heavy for his fragile heart to be pressed back into drawers.

He rose to his feet and stumbled on the stool; a half-finished blouse lay abandoned over it, a needle paused mid-stitch. He had felt so many emotions for his mother growing up; grief, love, anger and even hate, but it was in this moment as he looked at her in this state that he truly felt sorry. Sorry for the woman who once believed in love and not in its volatility, or its power to change forms.

Outside, the night pressed closer, the dogs had fallen silent at last, as though even the street had decided to overlook this scene.

Chapter 24

'You alright, Ira? Let me help you out!' The words dissolved before they reached Ira's ears. Beads of sweat clung to her skin. Panic clawed at her throat as she fumbled for the door handle.

'Ira!' Nihal said softly as if she would crack like an eggshell from his voice alone, but she scrambled back, bumping her head against the car window, her eyes tightly sealed. Chan draped his arm around her shoulder from the driver's seat, but she threw him off as though he were an infested fruit.

'It's okay, I'll take her.' Nihal helped her out of the car. Once out on the patio of her house, she sank her head into his shoulder.

He called for Amma and Shivani, then remembered the two had gone for three days. Draping Ira's arm over his shoulder, he led her toward the guest room on the ground floor. The thought of climbing the stairs seemed impossible in her state. She leaned into him, her steps uneven, her breath still jagged from what he thought was the bad dream.

Inside the room, the curtains were drawn, but the faintest line of light crept through, brushing the floorboards with silver. He eased her down onto the bed, smoothing the pillow beneath her head. Her fingers clutched his shirt, unwilling to let him go.

'Can you stay?' she whispered, the words trembling.

He nodded, brushing damp strands of hair from her forehead. 'I'm here.'

When her eyes closed again, he slipped out briefly, checking in Amma's room, where an old radio croaked softly in the corner. He filled a water bottle and, on his way back, he lifted two books from Aryaveer's study. *Design Homes* and *Monumental Homes around the world.*

Ira was already asleep, her hand adrift, swinging over the side of the bed. Gently, he placed it on her stomach and pulled the duvet just beneath her chin. Only then did he allow himself to sink into the armchair near the window that overlooked the garden. He opened the book on his lap. The night had deepened, the orange lamps cast delicate shadows over Amma's newly planted marigold saplings, their young leaves trembling faintly in the breeze.

Amma's garden brimmed with flowers—roses lifting their velvet heads, lilies pale and aloof, bougainvillaea spilling recklessly over the walls. Nihal admired them, but they never stayed with him. Roses wilted too quickly, lilies bruised at a touch. Beauty that fragile felt like a trick.

It was the marigolds that drew him. They grew in clusters, never solitary, crowding the soil with bursts of orange and gold. Ordinary, perhaps, but plentiful. Their sturdiness comforted him—the way they seemed to thrive without fuss, filling space with colour, multiplying until the whole patch blazed.

Something in them echoed what he wanted for himself: a life that wasn't fragile or fleeting, but solid, certain, overflowing. A life that didn't give way at the first gust of the wind.

He took a deep breath and began to read.

Eight hours ago, Ira had worn a shirt that knotted at the bottom, revealing a sliver of her belly. She felt beautiful in her mother's clothes until she saw Sonam when the four of them met for a musical.

It was Sonam's idea. Chandan had arranged the fake IDs for the three of them. He didn't need one, as everyone learned, Chan was a little more than twenty.

The deep blue tunic Sonam chose hugged her body like the scales of a snake, accentuating her curves. The very curves Ira was yet to welcome in her own body. The drops of rain on the skin of her shoulders glistened like strokes of sunlight brushed onto a wet canvas. Ira did not realise she was staring until Sonam's hand rose to gather her damp hair, pulling it into a high ponytail.

She tied a black bow with a satin ribbon, so gracefully it seemed less an accessory and more a signature—something that marked her, claimed space the way art does. Ira's fingers itched; she wanted to catch the image before it vanished, paint it before it blurred like rain sliding down the glass.

Nihal had once said Sonam was a storm, and Ira saw it now—in the way her presence unsettled, pulled, carried everything around her into its feminine orbit. Ira felt the same strange flicker again, a pulse she could neither name nor accept, when Sonam broke into her thoughts, 'This is the reason I hate monsoons. All this frizz in my hair.'

Dismissing the feeling, or burying it like contraband, Ira took a breath too heavy for the moment. She shook her head and followed her out, trying and failing to keep her eyes from tracing the line of Sonam's back. She wondered, briefly, how she herself appeared from behind—like a stick, she thought, a blank canvas.

The theatre was dim. The four of them slipped past the usher with their forged tickets, hearts thudding with the thrill of crossing into a place they weren't meant to belong. The seats folded beneath them with a soft creak, and for a moment, all Ira could hear was the furious beat of her own heart.

Nihal had already begun to doubt his decision to come here by the time the curtain rose on a grove drenched in painted light. Shakuntala entered, her saree the pale green of new leaves. She bent to water the plants, her bangles clinking. From the other side of the stage, the king appeared, watching her with a hunger dressed in poetry.

Ira leaned forward, chin in her palm, watching. The air inside was charged with both incense and curiosity. She tried to lose herself in the rhythm of the lines, but her body betrayed her. It was all so sudden when Chan's hand slid across the narrow gap of skin at her waist, warm and deliberate. Her breath snagged. She dispelled her thoughts, tried, failed, tried again. The more she resisted, the more aware she became of the heat of his palm. She briefly remembered another time, at the bookstore. She had wanted it then. Now, it was different. And yet, she let him.

Behind them, Sonam's fingers stealthily found Nihal's hand and held it lightly, as though coaxing a secret. Tilting her head, she whispered, 'They're both very lovable, aren't they?'

But Nihal's eyes were drawn to Ira and Chan in front, to the hand resting where her shirt gave way to skin. He could not follow the verse on stage, could not hear the applause for the lovers' first exchange. Only the sight of Ira's small shift forward—half invitation, half recoil. It burned him.

Sonam leaned closer, paused for a while before she spoke, 'Nihal, there's something I've been meaning to tell you for some time now.'

'What?' He said.

She said it swiftly, as if to get rid of a red ant, 'I've known Chandan before. He's... Sharan's friend.'

Disbelief had hardened his face. He looked at her with eyes sharp as his mother's needle, 'And you tell me now?'

'I couldn't keep it from you. Not anymore.' Sonam's jaw quivered as she spoke.

'Does Ira know?' Nihal asked.

'I tried to warn her once.'

'Tried?' The word scraped from his throat, sharper than he intended. Sonam's eyes faltered under it.

On stage, Shakuntala pressed a blossom into Dushyanta's hand, her innocence trembling. The audience sighed, but Ira was startled, laughing suddenly when Chan bent close, whispering something into her ear.

Behind her, Nihal's jaw throbbed, teeth clenched so hard it ached, and his hands curled into tight fists at his sides. Enraged, he stared at the stage.

Sonam gripped his arm with both hands, 'I'm sorry...but...I was keeping a close check.' Her voice was low, nearly swallowed by the applause as Shakuntala slipped offstage, leaving the grove emptier than before.

The play wound forward with anticipation in the air, but for the four of them, the night had already carved its own script—jealousy, desire, and silence woven tighter than the story they had come to watch.

The story of Shakuntala.

Chapter 25

On their way back, Chan drove, taking every chance he got to brush his hand against Ira's knee. Each time, her body stiffened. She did not pull away, not at first, even though the touch unsettled her, confusing her with a strange hollowness where she thought there might be excitement. Something in her recoiled, and yet she sat still, as if frozen in the role of girl she craved to become.

Nihal noticed from behind, his jaw tightening each time Chan's hand slid across the gearshift. Sonam, too, saw it, saw Nihal's shoulders grow taut with rage he did not voice. The air in the car seemed to grow heavy with silence, clashing against the blaring beat of Michael Jackson's *Black or White.*

Ira turned her face toward the window and closed her eyes. The whoosh of wind against her skin drowned out the noise, carrying with it the faint scent of rain and petrol.

And a *memory. The first recital.*

The air was thick with anticipation. Velvet curtains hung high, their folds heavy with gold embroidery. Chandeliers spilled molten light onto the gilded mouldings and polished wooden floor. Golden sconces along the carved walls dimmed as the house lights fell, leaving only a halo around the lone piano.

When Mandira appeared, the auditorium seemed to inhale. Her dress, a deep emerald silk, shimmered with each step, catching the light like a ripple of water. She lowered herself onto the bench with unhurried grace, her spine straight, her profile sharp against the halo of stage lights. Only Ira, watching from the wings with her sister's hand locked into hers, could see the faint tremor beneath her mother's fingers.

Silence swelled.

Then her fingers found the keys. She touched the trail of black and white as gently as if she were braiding Ira's hair.

The first notes quivered. Ira's grip tightened with her sister's hand. Their father watched with moist eyes as if he were a statue that could break if interrupted. Soon the music unfurled. A melody the sisters knew as intimately as their own breath, the tune that had often drifted from the drawing room at midnight, threading their dreams.

Under the chandeliers, Mandira's face transformed. Her usual animation melted into a radiant stillness, brows drawn, lips parted slightly as if in devotion. Like she was praying for the first time in her life. Her hands moved like water as each note bled seamlessly into the next, a tapestry woven in longing and poise.

The audience sat spellbound as if Mandira was not simply playing but conjuring — pulling something ancient out of the air.

When the last chord rang and dissolved into silence, the room erupted. Applause thundered against the vaulted ceiling, crashing down in waves. Ira's heart swelled painfully in her chest as her father hugged his daughters from behind. Her eyes stung. Mandira bowed her head with shy grace, offering a smile that outshone the sun.

Later, in the soft lights of the diner, Ira buried her face in the folds of that emerald dress, breathing in the faint perfume of her mother's skin mingled with the sweetness of chocolate and vanilla. The warmth seemed boundless, unbreakable.

The night had stretched longer than a lifetime. The sisters drifted to sleep, lacing their hands into each other's long before their parents decided to bring an end to the day. Back in the car, the tyres hummed a lullaby against the highway. The moonlight poured silver through the window.

But the serenity broke soon, splitting their lives into two halves.

A sound both monstrous and unnatural jerked the night awake. The car lurched violently. Ira was hurled against the window. She croaked as pain seared through her shoulder where shards of glass had buried themselves deep. A heavyweight pinned her flat against the seat.

The air reeked of smoke, iron, and gasoline. 'Aarya!' Her voice was raw.

Aarya didn't speak or move. From the front came a low, guttural moan that sounded like her father. Ira reached again, her fingertips grazing something slick and cold. Blood. A sob tore through her chest, hollowing her from the inside.

Rain lashed mercilessly against the twisted steel. Somewhere in the distance, sirens wailed.

'Two are not breathing,' the officer said.

Ira clung to Aarya's limp hand, not letting go. A single tear cutting through the soot and blood on her face. A sharp rap against the shattered windowpane startled her. An officer peered in, his silhouette blurred by the rain. He pulled the mangled door open and fastened his grip around her arm. His uniform smelled faintly of sweat—and flowers.

She could not tell if it came from him, the sweet scent of festivities, or from the flowers huddled in the chipped clay pots along the pavement. The orange heads bowing under the storm. Ira's last sensory memory of her sister.

Marigolds.

'Are you alright? I'll help you out.' Ira turned her face slowly towards the officer.

'I love her so much,' Ira's eyelids fluttered, half-lifting, half-sinking back into the pillow.

Nihal closed the book resting on his thighs. He watched her chest rise and fall in shallow, uneven breaths. 'I know,' he murmured, though he wasn't sure she had even heard him.

Ira shifted again, adjusting the hair tie of her ponytail against the pillow, a soft hum escaping her lips. Perhaps, she was still with Aarya in her memories, Nihal thought.

'You should sleep,' he said softly, stifling a yawn. Ira's breathing gradually evened out. He leaned forward and caressed her forehead, the way his father did to him, once. 'It isn't so easy to unlove someone,' he said.

The quiet stretched in the room. Gently, he pushed himself out and made his way to Aryaveer's study next door. He stared at the drawing plans pinned neatly on the wall. He was running his fingers lightly over them, tracing each line, when the soft sound of footsteps approached, breaking the silence of the house.

'You're here, son?' Aryaveer's voice sagged under the weight of exhaustion. His tie was loosened around his neck.

Nihal was startled, briefly. 'Mr. Lall,' he faltered, then steadied. 'Ira… she's not well. We were out with friends, and something reminded her of—' His voice dropped.

'Oh dear.' Aryaveer closed his eyes, as if to brush away the ache that clung to Nihal's words. When he opened them again, he crossed to the desk and lowered himself heavily into the chair. Nihal stood awkwardly, unsure if he should speak or go.

'Should I get you water, sir?' he offered softly.

Aryaveer lifted a hand, brushing the suggestion away. 'It's not been easy for me either.'

'I'm sure,' Nihal whispered.

'I lost a child too, you know,' Aryaveer's voice was flat, controlled. 'But I'm a man—and man must I be. I can't collapse like Mandira, or cry away my days like Ira. A man must work.' His gaze hardened on the empty tumbler before him. 'It feels like I'm working only to afford the grief of this family now. While they sulk, someone must keep the lights on.'

'I understand, sir,' Nihal said, though his voice trembled with hesitation.

'You better do, son. Because *that* someone is always a man. And you have to become that man one day. How can you cry? You are a man. You have to be strong for the ladies—that's what they tell you.'

Nihal pressed his lips together, uneasy at this glimpse of vulnerability from the man he had always seen as unshakable. Aryaveer Lall had always been the figure who had everything: respect, wealth, power and stability.

'They told me—give Mandira time alone. I did. Take her to work. Be with her, don't talk about the past, don't say this, don't say that. As if I am some supernatural power, responsible for curing her grief.' His voice cracked on the edge of weariness. 'I'm trying, Nihal. God knows, I'm trying.'

'Can I get you something?' Nihal asked again, almost pleading.

'Whiskey. Second cabinet behind you. The only friend of a man.'

Nihal obeyed. The cabinet door swung open to reveal rows of rare bottles, their labels faded with age but catching the light of the lamp as if telling they are still alive. He had spent countless hours in this study, marvelling over the collection of books, imported electronics, but never once noticed this hidden village of bottles. He passed Aryaveer one.

The middle-aged man poured generously into a crystal glass, the amber liquid swirling. He downed it in one go, then refilled it with a practised hand.

'I always knew you were a decent fellow,' Aryaveer said, his tone softening. 'God knows you came to us at the right time. I asked you to watch over Ira in school after...because I couldn't do everything myself. I thought—with you by her side—I could breathe easier.'

Nihal's chest warmed, pride mixing with unease.

'She doesn't live in the real world, Nihal. People think she became like this after Aarya died, but the truth is—she was always different. Even as a child, she never quite fit in. While other children laughed and played, Ira sat quietly, observing.' Aryaveer's eyes softened, a quiet smile tugging at the corners of his mouth, 'Always drawing from her memory.'

He paused, staring into the amber in his glass as though the words floated right there, 'She must have been four when we took the girls to the zoo. At bedtime, we asked which animals they liked. Aarya rattled on about peacocks, hippos, and the wonders she'd seen. But Ira's eyes filled with tears.'

Aryaveer leaned back, his voice dropping lower, 'She said the animals looked sad. How could they be happy in their cages?'

The room fell silent. Nihal looked at him, awe and sorrow mingling in his gaze. Even in her strangeness, Nihal thought, Ira seemed to carry a weight beyond her years—something her father, for all his strength, had only just begun to admit.

Chapter 26

The next morning, Nihal dressed before Prajakta woke up. He had been avoiding her. Perhaps it was the awkwardness of having seen his mother half-naked in a moment that belonged only to her. Or maybe it was anger. She had reprimanded him for clinging to thoughts of his father, yet there she was—drunk, stripped of composure, immersed in her own memory with the same man.

He tucked the delivery packets she had labelled under his arm and left. At the grocery store, while counting out a hundred and seventy rupees for a small packet of cumin and dried red chillies, he hesitated. His fingers lingered on the notes, as if the decision of where to go next weighed more than the purchase itself. He stopped at the bookstore to work a quiet shift, agreeing with himself that it was too early to visit Ira.

The cleaning lady was quietly sweeping the floor while the fan hummed overhead, pushing warm air in slow circles. There wasn't much to do and no sign of a visitor. He made tea for himself and the lady, nibbled at two biscuits that left a trail of sugar dust on the saucer, and curled up with *White Nights* by Dostoevsky. When he finished, about two hours later, he scribbled a small reflection on a scrap of paper and slipped it into the book — something he often did, leaving behind fragments of his thoughts for strangers to find.

The bell above the door jingled. A woman walked in, her eyes thick with kohl, and the handle of her glossy handbag looped tightly around her wrist. Her lips curved in a quick, pleased grin when she saw the cover in his hand.

'My favourite author,' she said, her tone casual, like they were already in agreement. She added that Dostoevsky's epilepsy had shaped characters like Prince Myshkin in *The Idiot,* her other favourite. Nihal nodded politely, but all he could think about was the sharp floral scent of her perfume.

The woman purchased a few coffee table books without really looking at the covers and got them gift-wrapped. She left smiling at Nihal. Dostoevsky had left him both softened and unsettled. On his way to Ira's, he wondered if love was ever worth the ache it carried.

Had his parents, even briefly, loved each other with the intensity novels spoke of?

Or was all love doomed to be sincere only until it unravelled itself into tragedy?

Nihal stepped into the study and found Ira already there. Her bath gown hung loosely around her waist, her hair still heavy with sleep, a few strands sticking to her cheek. Behind her, Aryaveer's new sketches were pinned to the wall—fresh pencil lines where none had been the evening before. Nihal wondered how he had worked at all after how much he had drunk last night. Perhaps whiskey was really a man's friend.

Ira gleamed like a child, 'I want to paint you!'

He looked at her quickly, then away, a nervous laugh breaking from him before he realised she wasn't joking, 'Where's Amma? And Shivani?'

'Not back yet,' she said, already searching for a spot near the window.

'Did you sleep well?' Nihal asked, but was already glad to see her up and about.

She nodded, tilting the chair toward the sunlight where it poured in, her voice already elsewhere. 'And now I really do want to paint you.'

'You mean for me to strip down and be your muse?' Nihal laughed.

'I don't mind if you're comfortable,' she replied, adjusting the chair with care, 'but I was talking about your face. Only your face.'

'I can barely sit still for ten minutes. And you should get dressed first,' he said.

She stopped, turned toward him with a half-smile, 'I *am* dressed.'

'I meant proper clothes,' he muttered, then winked, 'in case your uncle drops by.'

'I wouldn't mind him. Not this time,' Ira said.

The memory returned like a knot in his chest. He forced it away.

Exactly five minutes later, Nihal was perched gracefully in a wooden chair, pretending to read a heavy book Ira randomly handed him, to match the bright white of his shirt. The handle was warm on his skin where the sun caught it.

Across the room, Ira stood before the easel, still in her bath gown, only the belt pulled closer around her waist now. The oil colours were resting on the desk beside her.

Her gaze lingered on his face as she studied the slope of his cheek, the shadow beneath his brow.

'Dad told me that you stayed to look after me last night,' she said.

They had both known each other's secrets. Things about their lives they would never reveal to anyone outside, and these secrets tied them like strands of wet threads.

Nihal made a *hmm* sound.

She dipped her brush into a dab of raw umber, touched it to the paper, and made her first stroke.

Between one stroke and the next, she felt herself knowing—this was a moment she would carry for the rest of her life. In the stillness, Ira felt how time both slowed and quickened.

Nihal softened everything just by being there. With him, language felt almost unnecessary; sometimes it even jarred her to be around others, because behind the façades, she and Nihal could see each other stripped bare. It was something they could only admit to themselves later, when no one else was there.

But today was different. The feelings that stirred in Ira were no longer hers alone.

When she was not looking at him, even *his* eyes found her. He did not look away when her bathrobe slipped from the side of her shoulder. Neither did she bother to pull it back. All she saw was colour, or was it Nihal, as she captured him in the only language she had known.

The intensity to touch her had begun to take over him. On the skin of his fingers, he already felt the warmth. Or was it the sun? He couldn't say.

Ira caught his gaze. 'What?'

'Nothing.'

She went back to her painting.

'Ira?' Nihal said, after a while.

'Yes?' A brush caught between her lips.

'Do you ever think of the future?'

She plucked the brush out and tucked it into the pocket of her gown. 'I don't. Do you?' Her eyes stayed fixed on her fingers as she painted the line of his eyebrow on the paper, her teeth worrying her lower lip.

'All the time.' He peeled his eyes away from her now.

'And what do you think?' Ira asked.

Nihal drew in a breath, 'I think of another world, when we'd be free from exams and school, you know? Finally making something of life,' he said.

'I doubt I'll make anything worthwhile out of mine,' Ira said, matter-of-factly.

'You could be a writer,' he said. The idea was so absurd to her that she laughed, her hand freezing mid-stroke. 'A writer who has never read a book.'

'You're smart. And I didn't mean a novelist—I meant a poet.' His tone was sincere.

'If I could ever find words beautiful enough.' Ira sighed.

'They're never beautiful to begin with. It's the wretched words that make a poem beautiful.'

'Then I'll leave that to you,' she teased. 'Finding wretched words in your wretched books by authors with impossible names. I'll be an art teacher. Maybe even an artist. Perhaps I'll leave something behind in this world. Not something worthwhile, but something that would tell the world I existed,' she said between the strokes.

'Well, it's the same thing,' he said.

Ira squeezed her eyes, 'How is it the *same*?'

'It's like poetry but visual,' he said.

Ira breathed out heavily, 'Okay, chatterbox. Don't fly off in time just yet.' She chose burnt umber for his hair. For the curls that fell on his ears. 'You need a haircut.'

Nihal didn't answer. He was already gone, lost beyond their years.

'You'll be a good mother one day,' he said, almost dreamily. 'When I come to visit you and your husband in a mansion bigger than this one, would you remember me?'

His words struck sharply inside her, a picture she wanted to erase as soon as it appeared.

'And what about you?' she shot back. 'Already planning children with Sonam?'

'I don't think I'll ever have any… or even someone to marry,' he said.

Ira smiled, 'Then we're the same.'

'Hmmm.' He looked out in the garden at the rows of marigolds they planted together.

'Can I ask you something?' Ira said, glancing at him between her strokes.

He was now examining the length of his hair between his fingers. Not long enough for him to spend money at the barber, he thought.

Ira sipped some water, 'Did you and Sonam… you know?'

'No. We're just friends,' Nihal said, before her question was even finished, 'Good friends. But I saw you with Chandan at the theatre.'

'And what did you see?' Ira laughed lightly.

Nihal was really looking at her now. 'Your body is sacred, Ira. Don't let some wayward idiot to—' he stopped, his eyes searching for the right words.

'What about you?' Her eyes were on her brush.

'What about me?'

'You're not wayward.'

'You're being stupid.'

'You said I was smart.'

He sighed, weary now.

'Tell me something?' she pressed, keeping her brush in the pocket without cleaning it.

Nihal began to rise, 'No, I won't. And I think I'm done being your model.'

'Do you think I'm beautiful?' Ira asked, nevertheless.

'What?' He halted, confused.

She was looking at him solemnly. 'Tell me.'

'I think you are…' His eyes moved over her: the stray hair falling across her forehead, the fragile collarbones, the raw corner of her lip where she had peeled the skin and the blood had dried up. 'very… beautiful.'

'Have you ever felt like…' She didn't look at him. '…touching *me*?'

He threw his hands in the air, surrendering. 'You're mad.'

'So you have?'

'I hate it when you talk like that,' he protested, but weakly.

'You can simply say no, and I'll shut up.' Her voice was sharp.

'Enough of your art,' he snapped. 'I have an assignment due. I'm leaving.'

Nihal picked up his bag and left without looking at Ira's painting, even though he was curious all along.

It wasn't really Ira's question that unsettled him, but the answer he couldn't bring himself to give. Did he even know it yet? Or was he still trying to deny what had been pressing at him these past few days?

Nihal climbed straight to the terrace, both to avoid meeting the eyes of his mother and to make something of the noise running in loops in his head. The cement beneath his sandals was still hot, holding the weight of the afternoon sun. When he leaned against the low wall, the grit pressed into his forearms, the warmth seeping into his skin as if the stone itself refused to cool down. Shadows stretched long across the lane below—children running after a ball, their laughter rising and falling, a pressure cooker shrilling from someone's kitchen.

He closed his eyes tight until sparks flared against the darkness. And there she was—waiting behind his lids, as if she had never left. Ira, her face tilted toward him in that light, her robe slipping carelessly at the shoulder. He should have looked away then.

And yet, even now, he let the image hold.

Heat swelled in his chest, ran down his arms, caught in his palms. It was the same stubborn heat refusing to leave even when the day was nearly done. He wanted to touch her then—just the curve of her wrist, and the faint hollow where her collarbone showed. He had stopped himself before. But here, in the emptiness of the terrace, he let the thought run its course; he let his fingers explore the parts of her body he had never seen.

And then, just as quickly, another face flickered in—Sonam's. A laugh of hers, careless, from some forgotten afternoon, brushing past him like a draft through an open door. He didn't want it there, but it was. He pushed it back, clenching harder, until only Ira remained.

The remorse came almost as quickly. He opened his eyes, staring at the cracked edge of the wall, at the street below, where nothing at all had changed. Only inside him, something had shifted, and he wasn't sure if it was desire, or shame, or both tangled together in a way he could no longer separate.

On the two days Ira came to school, he took her to the playground at recess, where it was easy to disappear into the noise and the motion so Sonam would not spot them. On other days, he stayed in the library, hunched over application forms for the internships Aryaveer had suggested. The pages felt less like paperwork and more like small gateways—thin doors leading into a world he had sketched a hundred times in his head. A world where he wore shiny leather shoes, where a glossy bookshelf stood by his desk, stacked with hardcover books he had bought for himself, not borrowed or begged for.

Ignoring Sonam required almost no effort. Somewhere, he even felt a strange satisfaction at having a reason to avoid her.

At the same time, he felt the slow, certain thing forming around Ira—a tenderness that looked dangerously like… love —and he didn't know if he could return it. He wasn't sure what he wanted. How could he? The only thing he knew was the hollow ache of being unloved by someone you loved deeply.

He had seen it in his mother: the way she became a shape he barely recognised, how sudden small irritations could erupt into fury, how she would vanish from conversations. She would avoid coming to bed until exhaustion finally dragged her under, and then sleep swallowed her so completely it seemed she'd never wake. He had often imagined what that felt like to be in love: shouting into a cave and only your own echo answering back, louder and lonelier until you convinced yourself someone was listening.

He wondered what it would be like to still desire someone you had convinced yourself to hate for so long.

That afternoon, after the recess, Sonam followed him into the boys' washroom and waited outside the stall. She still stood there with her kohl smudging into thin black rivers on her face.

'I just need a moment,' she said, watching him wash his hands under the tap. He stared at her, jaw tight; the water still running.

'I was a fool not to see it earlier,' He went on, 'I doubted a few times that you and Chan knew each other already. At the movie, you knew he didn't like popcorn and took his cola without ice.'

'I've known him two years?' the words wormed out of Sonam's mouth.

Nihal stared at her in equal amounts of anger and amazement. Sonam's face fell. For a moment, she looked so small and beaten that his anger felt wrong.

'Clearly you didn't come just to confess an observation,' he said after a pause.

She drew a breath, steadying her voice into a near-whisper. 'He has had a past, yes. With girls. But I believed him this time—I believed him when he told me he was *different* with Ira.'

'Girls,' he repeated, the word flat and brittle. 'Does that include *you*?'

Her lips trembled. 'He told me he was serious…for Ira. And that he was falling in—'

Nihal's anger pressed at the edges of his voice, 'Who are you, then? His conscience? Or are you trying to be some matchmaker here?'

'I'm trying to be honest,' Sonam said, and in that honesty, there was a small, hurt dignity. And guilt.

Nihal ran a wet hand over his face. 'Then tell me again—why did you break up with him?' The question was sharp.

She wiped at her cheeks and looked down. 'People change. I wanted to believe him.'

'Look where you've left Ira,' Nihal said finally, the accusation more exhausted than righteous.

'I'm sorry,' Sonam said, earnest and raw. 'I didn't mean for any of this. You can ask Ira, he hasn't done anything with…'

'He hasn't yet—for his own sake.' Nihal's voice had gone quieter, colder. 'But I can't make Ira wait to vouch for his changed character. She's not some little experiment you and your ex-boyfriend want to run.'

Later, in Maths class, the equations blurred into each other, numbers and symbols dissolving into a haze. When the teacher asked him to explain a trigonometric problem, he muttered an excuse, pushed back his chair, and slipped out. The corridor was cooler, quieter. By the time he reached the library, it felt like the only place where the air wouldn't press so heavily against his chest.

Chapter 27

At the dispersal, he told Ira to inform Mr Ghosh of his absence from the bookstore, nor did he walk Ira home. He went straight to the bedroom he shared with his mother. He took off his shirt and hung it on the hook at the back of the door when it was pushed open from outside with force.

'Did *you* keep the bottle back that night?' Prajakta was in her nightgown. Small, unruly strands of hair curled over her head.

Nihal was furious and tired. 'It's only you and me.'

'Don't act smart with me.' She gritted her teeth.

'I'm *not* acting.' The scream never reached his voice.

'Did you look at the pictures?' She asked, calming herself and veering her gaze away from his eyes. Her nostrils flared.

His tone was calm, 'I did.'

'All of them?'

He shook his head.

'You shameless pig.'

Nihal took a long breath. 'Why were *you* looking at them, wearing those… clothes?'

'And you think you have become the man in my life to control me. I need your permission to choose clothes now?'

A dry mocking laugh escaped his lips, 'And why did I need yours to write him letters?'

'He kicked you out of his life like a stray dog, you fool. I didn't want you to lick his boots. You were a child, and all I wanted was your safety.'

'Licking his boots was safer than being beaten every day,' he said.

Prajakta's chin quivered. Nihal felt a sharp pain seeing his mother like this. Why does he end up hurting everyone? His own eyes began to tear.

His voice fell, 'Ma, I was a fool to not see how that man walked out on us. I was just eight, and you were right. If anything, you helped me see better. And that's what I'm doing right now. After everything he did to you, you should be hating on him, burning all those goddamn pictures of him.'

Prajakta gritted her teeth so loudly they were audible, 'Have you burned all those letters you wrote him?'

'I love you, Ma. I don't want you to suffer over an asshole,' he pleaded.

Her eyes grew large, 'Don't you dare use that word for your father again.'

'He didn't even want to be my father. He was the one who told you nothing would happen. He didn't care that you were just a child.'

Prajakta's shivering palm was hot on his face. A tear found its way and paused between his lips. 'Ma, don't you see where he has got us? The man is fucking his bitch while you are longing for him half naked, drowning in alcohol and yearning for him just like a stupid school girl that you were in those photos.'

Prajakta didn't look at him, 'Get out of my house.'

She sobbed in her palms and whimpered again and again until he obeyed, like always.

~

'What are you seriously? Her brother?' Chandan looked confused, squaring his shoulders but maintaining his calmness as Nihal plucked Ira's school bag from his motorcycle.

Ira reciprocated Chandan's reactions. Only, she also rejoiced in Nihal's angst. Sonam stayed silent like a spectator in the distance.

'What I am to her is none of your business. And a brat like you would never be able to comprehend that anyway,' Nihal spat.

He held Ira tightly by her elbow, throwing a furious glance at Sonam.

Chandan calmed himself, 'Look, brother, you can't tell me what to do and not to do with my girl.'

Nihal's jaw clenched, the muscle in his cheek twitching. His voice came out rough.

'Ira is *not* your girl.' He turned to her, eyes blazing, 'You're coming with me — now. Or I swear I'll go straight to your Uncle.'

Ira's father was travelling, and she knew with a certainty that Nihal could never go to Lalit. Her jaw tightened, annoyance prickling under her skin, yet a strange obedience tugged at her—a wish to do as he said, if only to end the storm in his eyes.

Chapter 28

The week that followed, Nihal had gone on another of his educational trips to Kerala. Ira went to school hoping to see Chandan at the gates. Day after day, her anger swelled—at Nihal, at Chandan, at the boys clustered around—until it thickened in her chest like smoke by Thursday.

On Friday, she finally saw him—not at the gates, but in a car park a few blocks away. His body was pressed into hers, his face buried against her throat, the sound of Latisha's moaning cutting across the ordinary traffic noise. Or so Ira thought.

By the time she reached home, her skin itched with a restlessness she couldn't name. It was as if the world had decided to move on smoothly, refusing to acknowledge the storm tearing through her. She wanted to wound something. Herself, if nothing else. She dug at the cuticle on her index finger until blood welled, sharp and deliberate.

She pulled out her art from the closet, and the one still stapled on the stretcher. She carried them into the garden. The evening sun had dulled to a copper warmth. Ira knelt on the grass and fed one drawing after another to the small fire she had coaxed from a match and dry leaves.

The edges blackened first, curling inward, and the faces she had poured her time into went soft and molten. Each sheet made a small, hungry sound, like a breath leaving the chest.

Nihal came running, his small bag thudding onto the grass. 'Wait—are those—?' His voice cracked with panic.

He grabbed a book and beat at the fire, coughing as smoke rose. At last, he snatched a sketch away from the flames. The edges were scorched, the paper trembling in his hand. 'Are you out of your mind?'

'Why do you care?' Her tone was flat, almost bored. 'You think they are pathetic anyway.'

'No,' he said quickly, breath still uneven. 'I never meant that. I'm not an expert—I can't even draw a tree.' His eyes dropped to the half-burned page. 'But this one. This one's beautiful.'

She glanced over. 'That's you,' she said, with the faintest trace of bitterness. 'Keep it. Maybe you'll like yourself better than I ever did.'

'Ira…' Nihal's voice softened, 'C'mon now…smile. Will you?'

'Why are you even here at all?' she asked, her eyes raw. 'Or is it that your new friends have finally given you permission?' Ira's words didn't make sense even to her.

'They're not my friends,' his jaw tightened.

'You know what they say about us. About me.'

'I don't care what they say,' Nihal said.

'Of course you don't. You're a boy.' Her laugh was small but sharp.

'Yes, I'm a boy,' he said, suddenly fierce. 'Do you really think that makes life easy for me? That the world is handing me blessings?' His voice broke on the last words. He dropped the sketch, and it fluttered down to the grass between them like a witness.

The garden around them cooed the sounds of the world moving on—the clatter of a pot from the kitchen, the dull drone of a scooter starting somewhere in the lane, but the air between them thickened.

'Do you think it's easy to be made the man of the family at eight?' Nihal's voice cracked, though not from weakness—it was the strain of holding too much. 'And then to watch your mother work herself into the ground just to keep food on the table. While I sit in this goddamn fancy school, wasting time with boys who've never carried anything heavier than their cricket kit.' He let out a bitter laugh, 'and when I try to find work, anywhere—*anywhere*—they say I'm too young. A child.'

He looked at her as if daring her to answer. 'Do you think I'm a child?'

Ira knelt and let her hand drift to the sketch Nihal had saved from the flames, her thumb tracing the burn marks like they were veins on the skin. 'Do you even know how it feels to be a girl?' Her words were softer, but sharper too.

'All this—' Nihal pointed at the embers in the grass, at her swollen eyes, at the restless evening coiling around them—' all this just because you think your heart is broken?'

Her breath hitched. 'It's because of you. He wouldn't have gone back to her if you hadn't—'

'He would've gone anyway,' Nihal said. His gaze soft, as if explaining a life lesson to a child. 'A day later, a week. You think he was going to stay forever?'

'You don't even try to understand my pain,' a sob caught in her throat, 'you brush it away like it's nothing.'

'If you call that love—that's not, Ira. That's a shadow dressed up to look real.' His chest heaved, words pouring out, ragged. 'You sit here in this palace, painting your sorrows like they're storms, while there are girls your age—' He stopped, swallowed. His voice lowered, carrying something personal, heavier than just anger. 'Some of them never even choose the men who ruin them. Some of them get dragged into lives they didn't ask for—fifteen, sixteen, with a baby on their hip before they've had time to grow. And the man who gave it to them?' He looked toward the iron gates, let out a breath, 'already gone in the arms of another.'

His jaw tightened as he paused. The words settled heavily. Smoke drifted, faint, as though the fire was still hesitating between them.

Ira's eyes were raw but dry, like a canvas that had absorbed too much pigment.

Inside, she poured a glass of water and placed it in his hand. Nihal drank slowly, drained it in himself, and asked for another. He placed it beside him on the table as the two sat side by side on the couch in the lobby. 'I think I'm just…frustrated,' he said, falling back and looking at the crystal chandelier above them.

'With me?'

'Everyone.' Nihal leaned over the paper in her hand, squinting at the colours. 'You know… from up close, this doesn't even look like me.'

'Trust me, with that hair, you really don't want to see how you really look.' A quiet, private grin tugged at her lips at the thought that invaded her. She would not tell him that he looked beautiful still, in the curls that tumbled on his face and ended just above his eyebrows. In school, he pushed them back. Perhaps with oil, so they obeyed him. But they hid his scar, and that she didn't like. She liked his scar. It gave her some sort of triumphant feeling that only she knew the story behind it. Like it wasn't just his but hers too.

Ira tilted her head, letting the pale light of the lamp catch the faint ridges of oil on paper. 'It wasn't supposed to,' she said softly. 'I wasn't trying to capture you exactly as you are. Just the impression of you… the way you… *feel* to me.'

He traced the line of the scar she had softened on the paper, noticing how it became almost a shadow rather than a mark of injury. The colour bled into this finger. 'So… this is how I *feel* to you.'

She nodded, almost to herself, feeling the texture of the paper under her fingertips. She didn't touch his face, not yet. Painting him was her way of acquiring him, marking him, even explaining him to the world through her eyes.

Her gaze drifted to the open book of Monet on the desk where she'd left it this morning, the *Water Lilies* spilling colour across the page. The brushstrokes seemed to ripple even on the paper. He followed her gaze.

She told him how he painted the impression and not the exact subject. The light, the air, the fleeting moment. She told him how she wanted to do the same with him.

'I always thought a painting had to be perfect to the subject,' he said.

It doesn't, she told him. Her fingers were brushing against the paper almost reverently now. 'Details can lie. Feeling… that's the truth. I painted you this way for honesty.'

Nihal read the heading on the page, 'Impressionism.' He murmured, 'Capturing what matters, not what is.'

She looked at him, the corners of her lips twitching into a small, knowing smile. 'So it's the two of us again. Like the beginning?' She whispered.

'Like it should be, I suppose.' He took a sip from the glass.

A long, thoughtful pause later, he said, 'Saksham invited me to his birthday tonight.'

The words cut strangely, like paper against skin. Ira pressed her lips together, tried to stop herself, failed. How foolish of her to think she had won him for herself again. 'Let's see whose life you save this time.'

'I'm going for Saksham,' he said flatly.

'Then why say it like you need my permission?' She closed the book.

'I'm not asking. I'm telling you,' he said.

Ira lowered her gaze. The sketch still trembled faintly in her hand; edges singed, but her strokes alive, despite the smoke. Nihal took it and folded it with care, once, twice, and slid it into his jeans pocket—close enough to feel it as he rose.

Ira's eyes lingered on the motion. In that second as he walked away from her, he no longer seemed like the boy she had known but only a figure she might have painted, half in shadow, half in flame, holding on to something fragile only because he didn't know what else to hold.

Sometimes, she knew him like her own blood, and sometimes, she failed to even recognise him. But maybe that's enough, she thought. To understand him in the only language whispered between her fingers.

Chapter 29

The garden was quiet under the night sky, the moon casting a silver glow on the hedges and the fountain. Somewhere beyond the glass doors, bass thumped through the house, a persistent pulse that seemed to shake the air and his chest alike. He lingered at the edge of the lawn, watching fairy lights wrap around the trees and railings.

Inside, the house had been transformed. The living room swirled with bodies, laughter, and the clinking of crystal glasses. Boys leaned against walls, their voices low and sharp with bravado, while girls laughed in tight circles, posing with disposable cameras. Everything was polished, rehearsed, and controlled—but beneath the glitter, Nihal felt the quiet ache he left with Ira.

He remembered the first time he had come here. The whispered jabs, the games, and the cruel question. *'Are you riding the freak because her father owns the school?'*

The memory tightened his chest.

Saksham and Sharan commanded the centre of their circle, grinning like kings of the night. Saksham waved at Nihal, teeth flashing over a sequined shirt, but Nihal only nodded, unwilling to step into their performance just yet.

Then—just like the last time—his gaze found her. She was wearing the red dress he had seen between his mother's fingers so many times. He remembered Sonam trying it in the mirror of his living room. A piece of clothing he had himself delivered, now glowing on her body as if it has a life of its own. The memory hit him again: the pull, the irritation, and the fascination. He hated that part of himself, how a small thread of him still clung to her, stubborn and unyielding, impossible to untangle.

Ten minutes later, he was at the bar asking for a Coke when he spotted Chandan, leaning against the counter. He watched him slip something small and white from his pocket, a tiny, almost invisible gesture as he turned his back to the waiter.

Chandan stirred it into one of the lemonades. He gestured to Sharan, who grabbed two glasses and charged towards Sonam.

Nihal's heart pounded. It was all happening too fast.

Meanwhile, Sonam reached for the glass, her fingers curling around its cool surface. Her eyes were searching in the crowd. Nihal moved. He crossed the distance between them in a few swift strides, his focus narrowed as the music faded into a dull roar. He reached Sonam just as she lifted the glass to her lips.

Without a word, he knocked it from her hand.

The lemonade splashed across Sonam's dress and the floor, the glass shattering with a sharp, explosive sound that cut through the party noise. The sudden action drew gasps and stares. Sonam stood frozen, her eyes wide with shock, the front of her dress now stained with the sticky liquid.

Sharan jumped back with a pale face.

'I saw what you did there,' Nihal spat.

Sonam's eyes glinted with tears as she looked at Nihal.

'Seriously! Do you think you are some messiah?' Sharan said.

'Why are you such a jerk?' Nihal's voice was half anger, half disappointment.

Sharan now stepped forward, his hand clenched into a fist. 'Chandan was only being nice to your freak, but Sonam spoiled it all for him. Guess she still wants Chandan for himself. Or maybe you're not as good at everything,' He said, then lowered his voice, 'Or was it that you wanted the freak for yourself?'

A brief, clumsy scuffle erupted, a flurry of limbs and hushed curses, before Saksham intervened. His voice, both pleading and authoritative. 'Easy, easy, what's going on here?' He stepped between them, pressing a hand against each of their chests to pull them apart.

'I saw Chandan mix something in Sonam's drink.' Nihal raised his gaze to find her, but Sonam had already left.

Faces, previously animated, were now frozen as they turned towards Nihal. They watched with a detached curiosity, like spectators at a staged spectacle. A raw heat surged through him, a mix of adrenaline and something darker, a simmering anger that threatened to boil over. Saksham's face wore a mask of controlled annoyance. He gestured sharply towards Chandan. 'Apologise.'

'Fuck you all,' Chandan barked and left.

Sharan was still there, his profile slightly relaxed now. Saksham took Nihal to the bar and offered him cold water, which he refused. 'I'm sorry it's always too ugly for you.'

'It's not your fault,' Nihal said, meaning it.

'Can I ask you to stay for a little longer?' Saksham said.

Nihal pursed his lips, 'This isn't a place for me. Both of us know this.' He struggled to scour his pockets for the pen he had bought for Saksham, but found nothing. After some thought, he tried recalling if he had lost it when he pounced on Sharan. There were simply too many people in his line of sight, rendering his search—if he decides to do it—implausible. However, it was only when he stepped out and boarded a bus for his house that he realised he had also lost something else.

Ira's impression of his truth.

CHAPTER 30

Nihal slept on the terrace again. Only this morning, there was a plate of buttered toast and tea by his mattress when he woke up.

He hadn't eaten dinner for the past few days, and he knew his mother hadn't either. He dipped the toast in the tea and gulped it like it was a forgotten song he just recalled.

'I had stitched something for Ira. Would you give it to her?' Prajakta said when she saw him in the lobby.

'I will, Ma.' His gaze stayed on her as if waiting for her to reveal herself from behind the exhaustion.

Her chin quivered, and a sob left her throat, 'I shouldn't have…'

'I'm sorry, Ma, I wish I were a better son.' Nihal sobbed with her.

Prajakta covered her mouth with her fist as she cried. 'You are the best son in the world.'

Nihal patted her shoulder gently until she gestured for him to go.

And he obeyed.

~

Ira was having her breakfast in her room when he saw her. She lit up like dawn and gestured for him to sit next to her.

'You ok?' She asked with a mouthful, sliding her mother's pearl dressing mirror beneath the cushion behind her.

He looked at her and shook his head weakly. When his eyes fell on the bruise on her wrist, she wore an animated tone, 'I cannot look at your hair anymore!'

Nihal let out a sigh, 'Then cut it.'

'How was the party?' She asked.

'I left early.' He closed his eyes and rested his head on the back of the chair.

'Do you want some?' Ira brought a bowl of roasted foxnuts with only a few left in it to his face as she rose to get it refilled.

He gestured that he was fine with a wave of his hand.

She appeared a few minutes later with a packet of cookies and a pair of scissors. 'Are you wearing something underneath?' she asked, her voice cutting through the lazy quiet. Nihal blinked, half-asleep. 'What?' She tilted her head slightly, a mischievous glint in her eyes as she flashed the scissors. 'I'm going to cut your hair. Just take your shirt off.'

He curled his lips in a faint confusion and then glanced toward the door. 'Uncle is with my parents in Pune,' Ira said, dragging the chair in the direction of the mirror.

His vest was white—the kind that showed every line of muscle and shadow of skin beneath. There was something new about him, Ira noticed. A weight in his shoulders, a quiet strength in the way he stood. The soft edges of a boy giving way to the frame of a man.

She filled a spray bottle and misted his hair. Tiny droplets caught the light as they fell, glimmering before they vanished into his dark curls. She raked her fingers through them, separating strands with slow precision. 'Do they still play that game?' she asked, her tone light. 'What game?' His voice was low, rough.

She met his eyes in the mirror. 'Latisha once told me.'

Nihal rubbed his temples. 'I told you I left early.'

'You're not talking to Sonam these days… why?' Her fingers slid through his hair again, the comb gliding close to his scalp. 'Nothing like that,' he said, though his voice betrayed fatigue.

'Something happened between Chandan and Sonam,' she said quietly. 'Did she tell you something awful about him?'

Nihal exhaled, leaning slightly forward. Ira gathered a section of his hair between her fingers and trimmed the ends. Each snip landed softly on the floor. 'I'm saying this because Chandan had already told me about his past.'

'Past?' Nihal asked, meeting her eyes.

'Yes. About all the girls he—' She began.

'Slept with?' He said.

She paused mid-motion. The scissors hovered near his neck. 'Yes.'

The quiet that came after felt heavy. Her breath touched the back of his ear as she leaned in to even a lock.

'I'm surprised you didn't care about this information,' he said, eyes closed, 'and honestly—' he pressed a hand to his forehead tightly, 'I'm too exhausted to talk about anyone right now.'

Ira set the scissors down for a moment. 'I thought you had begun to love her,' she said, her fingers brushed the trimmed hair from his shoulders, slow and deliberate. When she lifted the scissors again, her hand trembled slightly. She gathered another lock, the comb grazing his neck. He shivered, and their eyes met in the mirror again. Only this time hers were as steady as his seemed uncertain.

She leaned closer until her breath touched his face.

'I'm terrible with everyone I'm supposed to love,' he whispered, but his eyes were closed. His lips, grazing the skin behind her ear.

'I know,' her voice was so low it barely reached him.

Her hand found his shoulder, fingers warm against his shoulders. He turned slightly, and the movement brought her face inches from his. The smell of soap, paint, and something familiar—something like a memory—filled the space between them.

For a heartbeat, the world seemed to stop. Then he pressed his forehead to hers, a soft, broken and apologetic sound escaping his throat. Her hand slid up to his neck, and she felt his pulse beating against her palm.

'I can't,' he breathed, pulling back.

'It's alright,' she whispered, though her voice trembled.

Nihal shook his head. 'No… no, you're too young and—' He was breathing fast.

'I'm just a year younger,' her words came out almost as a plea.

He stepped back, wore his shirt in a hurry and grabbed his backpack.

He left without looking at her.

For a long time, Ira stood there, the mirror still holding their blurred reflection like a painting she imagined before creating—the white vest, the fallen hair, and the faint trace of warmth in the air that she wished never went cold.

Chapter 31

The morning was already charged, humid and scented with the sweet perfume of flowers blooming in the garden. Aryaveer was talking on the telephone about the Aarya Foundation, which was to be inaugurated in the coming week, a cause Mandira had willed into existence. Lalit, predictably punctual in his expensive suit, had arrived just as the silver dishes of parathas were being cleared. He took a seat next to Amma at the dining table.

Shivani had just brought in the black coffee when Lalit lifted the pile of papers positioned on the corner of the table and began to scan them. 'Is it for that boy?'

'Nihal, yes,' Aryaveer said, warming his palm on the coffee cup.

'Are you sure about it? I mean, you know the reputation of his father?' Lalit said, raising one of his eyebrows.

'He is not his father,' Aryaveer's tone was final.

Lalit twisted his lips, unsatisfied.

'The boy is exceptionally brilliant. Do you know how many of his articles have been published in The Architectural Digest Magazine already? You should read his opinion piece on the Neuschwanstein Castle. He called it *Ludwig's compulsions for building heaven on earth*.'

Lalit's expression tightened, defeat clouding his face. 'I'm sure you have reasons to vouch for him, putting your own reputation at stake, but if you ask me, I have my qualms about him from the very beginning. You know his father is still…'

Aryaveer brushed his hand impatiently. 'The man destroyed his own family. I don't want to talk about him.'

The coffee's strong aroma was cutting through the air. 'And where is Ira?' Lalit asked, his voice too casual now.

'She is in her room,' Shivani answered as she replaced the used napkins with the fresh ones that bore Amma's floral embroideries in the corner in purple and brown.

Aryaveer's eyes sharpened, 'Ira hasn't gone to school?'

Shivani gestured a no, pressing her thin lips in a line.

'Can you get her here?' Aryaveer said.

Amma's voice, calm and steady, interrupted from around the table, 'Your coffee, Lalit.'

By then, the men had already launched into a discussion about the foundation's management, the pragmatic details of selecting a suitable, preferably a female manager for the Aarya Foundation. The stark reality of abandoned children in the country, especially girls, and the urgency of the housing project for the boys.

Mandira, who had just appeared on the table scribbling in her diary, stilled her pen, the scratching sound abruptly ceasing. 'I was thinking,' she said, her voice soft but firm, 'I could manage it myself, at least initially.'

An uncomfortable silence descended on the table, accentuating the sounds of the kitchen. The hazy chatter, the clink of cutlery, water running in the basin. Amma, with a silent, knowing glance at Aryaveer, pushed the cup of coffee towards him.

'You mean you will shift to Pune?' Aryaveer asked softly.

Ira showed up and was unpleasantly surprised to see Lalit, who feigned a cough to indicate the change of topic. 'How are you doing, sunshine?' his tone was falsely sweet.

'I'm good, thank you.' Ira took her seat opposite her father.

'Not coming to the park anymore?' Lalit asked.

Ira's face heated, only this time it wasn't fear. It was anger. 'I just met him that once in the park, and he is not my boyfriend before you begin your investigation again this time.'

'Ira, watch your tone.' Mandira looked at her daughter.

Lalit chimed, laughing to himself, 'A guilty heart needs no accuser.'

Ira surged to her feet, the chair scraping against the floor with a harsh, discordant sound. She shoved it back in rage. The wood slammed against the table, a sharp punctuation to her abrupt departure.

'The first signs of a girl becoming a woman.' Lalit's eyes followed Ira, just as everyone else's.

Mandira followed her, but Ira banged the door of her room and screamed, 'Stay away.'

Aryaveer wrapped his hands on his head and closed his eyes just when he felt Amma's hand land on his shoulder. 'You have left your coffee for too long, and it's running cold now.

'I don't care about the damned coffee, Ma,' he barked in resignation.

Amma leaned towards him, 'I'm too blind and too old to care about the coffee myself, but I believe you are wise to know that I wasn't just talking about the coffee.'

~

Confined restlessly in the car's hum, Ira pictured many scenarios in her head. She could tell him to keep their story a secret. Perhaps he was afraid Aryaveer would give up on him, and she knew how much his future meant for Nihal. Why does her father need to know everything?

She wanted to tell him she could wait for him, for as long as he wanted.

Yet whatever future she imagined, her thoughts drifted inevitably back to the fleeting, electric intimacy of the day before. She curled inward, remembering his touch. Tentative, yet burning. She saw his eyes closed in her mind, his breath syncing with hers. She recollected the feel of his touch and imagined it on parts of her body that she had touched last night, thinking about him. The truth was, he had opened a door inside her. A quiet, unsuspecting door that led somewhere deep and disorienting, like the rabbit hole Alice had stumbled into, and so suddenly.

The bell wasn't working, and the metal handle was cold and rough beneath her fingers when she pushed the door open. Memories rushed in like warm air rushing out of a long-sealed trunk. She remembered coming here for the first time. Nihal's mother was still polishing the low table; a sling bag draped around her body like it was a part of her. Her hair was uncombed. She looked completely different from her own mother. Seeing Ira and her father, she had hidden the rag cloth behind her back and asked them to sit with a hesitant smile.

Nihal had brought over glasses of water, handing the one with the cracked rim to Ira without a hint of embarrassment, unlike his mother, who seemed flustered and small as she settled beside her son. She began to thank Ira's father, her voice catching between the emotions.

'Your girls are lovely. Nihal told me they are twins. How beautiful.'

Aryaveer's lips curved in a gentle, proud grin as she continued.

'We would have been lost without you.'

Ira couldn't help but notice his mother's hands, rough and calloused, appearing to belong to someone far older. She recalled her own mother applying sweet almond oil to her hands each night before bed, saying with a smile, 'Our hands age faster than our faces, girls,' as she gazed into the mirror.

Aryaveer had gulped the water quickly. 'Your boy will turn into a fine man one day, mark my words if you must. I just showed him the way, now it's up to him to walk or run.'

Aryaveer asked Nihal about his plans for the future. Nihal told him he had already decided to follow Aryaveer's footsteps. It seemed slightly preposterous to Ira; Nihal's decision in three days. But her father was flattered. He told him about a similar neighbourhood he grew up in. Ira had never known her father had once had to choose between eating and buying school supplies. She had known he and Amma were not rich like her mother's family, but not the intricate struggles of their everyday life.

Prajakta had taken Ira's hands in her own and kissed them. Surprisingly, they were soft and warm like freshly kneaded clay. 'My truest blessings are with you and your sister. I hope we could be of any help,' she said between the sobs.

Ira let out a slow breath, bringing herself back in the present. The room seemed almost the same. Dust motes floated lazily in the single shaft of sunlight that pierced through the windowpane, illuminating the peeling paint on the walls. A wooden chair sat with a battered table pushed against the wall. A single, bare bulb hung precariously from the ceiling above it. Ira imagined it casting a dim, flickering glow as Nihal spent his nights under it, reading with his eyes squeezed in focus. His fingers drumming the surface like they do when he is deep in thoughts of a thousand possibilities. Soon, she imagined him weary and crashing on his papers during the early morning hours of exam days, until sunlight spilled across his face. And that scar that claimed it.

She walked past the living room and heard a faint intermingled chatter emerging from the balcony. Laughter, a pause, then a softer voice. Perhaps he was sitting with his mother. A warmth bloomed within her. Mother and son. Ira cleared her throat, a subtle announcement of her presence as she continued across the room with an organic smile on her face. The woman had always lit up like a Christmas tree at the sight of her.

She caught a glimpse of his back through the window. He was wearing a brown T-shirt. She had never seen him in anything other than crisp, ironed shirts. No matter how closely you know a person, you don't really know them until you watch them in their home. She knew him to be a devoted son, but the quiet dynamic between him and his mother was something she hadn't yet witnessed.

His shoulders seemed broader than the previous day's memory, the simple t-shirt revealing a strength she hadn't consciously registered. He spoke, his voice too low to discern the words, and then a hand, small and familiar, settled on the dark, damp circle of sweat on his back.

There was no reason for her not to be happy. After all, Mrs Sagg had always held a quiet fondness for her.

As she stepped closer, the murmurs sharpened into clarity. Her gaze caught a glint. A pink mother-of-pearl bracelet encircling the wrist of a woman's hand.

Sonam's hand.

A sudden wave of despair surged through her.

'I know something about you that you don't know yet. Or maybe there is something that's holding you back in accepting it,' Sonam spoke gently. Her loose hair was dancing in the breeze, landing almost on his face before drifting away.

'Why do you overanalyse everyone else's life?' Nihal said.

Sonam wore a black top with tie-on straps. The fabric clung softly to her perfect frame. She scanned the branches of the bougainvillaea plant placed in front of her alongside the grille. 'Just the people I care about,' she said.

'Is there anyone you don't care about?' Nihal grasped the base of a yellow leaf between his thumb and forefinger, giving it a gentle tug.

Sonam lifted another branch, revealing a cluster of discoloured foliage beneath. She released it from her grip and looked at her hand as she spoke. 'You know I would have loved it if you felt for me what I feel for you, but…'

Nihal briefly dropped his face into his hands, the tension in his shoulders betraying the weight of his thoughts. As he did, Ira's eyes were drawn to the graceful curve on the back of his neck, where the delicate line of his bone subtly emerged beneath his skin. That fragile, floating bone seemed like a symbol of his vulnerability. Something that only she had noticed, touched, and painted. She remembered how her fingers had rested there, cradling the nape of his neck. The memory of his breath against her skin surged back with aching clarity. She had held him there, and he had anchored her in a moment that now felt impossibly distant.

'Look, I'm sorry if I've messed with your feelings and have let you believe something which isn't true,' he told Sonam.

Sonam took his hands into hers. 'On the contrary, you have been honest. So honest that a part of me wished you weren't. So there could still be hope in my heart.'

Ira held her breath and listened, stepping even closer. Nihal was now looking at Sonam, her dark, moist eyes. 'You amaze me. How are you always so clear with what you want?'

'Not always. I just have a keen interest in people, and that particularly includes myself.' She held the cluster again and began to pluck the leaves one by one.

Nihal placed the wicker basket, the one his mother uses to collect flowers for deities, between them, 'You're just fifteen, and you always know what to do?'

Sonam's laughter was strained, painful. 'I don't. But if I were in your place, I would tell her.'

Ira's heartbeat quickened. Her chest inflated like a balloon on a child's mouth. Was Sonam referring to her? What is it that Nihal had told Sonam for her to say this? What was he supposed to tell her?

Nihal looked away, 'You don't know everything about me…about us…Ira and I…'

'I think I know enough.' Sonam dusted her hands on the napkin she dug out of her pocket.

Meanwhile, once again, Nihal's thoughts were consumed by Ira. He, too, recalled the time he had touched her and how badly he had wanted to. He was aware that she would not have denied him; in fact, he had always known this. This realisation inflated his self-esteem. Yet, he took pride in restraining himself, believing that by doing so, he was embodying the virtues that Ira's father believed him to. However, the memory of having touched her without the intention of commitment weighed heavily on him. He felt that he had betrayed not only Ira's trust but also his own principles as well as Aryaveer's trust. This internal conflict was something he couldn't share with Sonam, not when it concerned Ira. After a long pause, he said, 'Everything I have, even my school life, is borrowed from her father.'

Nihal continued, his voice a fragile snowflake on the verge of melting, '…being with Ira wasn't easy. She has this... overwhelming need… to surrender control entirely. It's as if she hands over the reins of her life, expecting someone else to steer. At first, it feels empowering, even flattering…but then…it's also a burden…not burden literally…I don't know if I'm making any sense. There were moments…with Ira, I mean, when I wanted to run, to escape the weight of responsibility I never asked for but felt compelled to bear, especially given the favour her father did for me.'

Ira choked back the sob that clawed at her throat, her hands instinctively flying to her mouth, muffling the sound. The sudden rush of tears blurred her vision. She spun and stumbled towards the door. The wooden floorboards creaked slightly, cool and unforgiving beneath her bare feet.

Outside, on the balcony, Nihal pressed his hands on his temples. The bougainvillaea's pink bracts trembled in the soft breeze. Their motion added a gentle energy to the tranquillity in his words, 'And then suddenly, everything changed. This lonely, sad girl became my home. No matter where I go and what I do, I always want to go back to her for that calm a person feels only at home. Where I can take off my façade. Be ugly. Be myself. Ira is my home.'

Sonam stiffened. Her heart was crashing against her chest, causing the pain she had never felt before. 'I tried hard convincing myself that you and Ira are…just friends…and then she started dating, so I thought maybe I was wrong all along and that you don't…'

He cut her words, 'I keep telling myself not to fall in love with her. I should not.'

Sonam's voice choked, 'You are the best person to fall in love with...'

'When I said Ira was different. I meant she is both fragile and strong at the same time. Like… a sharp piece of broken glass in the sea, smoothened by the waves in time. She is not scared of anything, and that's the scariest thing about her. When she gives herself to someone, she will also give the power to destroy her. Knowing her, she would even find some calm in that destruction. And I can't do that to her. Not ever.'

'Why would you do that to anyone?' Sonam wiped the tears on her face with the back of her palm.

'What?'

'Destroy… like you said,' Sonam said.

Nihal scoffed, '*Love* would do that.'

'I don't know how you define love in your head, but…that's not love. Not all of it.'

His eyes grew distant, as if he was reading the sentences swinging in the air. 'Her presence calms the chaos in my head.' He began, 'I feel we are the two pieces of a child's puzzle, fitting together like we are meant to be and for that I am truly grateful to Mr Lall. But love is fleeting, unlike friendship.' He looked into Sonam's teary eyes, 'Dostoevsky once wrote, 'Beauty is a terrible and awful thing.' I think the same goes for love.'

Sonam laughed, a single tear tracing a path down her cheek, 'You need to first stop reading depressing novels.'

'If I break her heart eventually and she tells me she does not want to see my face, I don't know what I'll do without her. Without a home. Let alone, living with the regret of doing it to her while already knowing what I'm truly capable of.' Nihal picked a yellow leaf from the basket and inspected it between his fingers.

'Capable of?' Sonam's voice was broken glass.

He crushed the leaf between his fingers, the sap seeping onto his thumb, cool and slick, 'Breaking her.'

'You are not your father,' Sonam stated matter-of-factly, steadying herself. Her eyes were large and staring.

'I am his son.' He tossed the leaf in the air. 'An apple doesn't fall far from the tree, does it?'

Chapter 32

'How is your friend doing these days?' Aryaveer's voice reached Ira in fragments. It was becoming difficult for her to exist in the real world.

'Which friend?' Ira asked after a pause.

'I didn't know my daughter had more than one,' Aryaveer said, looking at his wife, who sat quietly next to him.

'I haven't seen him for days,' Ira spoke between mouthfuls.

A brief glance was exchanged between Aryaveer and Mandira as she picked up the bowl to serve the pudding she had made for Ira, which was refused. She had grown past the taste of vanilla and blueberry, but Mandira was too absent for too long to know that.

'You didn't inform me about the parent-teacher meeting at your school yesterday.' Mandira made a hesitant attempt at talking to her daughter.

Ira exhaled in frustration and began to stuff large chunks of bread in her mouth.

Aryaveer glanced at his wife, whose eyes stalled on Ira, expecting an answer. When Ira spoke nothing for the next few minutes, he cleared his throat. 'Ira, your mother is talking to you.'

Ira pushed her plate for Shivani and prepared to rise.

'Ira?' Aryaveer's voice was anxious, urgent.

She snapped back at him, 'What?'

'Sit down.' He gritted his teeth.

Ira drew in a deep breath with her eyes closed, calming the frustration mushrooming within her.

'When was the parent-teacher meet at school?' He asked gently now.

Ira exhaled heavily, 'Why are you both putting up this show, really?'

'Don't forget your manners, young lady,' Aryaveer said through flaring nostrils.

'Why is she suddenly asking about me? Are all the orphans already adopted?' Ira said.

'Ira!!' Aryaveer rose to his feet when Mandira grabbed his hand. Her own eyes were full of tears. Ira's features softened slightly, but there was anger lacing her voice, 'Really, mother, when was the last time you cared for me or my school life?'

'You probably don't know, but we make sure to speak with your teachers every few weeks over the phone,' Aryaveer said loud enough to mask the lack of his confidence. 'About your progress… at school.'

'My progress,' Ira repeated the words in sarcasm, throwing her hands in the air. 'Will the teachers tell you the boys call me a 'flat-chested bitch' at school, all the nasty senior boys?' She laughed wryly, 'Huhh? I'm sure they hadn't… because only I could tell that to you if you had ever cared to ask.'

Aryaveer shifted uncomfortably in his chair. He looked at his wife, who was looking at her recoiled fingers, crying.

'Mother, you say you care for me… do you know when I got my period or that I have got them at all? Do you know what I go through every month…all by myself. Do you know I am a woman already?' She paused, 'The truth is…I can make out with a horse in my room, and my parents will never get to know…' She laughed, 'Because they are never home.'

Ira must have slept through the day because when she woke up, the sky was dark outside the window. And yet a blank stretch of white waited impatiently. She stood barefoot, facing the canvas like someone facing a confession.

The painting was still taking shape — two trees, standing apart on a pale field, their roots nearly touching beneath a thin wash of colour.

'I think Nihal was always right about love,' she whispered, her eyes stinging from tears or colours she couldn't say. 'There is nothing that can hurt like love.'

Her brush slid downward, leaving a faint red line that bled into the lighter tones.

'I'm terrified, Aarya. What if I'm trapped, thinking about him forever? If love is as strong as they say it is, I doubt it will fade with time.'

She rinsed the brush and looked at the water clouding in the jar. 'I doubt I'll ever be able to tell myself it was too long ago. That maybe it hurt only because I was young.'

She pressed her lips together, a faint tremor in her jaw. 'Will I ever get over it? Like I used to get over the howling and crying over the leftover piece of cake that you ate before I could, because you always woke up early?' She paused, closed her eyes, 'but this is not a cake. This is a limb torn away, a vital organ ripped from my chest, Aarya.'

Her voice softened as she added colour to the space between the trees. 'I don't want to be fifty and still thinking about him, or painting the idea of him with my fingers like some tragic painter Kabir tells me about, trying to find his traces in everything around me.'

She leaned closer, almost whispering to the canvas now, 'It may be easy to fall in love with a boy who doesn't love you back… but it's the hardest thing in the world to teach yourself to unlove him.'

She stepped back and observed the paint on the canvas in front of her. 'I am trapped, Aarya, in this suffocating amber of unrequited feeling. I'm a fly caught in a sticky, golden death.'

The two trees stood quietly — apart, but bound by the same root beneath the paint.

Chapter 33

The corridor outside the principal's office was bathed in the afternoon sun. Ira stood by the bulletin board, her fingers deftly guiding a brush to paint a black border around a poster titled 'Importance of Discipline.' The bristles whispered against the paper, leaving a trail of wet ink that glistened momentarily before drying.

A shadow suddenly loomed over, and a familiar, unwelcome voice broke her rhythm. 'Are you going with someone?'

Ira's hand paused mid-stroke. She didn't need to look up to recognise Sharan's voice, laced with its characteristic mockery.

Her fingers continued their precise path. 'I'd rather be dead.'

'Your boyfriend's going with my sister. You know that…' A cruel twist of his lips punctuated the statement.

The words hung in the air, heavy and intrusive. Ira's grip on the brush tightened, the bristles pressing harder against the paper.

'So you don't know they are an item now?'

She met his gaze. A knowing glint shone in his dark eyes, enjoying her discomfort. Her jaw was tight when she uttered, 'He is not my boyfriend.'

'I'm glad he is not. A girl like you shouldn't be with that pauper anyway. The beggar cannot even afford the school without the scholarship.'

Ira rose slowly, clutching the other poster like a shield. 'Does it appear to you that I'm interested in talking to you?' Her voice was low, a dangerous calm that hinted at a storm brewing beneath the surface.

'I saw your painting of him. Was it after you went to that erotic theatre? But you went with Chandan, right?' His eyes held a taunting curiosity.

A flush stained Ira's cheeks. 'That's none of your business.' The cardboard was digging into her palms.

'I heard you broke off with Chan over Nihal.' Sharan's tone shifted, a feigned concern that didn't reach his eyes. 'He did care for you, you know? I have known him for a long… He was a changed man for you.'

Ira took a deliberate step back. A teacher offered a tight smile without waiting for a reciprocation and passed by.

'Did I do something wrong to give you the impression that I'm interested in talking to you?'

Sharan held out the folded piece of paper, 'I thought I'd return it. Must have taken some effort.' He unfolded it and looked at the paper briefly, 'Is this it?'

Ira's breath hitched; the sight of her private offering, now soiled in his dirty hands, ignited a fresh wave of anger within her. Her hand shot out, snatching the paper with a fierce motion. She crumpled it into a tight, unforgiving ball. The paper protested with a sharp crackle. She shoved it into the pocket of her skirt.

'Why are you always so bitter with me?' his voice softened.

'Perhaps because I'm a flat-chested bitch.'

Sharan looked around, then his gaze flickered down her body, a brief, insolent appraisal, before returning to her face with a smirk. 'Actually, you are not that anymore. None of the two.'

The bile rose in her throat. She looked away.

'He hurt you really bad, right?' Sharan persisted, his voice taking on a strange, almost confiding tone, as if they shared some twisted understanding. 'That's what Sonam does to me all the time. My father doesn't even trust me with my pocket money anymore… She has literally ruined my life. Did she tell you she was dating Chandan until last year?'

Ira froze, her back rigid with a mixture of disgust and a reluctant wave of interest.

'The two were an item, really. The reason she came here from Manali. You can ask anyone around here.' He squared his shoulders.

Ira slowly turned back, her eyes wide with a dawning shock. The hallway's ambient noise faded into a dull roar.

'So she didn't.' Sharan's smirk widened into a predatory triumph. 'I bet Nihal knew. What a bastard, isn't he? You were there for him all these years, bringing the pauper some fancy lunch like a good old wife.

Everyone around here knows it's your father who gave him the early scholarship. And the asshole couldn't even value your sympathy.'

His words burned Ira's heart. 'It wasn't sympathy,' she said finally, her voice low and trembling with a potent mix of hurt and anger. 'Guess a person like you would never understand.'

'I hardly think *he* understands.' Sharan's eyes narrowed. 'Guess what you have for him, he has already thrown upon her.'

'I don't care,' Ira's voice gained a brittle strength, though the tremor betrayed her. 'And please leave. I have work to do.'

Sharan leaned in and whispered in a low, insidious voice. 'If I were you, I would give him back in the face.'

Ira stared at the ugliness of his soul, 'Aren't you all the same anyway?'

'Think about it.' Sharan took another step closer, his voice dropping to a conspiratorial hiss. She could smell his sweat. 'We don't have to be buddies. The asshole should have at least kept your drawing.'

Ira stood there, watching him saunter away, with the crumpled drawing like an ember burning in her pocket.

Chapter 34

'I've sent the letter of recommendation.' Aryaveer held a glass of whiskey in one hand. The light from the chandelier fractured across the crystal, casting delicate golden shards onto the papered walls. In his other hand, he held a slim paper folder.

The study smelled its usual: aged wood and the soft musk of old books, but the air was still, heavy, as if it, too, understood something was ending.

'Thank you, sir.'

Nihal stepped in with a stack of old magazines that he had taken over the years he had spent in this house. He approached the bookshelf—tall, dark, familiar—and carefully slotted each magazine back into its home.

Aryaveer took a slow sip, the ice clinking against the glass. 'I am certain you will do wonderful things in life. If you need any support — as a mentor… or even a father—just think of me.'

The words soothed him briefly, soft and endearing like always. Nihal's smile was genuine but distracted. His eyes wandered to the window, or perhaps to the memories stitched into the room. 'Thank you so much for everything, sir.'

He bent down and touched Aryaveer's feet. The benevolent man placed a warm, steady hand on Nihal's head. A silent benediction, weighted with emotion.

'Write to me anytime you feel like, son,' Aryaveer said.

A silence followed, not awkward but large. The kind that settles only between two people who have known both affection and disappointment.

'Is Ira not home?' Nihal asked, finally.

Aryaveer placed his glass on the table with a soft clink, then exhaled through pursed lips, the sound low and tired. 'She is… but…'

'Is she not well?' Nihal asked.

'I think so,' Aryaveer said, his eyes drifting towards the hallway. 'Let's leave her to her canvas today.'

Nihal nodded with a tight, pained smile. He turned to leave, but Aryaveer stopped him with a motion of his hand. 'Before you go, I want you to know something.'

He patted the seat beside him on the carved teakwood bench where he now sat comfortably, crossing his legs. Nihal obeyed.

Aryaveer emptied his glass in a single, purposeful gulp and set it down on the coffee table. 'Don't ever think I'm helping you in exchange for what you've done for my daughter. Although I'm truly grateful you respected my request. You were a hardworking boy. And you've become a remarkable man. You deserve everything that's come to you. Even more.'

Nihal blinked hard. The sting behind his eyes was rising like a tide. What would his own father think of him if he saw him today?

Aryaveer placed his palm reassuringly on Nihal's knee. Nihal looked up, eyes brimming but steady. 'Mr. Lall… thank you for believing in the boy whose own father abandoned him.'

Aryaveer's face softened, and a tender warmth coloured his words. 'He will never know what he missed. I'm glad we came across, son.'

This time, the tears flowed freely down Nihal's face—quiet and unashamed. 'If there's anything I can ever do for you… I'll consider myself fortunate.'

~

In the entry foyer, the air was cold like a memory. Ira stood near a low table, tapping hardened Plaster of Paris against a cracked glass teapot. She was transforming it into a vase.

'Ira… I was… I was looking for—' His voice was hesitant.

She cut him off with a lift of her palm, fingers stained white, 'Don't you speak my name.'

Nihal sighed, eyes flicking around the space — the hallway walls where her unfinished canvases leaned, the paintbrush rested in a chipped mug on the console. He took a careful step forward and gently reached for her elbow. Her skin was cool on his fingertips. She jerked away.

'I know you're hurting because of me,' he said softly. 'Whatever I did—'

She said nothing. Instead, she stared at the vase, now barely resembling a teapot.

His eyes only stayed on her. 'One day, you'll know it was for the best.'

Her lips curled into a brittle smile when she caught sight of the file in his hand. The laugh that escaped her throat cracked like dry earth, 'Good for you or me?'

'Both,' he whispered quietly. 'Both of us.' He looked down at his fingers that had begun to tremble slightly. 'There's something I want to tell you.'

'Get out of my house and never come back here again,' she spat before he could say any further. Her voice had gone sharp, almost childlike in its pain. 'I shouldn't have let you in. Oh, but… that was your plan with my father, wasn't it? So what did you get in exchange for the torture of my company all these years?'

'I got to spend the most beautiful moments of my life here,' he said, not wiping the tears that glided through his face. 'With you. That's what I got.'

Her jaw clenched, and she turned her eyes from looking at him as if, if she looked for long, she would melt like a candle. She inhaled angrily, 'I wish my father hadn't stopped for you that day. Maybe you were right… maybe you do bring heartbreak with you.'

Nihal's breath hitched, a long and heavy sigh escaping through his nose. He closed his eyes, fighting to keep the sobs inside.

'Can we…' His voice cracked. 'Can we please talk for a while?'

Without a word, Ira reached behind her and lifted the vase from the table — her recent creation. And in one sweeping motion, she smashed it against the floor. The sound was sharp and final. Shards scattered across the marble like stars collapsing through the sky.

'Shivani!' she screamed, her voice echoing up the staircase. 'Clear this trash before it cuts through me. I shouldn't have wasted my time on this stupid teapot.'

'Don't do this to me, please,' Nihal begged, voice thin, shaking.

She grabbed another vase—smaller, heavier—and lifted it just enough to let the suggestion of danger linger in the air. Nihal stiffened. He knew this look. He remembered the last time she hurt herself.

'I'll go,' he said, holding his hands up.

Ira looked away, her heart exploding in the pain she knew she was causing him.

'You'll never see me again, alright. Just… be safe. Please.'

The door closed gently behind him, the click echoing in the quiet foyer like a verdict.

Ira stood frozen, staring at the empty space where Nihal had just been, her breath caught somewhere between fury and heartbreak.

Then, as if her legs had finally given up pretending to hold the weight of her pride, she sank to the floor. Her fingers trembled, dusted in flakes of plaster, now useless in their artistry.

She had driven him away. She had planned it, practiced it, armed herself with sharp words and sharper silence—but the moment he walked out, she felt the something crack open inside her.

She would see him again. She knew that. And in the stillness that followed, regret curled inside her like smoke. She knew the weight of the pain she was yet to cause him.

The pain, she wanted to cause him.

And to herself.

Chapter 35

Sonam wore a soft pink saree that flowed around her like the first blush of dawn. Nihal had brought it to her on careful instructions of his mother. 'How I wish I could see her in this,' Prajakta had said. The sleeveless blouse had pearls sewn around the neck and revealed the gentle curve of her back.

They moved in a slow rhythm under the dappled glow of the overhead lights. Her bangles chimed faintly with her mother-of-pearl bracelet every time their hands shifted. His palm hovered respectfully over the small of her back, suspended like a breath never exhaled. Around them, their classmates twirled and laughed, but *their* world had drawn in a quiet, invisible glass dome of unspoken things.

'Last night I was reading a book… and I came across a word…' Sonam murmured, her voice barely audible above the music.

Nihal's hand tightened slightly on her waist as they glided across the floor. 'Hmmm.'

'Soul crossing… do you know what it means?' She tilted her head, searching his eyes.

'I think I do,' he said.

Sonam smiled knowingly, 'Can I still tell you?'

Nihal nodded, and she began, 'It means a fleeting encounter with another soul. Like two ships passing in the dark of the night, where a connection is felt and could have been nurtured, but life, as we know it, keeps it from happening.'

They completed a turn, their bodies moving as one. Sonam's voice was distant, 'Sometimes the pull of fate is too strong, and our courses are already charted.'

Nihal spoke as if speaking to the rhythm of the music itself. Sonam lifted her face to look at him, but his expression was veiled. 'If we are still talking about the ships…let me tell you, to remain suspended in that moment, was to invite a slow death, a descent into the deadly currents below,' he said.

Their dance slowed, their movements becoming less defined as the music began to fade, or was it fading only to their ears, hinting at the finality of their time together.

Sonam pursed her lips, trying to soften the lump that formed in her throat. 'Can we please leave?' She said after a while.

The plush seating in the foyer seemed to absorb the remaining sounds of the nightclub as they walked towards the heavy oak doors leading them outside. Sonam's voice, when it came, was a poignant mix of resignation and sorrow.

'So I guess this was the end of it?' she murmured, her gaze fixed on a large, potted tree standing near the exit.

'Or maybe it is a beginning,' he said, checking his pocket for the wallet.

The night air held in its belly the scent of the lingering summer. Of urban jasmine and diesel.

He watched her pull a cloth out of her small handbag. She drew the scarf around her shoulders, eyes fixed on the dark outline of trees beyond the gate, as if they could somehow rise into the hills she grew up in.

They walked in silence, the joyous energy of the party around them a stark contrast to the quiet sorrow that was consuming them. As groups of brightly dressed young men and women streamed past, their laughter echoing with the promise of a night just beginning, Sonam and Nihal offered them brief smiles.

'Have you thought about the offer?' She asked. Nihal looked at her with a tentative smile, 'For someone like me, that's as good as dreams get. Aryaveer Sir even sent them a letter of recommendation.'

Her face grew solemn, 'Don't sell yourself short. You worked hard for it—you deserve every bit of it.'

'Will you write to me?' He asked.

Her lips quivered despite her resistance, 'I don't know. Do you want me to?'

He shook his head before he spoke, 'I think that would be good.'

Just as he finished speaking, a sleek, white car pulled up to the entrance. The door opened, and Sharan stepped out, but he wasn't alone.

Sonam narrowed her gaze, squinting at a figure approaching. 'Wait… is that… she has come with…'

Nihal turned slowly. His spine straightened so suddenly as the ripple of whispers filled the space like wind rustling through the foliage. He watched her disappear into the brightly lit hall. Ira. Sonam trailed silently behind Nihal as he followed her, the merry atmosphere feeling increasingly alien now.

Ira glided into the room like a storm, wearing her mother's silk gown. Her defiance wrapped in emerald green that skimmed her frame, each step causing the delicate fabric to shimmer like wet leaves in moonlight. Her dark hair fell around her face, soft and severe all at once.

Sharan's smirk carved a slash across his face as he leaned in and whispered something, coaxing a brittle, echoing laugh from her lips. Her arm rested in the crook of Sharan's elbow like a gesture too practised to be casual.

Nihal's chest tightened. He knew that laugh. It came from a place within herself she had never visited in his presence. A place as dark as the shadows she painted beneath the eyes.

Through the evening, Ira played her part with theatrical precision. She swirled her wine, tossed her hair like a banner, and spoke to strangers like they were her lifelong friends. Most of them were her seniors she had never bothered to look at in school. She didn't glance at Nihal even once. And yet, he could feel her eyes on him.

Nihal snatched a glass from a passing waiter, the clear liquid catching the light of the youth. Without a word, he tilted his head back and emptied it in a single, swift motion. The raw burn of the vodka seared his throat and chest. Yet, even that jolt felt dull compared to the icy ache that clenched his heart as he watched Ira across the room. Maybe he was lying to himself. Maybe she belonged here now, among people whose lives were measured in vacation homes and antique clocks, who inherited rooms filled with notes of a glossy piano that no one has time to play.

Later, after the noise thinned and the crowd mellowed into a warm intoxication, a small circle formed on the floor. Heels were kicked off, scarves and ties were loosened, and the scent of perfume and alcohol blended with the laughter textured in youth. Out of the people who remained, most of them were final-year students, plus the ones they had brought along. Nihal remained on the margins, his presence quiet, nearly invisible, yet he radiated the weight of watching. Sonam stood beside him, still and stiller, watching as he drifted away from her in every breath like a dandelion seed.

He would have left, Sonam knew—if not for Ira. She knew it was his instinct that kept him rooted. A misplaced belief that he still had a duty to protect her from the world. The irony, however, didn't escape him. He had already hurt her worse than anyone here could.

'Truth or dare,' someone called out, the voice buzzing with anticipation.

Nihal's turn came even before he registered that he was a part of the game. 'If you were to choose between love and money…what would it be?'

The room hushed. Ira rolled her eyes, but every nerve in her body leaned towards his answer. Towards him. She hated herself for it, hated how he consumed her. She looked at him, this familiar face. A portrait in oil. Intense, unfinished, beautiful in its ruin.

Nihal's features grew unreadable, the tension around him flickering like heat above summer asphalt. Ira noticed how his jaw flexed once. Then, 'I'd save myself the tragedy and take money.'

The response landed with a hush. No laughter. No teasing.

The game carried on. Saksham kissed Aditi with boyish triumph, cementing the rumour about the two dating outside school. Moni was asked about a wet dream and blushed in her palms. She had come with her older cousin, who wasn't allowed a male company. The group moved on without prying.

Then Sonam chose truth. 'Is it because Nihal is graduating from school that you are leaving for Manali?' 'Yes.'

Hoarse hooting followed, but it sounded distant. Hollow echoes in a hall that now felt colder for a summer evening. Ira's turn came in the end. Her facade was now fraying at the edges, lending a tremble to the wine glass in her grip. When her eyes met Nihal's, her smile vanished.

'Dare,' she said, closing her eyes in rebellion. A ripple ran through the circle.

'Since it's your first time with us, you can choose any boy, but kiss it should be,' said some boy Ira hadn't even noticed before this moment.

'On the mouth,' added a girl with a nose ring and a cleavage too loud for her young age. She was shrieking with her eyes closed.

Nihal watched Ira in a screaming silence, his insides clawing toward her. He wanted to hold her hand. Tell her he'd take her home — to her closet, to her canvas, to the quiet that healed. He would make her tea till she feels better. He saw her fingers moving, conjuring a painting in the air that only he could see. He longed to be her audience again, if not her muse.

In this moment, he could leave the world behind to be with her.

STOP STOP!

Sonam curled her hands into fists in her lap. Her own heart ached with clarity. How effortlessly Nihal slipped through her fingers in Ira's presence.

Ira stood finally, her spine rigid. She walked to Sharan, where he sat next to the silver statue of a woman. His hands met her waist with an ease she despised. The heat of his palm on her skin nauseated her.

She swallowed the bile that rose in her throat.

She would tell this to Aarya. She knew she would. About how this moment would never leave her body. How this shame had found a home under her skin. She wanted to scream at Sharan, hurt him for his cruelty, for insulting Nihal, for turning her into a pawn.

But she did none of it.

Instead, she clung to the devil, fingers grazing the back of his neck. Her soul curled inward, shrinking into a ball of wet thread. She closed her eyes.

Black. That's all she found.

And then she saw Nihal. And Sonam. On the balcony.

She kissed Sharan on the mouth. His lips parted, tongue reaching greedily into hers. Her stomach turned, and she shoved him hard.

'Easy, easy,' Saksham said, catching Sharan, handing him a glass of water from the table.

Finally, Ira looked across the room. Right at Nihal. No pretence, no masks. Just the raw ache of a girl drowning in her own theatre. Her makeup had melted into tears. Mascara streaked down her cheeks like black rain over pale earth.

Nihal was gone.

By dawn, he was already on the train to Mumbai—leaving behind a city of echoes, a girl in green silk that belonged once to her mother, and the heavy fragments of a juvenile love neither of them knew how to carry anymore.

Chapter 36

The classroom air pressed down on Ira like an invisible weight, mirroring the dread that had settled in her stomach. A rebellious defiance had flamed within her earlier, a thought that she didn't need Nihal to claim her right to education in the school that was owned by her family. Yet, as she stepped across the threshold, that bravado faltered, replaced by an instinctive reluctance to meet the judging eyes she imagined were waiting. Moving with a deliberate quietness, clinging to the illusion of invisibility, she slid into the first desk.

A strained smile touched her lips as her gaze landed on Moni, already hunched over, retrieving notebooks from beneath the desk. Moni's movements were jerky and hurried. She was stuffing the books into her bag as if fleeing a danger. Once done, she moved towards the back of the classroom.

Ira's courage deserted her; she couldn't bring herself to follow Moni's retreating figure with her eyes, couldn't bear to see the confirmation of her isolation. It wasn't the usual indifference from her classmates; this felt different, charged.

Closing her eyes, she inhaled sharply, a silent gasp against the rising panic. She desperately sought a distraction, a stray thought to latch onto, anything to pull her away from the present. But her mind offered only the vivid, unwelcome replay of the previous evening.

Her eyelids squeezed shut with a painful pressure behind her eyes. When she finally opened them, the space beside her was no longer empty. A boy had settled there. She shifted, and he shifted. Behind her, a sudden burst of laughter erupted, sharp and mocking. Just as she felt herself teetering on the edge of sobs, a hand appeared near hers on the wood of the desk. A jolt like an electric current. She recoiled, snatching her own hand away. His hand retreated too, and in its place, a folded note lay on the desk. He tapped it once with his index finger, like it was some silent invitation.

With fingers that trembled with a longing she usually reserved for the feel of a paintbrush, Ira picked up the note. She yearned for the tactile comfort of a brush, the one that Nihal had gifted her. She wanted to swirl the colour onto a canvas, blending it until its original identity is dissolved into something new, something no one had ever seen.

Mrs Ketu's entrance brought a sudden hush to the classroom. The sounds of notebooks scraped open, bags softly zipped, and pen caps clicked punctuating the new silence. Ira tucked the folded paper into her pencil box. Her fingers fumbled as she turned the pages of her history textbook.

'The iconic figure from the history we are going to read about today is someone who gifted us so much. Rabindra Nath Tagore,' Mrs Ketu's voice soared.

For a fleeting moment, the edges of misery softened. But beneath the surface of the teacher's words about a long-dead poet, the insistent, almost physical ache to lose herself in the vibrant chaos of colour persisted. She found herself pondering the strange glory of being remembered long after death.

It struck her then, the cruel, almost comical irony of recognition often arriving only in absence, the weight of a life truly appreciated after it was gone. The more tragic the narrative, the more luminous the fame.

How would Van Gogh have felt, witnessing the world's belated adoration of the swirling colours of his canvases, the very works once met with scorn and incomprehension? And what brutal calculus of power would Caesar have employed had the cold steel of the assassins' blades missed their mark? How did Cleopatra navigate the suffocating emptiness of a world devoid of her lover's presence?

How was Aarya in her afterlife? Was there colour there? Or just silence?

By the time the cacophony of recess soared to life, her appetite had shrunk, leaving behind a hollow feeling. The cafeteria was unbearable in the absence of Nihal. But where was he?

Ira sought refuge in the sterile quiet of the girls' restroom near the teachers' cabin. The sharp, chemical smell of disinfectant filled her nostrils. The first person she saw was Moni, standing at the porcelain sink, washing her hands under the steady drip. This particular restroom was Moni's sanctuary, a place to avoid the messy social entanglements of the main toilets where most girls went. A space to guard her precious time and prevent unwanted requests for notes or homework.

Ira stood silently, the cool ceramic of the wall pressing against her back, observing Moni's deliberate movements, the way the water beaded on her hands before disappearing down the drain. Without turning her head, Moni said, 'You know what they're saying about you?'

Ira nodded.

'So is it true?' Moni finally turned, her gaze cool and assessing, the fluorescent light above casting harsh shadows on the acne marks on her face.

The squeak of the door hinge announced the arrival of another girl, a ninth grader with bright pink hair ties. She hurried into the first stall and locked it with the metallic click of the latch. Moni resumed washing her hands, the silence stretching, thick with accusations, punctuated only by the rhythmic dripping of the tap. The girl walked out in a rush without washing her hands.

'I kissed him. So many of them kissed each other...' Ira's defence sounded weak and hollow. The words echoing, 'You were there.'

'Why were *you* there? Class 10 wasn't invited.' Moni's gaze sharpened. Ira noticed her dark eyes for the first time. She had long lashes, but not as beautiful as Nihal's.

'I went as Sharan's partner...'

Moni's expressions held a sharp disapproval. 'Don't make it sound like it's the same thing.'

'It's not...the same...I know.' The admission was a soft surrender. Ira felt the heat rising on her cheeks.

'Are you two seeing each other? You and him.' Moni had crossed her arms just the way she did when she asked Ira and Latisha about the status of their project work, which she had assigned to each of them.

Ira's denial was immediate.

'Then why did you kiss him?' Moni asked.

'It's all they do in that stupid game.' The words tasted like ash in her mouth, the metallic tang of shame returning.

Moni shook her head as if in denial, 'You know how mean he is to Nihal. He was the one who complained and got Nihal disqualified from his project on Rome. My Mother told me. All the teachers felt bad for him, but they were helpless.'

Ira's world crumpled as Moni continued, 'Sharan is telling everyone that you two were together in his car in the parking after the party got over at night and…' Moni paused, her eyes flicking towards the closed stall doors, the silence amplifying the distant sounds of the bustling school. She bit her upper lip as an involuntary gesture. 'Sharan told everyone that you…touched him…because *you* wanted to.'

The words stung Ira like a swarm of angry bees, each leaving a burning mark on her already beaten heart.

A long shuddering sigh escaped Ira's lips. She pressed her palms against her face.

'Look, I know half of what they're saying isn't true. I knew it from before…because I know you quite well…I think. But then you also showed up with the most hideous boy in school…hand in hand.' Moni's voice softened slightly, a reluctant understanding colouring her tone, 'I cannot be seen with you. Not after all this.' Moni's words were firm, a definitive closing of a door.

Ira's body shook with silent weeping.

Moni didn't look her in the eyes this time. 'I worked really hard to be here and get this scholarship that I believe I deserve. The teachers will recommend my name only if they can trust me. For some of us here, scholarship is our only hope.'

Ira could only nod as her chin trembled.

When the recess bell rang, Ira was already huddled in the corner-most stall. She had read the note the boy from her class had left for her. Two hours later, the final bell shrilled, announcing the end of the school day. But Ira remained there, a small, desolate figure, with her arms wrapped tightly around her knees. The note crumpled beside her, wet in her tears.

Sharan told us everything.

R.S.V.P

All the boys

Ira never went back to school again.

Chapter 37

'So you have made up your mind?' Sujata's voice was barely louder than the slow hum of the ceiling fan above them.

Mandira didn't answer at first. She was kneeling beside the bed, carefully slipping photographs into a designer suitcase with metallic edges. Her fingers lingered on one—a picture faded at the corners—and she brushed a tear.

'I should have done it long ago,' she whispered.

Outside, the afternoon sun dipped behind the thick clouds, casting a gauzy twilight.

'Leaving a young daughter behind?' Sujata's voice sharpened as she stooped to pull a glass from the cabinet beneath the side table. It clinked faintly against the wood. 'Seriously, if there was ever a time she needed you… it is now.'

Mandira sat on the edge of the bed, the mattress sighing under her weight. 'She had always needed me.'

The bottle murmured as Sujata poured the amber liquid into the glass. She handed it to Mandira.

'Only I was never there.' The glass trembled in Mandira's grip before she drank.

'What about Aryaveer?' Sujata asked, her eyes pleading now. 'The man's worked himself raw trying to bring you back to yourself ever since…'

Mandira took another sip. 'He's adamant… maybe a fool. His colleagues call him that now. Always chasing the unachievable.'

Sujata laughed a short laugh. She drained her glass and filled it again, like a mechanical ritual. 'But he always got what he wanted, didn't he?'

Mandira finished her drink in one motion and placed the glass beside her. It slipped and fell on the mattress, a few droplets splashing onto the sheet like the raindrops on the stone before they disappeared, leaving behind a halo of grey.

'He's been kind, yes. Everything a good husband could be. A lover. A friend. I know he is hurting too, perhaps more.'

The silence between them stretched like a bruise. Sujata placed her palm over Mandira's. 'He has never blamed you. Not once.'

'It would have been better if he had. Then I wouldn't have to search it over and over in his silence, the way he averts his eyes whenever he spots two little girls together. His eyes speak to me in a language that breaks my heart. *I told you not to do it.*'

'Well then, talk to him,' Sujata urged, leaning in.

'You think I haven't tried?' Mandira's voice cracked so suddenly, almost like the spine of an old book. 'It's been years, Sujata. Years. And that night still sits between us like a goddamn monument. He never speaks of it. And I… I can't live with this feeling of being a demon anymore.' Mandira grabbed another bottle — didn't bother checking the label — and drank straight from it, the liquor trailing down her shirt. 'I've known for a long time now. My life doesn't belong to me after that night… not in a way that ever felt right. So maybe I can give it to someone who needs it more than I do.'

Sujata lay back on the bed, her hands behind her head, staring above her. The glass chandelier hung above like a memory. Delicate, almost too proud to swing. Its tiny brass chains trembled as a stray gust slipped in through the half-shut window. 'You know what? I always wanted to live your life.'

Mandira turned her head slowly, surprised. Her eyes were trying to focus.

'We were little girls with white ribbons tied to our braids. You were always ahead. The same clothes, even the same grades… they fit you differently. Your voice. Your heart. Everything. I used to think to myself… is your life even real? I thought you had everything,' Sujata said.

The scent of tempered spices wafted up faintly from the kitchen below. Mustard seeds popping in ghee, curry leaves hissing against hot metal, grounding the silence between the two women into something familiar, something aching.

After a long pause, Mandira slipped to the floor, resting her head against the wall, 'I didn't know you envied me.'

'Neither did I. Not until high school happened,' Sujata said.

Mandira looked up, squinting her eyes, 'What happened in high school?'

'Love,' Sujata said simply, rising from the bed. The air shifted with her as she dug out a memory. 'We both fell in love… at the same time.'

Mandira blinked. She tried to stand but stumbled; Sujata helped her up, and the two sat side by side, like schoolgirls again.

'You… you liked Aryaveer?' Mandira's words were half horror, half amusement.

Sujata shook her head. 'Ahh…' She laughed dryly. 'The whole school, but you knew he woke up in the morning only so he could see you. As for me, he was always like a brother…determined to set me up with someone so I don't feel lonely when you two begin your little love story.'

Mandira stared at her, the bottle cradling loosely in her lap, 'You said you were jealous of me? Why then?'

'Do you really not know?' Sujata turned to look at her, as if trying to find something, an answer to the question that was never asked.

Mandira sat straight, gathering all the attention she could, 'What are you talking about?'

'The day we met them at the protest outside school, the day you actually noticed Aryaveer for the first time. The boys were in their gum boots and helmets, remember.' Sujata took a long pause. 'I kept waiting for him to look at me just once, but his eyes, Lalit's eyes, were only for *you*. Of course, you were smitten by Aryaveer. You didn't hear how loudly Lalit's heart was shattered. But I heard it. The thunderous sound of it.' She wiped her tears and whispered, as if only to herself, 'I still do.'

'He helped you all these years, not for Aryaveer or your family. He did it for you.'

'Sujata… No…' Mandira held Sujata's hands in hers, eyes wide, as if trying to undo years with her fingers.

'Do you think he shows up because of Aryaveer?' Sujata let her tears flow now.

Mandira hugged her dear friend, but Sujata was a stone. 'When Aryaveer was away, all he cared about, my husband, was to accompany you to the vaccination of your girls because one of your nannies didn't show up while his own wife rolled in bed, raw and agonising in the want of a child. How jolly he is with your family, right? Lalit Uncle!!' Sujata's silence screamed.

'I'm sorry. I'm so so sorry,' Mandira said, her features curled in bewilderment. She buried her face in her palms and howled. Her cries were raw, ancient, 'How many lives have I ruined…just how many?'

'Only one,' Sujata's voice was like porcelain at a junkyard. 'Your own.'

She placed her hand on Mandira's shaking shoulder, 'My point of telling all this to you is that you had everything a woman can desire. Yes, you have lost a lot along the way. But such is life, and if you look at it with a little heart…you still have enough. You have Ira. That child is burning, Mandira. I've seen it. The way she moves her fingers over a blank page, like she's trying to draw something just to destroy another. Don't turn her into… another you.'

'I don't know how to live anymore,' Mandira cried.

'Then learn. Heal. Because if you don't, no one will. Not her.'

Sujata paused, 'Not anyone *after* her.' Sujata whispered, as if she could see who came after Ira, through Ira.

The room went very still. The air, heavy.

Shivani came to drag the suitcase out. Sujata sat motionless, fingers clenched in her lap, eyes burning. Mandira paused at the door. Over her shoulder, she said, 'Tell that husband of yours… that you were always the better deal.'

But Sujata was not thinking about her husband, not in this moment.

Chapter 38

A week had passed since Mandira left. Her final goodbye echoed in the house like the last note of the piano. With the blinds drawn, Ira was battering a canvas with texture using a spatula. Without looking at the door when it was knocked, she declared, 'I'm not hungry.'

It was true, she had forgotten hunger. The idea of food repulsed her. She wanted to throw up just at the thought of food and had been surviving on the biscuits kept in her drawer. Feeding on a few late at night as she stared at her art.

'Me neither.' Sonam bent to straighten the slippers by the door, aligning their edges until they matched perfectly, before stepping into the room.

Ira looked at her and sighed. She didn't hide her irritation.

'I didn't see you in school for a week and wanted to check on you.' Sonam said.

Ira scrunched her face, 'I'm not an orphan that anyone would need to check on.'

Sonam glanced at the canvas, then at Ira, 'I'm glad to see you are doing well.'

Ira laughed coldly. 'What did you expect? I'd be here beating my chest because some girl thinks she had won against me?'

'It's not a game we are playing against each other. It never was.' Sonam said.

Ira pursed her eyes in irritation as she spoke, 'Have you come here with a plan like your brother?'

'I actually came to tell you to let you know I'm still here for you. Even if Nihal is gone. You can still...'

Ira's hurt was tangible. It burned her eyes. She cut her sentence, 'Gone?'

Sonam's palms curled in the fists by her side, 'You…you didn't know?'

A torrent of grief threatened to break free. Ira didn't attempt to conceal her tears.

Sonam leaned forward to hug her. Too weak to protest, Ira let her.

'I'm so so sorry. I had no clue he didn't tell you. How could he be so… tough…' Sonam whispered.

Ira pulled away suddenly, hands shot to her head in disbelief, 'You could have had anyone…anyone...why did you do this to me? To us? Why couldn't you spare him?'

A tear rolled down Sonam's face.

'Please go,' Ira screeched.

Without saying another word, Sonam left.

The months that followed, Ira spent on stretching and fixing canvas rolls on wood. The ailments that she thought were reserved for older people had begun their way through her. Chest pains and headaches. A heavy, lumpy feeling she could not put a finger on. Pains that Amma didn't have tea for, and then there were long stretches of inactivity. She would sit under the shower and let hours pass by, watching her skin wrinkle.

'Did you sit in the tub for long again?' Amma would ask.

'I was cleaning the brushes,' She'd tell her.

Today, she was painting a woman. Filling oil in the contours of her breasts as she felt a bead of sweat slide down between her own. The canvas shimmered with life—the deep, umber tones of Cleopatra's skin, the glint of gold and the emerald green of the Nile reflecting in her eyes. As she painted, a strange ache bloomed within her. She imagined her yearning, the subtle tension in her muscles as she awaited her lover's arrival.

The scent of linseed oil, thick and musky, filled the air of her studio, as she calls her room now. And like always, it mingled with the phantom scent of Nihal—the earthy aroma of the pages he spent his time with, the faint tang of his sweat after a long day at the bookstore. Ira felt the ghost of his touch, the rough texture of his fingers tracing the delicate curve of her jaw, the warmth of his breath against her skin. She closed her eyes and let herself imagine the gentle pressure of his lips.

The soft hum of Amma's tools in the garden outside the window seemed to fade, replaced by the rhythmic crashing of waves against the shore. She pictured the Egyptian coastline, the salty air heavy with the promise of union. The longing that burned inside her was so great it made her gasp.

Why is it that the heart almost always desires the forbidden?

She longed for Nihal, for his embrace, for the comfort of his presence to quell the storms raging inside her. And then, she touched herself, as if it were him guiding her fingers.

Later, in the bathroom mirror, she remembered a dead animal she had once seen in the zoo as a child. It may have been a deer. She stood there watching how the other animals completely ignored that one of them was lying there, lifeless. When Aarya pulled at her sleeve to move ahead, she told her to wait, and she waited until it moved just so much to reveal it was only as dead as it was alive.

Existing.

Ira removed a bottle she had earlier hidden in the cabinet above the bathtub. She knew Kabir was about to come for her art class, and yet, she filled two glasses.

'I don't think it's right.' Kabir's face was washed in terror as he sat near the canvas, removing stationery from his pouch.

Ira laughed, 'Really! I don't know what is right anymore.'

'Oh boy! Ira, you don't seem alright to me. Maybe you could—' Kabir began to cap his pencils.

Ira walked closer, glasses in her hands. 'Nihal left the city…you think that is *right*? How many years of your life will you spend teaching people like me when all I want to do is vomit my pathetic life on the canvas? You know who killed Julius Caesar. His closest friend. You know how old Plath's children were when she died? And you say this world is not brutal? That there is a God. You know how old she was? Ten.' Ira shrieked, 'Ten. Aarya was ten.'

'Ira! you need to stop. Where is Amma? Your mother?' Kabir picked up his sling and swiped his handkerchief on his forehead. 'I think I should leave. Is there someone I can call for you? Your father?'

'He is probably somewhere doing exactly this.' She brought the bottle to her mouth and sucked it until it was less than half full.

'I'll dip the brushes in the oil. You can clean them tomorrow and.... and I'll see you on Monday.' Kabir slid his sling across his shoulders. He knew Ira was not talking to him anymore. Her voice grew shaky as her fingers reached her lips. 'I always thought it was a lie when Amma said Aarya went to a better place. How stupid was I?'

Despite being petrified, Kabir offered her the napkin she'd used earlier to wipe the extra colour from the painting. 'Ira... would you be alright?'

'I'm very lonely.' She looked him in the eyes. 'Can you sit with me. Please?'

He checked his watch. Then glanced at the door, which was closed, barring a chink through which a wedge of orange light from the lobby made a dash.

In measured steps, he placed himself beside Ira on the couch. His own heart beat rising.

'Tell me something?' She sipped from the glass that she had filled for him and replaced it on the coffee table. 'Do you still think of Aarti?' She offered the glass to him, which he reluctantly accepted. In a gentle motion, he brought it to his lips. 'It will be a complete lie if I say I don't.'

'So it's true what they say about first love,' she said, taking another sip.

'You take it to your grave.' Kabir finally eased in her company. He emptied the glass into his mouth. 'Just know that this... won't make you forget your pain...or loneliness. I tried that already.'

Ira nodded gently. Smiling. 'Sometimes I think, why do I do it again and again? Put myself in places of hurt and pain. I knew my mother would leave one day. I was scared Nihal would, too. I know a feeling worse than the feeling of pain. It is that numbness. A feeling of no feeling. Like, I am dead. With that feeling, I cannot even paint.'

Kabir shook his head, but he wasn't really listening. 'She is a mother now. So I'm told. Twins.'

Ira looked at him softly, 'I will be a terrible mother if I become one someday.'

Kabir laughed, took another mouthful from the bottle, which was nearly empty now. The two sat in silence for a while. Ira glanced at him, trying to figure out his face, but there was only a little she could see.

'Do you want to kiss me?' She asked.

Kabir looked at her knowingly, his eyes dropping to her lips, 'I can?'

'Did you ever want to?' She asked, leaning closer.

'I may have once or twice. I am a man…a man who has never touched a woman,' he said.

'Come here,' she spread, her arms for him. 'It will make you feel better… if only for a while.' Ira held Kabir by his hair just beneath her neck. They were soft under her fingers. His own hands draped her back hungrily. He smelled earthy, almost a mineral scent, like clay dust. Sweet, but nothing like Nihal.

'Kiss me,' she whispered, leading Kabir's hand to her neck, bringing it further along her chest. Kabir's breathing was loud. His fingers felt cold on her skin.

Somewhere down the stairs, a door creaked open. Boots tapping on the wooden staircase. The incoherent chatter echoed in the hallway within a matter of a few seconds.

'Your father is home.' Kabir wrenched himself out of her grip. Straightening himself, he flattened his shirt in panic, 'Oh my god, oh my god!' He held his head between his arms.

'Why do you always hold back?' Ira patted the upholstery beside her, her eyes unfocused somewhere behind him.

'You freak! This was the only job I had. I should have believed what those boys in your school were saying about you,' he shrieked.

The door opened. Aryaveer entered with the mask of excitement he always wore for his daughter, especially after Mandira left.

Kabir fumbled, 'I…I came here to drop the brushes. I found her like this… so I stayed. I was trying to help her. Amma isn't here…and I thought I'd stay till someone comes back. I don't think she is…well.'

Ira never found out if Kabir stopped coming because of her or her father.

Chapter 39

Time tore through her days like a clan of hyenas—hunting, circling, sparing only what it wished to leave behind. The lobby walls overflowed with Ira's portraits—a quiet proclamation that she lived here alone, and that the house, with all its rules and silences, belonged to her to obey or undo. All the faces she painted bore a fleeting resemblance to Nihal, his scar, his sharp jawline, the curls invading his forehead, though she never intended them to. His presence seemed to slip, uninvited, into her colours and textures.

Amma's eyesight had finally surrendered to time. She now saw with her fingers, tracing the petals of roses tended by the young gardener who had replaced the old one. Shivani was married and gone, her place taken by a quieter woman who moved about the house like a shadow, careful not to disturb the stillness.

Aryaveer had brought Ira a Nokia phone from Singapore, sleek and hopeful in its promise of connection. But there was no one for her to call. Sometimes, her mother's voice came through the receiver late in the evenings, soft and uncertain. Ira would tell her she was in the middle of a painting, her hands too full of colour and turpentine to talk.

She often thought of Nihal. She knew, somehow, that he must be in touch with her father. But he had never called Ira. Not once.

In the closet, behind the emerald lace dress she had worn on her farewell day, something else began to grow—a secret life of its own. Each bottle was a quiet theft from Aryaveer's study, each sip a defiance whispered into the silence of her life.

Meanwhile, in Mumbai, Nihal had finally found a place where he felt he belonged. His college was more diverse than the school. He made some friends, too. After his classes, he would spend all his time in the library until his eyes grew heavy and he could read no more. However, once back in his hostel room, exhausted in his bed, his thoughts would invariably drift to Ira. Each night, he prayed she was safe and happy. Sometimes, the boys took him out drinking. He held a glass but never drank because that would affect his attention in the lecture the next day. So he just pretended to enjoy his drink. He had learned that a major part of growing up was pretending.

One evening, he entered his room and saw the naked back of a girl on his own bed.

'Dude!' His roommate screamed.

Nihal ran out and hailed an auto rickshaw, heading straight to Juhu beach. The city sped past him in a blur of noise and neon. At the shore, the air was thick with the scent of salt and dreams. Someone nearby was tearing open a packet of chips, laughter spilling like crumbs into the wind. And then—among those giggles—he heard one that stopped him.

A stunned, joyful light spread across his face. 'Why didn't you tell me you were in Bombay?' His smile beamed in his eyes.

Sonam swiped the strands of her hair behind her ears, 'I didn't want you to think I was following you.'

'Were you, though?' He said, still unbelieving of the events.

'No and Yes. I had three places to choose from. Obviously, I chose Bombay,' Sonam said.

His eyes travelled to the leather diary in her hand, 'And yet you never wrote?'

Sonam pushed the diary into her tote bag. 'I'd heard you were doing well without me.'

'Saksham,' Nihal said to himself. 'What about you? Do you still go somewhere every Sunday?'

Sonam gestured to her friends to go on without her, 'I've got my grandfather to live here in the old age home near my hostel.' She pushed a long strand of hair behind her ear, 'I couldn't leave him alone in Manali. I see him and his friends on Sundays. We play tambola.'

Nihal smiled at the warmth of her words. Sonam hadn't changed one bit, except her eyes. They somehow looked a deeper shade, and she wore thick mascara.

The two met every Saturday after their classes—sometimes at the beach, sometimes at the movies, and on quieter days, in the library where Nihal liked to read while she wrote her assignments. One such evening, when the librarian finally asked them to leave around ten, Sonam turned to him with a sleepy smile and said she was craving vada pav.

They sat by the tea stall at the beach, talking about everything and nothing. The sea murmured behind them as if listening in. They laughed over things that had once drawn tears, the kind of laughter that comes only when the years have softened the edges of pain and memories. Sonam told him she had joined the debate club only to be near him back in the school, and about the sports teacher who once proposed to her—how, when she refused, he had begged her not to tell anyone, and she didn't. Nihal told her he threw all his trophies in the bed trunk once home. He never liked to see them. He showed her his new Walkman in which he taped Bryan Adams from the radio last night.

Together, they wandered through every corner of their shared past except one: Ira. When Nihal said something mildly funny, Sonam laughed as if it were the most delightful thing she had ever heard. And when her laughter finally fell away one day, she looked at him—eyes tender, uncertain.

'Do you want to come to my room?' She asked.

Once in the room, Sonam excused herself. The room was exceptionally small but neat. There was no bookshelf, so the books were neatly stacked on the bed back according to size and colour. A small pink ceramic pot with a pair of lilies sat in the corner of her study table by the window. The flower seemed fresh, as if it were placed there just this morning. A cream jute basket held a few pens, lipsticks and hair ties. The single floral curtain cloaking the window was frayed, but clean.

Nihal sat on the chair and began leafing through a book on pop fashion when Sonam appeared.

'Are you going to spend the night on that chair?' She asked, folding a piece of cloth. Perhaps, a scrap.

Her words confused him. Did she want him to spend the night here? 'I don't think the coffee would let me sleep,' he said.

'Me neither,' Sonam said, pulling a pyjama and a t-shirt from a small chest that he had missed noticing before. Perhaps the room wasn't as small as he initially thought.

'The floor has a common bathroom for all the paying guests,' she told him and went outside with the change of clothes in her hands.

When she came back fifteen minutes later, the room was dark. Nihal was on one side of the bed, already asleep. She placed a duvet over him and watched the moonlight paint his features through the window. He seemed to be in deep thought even while asleep. Sonam leaned closer and flattened the lines on his forehead with her fingers. She closed her eyes and let his warmth seep into the pores of the skin on her fingertips. She knew, in that moment, she would never be able to love another boy the way she loved him.

Around five in the morning, Nihal stirred beside her. In a sudden rush, he sat up and began fumbling for his shoes. Sonam looked up from her book, her back straightening, the early light pooling faintly across the sheets.

'Leaving?' Her voice held no trace of sleep. The night hadn't spared her a wink.

'Site day. I almost forgot,' he lied, bending to tie his laces without meeting her eyes.

She noticed how his fingers halted. She closed her eyes as if to push away an impending storm, 'The week after you left Delhi, I went to see her.'

He sat up straight, looking at her but not speaking yet.

'She didn't look very good,' Sonam continued.

Nihal's face was sour when he turned around. He didn't say anything. Not for a while. He rose to his feet, but was not ready to leave yet. 'I'm the reason, right?'

Sonam pulled out a scarf and a pencil box from the drawer. She wrapped the scarf around her shoulders. She asked him if he wanted to go to the terrace. It was silent up there, she said, the best place to search for answers.

The sun had not shown up yet, but had sent an announcement through the twilight sky. The city underneath was yet to roar to life.

Sonam extracted the cigarette from the box and lit it between her lips, cupping the flame against the breeze. She drew in and let the smoke out slowly.

Nihal stared at her in disbelief.

'Relax,' she said, her lips curling. 'I'm not addicted. I just like the drama of it.'

He shook his head, half-smiling now. 'It doesn't fit the idea I have of you.'

'I'm used to being a misfit,' she replied, handing him the cigarette.

He pushed it back. 'I prefer destruction in quieter forms?'

Sonam's laugh came out as a cough. Nihal looked at her. His eyes were soft.

'Overthinking,' she answered from his side, then extinguished her cigarette on the brick parapet. 'For me, it is not the destruction that pulls me, but the pause it gives. A moment I steal from the world for myself.'

Nihal observed the city slowly coughing to life beneath them. In a way, he felt, they were in it but not a part of it. Outsiders, but not really.

'You were not the only reason, Nihal, well not entirely…' Sonam began to speak carefully, 'I was told Ira's mother had left home.'

'Her parents had lost the capability of hurting her long ago,' Nihal said.

'And you think you were the only person left with that power,' Sonam asked.

Nihal blinked the tears forming at the back of his eyes. Sonam placed her hand over his palm. Pressed it like making a point. 'You can keep someone afloat only as long as you can keep yourself from drowning with them,' she said.

'I can't say who was keeping the other afloat,' Nihal said.

'Look at me.' She yanked his elbow. 'You needed this city, this college and the degree it will give you.'

He shook his head. Sonam watched him as his lips twisted, as if to avoid the surge of grief that he carried within him.

'Only you could…' She held his hands, 'You should have given her a farewell she deserved…you took it too far.'

A lone tear made its way through his face. 'I didn't even tell her I was planning on leaving.'

'And it broke her… that you vanished so suddenly and how!' She said.

'The reason I restrained myself, told myself I couldn't, just couldn't, was only to keep myself from breaking her heart again and again, but that's what I did eventually. She called me trash, a bad omen.' Nihal fell into her arms as she spread them out for him. 'I grew up believing I was really a bad omen. My mother kept telling me I drew my father away. I was the reason she stopped being attractive to him, and so someone else took her place. Ira was the one who made me believe it wasn't true, but then I came here…changed everything about myself…only one thing that I couldn't change is that I…'

'Nihal...' Sonam held his face in her palms before he could say out loud how much he longed for Ira, 'You are not the reason your father left.'

In the darkness of her eyes, he saw himself. Broken, but not completely, yet. He also faintly saw a hope. A glint of the love that the child in him had wanted during the nights, his tears drenched the pillow. He saw his mother, singing in the kitchen, a hand on her hip.

And then he saw Ira, tongue between her lips, filling sunlight in the petals of a rose on the easel.

A dull sun grew larger behind them, casting a dark glow on Sonam's face when she kissed him. It was brief. Moist, like an oasis. Then again.

The Saturdays that came after, Nihal spent in Sonam's room or on the terrace while he watched her smoke. He told her about Anna Grigoryevna Snitkina, Dostoevsky's second wife, who was his stenographer during the frantic writing of *The Gambler*.

'They married shortly after completing the book, and she helped stabilise his life financially and emotionally.'

He told her about the girl in his class who leaves notes for him in his books. How she always sits around him but not with him, even when there is a place. He spoke about the shopping complex he was designing with his seniors. About the books he read. About poetry. He told her how beautiful his mother looked when his father had not left yet. And he finally told her about his father. Both before and after he was gone.

The two made love quietly, like it was some sort of meditation, and went back to reading their books on their sides of the bed, sometimes even before they put their clothes back on.

Nihal began to bring his pencils and drawing plans. Sonam watched him draw straight lines on the paper from her bed until her eyes became heavy with sleep. He would sit by the window and work for hours into the night. The window reminded him of home.

One day, he told her that he was sending an entry to one of the competitions held by an architectural firm in Rome. He hadn't planned on telling his classmates he was participating.

'What will they give you if you win?' Sonam asked over her book.

'Internship. And maybe…'

'Cash?' She asked.

He shook his head.

'There we go!' Sonam laughed, and he laughed with her as he watched how the streetlight that spilled through the window struck in her long hair like tiny drops of stars.

Chapter 40

One Saturday, Sonam and Nihal lay in her bed after making love. She was absently tracing a circle on his chest when he held her hand, 'There is something I want to tell you.'

'Me too.' Sonam said.

Nihal released her palm, 'You go first.'

'I'm going to Manali on Tuesday,' she said.

His eyes crinkled, somehow accentuating the stitch mark on his forehead.

Sonam had wanted to ask him about the story of this scar, but she would hate it if he didn't tell her. So she had never asked, 'It's my mother's death anniversary. Three days. Five Max.'

Nihal rose to sit on his side of the bed, grabbing his shirt from the side table. He began to swipe his arms in the sleeves, 'Try to come back on Saturday.'

'Why Saturday?'

He halted buttoning his shirt. 'So I can see you.'

Sonam's face fell, 'You don't have a reason to think of me for the rest of the week? Do you?'

'Are you mad?' Nihal said, confused.

'Is it the only thing you need me for?' She sat up straight and threw on her tunic from beneath her pillow.

Nihal watched her, waited so she would look at him again. She didn't. 'I've never forced myself on you. We have sex because you want it too. Don't make it appear something it isn't,' he said, still searching her eyes.

'You wanted to tell me something?' she asked, trying hard to hide the hurt.

'Nothing. It's nothing.' He wore the rest of his clothes, plucked his backpack from the lone hook on the wall and let himself out without saying goodbye.

Sonam didn't come back on Tuesday. Only a message from her.

Sonam: *Saw your photo in the magazine today. Your interview was fantastic. I knew you had to win.*

Nihal: *Why aren't you back yet?*

Sonam: *Nana is not well. I don't know how long it will take, but he wants to be here, in the hills.*

Nihal: *Take care.*

Sonam: *Yes.*

Nihal: By the way, m*y entry was disqualified shortly after the announcement.*

Sonam: *Oh*

Nihal: *But they have chosen me for an internship. I wasn't sure if I wanted to take it.*

Sonam: *That is great news.*

Nihal: *It would mean three years outside the country, in Rome.*

Sonam: *So...have you decided yet?*

Nihal paused. Searched for the glass of water that he had filled for himself a while ago. He found it on the top shelf of the wall. He didn't drink it. He dialled Sonam's mobile instead.

'I'm going to Delhi,' he said and noticed how she went quiet, like she wasn't there at all. There is a tap running somewhere behind her. And someone coughing.

Sonam cleared her throat, 'You want to meet your Mom?'

'Yes and—' he began.

'I've been meaning to tell you this, Nihal.' Sonam's voice was devoid of emotion. 'You both deserve closure. Go see Ira.'

He inspected his fingernails one by one. 'You... want to come along?'

'Trust me,' Sonam's smile was sour, he could tell. 'You don't want me there. Don't worry about me, alright.'

'Hmmm'

'Nihal.'

'Yes.'

'I love you.'

Nihal scrunched his eyes. That's how he said it to someone for the first time.

With a regret that came straight after.

'I love you too.'

Chapter 41

Ira watched the teardrop fall onto the thin paper stretched across her thighs. It had arrived that morning, in the post from Bombay, along with a box of roasted cashews. Addressed to Aryaveer Lall.

Another drop followed, then another—until the salt blurred the ink and softened the page, erasing in moments, the triumphs of a young man the article called a phoenix, risen from ashes with discipline and grit. She rubbed her eyes with the heel of her palm and stared at the place where Nihal's face had smiled—beaming in the way only someone who had learned too much, too young, could smile. It was gone now. A pulpy void stared at her in place of his face.

'Ira?' Amma's voice crawled after a soft knock on the door. 'I'll be back in a while. Is that alright?'

The door creaked open, warm daylight breaking across the floor in a clean line. Amma stood there, saree crisp, braid tight, a red bindi pinned above wrinkled brows. Amma's failed eyesight hadn't really altered the way she perceived life. Ira could hear the hesitation before Amma spoke again. 'I have to go to the nursery. And then…'

Ira didn't need her to finish. She lowered her gaze, scratched her neck where the paint had dried into her skin, 'I haven't washed yet. And I'm still working on a…'

'Yes, yes…' Amma paused briefly, studying Ira. 'Nihal has come from Bombay. I'm going with him.'

Ira thought she had heard it wrong. The air around her seemed to press inward, heavy and close, as if the room itself was holding its breath. She didn't move. Couldn't. Had she heard it right?

'He came to see you in the morning, but you were fast asleep. He waited with your father in the study for over an hour. Said he'll meet you in the evening. Something he wants to tell you.'

Ira didn't move. Couldn't. The words dried and cracked in her throat.

'I'll take a bit longer, I was saying, after the nursery he wants to see something for his mother, at the jeweller.' Amma laughed endearingly, 'Silly boy wants a blind opinion.'

Ira wiped her face with the back of her palm, still painted in the patches of red colour from last night, or a day before, she couldn't say. Red, the colour of beginning.

Amma closed the door gently behind her. Ira felt her stomach grumble. She hadn't had the poha that was sent hours ago. The potato chips she retrieved from her bedside table had turned limp and soft. She ate what was left and let the empty packet fall on the floor.

The day was hot. Beads of sweat crawled slowly down her back like snails. The scent of oil paint hung thick in the air, clinging to the walls, coating her tongue.

She poured turpentine oil in the jar of colour and stared at the white of the canvas for a long time. An emptiness so familiar to a young girl in a white cotton bra and purple pleated skirt that she had been wearing for three days. Ira didn't remember the last time she washed her hair. She began making large strokes of brown and black overlapping one another, her movements fierce and quick like the crashing waves in the storm, her worn arms suddenly catching strength. She hated how her mind was drifting towards him. She hadn't seen him in more than a year. The mark on his forehead only she knows about.

How was she supposed to wait now?

How she craved to consume him with her eyes. To lock him in her sight.

Chapter 42

Near the window of the closet, Ira's fingers hovered over her sketchbook, restless, as she looked at the blurred reflections in Monet's water lilies. Kabir had once told her that Impressionism began as a rebellion, a refusal to be bound by rigid rules, to capture life as it flickered in light and feeling rather than in exact forms. She thought of her own work, the smudges and hurried strokes, the unfinished edges that nobody else might understand. Maybe this was her rebellion too—against the emptiness of quiet rooms, against the absence she felt in the spaces around her, against a world that never waited. Each line, each dab of colour, was her way of marking herself, of holding onto the fleeting, of staking a claim in a life that was always slipping away.

She grabbed the magazine like a mother runs for her child in danger. Nihal was smiling in the photo. Was. But she didn't need to see it. She knew that smile. Plain and meaningless. Created for only the camera.

The door inched open. Without looking behind, she said, 'Come back later.'

'For a moment I thought you were Mandira.' The voice sent a shiver through her bones.

'Uncle!' She rose, covered herself using what she could. The magazine.

'Wow! Every time I walk into this room unannounced, I see him, and how,' Lalit's voice had a hint of something strange. Something bitter, like a venom.

Ira pulled her shirt from the easel and threw it over her arms. She clumsily did the buttons, turning her back.

'You know I had believed that you two would eventually turn into lovers?' Lalit's eyes glared at the photo in the magazine that she had dropped on the bed. 'But I'm told he never writes to you, nor calls.'

Still facing away from him, Ira looked at her fisted palms.

'At this age, it's natural to find someone in college. I'd felt love for the first time myself in my college,' he said, walking closer.

Ira walked past him to go out of the room, but he stopped her, 'Where are you going?'

'I need to have lunch,' she said and shrieked for the housekeeping lady.

Lalit prowled like a wild animal on a hunt, careful and measured, 'Oh, she had gone for groceries, and it's too late for lunch now, isn't it?' He sighed. 'So…I was saying, so many of us have our first love in college. Some even have their hearts broken for the first time. You would know if you were to study,' he looked at her boldly.

Ira couldn't move. Was she frozen? Scared? or just numb?

'You look just like your mother when I saw her for the first time. If I were in his place, I would have been so ruined to even think of another girl,' he whispered.

Ira sucked her breath, suddenly conscious of his nearness. In her mind, she went back to that day with Sharan. The reek of his perfume. His breath burned her like coal. The ugliness of that night still lingers within the four walls of her soul.

He was speaking, but his words didn't reach her, 'I see a spark in you, a waiting…a sort of longing to be…'

She scrunched her eyes as she felt Lalit's hand graze the back of her neck, but she could not move, not yet in her stoned state.

When he looked her in the eyes. A new fear erupted like a volcano in her. An urge to move sparked in her muscles. She pulled away quickly, crashing into the easel. The large painting, still wet in colour, fell on the floor with a loud thud that shook her.

'One day the world will marvel at the magnificence of your artwork, but the greatest artwork, if you ask me, is you. And only your mother could have created it.' He had grabbed her by the shoulders. Her body fell limp again, like seaweed. She felt his mouth on her lips. His tongue darting inside, his arms running like blades of iron around her waist and shoulders.

In front of her eyes, Chandan's face flashed, the last time she saw him in the back of the car. She saw white, a blinding white across her eyes. Afternoon sky. Her body was like a piece of paper on the top of the ocean current. Melting. Lost.

He was breathing heavily. With one hand, he tore open her shirt and with another, he pulled her hair so hard a cry left her mouth. A sudden strength dashed across her. A feeling so repulsive that she could throw up. She jerked him away and helped herself out of the stifling closet.

She remembered the backseat of the car as she slept. A fog of black smoke enveloped her. Aarya's hand was limp on her grip. With a hand, she wiped the sweat on her face. A jar of paint dropped behind her, spreading like darkness on the wooden floor.

Then she saw something shift in Lalit's eyes. Something bordering on fear and disbelief? 'For God's sake, you're like my child,' Lalit barked, running behind Ira's father, who stood on the door, as if to save himself from danger.

'I guess what they are all saying is right…your daughter has lost all morality…she is no less than a…' Lalit feigned a cry for help.

'No,' Ira's father said—not loudly, but with a finality that seemed to tear through the air between them. His eyes were angry and deeply wounded.

Lalit's words crawled out shaken, 'I'm sorry, but I never want to come back here again unless this girl minds her morality. Today it was me, tomorrow it could be…'

That night, Aryaveer sat in his study until dawn. The lamp burned low, shadows stretching across the room like silent witnesses. He drank whiskey straight from the bottle—one, two, and then he stopped counting.

By the time morning broke, his eyes were bloodshot, but his mind felt sharp, almost cruelly clear. He stepped out, the sun just beginning to climb over the city, and told the driver, in a voice that allowed no hesitation, 'Go to Nihal's house. Bring him to me.'

Chapter 43

The night sky hung like a velvet curtain above them, scattered with stars that blinked like ancient secrets. A silver moon carved a gentle arc through the darkness, casting a soft, cold glow over the tiny bulbs of marigolds.

Amma sipped her turmeric-ginger tea, the steam curling like the wrinkles on her face. 'The problem with your generation,' she said, 'is that you tell yourselves you've fallen in love every day, yet treat love like some jewel to be locked away in a safe—' she chuckled softly '—for fear someone might steal it.'

Amma closed her eyes and inhaled deeply, as if to fill her lungs with the magic floating in nature. 'Love is like a rose, my girl. It grows, it wilts, and then it grows again—sometimes in different colours, in the same garden. If you work hard, it will surprise you. If you give up too soon, it never will.'

'But shouldn't every relationship begin with the truth?' Ira whispered, shame swelling in her chest.

'Truth,' Amma said, with a sigh that trembled like old silk, 'is like morning prayer—noble, of course—but not something meant for the darkness between wedding sheets.' She released a long breath, the kind that carried years of knowing. 'Now listen to me. Every woman walks into her marriage with a heart full of secrets—and secrets they must remain.'

'But it's not me his heart wanted. I will be like a cost he would pay for the rest of his life. What if he never stops loving her?' Ira's voice cracked.

Amma turned her head toward the rose patch where she'd spent half her life, watering and pruning. It was hard to tell that her eyes no longer saw. She swatted at a fly. 'Oh, nonsense. Grief is dramatic, not permanent. Give a man a little comfort, a warm hand to hold—and he'll forget faster than you can finish your ginger lemon tea.'

Ira rested her head on Amma's lap and fished out the sketch she had made of him. Its edges burned as if to mark it so no one can claim it ever again. It was the first time she felt her body ache for him as Nihal sat by the window, the two caught in their almost-touch.

Maybe that's what she will remain, too, she thought.

Always almost. Always unfinished.

PART 3

Rome, 2018

When Stories Refuse to Die

Chapter 1

I refuse to let my mother's story remain unfinished. Her life will not be defined by her tragedy.

Wiping my eyes, I pull a sheet of paper from the folder beneath the script and begin jotting down names—people, magazines, anyone who ever interviewed Mom. There aren't many, so the task is quick.

There were plenty of articles and reports written about her, but almost none by anyone who had actually met her. They had all written from a distance, painting her life in broad, careless strokes.

Nevertheless, I finally land on a name.

Lina Moretti.

There are photographs of her with Mom, taken in a dim café in Florence. The light is low, almost secretive, falling in amber pools across their faces. Mom is leaning forward, as though confiding something, and Lina is listening intently.

I look up her employer and discover she once worked for an art magazine in Rome—a small publication that focused on women and immigrant artists.

The photographs clearly suggest an interview took place, yet I find no trace of it online.

I check Lina's Instagram, only to find it locked. There are no other interviews attributed to her either. It almost feels as though she vanished—perhaps she left the job.

The next morning, I tell Gaius everything that has unfolded—everything except that I told Solo about us. But I tell him I won't see Solo again, and that I need him beside me in my investigation.

He is revered in Rome; people know his name and respect him. He promised he would help me in every way he could. And yet, beneath his assurances, I sense it—that small, quiet doubt.

He didn't believe my certainty that Mom was murdered.

'Didn't you say your dad was against your mom giving interviews?' Gaius's voice breaks the quiet as he watches me trace the bus routes on Google Maps, the blue lines shifting across the screen like veins.

'Yes,' I say, still focused on the screen. 'The only person he was comfortable with Mom opening up to was Solo.'

He folds his arms, his brows tightening into a sharp line. 'I think Solo may have more to her than what she shows you.'

I lift my head slowly. 'I know you don't like her,' I say, my voice low but steady, 'but I know it in my heart,' pressing my hand to my chest, 'that she always meant well.'

The room hangs suspended for a breath. Gaius doesn't argue. He just watches me.

He accompanies me to the magazine office. The owner was a wiry old Italian with a velvet scarf looped three times around his neck, even though it was warm inside. His fingers, long and stained with ink, tapped restlessly on the wooden desk, as if playing an invisible piano.

'I am Marigold, Ira Lal's daughter.'

His lips twitched, a gesture that never made it to his eyes. He looked at Gaius when the hand was offered, but didn't take it; his focus returned instead to the scarf, as if it gave him an excuse not to engage with Gaius. I've seen it before—people often draw back around Gaius, intimidated.

The air in the room smelled faintly of mould and mint tea, but something sharper lurked beneath, something that prickled my nerves. I want to leave already. But I stay. 'I wanted to talk to you about my mother.'

'Who doesn't know her,' the man says, voice thick with reverence and weariness, 'your mother…'

I swallow before I speak. 'Yes. And I believe your magazine knew her better than most. A woman who works for you—Lina Moretti—was the only one my mother ever spoke to. It was just a week before she…' I halt.

'She committed suicide,' he says it like it is, as normal as discussing the weather.

'Yes,' I say, the word scraping my throat. 'But I cannot find that interview anywhere.'

His fingers pause on the table. 'What do you imply?'

Before I can answer, a petite woman barges in. She has straight blonde hair covering her forehead like a curtain, heavy black glasses swallowing half her face. She marches in and thrusts her phone at him. 'Why aren't you answering my calls?'

The man's face tightens. He snatches her phone and tells her curtly to wait outside. Immediately, she turns on her heel, but not before pausing and flashing me a strange look on her way out. Her eyes linger too long on mine, searching, as if she recognises me from some forgotten dream.

I turn to Gaius. He blinks in a quiet reassurance. He clears his throat and says, 'Ira Lall did not kill herself.'

I carry it from there. 'I don't think my mother killed herself,' I say softly, words tumbling out of my lips like stones. 'And I believe that interview may have something to tell me about how she felt on those last few days before...'

The man's laugh was sharp, dismissive. 'And you expect us to solve murder cases in an art magazine?'

'No. I only want the October issue. That was the only interview my mother ever gave. I need to read it.'

His hand drifts to the scarf again, fingers clutching at it nervously, like he fears it will choke him. 'I'm afraid to disappoint you, signorina. That issue no longer exists.'

'Why?' Gaius and I ask together.

'Legal reasons.' His eyes dart to Gaius, or the window behind him where a bird had perched, before they come back to me, restless and irritated. 'Every copy was destroyed—print and digital. I cannot say any more.'

The silence felt heavy, suffocating.

'Confidential,' he adds, his voice dropping low. 'Now, I'll have to ask you to leave.'

And then I felt it, even before Gaius and I entered the elevator—a gaze brushing against my skin like a cold breeze.

We were not the only ones piecing my mother's life together.

We were being shadowed.

CHAPTER 2

We duck into a small café between two leather boot shops, the kind with faded awnings and a handwritten menu board chalked in looping Italian. The warm hum of conversation and the hiss of the espresso machine meet us as we step inside. The air smells of roasted beans, and the faint salt of sweat carried from the street.

I order an espresso, its porcelain cup trembling slightly on the saucer as the waiter sets it down.

Gaius shakes his head, 'The doctor told me to stay away from coffee. It triggers my epilepsy.' He sounds half-resigned, half-wistful, as though refusing coffee in Rome were its own kind of cruelty.

I glance toward the doorway. A woman stands there for a heartbeat, and the moment our eyes meet, she spins on her heel—gone before the thought of calling out can form.

'Excuse me!' I call after her, scraping back my chair, running, but she is already gone. The moment breaks, and I sit down again, my espresso cooling untouched. I take a long sip and feel the caffeine relax my senses. I don't know why, but I do not tell Gaius about the mysterious woman.

'Solo said Mom died of an overdose,' I say instead. 'But she had no access to alcohol. Not even her pills. It was always Dad or Donna who gave her the medicines.'

I am spun back into the past so suddenly it feels as if I've slipped into a science fiction novel. A memory throbs through me. A sharp, familiar ache of being kept out.

'Are you alright, Mari?' Gaius presses my palm on the table. I speak through my memory, unsure if it is Gaius I am talking to.

'Once, I had begged them to give Mom the medicine myself—just once. I wanted to be the one she trusted. But the door was always closed to me. I could only peer through the keyhole as my father or Donna placed the glass to her lips. I used to wonder if that small ritual was love—or control. Whatever it was, I wanted it for myself. Only myself.'

He leans forward, voice low but steady. 'You know the easiest way to kill an addict is through an overdose. We need to find the people who knew how dangerous it was for Ira to go back to drinking.'

It feels strange to hear Mom's name on Gaius's tongue. He says it with an ease that doesn't belong to someone who never knew her.

I stir my espresso—whatever is left of it—though I've long lost the desire to have any more. The surface in the cup swirls like dark marble. 'It wouldn't have been a secret. Everyone close to Mom knew. She was a morbid alcoholic. And they all knew it could kill her.'

'Not everyone,' Gaius says. 'Your father hid her rehab stays well. There's no article, no public mention. Every time she fell back, he slid her quietly into that clinic owned by his trusted friend.'

'He did it for her,' I snap. 'Would you want him announcing it on the evening news? My wife, the celebrated Ira Lall, is drowning in alcohol again?'

Gaius doesn't flinch. He only looks at me with those calm, unblinking eyes. 'Maybe the rehab still keeps something. Records. Notes. Or just someone who remembers.'

'She died at home. Not the rehab,' I remind him.

'But she was there the whole week before the day she died. Didn't you tell me that she only returned the morning of September 25—the same day she died?' he says.

I nod, absently. I don't remember telling Gaius about her last stay at the rehab. Then how does he know?

I sigh. It is all so confusing.

'Perhaps someone met her there and persuaded her to...' Gaius continues.

'She did not kill herself,' I announce, getting back on my investigation. The clink of cups and spoons around us suddenly becomes too loud and cheerful.

'Can we go there?' he says.

'I can, but they won't let you in,' I tell him.

A wry smile reaches his lips despite the heaviness pressing in on me.

'Don't worry about me. I've never needed permission to enter a place in Rome. I'll see you there tomorrow morning.' He smiles that adorable, mysterious smile that always gets through me.

Outside, a scooter buzzes past, leaving behind a ribbon of petrol and summer heat. I walk alongside Gaius, but somewhere in the back of my mind, the echo of that woman's retreating steps lingers, quick and purposeful.

As though she knows something I don't.

Who could she be?

Chapter 3

Matteo is watering the plants on his desk when he sees me. The spray bottle catches the sunlight, scattering droplets like shards of glass across the leaves. He stiffens and hurries toward me.

'Everything alright?'

'Yes, Matteo. I just… felt like coming here.'

He rests a hand lightly on my arm, guiding me down the corridor. The air carries its usual mixture—disinfectant and something faintly metallic, like wet coins. A patient in slippers shuffles past, humming tunelessly. Somewhere down the hall, a door clicks shut. It isn't such a bad place for people who need it, I think to myself.

Once in his office, Matteo begins to make two coffees. The machine gurgles, hisses, and the aroma of hazelnut curls into the air. I lift a cup. The heat presses into my palm, the first sip flooding my mouth with syrupy sweetness. Too sweet for me, I decide, and leave it.

'So what brings you here all of a sudden?' he asks, settling into the chair across from me.

'I've been thinking about Mom a lot lately. This is one place where she spent most of her time in the last few months. I wondered if I could find some memories of her here.'

Matteo's face softens. He believes me, I can tell. He spreads his palm flat against the table and turns toward the window. The garden outside shimmers in the Roman noon—olive leaves trembling, a cicada buzzing faintly somewhere nearby.

'It is lovely to see you finally warming towards us, Mari. We are always here to help. The other day, Nihal told me you organised his papers after he crashed into a debris of them. Welcome back, my little girl,' he smiles.

'Thank you, Matteo,' I say.

'Your Mom…' He sighs. 'I've never seen a woman more incredible. She painted day and night here. You see that bench?' He points to the far end of the garden through the window, where a stone bench glows pale in the sun. 'Your father sat here with me and watched her through the window. Sometimes for hours, not moving, just watching.'

'Why didn't he go to her?' I ask.

'She liked to be with herself. That's what she told everyone. Wouldn't even allow our housekeepers. Only Donna was permitted to enter to clean and feed her.'

'So no one ever visited her here?' I ask.

Matteo's pause is brief and light, but it presses into me like bricks. 'No one, as far as I know. Only your father, and sometimes Lorenzo. But Sherry will tell you better.'

I run a finger along the rim of my coffee cup, the aroma of its sweetness now making me slightly nauseous. A sparrow hops along the garden ledge outside, pecking at crumbs. The sunlight suddenly makes the room too bright, too sharp.

'Can I see the room where she…' I hesitate.

'Of course.' Matteo's voice is quick, almost eager, too kind, 'Sherry will take you.'

Chapter 4

I follow Sherry through the narrow alleyways where tall windows with iron railings let in sheets of pale sunlight. The air is cooler now, carrying the faint scent of damp stone and fallen leaves from the garden. Shadows of climbing vines sway across the walls, their leaves already bruised with autumn.

We climb a short flight of steps, the corridor echoing with each footfall. A draft slips in through a half-open window, carrying with it the distant sound of church bells and a fountain.

At the end of a circular corridor, Sherry opens the door to a large room. Daylight pours in unhindered; the single lamp overhead hangs unlit, unnecessary in this golden season. Bare walls rise around me, except for faint pencil sketches—shadows of figures, half-formed flowers that still cling like whispers of the past. Three tall easels stand by the windows, their wood streaked with dried acrylic. The floor is littered with stains of paint, a red streak running almost to the wall, as though the colour itself once bled into the room.

'Here is where all the masterpieces were created,' Sherry says, her voice reverent, as if she were standing inside a chapel.

'No one stays here now?' I glance at the single bed without sheets that sits pressed to one side. Two heavy tables stand nearby, their surfaces marked with knife scratches and hardened drops of pigment.

'No,' she smiles faintly, her eyes flicking to the easels. 'I am hopeful this will be a museum one day. Your mom was very famous. More now after she…'

I don't answer. My throat feels tight. 'Would you leave me alone for a while?'

She hesitates, jingling the keys in her hand. Outside, a gust rattles the branches against the glass. 'You know where to find me. Or dial zero for reception,' she says, pointing to the intercom I failed to notice before.

The door shuts softly behind her. Silence settles. The light is warm but brittle. I test the windows. They are low, almost at ground level, but the railings are fixed tightly into the stone. Beyond them, I think I see Gaius in the garden, half-hidden beneath an olive tree. He looks older in this light, his shoulders bent, his hair more silver than I remembered.

On the table to my right, I open a drawer and find a stack of newspapers, brittle with age. Beneath them, a yellow slip of paper: a gallery's name scrawled in an impatient hand, and a date—September 25, 2017.

Not my mother's handwriting.

A cold prickle crawls over my skin as a hand touches my shoulder. I gasp.

'Mari, relax—it's me,' Gaius says. His breath is heavy, his white tunic damp with sweat despite the coolness of the season. His face was lined, but his eyes remain restless, alive. 'How did you get inside?' I ask.

'Bathroom window. It's broken,' he says, wiping his forehead with the back of his hand.

Together, we search—under the mattress, in the drawers, behind the easels—but the room offers nothing. I don't tell him about the note I found.

When we step into the hallway again, a patient in a wheelchair glides past, pushed by a man in blue scrubs. The patient hums a broken tune, eyes unfocused. The orderly nods at me politely; I return the smile, hugging my bag close.

At the reception, Sherry is already gone. The clock on the wall shows two in the afternoon. Matteo has taken Dad to the site of his new property and won't return until evening. I crouch by Sherry's cabinet, my fingers brushing dust before finding the thick visitor register for September 2017. I slide it into my bag.

Outside, the sun sits high but softened, bleaching the tops of the trees. I look at Gaius. He meets my eyes with a steady nod.

'We should leave,' I whisper.

'I'll take you home,' he says.

Chapter 5

The studio is dark. The curtains have stayed half-drawn since Mom's last summer here, and the air is thick, stale, as though no one has opened a window for years. I switch on the yellow bulb dangling from the ceiling, but it doesn't help much—its weak glow pools in the centre of the room, leaving the corners to the shadows. The shelves, once crowded with paints and brushes, are now warped with my books. Their spines jut out unevenly, some lying sideways, some stacked in piles that tilt like ruins.

Gaius follows me quietly, sandals in his hand so as not to make noise. He coughs once, brushing the cobwebs from the doorframe.

'Somebody really lived in this place?' he mutters, half in wonder, half in pity.

I climb the ladder, the iron cold and sticky beneath my palm, and tug the wooden box from the highest shelf. Dust explodes in a little cloud, catching the weak light before it scatters into the gloom. The smell of soot and mould clings to the box.

Inside—relics.

Ghostly, ordinary, grotesque.

Napkins smeared with deep crimson stains. Lipstick, not ketchup. A sickly-sweet, rancid smell hits us at once, like old perfume mixed with rot. Gaius pinches his nose.

'This is disgusting!'

I don't flinch. Instead, I press one napkin close, as though memory might seep through the fabric.

'They smell like her,' I whisper. 'Someone wanted to keep her close, so he stole what was closest to her.'

One by one, we spill the contents onto the floor. A hairbrush with strands of Mom's dark hair knotted in it. Paper cups, their rims still bearing faint prints of lipstick. Bottles with dried paint, stuck lids. Pens chewed to their ends.

These are the remains of a woman people called famous. Reduced to trash—and yet I can feel her here more than anywhere else.

The visitor register lies heavily in my bag. I pull it out, laying it on the dust-coated floorboards. My fingers tremble as I heat the knife over the weak flame of the candle, the smell of burning metal sharp in my nose. The correction tape lifts smoothly under the blade.

Lorenzo.

Gaius stiffens. His shadow on the wall seems taller, looming. 'Why would he erase his name in the visiting book?'

I nod, throat dry. My mind circles back—Mom's funeral, Lorenzo's absence, the note in the rehab drawer. The handwriting that is not Mom's. The threads knot together. We search again, slower this time. It's then I find it—an envelope glued stubbornly to the casket's bottom. My nails peel it away. A folded sheet, the ink still sharp, letters slanting in haste:

> *I'm sorry for taking what was most precious to you. Your beloved portrait. I just wanted to hurt you the way you hurt me. But in the end, you win. Returning all this because it belongs to you.*

It was in this casket that I had found Mom's lost portrait. The handwriting is the same as the one in the gallery note. The same as the shadow we've been circling around.

'Lorenzo,' Gaius whispers, as if saying it aloud might summon him here.

The air in the studio grows heavier. I watch a spider crawl across the edge of the casket, slipping into the pile of stained napkins. I don't move. My hands are full with the brush, strands of her hair still clinging, fragile as threads of smoke.

I whisper to the shadows, to the books, to the ghosts in the room: Why did he hurt her?

Chapter 6

'If we believe the letter was from Lorenzo—' Gaius draws his eyebrows into a single dark line. His face is serious, and for a heartbeat, I lose the thread of his words.

He looks beautiful. Like one of Mom's paintings. Not the sketches, not the half-finished canvases, but the one life-size mural right across from me—the Roman emperor. The one whose gaze followed me whenever I crept in as a child, clutching at the smell of oil and dust.

Gaius has that same stillness, that same command. His cheekbones rise like careful brushstrokes of light, outlined in charcoal. The water in his eyes catches what little light the room offers, sparkling the way Mom's blues always did on canvas—never flat, always alive, always shifting. Even the shadows clinging to him seem painted, blended carefully to deepen the brightness at the centre of him.

Looking at him is like standing before one of her portraits: I want to step closer, study the texture, yet I feel I'll never truly touch the mystery of what she placed on him.

'Mari, are you listening?' His hand waves before my face, breaking the spell.

'Yes. Yes.'

'I was saying—if we believe that Lorenzo secretly loved your mother, it makes no sense why he would kill her?'

I think of a book I read a long time ago, as I waited for Mom to be done with her painting. She was preparing the base layer for the canvas. Brown. The book in my hand was an old copy of Shakespeare that Lorenzo had gifted me.

Desdemona is sleeping when Othello kisses her before smothering her. He wanted to kill her while she still loved him.

I gasp, 'Sometimes love is exactly the reason people kill. Mom never loved him. She could never love him.'

'Did she tell you that?'

She hadn't. I tell Gaius, 'Mom only shared everything she felt about anyone with Solo; maybe she could help us.'

Gaius scratches his forehead.

'I'd better not enter that place in Rome,' he says, half smiling.

Chapter 7

Solo is humming softly to an old Hindi song—the kind that carries both longing and comfort—while dusting the brass lamp in her living room when I enter. The place smells of sandalwood polish, neat as always, cushions aligned in their corners. She uses the sleeve of a faded T-shirt as a rag, wiping with the same tenderness as if she were tending to someone's face.

'I've been taking the medications,' I announce quickly, almost rehearsed. 'And sleeping absolutely well, Aunt Solo.'

Her eyes flick toward me, a look that tells me she knows I'm lying. But she lets me continue.

'I'm thinking more and more about Mother,' I say, lowering myself onto the sofa. 'Talking about her makes me feel calm.'

Solo sets the lamp down and turns, her hands on her hips.

'When Mom was seeing you, was it because of Lorenzo?' I ask as casually as I could.

'I told you before—he wasn't the only reason,' she says.

'I often heard the two quarrelling. Even when he visited home, they were always on tenterhooks.'

Solo puts away the rag. The corners of her mouth lift, then fall. 'Yes. Their relationship started beautifully. In fact, there was even a rumour they were… more than friends, you know. Nonsense!' She laughs once, sharp and quick, then her face hardens. 'They were great friends. And he loved you like his own. But yes, it scarred over the years, their bond.'

'Scarred to the extent that he could not even attend Mom's funeral?' For the first time, I notice the faint wrinkles spidering around her eyes as she straightens.

'He sent his apologies. He had invested so much in Ira's exhibition in Rome; he could not risk letting it fall apart. Especially after Ira refused to go.'

'Mom refused?'

'Yes. You were there, Mari. The morning before the exhibition—24th September—Ira announced she would not exhibit anymore. Wouldn't even sell her work. She said she'd lost an old artwork, but of course that wasn't the reason. She still wanted to paint. She began a new painting that very day, remember?'

I remember. I do. Mom had set her easel with a small canvas, three feet square. I kept asking if I could make her a cup of tea. She always felt better with a cup of tea. Donna wasn't there, so I wanted to take care of her. She kept shaking her head, brushing me off. She was in an old gown—once white, now a battlefield of colours, stains from years of living against the canvas. Her face was wet with tears, and her hands trembled with each stroke. I brought my book to sit beside her. She hadn't eaten, hadn't sipped water—only painted as though the world could only be held together that way.

'But why didn't she want to exhibit?' I whisper.

Solo seems to drift somewhere far from the room.

'Your mother was tired. Painting for her was like breathing for you and me. She was tired of making a spectacle of it. The commercial demands, the collectors, the changes they asked of her palette… it disappointed her deeply.'

She sighs, blinking as if pulled back from memory. 'But why are you asking all this, Mari?'

Tears blur my vision. 'I feel I didn't know Mom at all.'

Solo crosses the room and lifts my chin with her fingers, the faint smell of cigarettes clinging to her skin.

'Every person is full of mysteries no one can uncover in entirety. Stop running your memory in circles, Marigold. She loved you with her whole heart—that's what you must carry.'

I swallow. 'Was Lorenzo fine with her decision?'

'Lorenzo gave twenty years of his life to shape Ira Lall as the world remembers her today. Could anyone in his place be happy?'

'So he wasn't?'

'A man will never understand the complexities of a woman's heart. He was angry. In fact, they had a long argument the afternoon of the day she—' Solo pauses.

'When he went to see her at the rehab? September 24th morning?' I ask.

'No. He met her at home the same day, but briefly. She told me so on the phone.'

'I was home the entire time. How did I not notice?'

'He met her in the garden briefly. She said he had somewhere to go.'

Solo abruptly excuses herself and leaves the room, as if something urgent has struck her mind. I let my eyes wander around her shelves while she is gone. One catches my attention—an entire row of white spines. On closer inspection, I see that they are her calendar registers. Lined up by year, neat and disciplined, like she had stored away time itself.

Unlike me, Solo carried her neatness not just in the polished order of her home but in the calm precision of her thoughts. Sometimes she reminds me of Elinor Dashwood from *Sense and Sensibility*. Everything about her is arranged, measured, admirable—yet never cold.

When she returns, she is carrying a tray with two small bowls of what looks like pudding, cashews and blueberries sprinkled generously on top. She hands me one and sits down beside me. Closer than I'd prefer. She lifts the spoon and places it into my mouth. The pudding is sharp and sweet at once, exactly how I like it.

She watches me finish the bowl with quiet contentment, as if feeding me has eased something in her. Then she speaks.

'Mari, I've found a perfect house help for you. She's Indian, can come by for a few hours of cooking and cleaning.'

I shake my head, 'I told you, I'll wait for Donna.'

Her voice softens, almost hesitant, 'Mari, there's something you should know.'

A knot forms in my stomach because of the way she said it. 'What?'

'After you told me you couldn't reach her… I went to her house.'

I stare. 'You went to Florence?'

She nods. 'Yes. Remember the train tickets you found in my bag? I met her brother there.' Solo looks down at the empty bowl in her hand. Her fingers tighten around it. 'And I didn't want to tell you this, but…'

I lean forward, my pulse quickening. 'What is it now?'

'I went to request her to come back because I thought you needed her now more than any other time.'

'And she refused?'

Donna was the only woman who had wiped my tears and shed a few with me when Mom was far away, creating her masterpieces. I remember the softness of her bosom as I sank into her fleece coat.

'Donna had taken her own life,' Solo says flatly, as if it isn't death she is talking about.

'When?'

'They won't tell me that.'

I feel my throat tighten. It is impossible for me to speak.

Somewhere in my mind, a sentence closed itself, and I knew I would not be able to turn the page for a long time.

Chapter 8

It is late in the evening, but I stop by the library, hoping to see Gaius. Around eight, he comes.

'I thought you'd gone home,' he says softly. 'But I wanted to check in once.'

I don't feel like going home, I tell him. I want to ask him for coffee at the café next door, but it is always awkward being in public with Gaius. People stare at him, and then at me.

It is better in the books, I suppose. Where love makes lovers equal—one. Just as Jane Eyre once claimed before God's feet, when she said she and Rochester stood as equals, spirit to spirit.

But in real life, it is so unusual for a twenty-one-year-old woman to love a man decades older. As if love really is to be measured in years and not heartbeats.

I cannot fathom the world at times—the world that lies outside the pages, I mean.

'How did it go? With Solo?' Gaius asks, his voice low, bringing me back to where I never quite belong.

He guides me between the shelves. The aroma of old paper consumes me, and yet, I feel whole again. This is what I live for—Gaius and this place. We sit on the cold floor, the tall wooden spines looming over us. The library is dark except for the pale spill of light from the streetlamp outside.

'He met Mom at home on September 24,' I say.

Gaius shifts closer, his shoulder brushing mine. 'If Lorenzo was meant to meet Ira at home, why would he visit her at the rehab that same morning? And why would Sherry mask his entry?'

Our knees touch. A quiet current runs through me at the nearness, the way the silence seems to bend around us. I feel him searching for my hand, and then his fingers close lightly around mine. In that instant, I know exactly how Elizabeth must have felt when she touched Mr Darcy's hand during the dance—an ordinary touch enough to upend the world.

'Maybe he did it on his own,' I whisper.

'It's hard to miss a tape.' His thumb makes slow circles on my skin, as if without thought.

'Perhaps he bribed Sherry. Maybe he tried in the morning and failed, so he returned later. He saw you and your father there, made an excuse, and left early.'

'Or maybe…' I hesitate, tracing the dusty spine of a book beside me with my free hand.

'…he waited. Waited for us to leave, or for Mom to be alone. Then came back and poisoned her with her own drugs.'

'But you said you were there the whole time. Even when she was painting in the drawing room, you said you were there watching her.'

'I must have dozed off while reading.' I feel his grip tighten gently, steadying me.

'Dad was with her then. But he left for some errand, and when I woke, Mom was crying. She was painting flowers directly onto the canvas, straight from the spatula, in thick oil paints. When I tried to talk to her, she said she wanted tea. So I went into the kitchen to make it for her.'

For a moment, we say nothing. The dark shelves rise around us like walls of silence. His thumb keeps moving across my hand, making circles.

'Perhaps it was then.' My words break into a hush, 'That Lorenzo slipped in through the garden… gave her something. Because shortly after that…'

I stop, the weight of the unfinished sentence pressing against my chest. Gaius says nothing, only lets his hand remain around mine, and in that stillness, I feel both undone and held.

After Gaius leaves, I finally step out into the night. The air is heavy, the streetlamps dim, but I walk quickly to the bus stop. On the ride home, I scroll through the photographs from the exhibition a year ago. My mother's paintings glow in them, alive and defiant. But my eyes catch only Lorenzo. He isn't smiling in a single frame. His mouth is pressed shut, his gaze almost elsewhere. Perhaps he was scared. Or guilty. Or just sad. I cannot tell.

My phone dies in my hand.

At home, I search through drawers for a charger and stumble upon something else—Mom's laptop, tucked beneath the table, still resting in its charging station as though waiting for her return. A thin film of dust clings to the lid. I wipe it off with my palm.

The screen glows to life, and the lock greets me like a challenge. I hazard a guess: *Marigold*. The letters fall into place, and the screen opens without hesitation; a shiver runs down my spine.

On the desktop, I see a folder titled: Ira Lall—Full Story.

Her email is still signed in. Rows of subject lines blink up at me—ad agencies, galleries, fan letters. I skim them all, though each one feels like trespassing, like pressing my ear against a door never meant to be opened.

And then I see it.

A starred mail from a certain Fiza Ahmed, New Delhi.

I type her name in the search bar. The inbox floods with her. Dozens of emails, one after another, stacked like hidden chapters of a book I didn't know existed.

I scroll to the very first one, dated 22 February 2017. Sent by Mom.

The mail opens.

My mother's words spill out, fragile and heavy at once.

Chapter 9

Fiza,

I am writing to you after holding myself back for years.

Time has not softened this need. It has only taught me how to live beside it.

I had never been nice to you, but how could I be? You were the stranger who got more time from my mother than I ever could. She gave you her hours, attention, care—things she rationed carefully with me. The day my fate was decided to leave Delhi, I decided to never think of my mother ever again, but her presence in my life is like water. Colourless, tasteless and yet, takes up the most place in my being.

Here, I have created a wonderful life for myself with my husband. Wonderful, let us both believe it for a while. We have a daughter, Marigold. Marigold often reminds me of my own childhood, and it takes a lot of effort not to bring my own grief upon her. For so long, I feared becoming a mother like the one I had, but I have had help, thankfully, to be able to navigate through that. In giving her all that I never received, I think I am finally able to begin healing the child in me. It's tough, I must admit.

There is so much venom in me for my mother that I curse myself when I think of her, and yet, I think of her every moment with love. I don't know if I want a closure from her, as my therapist says, or an apology, because I doubt she can even give me either of those.

There are days when I think of her in my moments with my own daughter, and how I wish things were different.

I miss her so much. It's also the reason I am writing to you.

Can you tell me how she is? Stupid to think, but does she ever talk about me?

Ira

I sit back in the chair, numb. My mother's voice stares back at me from the screen, but it is not the voice I knew. This is a younger, frightened, desperate Ira, still entangled in a mother–daughter war I never even knew existed. She has written about me, too—Marigold—as though I were her second chance at love, her fragile hope to be different.

For the first time, I begin to wonder: *Had I ever really known her at all?*

Dear Ira,

I cannot adequately describe how moved I was to receive your email. After you left Delhi, I searched for you for nearly two years. I went to your home, but your father told me he could not share your whereabouts. He said there were very few people left in the world he trusted, and that distance was, in his mind, a form of protection. Given all your family had already done for me, I did not go against his wishes.

It was only months before he passed away that I brought your grandmother to live with me. By then, she had already begun to forget the world she once knew—including, painfully, you. Alzheimer's had already taken hold.

In 2004, I finally found you on the internet. I followed your work from afar. I am proud of what you have built. I had always believed you were meant for something larger than the life you were handed. I tell the children here about you—how you once painted in a closet, and how far that instinct has carried you.

Your mother passed away quietly in her sleep in 2014. There were no warnings, no spectacle—only silence. It felt, in some ways, like the conclusion she had been moving toward for much of her life.

I hesitate to place my grief beside yours, yet I feel it is necessary to tell you what we shared. Perhaps it will allow you to see your mother from a different angle—not to absolve her, but to understand her.

On the night of the accident, when your sister Aarya died, it was not only you who lost a mother. I lost mine as well. My mother—my only parent—died that same night.

You would never have known this. I learned it much later myself. Your mother was driving the car. She was inebriated.

In hindsight, I believe her care for me was an act of penance. Your father and uncle shielded her from the police, but guilt does not require a courtroom to sentence us. Now that we are both mothers, you will understand the scale of such torment: to live knowing one child has died by your hand, and another has been left behind. I do not believe there is a harsher punishment.

I wish you could see what I saw. She was not a monstrous woman, Ira. She was a woman undone by remorse. I hope that, in time, you may find a way to forgive her, as I did—not because she deserved it, but because it allowed me to live.

Growing up in a children's home and later writing the lives of countless others has taught me this: We rarely receive everything we want. Yet in what appears empty, we often already possess what we need.

There are rumours that my mother deliberately stepped in front of your mother's car, believing the compensation from a wealthy family might secure my future. I do not know if this is true. There is, mercifully, no way for me to ever know.

Tell me about yourself. Beyond your work—which I admire greatly—there is so little of you in public view. I would like to know the woman behind the paintings.

Please write back.

With warmth,
Fiza Ahmed

Fiza,

I am writing to you from the edge of exhaustion and hope—both equally familiar to me now.

When pain grows this large, it becomes difficult to imagine another's, let alone be generous with it. I cannot decide whether what you have told me has shocked me or relieved me. I have lived with grief for so long that it has dissolved into my blood and bones; it is no longer something I carry, but something I am made of. Nothing you say can truly palliate it.

I live only with one quiet promise to myself: that I will not give my daughter even a trace of what was given to me. And yet, there are days when I fear that all I pass on is my own unhealed history.

We suffer in silence, believing silence to be dignity, unaware that it is also an inheritance. If only we had known how to speak. If only my mother had been able to place her pain in my hands. Perhaps then we might have shared something other than absence. My only mercy was the inscriptions I wrote on the back of my paintings as I spoke to her—thin threads that kept me tethered to my sister when everything else fell away.

I do not know what to do with those now. My body has begun to betray me in small, insistent ways, and since your last message I find myself thinking—actively, almost desperately—about speaking. About placing words where there has only been containment.

There are parts of my life I want my daughter to know. Parts my husband believes I buried long ago in the debris of the work I left behind in India. He does not understand that those memories are not buried at all—they are dissolved in me, like salt in water. I hid them out of shame, believing concealment might hasten healing. I am no longer certain that it does. I am tired of running from what persists.

If there is anyone to whom I wish to tell my story—whole, not in fragments—it is my Marigold. And perhaps, through her, to anyone who might recognise themselves in it and feel less alone.

I have read how you write women—how carefully, how without spectacle. I am known, even admired, for what I do, yet I do not believe I resemble the women you write about. They seem braver than I have ever been.

Still, I ask this of you: would you write my story? All of it. Stitched into the spine of a book, with its colours and its shadows intact. I know no other way to place the truth before my daughter, who reads as naturally as you and I draw breath.

I am sending you scanned copies of the words I wrote to my sister. They contain the marrow of my childhood.

My story is now yours.

With love,
Ira

Dearest Ira,

Some stories can only be understood where they first took root.

Perhaps it is time you returned to where yours began.

Fiza

Dearest Fiza,

I am afraid I cannot return to Delhi. To go back would only reopen wounds I have spent a lifetime learning how to live around. Some places do not loosen their hold on us; they only wait.

But I would be glad to host you here in Rome. The air is gentle this season, softened by light, and perhaps you and your family could use a pause from the weight of things. The city is kinder when one does not ask it to explain itself.

We also have a villa in Pisa, tended by a caretaker whose devotion has kept a rose garden alive against time. It reminds me, always, of my grandmother—of patience, and of things that survive without needing to be spoken of. You could stay there. It would allow us the discretion I feel this meeting requires.

There is much I wish to share with you. Some of it has been waiting a very long time.

For now, I would like the matter of my biography to remain between us—unseen, unspoken—until it is ready to step into the light on its own terms.

With love,
Ira

Dear Ira,

My son would be overjoyed at the thought of a holiday—it has been far too long since I have given him that gift. I am perpetually entangled in my work, and perhaps this is precisely what the three of us need: a pause and a change of air.

My husband is especially moved by the idea of seeing your work in person; to him, it feels nothing short of a pilgrimage.

We will meet you in July.

With love,
Fiza

Chapter 10

The next morning, Dad wakes me. I must have fallen asleep in the studio; the table has branded its edge into my cheek, leaving a thin welt like a scar that isn't earned.

Breakfast waits for me on the table—boiled eggs and wheat pancakes. Dad has shaved, even cut his hair short. He looks good, almost too good, like a man rehearsing normalcy.

He watches me eat for a while, then says, as though clearing his throat of something thick, 'Matteo and I have been thinking… about turning your mother's gallery into an institute for art and mental health.'

The food catches in my mouth. It is too dry, or maybe I have forgotten how to swallow.

'You'd tear down her gallery?' I say, 'She had only just—'

'It's been a year, Mari.' He looks at me steadily, the way people look at locked doors they don't know how to open.

'Did you ask Lorenzo?' I say.

'Lorenzo's moving to Paris. He's with some French institute now.'

'Oh.'

Dad hesitates, 'But we wouldn't do anything without you. We thought maybe you could… oversee it.'

'I can't,' I say quickly. 'The writing workshop, and the novel—it's too much.' The lie slides out neat and polished. I have practised it in a hundred small ways already.

His eyes fall on the tea cooling between us. He sighs, so quietly it might have been a thought escaping rather than a sound.

I roll the rest of the eggs inside the pancake, press it flat in my palm, and stand. 'It's the interactive session today. I have to go.'

I go straight to the attic and find them—canvases rolled and stiffened by time, a life deliberately folded shut. Behind each one, a word, a sentence. A story she chose not to carry forward. I read them again and again until my mother comes alive before me: a young girl attempting to paint not just flowers but something larger, Cleopatra and Julius Caesar, unafraid of desire or destruction.

The inscriptions repeat, in fragments, the same story as my mother's biography—the one Fiza had written. Only now do I begin to notice the girl my mother mentioned again and again, the one who slipped so seamlessly into my parents' sacred sanctuary.

Chapter 11

Solo is in the kitchen when I enter her house. A tall woman with a streak of white in her hair brushes past me, faintly smiling as she leaves. The air carries her perfume—sharp and expensive. It clings to the hallway walls as if refusing to be forgotten.

I set my bag on the cabinet above the shoe rack, the wood warm under my palm, and walk toward the living room. The books are piled carelessly, their spines bent, like tired shoulders. Between the stacks, I look for a diary. I open it. On the first page, her name stares back at me in clean, deliberate ink.

I feel stupid, as though I've stumbled into a room I have lived in all my life but never noticed the windows. She appears then, apron tied neatly around her waist, hair coiled high into a bun that sharpens her face. Her gold danglers catch the shards of sun as she moves.

'Hello, Sonam,' I pronounce her name like a verdict, the pride of an officer uncovering stolen evidence.

She arches one brow, lifts the glass on the table, and sips water. It leaves a wet ring on the wood. 'Hello, Marigold. Why are you acting so strange?'

The steadiness in her voice weakens me. 'You were practically my family. My only aunt in this country. Why do you think I never knew your name until today?'

She steps closer, cautious, like someone approaching fire. 'I didn't know that you didn't. I'm sure it wasn't on purpose…'

'I was never told. Not your name. Not how you met my parents. Or I should say—my father.'

Her face drains of expression, so unlike her.

I sit on the floral chair. The fabric has faded roses that I remember being bright. She takes the seat across from me, hesitating as if it might betray her.

'Rings a bell, Aunt Solo?' My words feel bitter in my mouth.

I place Mom's biography on the table between us. Their papers look fragile, as if the air might tear them.

Her gaze flickers, then softens, 'I have read it too. Your mother asked me to.'

'Out of every place in the world, why did you choose Rome?' I ask.

'If you'd ever felt what it was like to be entirely alone—no friend, no family—you'd understand my compulsions,' she exhales. 'To be honest with you, Mari, I came here for your father.'

'Do you still love him? Is that why you never married?'

'Yes.' Her voice doesn't waver. 'Your father is the only man I ever loved. But age teaches you that love isn't always about possession. Love has shades and textures, Mari, like your mother's paintings. Sometimes love is letting someone go. When we were young in Delhi, I barely cared for your mother. But it was impossible to know her and not... love her. That was my love for your parents.'

Tears trail down my face as I say, 'Was it easy for her? Seeing you and—'

'Nihal loved Ira with all his heart. In fact, I don't think he ever came close to loving me in the slightest way. He simply didn't know it back then.'

Her fingers trace the rim of her glass. 'Your mother came to Italy with a broken heart. It's one thing to be a friend—which she was to your father, and a loving one—but it's another to be a wife. There is no feeling worse than believing you're loved only out of duty, a promise given to someone. For a long time, she thought she was a punishment handed to Nihal by her father—that his heart belonged to... someone else.'

'You,' I whisper.

'Yes. But that wasn't true. Your father has a heart of gold. I've known him since he was sixteen, and even then, the only thing he ever feared was being unfaithful.' Solo lets her gaze drift around the room, as though the walls might hold the answers. 'Their love—though rooted in childhood—did not truly bloom until after you were born. Ira began to heal through her art. She painted obsessively, cocooning herself in the work. It was her way of unveiling. Nihal carried her paintings into the world. At a design exhibition in Milan, he met Lorenzo and introduced him to Ira. Lorenzo saw her potential at once. She was working in semi-abstracts then, and he fought hard to secure her a solo show.'

A quiet warmth passes over Solo's face, the kind that only memory can bring.

'She refused to collaborate with anyone, and thankfully so. Within months, Ira was a sensation. Collectors called her paintings *limited editions*, because by then, she painted less and less. At home, she prepared canvases—one after another—and abandoned them, spent hours with you… and drank. Rehab was the only place she flourished. It was only when she was alone that she painted. Healed.'

Solo pauses. The air between us is heavy, like a storm about to break.

'What about Dad?' My voice comes out weak.

'Your father found Matteo. He would not send Ira just anywhere. He struggled, Mari. Ira consumed him. Her addiction demanded more and more of him every day.'

'Was she always…'

'Yes.' Her eyes flicker with something like shame or regret.

'That part of her life never changed. Your father had to guard her—keep her from drinking, from buying alcohol. It drained him. He could never give himself fully to his own work, though he had longed for it since childhood.'

'Wasn't he frustrated?'

Sadness curls around her lips like the aftertaste of an old song. Solo smiles, 'Nihal had a gift. He could transform frustration into tenderness for the people he loved. But Mari… I think the void of not chasing his own dreams did gnaw at him. But then you were born.'

I cover my mouth with my hands and cry, the sound trapped somewhere between my chest and my palms. The tears fall anyway, slipping through the cracks of my fingers. For a moment, the room tilts, and all I see is the outline of Solo's face blurred into the floral wallpaper behind her. She doesn't move, doesn't try to console me—only watches, as if she has been waiting for this to happen all along.

'With you, it was as if he was handed a new purpose. A reason to begin, again.'

I stare at my hands. 'I feel like I've never truly understood my father.'

Solo leans back, her voice softer than I've ever heard it, 'It's never too late, Marigold.'

Chapter 12

On my way back home, I stop at the rehab. Something gnaws at me—a new possibility I haven't dared to name aloud. What if Mom was overdosed here, in this place, by Lorenzo himself, and only then sent home so it looked natural?

But then—I remember opening the door for her that afternoon, speaking to her. She had seemed fine. Anxious, yes, about the lost sketch, but alive. Present.

Sherry is in the common room, hunched over a pizza box. Grease stains her fingers, and she licks them absently, as if it doesn't matter who is watching. But that's Sherry. Two cans of Coke sweat on the table in front of her.

'Collecting memories again?' she says, asking me to sit.

I look around. 'Exploring the future museum, like you said, and the artist who lived here.'

'Your Mom was usually quiet when she stayed here,' Sherry begins before I can even speak, as if she expected my visit. 'She barely ate, slept at odd hours—mostly evenings. Sometimes, I'd find her sitting naked on the floor, staring at an old sketch in her hand. But mostly she painted. Day and night. Like she had no sense of the world outside. Once, she told me she tasted something different when she painted. Said it was like floating above the world. Like freedom.'

I swallow. 'Did you ever feel she could… do something like that?'

'Kill herself?' Sherry's tone is flat, almost rehearsed. She doesn't blink. 'Yes.'

'She spoke of it often,' Sherry says, tearing at the crust of her slice, her nails digging into the bread. 'Said the thought was always there, waiting. Sometimes she even woke with a plan of how she'd do it. But I'm positive she couldn't have. If she wanted to, she would've done it long ago.' Her eyes flick up to mine, too quick, before sliding away. Then, lowering her voice, she leans in, 'Should I tell you something?'

I nod.

'She was ecstatic the morning she left. Like she'd finally cracked a code. She had tea with me, can you believe? Talked about her initial paintings in Delhi. She said she only painted flowers back then. Then she ordered them using my phone. A bouquet of lotuses. Said they meant happy beginnings.' Sherry lets the words hang, almost savouring them, and then gives a small, strange smile before picking up the can.

'Did you tell anyone this?' I ask.

'I tried telling Matteo, but my father wouldn't listen. He'd already made up his mind. Easier to believe someone like your mother would kill herself. The police, too. No one wanted to know otherwise.'

'Who keeps the register here?'

'Mimi. But she's on maternity leave now.'

'Was she here when my mother stayed last? September 2017?'

Sherry's fingers twitch at her Coke can. 'Yes. What is it you want to know?'

'I want to understand the conversation my mother had with Lorenzo. The day he came.'

I notice a shadow cross her face, quick and cold. She licks her lips, fiddles with her hair, and finally says, 'He never met your mother in the rehab. Not on her last day here. September 24, right?'

I shake my head.

It is too neat. Too deliberate. Sherry is lying. She knows more than she will ever admit. And in that moment, I feel it—she is complicit. Not just covering for Lorenzo. Choosing to.

Her smile flickers back, brittle as glass. 'Do you want a Coke?' she asks, almost lightly.

I force a polite refusal and make an excuse to leave. My head is heavy with the weight of her words, of her silence. I need to find Gaius. I can't carry this alone. Where is he?

Chapter 13

Dad is in his bedroom, the lamp too bright for the hour. The magazine lies in his hands like a prop. He isn't reading it. Just holding on. His thumb slides back and forth over the gloss as if something might rise out of it if he keeps touching it long enough.

I sit in the chair by the wall. My knees drawn in. A strange shame presses at my ribs. I don't know why. Maybe because I can't begin. Can't find the way to talk to my father anymore. He seems to me like a language I have forgotten.

This is the man who used to wait at the bakery for cinnamon rolls—the sticky kind that left sugar on your fingers. Who clapped too loudly at my dance rehearsals. The man who gave me my first library card and taught me that books were not just stories but rooms one could enter and make home. When I said I wanted to own *Little Women*, he found me every edition he could—clothbound, leatherbound, hardbacks in faded jackets and gilded spines—lined up like variations of the same song.

He glances at me and tilts the magazine. 'That's me on the cover.'

I lean forward. It is difficult to recognise him—his face unlined, eyes free of the shadows I know too well. He looks distant in the photograph. Almost happy, but not quite. As if the smile had been borrowed for a moment and returned once the shutter clicked.

'Do you want tea?' I ask.

'Only if you'll have it with me,' he says.

So I fill two mugs, and we sit side by side with *Tom and Jerry* flickering on the TV. The room smells faintly of ginger and old times. The windows rattle in the night wind. Between the cartoon chases and slapstick crashes, we begin to talk. About her. The woman we both loved so deeply. The woman whose memory flowed through our blood.

He told me how he first saw her in her father's car; how she was always curious about the stories he was reading. About *Anna Karenina*.

And how she loved to paint—and loved him—long before she had said it.

And for the first time, he tells me how there had been another—Aarya.

I listen as though his words are my first lullabies, not telling him about the things I know. Even the things he doesn't.

After a while, his words drift into the stillness, and he falls asleep sitting up, his chin tucked to his chest. I notice how his breathing is uneven.

In that quiet, it sounds like the low wail of someone much younger. The boy from the magazine, who once had his own dreams before he was shipped away to steady the life of a girl meant to drown.

I realise then how my longing for my mother has taken up all the space in me, that I have forgotten to grieve my father.

Later, in my room, as I try to sleep, a memory slips in—not of my parents this time, but of Donna. We were in Pisa, at one of Mom's exhibitions. She stood before a canvas of two lovers by the Nile. Abstract in oils by my mother. Music and food were woven faintly into the painted air. Donna's eyes were filled with tears.

'It's a happy scene,' I had told her.

'It isn't,' she said. Her voice was soft but certain. It reminded her of a young Greek who drowned in the Nile—Antinous. His lover, the Roman emperor Hadrian, had fallen into a grief so bottomless it seemed to remake the world. He built a city for him—Antinoöpolis—stone and streets in memory of a body lost to water.

A colossal marble head of Antinous Mondragone is housed at the Louvre in Paris, Donna shook her head gently as she told me. 'Art isn't the emotion the artist puts into it. It's what you find in yourself while looking at it. It has the power to transport you to another universe.'

Of course, Donna knew all of this. I think of it now. She had studied history in Florence when she first met Mom. She carried stories inside her like relics, and she gave them away with such ease that you barely realised she was changing the way you looked at things.

My mother had painted the scene, but it was Donna who taught me how to read it like a novel. Since that day, every brushstroke of Mom's artwork has become layered—half her, half me. And a whole lot of the story I bring to it.

My Donna.

How could Solo think I could replace her?

I make a note to myself: I will visit her grave, bring flowers, something bright—like the first chapter of a new life. Lotuses.

When the street outside falls still, I open Mom's laptop. The glow lights the room blue as I search for tickets to Pisa.

Chapter 14

Mom's inbox has been open since the last time I checked her emails. Out of restlessness more than suspicion, I click on the deleted folder.

Most of it is the usual detritus—angry notes from gallery owners, accusing her of deception. They say she copied the Renaissance masters, passing their centuries of devotion through her brush, only to sell them at staggering prices. They say she stole stories that were not hers, painting over history until it bent toward her.

And then—an email from Fiza. September 17th, 2017. Deleted. Why?

Dear Ira,

There is something I must tell you. I could write it here, but it is better said face-to-face. I will be travelling to Cannes and will stop in Rome toward the end of the month. Please keep this private. Do not tell anyone—not even your family.

Love,
Fiza

I sit back, staring. She had been weaving my mother's life into her own writing for years—there could have been countless reasons for their meetings. But why the secrecy? Why does the weight of silence press into every line she wrote?

I type her name—Fiza Ahmed—into the search bar.

Photographs flood the screen: stages, podiums, cameras, her hair catching light as if it were always made for it. Awards, charity dinners, and colleges where she smiled at rows of young faces. It is a life written in applause. My eyes burn from staring too long, from scrolling through a version of her that seems infinite.

But one headline stops me:

From Absence to Inheritance: The Story of an Orphan Named Fiza Ahmed

I click.

The story spills out: a godmother, wealthy beyond measure, who had left her a decaying two-hundred-year-old mansion in Old Delhi. In the photograph, Fiza stands with her usual poise, but behind her, the house sags like an exhausted body—arches cracked, shutters half-closed like tired eyes.

Then the line that hollows me out:

Shockwaves followed the death of celebrated artist Ira Sagg in Italy, as her ₹150-crore mansion was revealed to have been bequeathed to Fiza Ahmed, an orphan adopted by Ira's mother. Mandira Sagg's will named both girls as equal heirs, with a clause stating that in the event of one's death, the surviving heir would inherit the entire estate, a revelation now fuelling speculation around the circumstances of Sagg's final days abroad.

I hear myself whisper, 'Gaius… are you thinking what I'm thinking?'

~

I want to ask Gaius where he has been, but I fear the answer will carry his wife with it, and I cannot bear her presence in my thoughts. We meet at six in the morning, the air still damp with night. Only one café is open this early. That is why Gaius agrees—fewer eyes, fewer whispers.

'You asked about her compulsion,' he says as we settle into the corner. 'Here it is. In the end, there are only two reasons people kill—love, or money.'

I shake my head. 'I can't believe she would be capable of that.'

'Did you call her?'

'Twice. She didn't answer.'

He opens his novel, and I pretend to open mine. But my gaze betrays me. The years have carved themselves into his forehead, yet the dawn light softens him, painting his features in muted pastels. No matter how abandoned I feel in the world, his presence, steady and unhurried, is a kind of shelter.

I look around and see that only one other figure lingers inside the café: a woman in a red scarf patterned with yellow seahorses. She has been turning the menu over and over without ordering, refusing the server twice. She seems to be waiting—for someone's mother, a forgotten friend, or maybe a lover. I wonder what story keeps her here at this hour.

Fifteen minutes later, the café door opens. A man in a grey suit walks in. Even from across the room, his silhouette catches me—something about the slope of his shoulders, the way he carries his frame.

I freeze.

Lorenzo.

Chapter 15

The woman straightens, smooths her hair, and rises to greet him. She kisses his cheek as she has rehearsed it.

I have never known Lorenzo to know someone in Rome. I lean toward Gaius, who is still immersed in Homer. I tell him in whispers. His grip tightens on the book. He urges me to leave before Lorenzo sees us.

I sign the bill with quick strokes—the café owner knows me, and they will collect everything at the end of the month. Outside, I ask Gaius to take the long way. Curiosity drags at me like a tide. Again, I feel someone's eyes on us. Like someone is following Gaius and me.

Gaius must feel it too. Abruptly, he kisses me goodbye.

I keep walking with the same feeling. I look back. No one.

From the wide café windows, I see him. And her.

He isn't with a stranger.

He is with Sherry.

The truth unfolds all at once, cruel and bright.

'She was the one,' I whisper. 'Sherry was the one who erased the evidence of Lorenzo visiting my mother in the rehab on the morning of September 24.'

Chapter 16

I had only just opened my book when a soft knock came at the library door.

'Marigold?'

It was the woman from the magazine office. Without her glasses, her face seemed younger, almost uncertain. Still, I recognised her immediately.

'You don't know me but—'

'I know who you are,' I said, closing my book. 'You interviewed my mother. You've been following me for a while now.'

She lowered her gaze. 'Yes. But only to talk to you.'

She brushed dust from the chair opposite mine and sat down. No one had ever sat there but Gaius. And once, Solo.

Her smile was tight, almost rehearsed. 'It was my honour to be the first person allowed into the world of Ira Lall. My first interview. I was trembling, but she… your mother was kind. She said I could ask her anything, and she would answer.'

'How was it?' I ask, swallowing.

'Just as she promised. Beautiful.' Lina's voice thinned, then steadied. 'But the response to that article… I didn't expect it. Fifteen thousand new followers. Job offers. Suddenly, everyone wanted me. My mother and I decided we would send her a gift. A crystal brush. But before we could… the news came.'

'She died,' I say, flatly.

She pressed her palm against mine, light as a butterfly's wings.

'I never believed she took her own life,' Lina whispered. 'She had given me glimpses of her story. She wasn't someone who would leave like that. There was a force in her—perhaps you, her family, or her art. And so, out of rage or grief, I wrote another article.' She paused, glancing toward the shelf behind me, as if the words might betray her.

'The magazine is my father's. The man you met was my elder brother. I knew they wouldn't let me publish it, so I did it quietly. The punishment was severe. My father clipped my wings, and my only job now is to deliver messages like a clerk.'

'And the article?' I asked.

'I wrote that it was impossible for her to have given up. That the art world had worshipped her one day and discarded her the next. That there was no real investigation. I used the *word*.'

She lowered her voice until it was almost air.

'Murder,' I say.

The word settled in the room like dust, refusing to move. I was right all along, I tell myself.

'The next day, my father received a call. Anonymous. A warning. Forgive me, but he did not care for Ira's life—he cared for money. A sum was demanded. They paid him three times more. In return, both stories were erased. The magazine went dark for weeks. It was as though Ira Lall had never lived—let alone died.'

Her eyes trembled, full of guilt that longs for release.

'Do you know who they were?' I asked.

'I traced the calls,' she said softly. 'They came from borrowed numbers—a grocery store, a flower shop. No cameras. But I heard the recordings.' Lina looks at me. 'There were two men. One spoke perfect Italian. The other had an accent—Asian, strong. He mostly used English. Indian, perhaps. Like Ira.'

Chapter 17

My phone rings, cutting through the hush of the library. A call from India. I let it buzz, then silence it.

I hug Lina goodbye and watch her disappear through the door.

It is Fiza. She sounds almost delighted when I tell her I am Ira's daughter, Marigold. She knows me. She knows nearly everything about me. The knowledge sits oddly inside me—that this woman, a stranger living continents away, could know my mother more intimately than I ever did.

The thought stings, like lemon on a paper cut.

Then I ask her directly.

There is a pause, long enough for me to imagine her lips tightening, the way someone does when disappointment presses at the edges of their composure.

'Yes,' she says at last. 'I bequeathed your grandmother's wealth and properties. There were others too—perhaps the article you read didn't mention them. But everything has gone into the kind of work your grandmother would have wanted. Marigold, I was born on the streets. I would have died there, too, if not for your grandparents. How could I do such a thing to Mandira Mam's daughter—and for what? A house?'

Her voice trembles, 'I was raised by your grandmother. A woman who lived only for children like me. How could I betray her?' Fiza is bordering on anger and pain.

'Then why,' I ask quietly, 'did you insist she keep your visit in September private? Why did you ask her to delete your email?'

'Mari,' she says, her voice steadier now, 'if you've come this far, you must have read your mother's letters. And you know there were many rooms to her life.'

I listen as she explains how she tried to keep the project quiet. But my mother was not only an artist—she was also a mystery. Rumours swarmed around her name. Every day brought hundreds of messages—curators, galleries, artists—all pleading to be attached to *the great Indian-Italian artist's* launch. She had told her assistants to ignore them.

Then one day, a peculiar email arrived in her inbox: *Ira grew up before my eyes.*

No name, no identity—just one line.

'At first,' Fiza says, 'I dismissed it as a trick. People invent all sorts of things to win attention. But then he began to reveal details—details so small, so intimate, they could only have belonged to someone close to her. He knew the exact corner of the house where she painted. He spoke of her afternoons with her twin sister, Aarya, before she died. Things not even in the letters.'

My chest tightens. 'Who was he?'

She says the name, but it tastes loathsome even in her mouth. 'Lalit…'

'When I met him, he already knew,' she whispers. 'He knew the heart of Ira's grief was him. He wanted me to cut that part out of the book. When I refused, he reminded me he was a lawyer, well-entwined with politicians and publishers here in India. He even spoke of the decision he had made years ago—the one that gave me this life.'

She pauses. 'I told him I would do as he said. But he knew I was lying. So I asked someone to watch him for me. On the morning of the seventeenth of September, I learned he was planning to go to Rome, under the pretext of a conference. He even reached out to Ira's curator, pretending to be a buyer. He had already purchased some of her works online. That same day, I booked my ticket and wrote to your mother.'

'You wanted to warn her,' I say. 'Why not just say it in the email?'

'Because he frightened me,' she confesses. 'And I knew Ira's state of mind. She was fragile. It wouldn't take much to break her. I thought… maybe my fear was justified.'

'What did you tell her?'

'I begged her not to see him. To leave Rome for a few days, to hide if possible.'

'And she didn't agree?'

Silence. Then, 'She said she was tired of running away.'

I swallow hard. 'Do you think he could have…?'

Her voice falls to a whisper, 'He had done terrible things before.'

'The man who paid the magazines to bury the story of my mother's death… he was Indian, I am told,' I say.

'And you're certain it was him?'

'There's no one else.'

'I'm sorry,' Fiza says. 'I should have looked deeper before.'

'You didn't,' I reply, 'because you believed it too, that my mother killed herself.'

'Marigold… your mother was depressed. And she wasn't taking her psychiatrist seriously. The only one she confided in was her friend Sonam, or Solo, who doubled as her therapist.'

I let her words hang between us.

Then she adds, 'Give me a day. Let me reach out to the authorities. In the meantime… ask around. Find out who visited your mother that day. Someone will surface.'

'That day,' I say, my voice tightening, 'I was home with her. She had started painting again after months. I stayed beside her in the drawing room. At some point, I must have dozed off—that's why I didn't see him enter.'

'And there was no one else other than you at home with Ira?' Fiza asks.

'Dad was,' I say slowly. 'But when I woke, he was gone too. He said he had somewhere important to be. He only came back after I called him… after I found her.'

Chapter 18

Wednesday morning, I take the train to Pisa. A bouquet of lotuses presses against my chest, their damp stems staining the paper with little green freckles. Merry beginnings, I tell myself, though the words feel borrowed.

The houses near the station stand in soft pastel shades—ochre, faded pink, sunflower yellow—each with iron balconies where laundry flutters like resigned flags. Cypress trees lean over tiled rooftops, their shadows stretching across cobblestoned alleys. When I reach the address scribbled in my notebook, I pause before the entrance: a tall wooden door is arched in stone, its paint cracked in delicate lines, like veins on an old hand. A wrought-iron knocker shaped like a lion's head glimmers faintly under the morning sun.

I knock.

A woman answers, her voice hushed as though the neighbours might be listening. Her hair is tied back in a loose bun. A faded apron is knotted around her waist, flour dusting her fingers as if I have interrupted her mid-preparation of bread. The corners of her eyes pull tight, not from suspicion exactly, but from years of worry.

'She doesn't live here anymore,' she says, almost muttering into her chest.

'Yes… yes, I know. I only… I cannot imagine what she must have suffered. I am so sorry for your loss,' I manage, my throat dry.

Her eyes flick to the lotus stems poking out of my tote bag.

'I brought these… for my Donna.'

The sound of her name unfurls every memory at once. I clear my throat, but the heaviness has already settled. My words break against sobs.

'She was the only friend I had… growing up. I really loved her.' My palm covers my mouth.

The woman's body shifts, a hesitation before kindness. She presses her lips together, then finally asks, 'Do you want to come in for tea?'

Inside, the air smells faintly of lemon polish and old wool. A wide lobby opens up, its ceiling frescoed with pale patterns, glass chandeliers dangling like frozen drops of light. Persian rugs soften the stone floor. The house seems too ornate, too assured of its place in the world. I can't imagine Donna—wild, searching Donna—belonging to it.

She seats me on a velvet sofa the colour of wine. A porcelain tray arrives with steaming cups and a plate of amaretti biscuits, their sugared tops catching the light.

'My husband, Donna's brother, is in the garage. He… does not like visitors. Especially those who come for her.'

'Why?'

She folds her hands tightly. 'Don't get him wrong. He loved her more than anything, more than his own children. He raised her himself after their mother abandoned them for a lover. Not everyone is cut out to be a mother. Anyway, he is the kindest man I know, but life hardened him. Abandonment does that.'

She pauses, as if weighing her words. 'Donna was not even his real sister. But he loved her as though she were. Until… until she walked out on us…with her lover.'

Her voice softens to a whisper, 'An apple does not fall far from the tree, my husband says, whenever grief circles back. I only wish this family could have been whole once more. Donna had so much love within her.'

She excuses herself, and the clinking of a drawer opening echoes faintly down the corridor. When she returns, a pen twirls nervously between her fingers. She slips a folded paper into my palm, the gesture half secret, half surrender.

'I can only tell you so much. But… please go to this place.' Her smile is thin, trembled by fear.

On the train back, I unfold the paper. The handwriting staggers across the page, slanting, uneven. I trace the words twice before they strike me fully. My face drains of colour.

The man sitting beside me, dark-skinned with rough hands smelling of engine grease, leans closer. His shirt is loose, collar frayed, as if it has known many summers.

'You alright, sister? Bad news in there?' he asks, passing me his bottle of water.

I nod. 'I'm fine. Thank you.'

He disappears into the crowd when we reach the next stop. I look down once more at the note in my trembling hand.

Three words.

Galleria Marigold, Florence.

Chapter 19

Dad's face softens when I tell him I want to visit Mom's gallery in Florence.

'Ira will like that,' he says, his voice carrying both pride and ache. He really did love my mother—and the awareness tightens something in my chest.

The drive to Florence is quiet, the late summer sun shimmering on the olive groves and terracotta rooftops that whir past the window. The road winds through the Tuscan hills, sun spilling across vineyards, air full of wild thyme and warm stone. Dad hums under his breath sometimes—an old tune I half-recognise from my childhood—until I break the silence.

'Did you know Mom wanted her biography written?'

He blinks, surprised. 'No... but it sounds like her.' His smile is small, wistful. 'She was made up of contradictions. Always wanted to be invisible and yet be remembered beyond her time.'

'Was there anyone who visited her that day? September 24th?'

He glances at me briefly, then back to the road. 'No one I can think of, Mari. Why?'

I shrug. 'Just wondering.'

I wait before I say, 'And Donna? Why did she leave a day before that day?'

A shadow passes over his face. 'They had a disagreement. It happens. Your mother loved her, but they drifted apart. It was... unfortunate.' His voice gentles, 'Things would have been different if she had stayed. But she wasn't there.'

He pauses, then mutters under his breath, 'So…it was only the three of us.'

'You went out in the evening, though, didn't you?'

His fingers tighten on the wheel for a second. 'I… did. I had to see a…client,' he says it quickly, as one spills a difficult lie.

I frown. 'But you never left her alone when she—'

His eyes flick to me—warm, almost pleading. 'I wish I hadn't that night. She was upset about that sketch going missing. I should've stayed. But sometimes, Mari…' He sighs. 'Sometimes things pull us away, even when we don't want them to.'

He reaches over, briefly squeezing my hand. 'I had my reasons. Do you believe me?'

I hesitate. 'What if someone poisoned her?'

The car jolts, as if my words have thrown us into a pothole. He grips the wheel tighter, his knuckles pale. 'Mari. Your mother overdosed. On her own. That's the truth. The only truth.'

He looks at me then, as though trying to force the words into me. 'Do you understand?'

I nod faintly. His words sound like a lesson repeated too many times—a story taught rather than believed.

I shake my head faintly, the way I used to when he asked me to thank Santa for the presents under my pillow on Christmas mornings, the way I used to when Dad told me Mom was really going to the art centre, when I was told Mom was fine.

I turn back to the vineyards slipping by the window. Blurry fragments of truth, passing too fast for me to catch.

Mom's gallery is bare as an abandoned theatre. The high white walls rise like cliffs around me, stripped of her spirit, emptied of her light. All her paintings have been sold, leaving only pale outlines on the walls where canvases once leaned. Marble floors echo our footsteps; in the corners, dust collects in neat shadows.

It is a pity—no, a tragedy—that she painted more than nine hundred works in her life, and I have only one with me. It feels like my mother gave herself to the world in fragments, brushstroke by brushstroke, never keeping enough of herself whole for any one of us.

As evening falls, we wait outside the gallery for the car. The cobbled street smells of leather from a nearby workshop, of pizza dough crisping in stone ovens. Students lounge on the steps, sketchbooks sprawled across their knees, pencils tapping like tiny metronomes.

My eyes fall on a hoarding across the road—*Florence College of Art and History.*

A thought stirs.

I tell Dad I want to visit there to discuss our initiative.

Chapter 20

The floor tiles are cool and mottled, their patterns worn by decades of footsteps. A heavy oak desk stands at the centre, behind which a receptionist in horn-rimmed glasses arranges files with meticulous care. She looks up as I approach.

'You used to have a student by the name of Donna,' I say carefully. 'Donna Rossi. I'm from her family.'

Her eyes brighten. 'Donna, yes. Should I call her for you?'

'Ah… no. I think you are mistaken. She studied here ten years ago.'

The woman smiles faintly, smoothing a sheet of paper with her palm. 'Yes, yes. She did. But she restarted her course last year. Such an inspiration to all of us. Do you want to see her?'

The floor seems to tilt beneath me, like a dream where the ground melts away. Not knowing what is fiction and what is not.

'Yes,' I whisper.

'Your name?'

'Marigold Lall Sagg.'

She dials a number, murmurs into the receiver, then presses her lips into a tight line.

'I'm afraid…Donna doesn't want to see you.'

My hands tremble, the air in the room suddenly too thin. I pull out my phone and scroll to a photograph—me and Donna, arms around each other, smiling in a field of marigolds. I hold it out to the woman.

'This Donna?'

She nods once. 'Yes. But she doesn't want to meet you. I'm afraid you'll have to leave now.'

On our way back, I hide my face behind sunglasses and weep quietly, the city rolling by outside the window in a golden blur—bridges arching over the Arno, lovers with gelato strolling under chestnut trees, vespas weaving through traffic like darting fish.

Dad doesn't ask.

Chapter 21

'Donna is alive. Do you hear me? She didn't kill herself as we believed.' I break down on Solo's shoulder, sobbing like a child. 'And she refused to see me.'

Solo doesn't seem surprised. Her hand moves slowly up and down my back, the way one calms a restless bird.

'Marigold,' Solo's voice is low, steady, 'your mother had layers about her. Always exploring, always mysterious. There are parts of her life that not even Aarya, nor Fiza, nor your father knew. Certain things were never meant to make it into her biography.'

'Will you tell me?' My voice trembles.

'Of course. She wouldn't mind that, I know.' Solo lifts my hand and presses her lips against it. A gesture both tender and heavy with memory.

'Donna was captivated by Ira—not only by her paintings but by Ira herself. So much so that she left her college, left her family in Pisa, and came here to stay with her. Her love wasn't an obsession; it was passion, the kind that makes a person glow. I saw it in her eyes the first time we met. And I also saw how much she nourished your mother's soul. Ira painted differently after Donna came. Brighter, freer, more alive.'

She sighs, her eyes glistening. 'I suppose I was selfish. I never warned your parents about what was in Donna's heart. I thought—she's harmless, like a lamb. I thought nothing dangerous could come of it.'

The air in the room thickens, as though even the curtains want to listen. 'But Ira...' Solo goes on, '...was always on a search for herself. Her mind, her body, even her desires. When your father left for India for his mother's funeral, I went too, for a week. I remember his mother's kindness—she stitched me my very first gown.'

Solo pauses. Her voice softens to a near whisper, 'When I returned, Ira was worse than ever. She had found another reason to punish herself. For a week, Ira and Donna had…'

'Oh God, no.' My stomach tightens until it feels hollow. I think I might collapse in on myself.

Solo pauses for a while before speaking again, 'Of course, Ira ended it. She told Donna to leave. But anyone who loved your mother would know how impossible she was to abandon. Ira existed beyond the limits of this world, and being near her unfastened people from themselves. Donna stayed, even though each day without Ira's attention hollowed a part of her. Death is the kindest way to be abandoned, they say. Then eventually… Ira asked her again. And that time, Donna left for good.'

Solo's eyes turn upward to the ceiling, as if she is seeking permission from someone above. Tears well at the corners. 'Perhaps it was her little way of punishing Ira, I thought.'

I am barely breathing. The room sways like a ship at sea.

'That's why,' Solo continues, 'I was so startled to see that sketch in your bag, the first day you came to me. I was certain Donna had taken it. And when I saw it with you, I thought maybe it hadn't been stolen at all—maybe it was simply lost.'

'The note…' I whisper, '…the note was not from Lorenzo. It was Donna. Her handwriting. Her casket. It all makes sense now—Hadrian, Antinous, the hairbrushes— the ordinary objects that held remnants of my mother.'

'What?' Solo blinks in confusion.

'I'll come back, Aunt Solo,' I say, standing abruptly. My voice is shaking but firm.

'There's somewhere I need to go.'

She catches me lightly by the elbow, 'Take care, Mari. And—how is your boyfriend?'

I try to smile. The image of Gaius and his wife and children cross my mind. I breathe and let the thought pass.

'Haven't seen him in a while.'

At home, I take the pills Solo's friend gave me, wondering which parts of me will still be awake.

Chapter 22

It is true. Gaius hasn't stopped by the library for days now, and the silence of his absence has begun to consume me.

On my table, beneath the weak yellow pool of the lamp, I write down two names:

Lorenzo.

Lalit.

The letters look stark on the page, like two shadows staring back.

The two men know each other. Fiza had told me that Lalit acquired some of Mom's artworks through Lorenzo. The two might have seen Mom on September 24. Both are powerful, both threaded into networks of influence. And one of them—one—had called the magazine office, forcing them to erase the article, to silence the investigation into her death.

I dial Lorenzo. He picks up on the first ring.

I don't have the patience for games. 'Were you behind halting the investigation into Mom's death? Did you call the magazine owner?'

A pause. Then his voice, calm, low, 'And what exactly would you achieve by asking me this?'

'Tell me.'

'No, Mari,' his reply is clipped, almost too neat. 'Where are you right now? Are you still in the library?'

'I have to go,' I disconnect.

But the unease remains, sharper now. Lorenzo's words have been evasive, stripped of their usual charm. He is never direct, never this curt. The lie pulses between his sentences like static.

At night, sleep stays away.

That night, when the house has fallen into its hush and sleep keeps its usual distance from me, I wander into the studio.

The mural rises before me—Caesar and Cleopatra, their first meeting.

Cleopatra seems to breathe out of the folds of crimson, her body neither wholly painted nor wholly withheld, as if the brush had conspired to reveal and conceal her at once. The curve of her shoulder shimmers into being, then dissolves into shadow; her mouth hovers unfinished, a promise abandoned mid-syllable. She is beauty not in completion but in suggestion, in the ache of what is left unsaid.

The carpet that bears her could have been an offering—or a burial cloth. And across from her, Julius Caesar stands like a rumour, scarcely shaped, a presence heavy with power yet obscured by darkness.

But it is not them I watch. It is the space between—the charged silence, the invisible current strung taut between arrival and recognition. In that unpainted distance, I feel history coil, alive with seduction and betrayal.

And then, impossibly, I feel Cleopatra's gaze slide toward me. Though no eyes have been given to her, something in the restless brushstrokes finds me out. I can almost hear her whisper, velvet and venomous:

Do you see what desire can cost?

Do you see how love becomes ruin?

My phone rings.

Fiza.

'Marigold—Lalit never came to Italy in September. He was in Goa with his wife. We've confirmed everything.'

Her words float somewhere behind me. I remain before the mural, watching Cleopatra lean forever forward, half-born from her folds of red, her allure shimmering like both a prophecy and a threat.

Lalit was never here.

But Lorenzo was.

And he knows of the library.

No one knows—except Solo.

Chapter 23

Sherry is half-slouched behind the reception desk, scrolling through Instagram reels with the sound barely audible—tinny laughter, clapping hands, a beat of some trending song. The desk itself looks like it has grown weary of its purpose: papers stacked in uneven piles, half-bent pens in a chipped mug, a faint ring of coffee staining the wood. The flicker of her phone lights her face with a blue glow.

I slip behind her chair and touch her shoulder. She jumps so violently that the phone nearly slips from her hands.

'Oh lord! You scared me, Marigold. Easy, alright.'

I don't wait. 'What happened between Lorenzo and Mom on the day she died?'

Her thumb hovers above the phone before she places it face down on the desk, though the reel keeps running, voices spilling like ghosts.

'I told you—they never met that day,' she says, almost confidently.

'Did he tell you to lie? I saw you at Caffè Doria with him the other day. Don't pretend. Something's going on between the two of you.'

Sherry lets out a long breath, eyes darting around the empty foyer, then curls her fingers around mine across the desk. Her skin is clammy.

'It's been a while…' she begins, then straightens her back as if choosing to confess in full.

'We're seeing each other.'

'You and Lorenzo?'

'Yes.'

'Does Matteo know?'

Her expression twists into something between defiance and guilt. 'He'd never approve. He's always hated Lorenzo, blamed him for Ira's breakdowns. But that isn't true. If anyone was worn down by Ira's moods, it was my Loren. I've watched him drink himself to sleep after gallery owners threatened him with warnings. Ira was the only artist he ever curated. He felt he owed her everything. No matter what people think of him—my father included—he really cared for Ira. And you.'

Her tone softens, almost wistful, 'I used to be jealous of how much space she took up in his mind. But eventually he let me in. He had a life outside of her, outside of work. Most of his visits here, in those last months, weren't for Ira at all. They were for me. And yes—I erased his visits from the records.'

I search her face. 'So they really didn't meet that day?'

'No. That day… Lorenzo wanted to take me out. He was excited about the show. We drove to Florence to meet his mother and came back the next morning, but by then—' she falters, 'the news of Ira's suicide was already everywhere. Poor him, he had to pay so much to make the whispers stop.'

My breath catches. 'What?'

Her hand flies to her mouth. 'I shouldn't have said that. Forget it. Please, Marigold… for Lorenzo.'

I pull my hand back. 'I suppose it's time to speak to the two of you together.'

Sherry rolls her eyes and checks her watch. 'He'll be here in half an hour.'

~

Lorenzo sits across from me, composed as ever. A picture of ease in his white shirt and jeans, as if nothing in the world can ruffle him. His voice is measured, almost gentle. 'You know,' he says, 'if it had been anyone else in my place, they might have welcomed a scandal on the eve of an exhibition. Artists who carry chaos in their wake—tragedy, controversy, broken lives—often sell more. The market loves a spectacle. Pain makes for a compelling story, and stories move art faster than merit ever does.' He pauses. 'But my relationship with your mother was never merely that of a curator and an artist. She was… family to me. I cared for her. I care for you, too, for your future. And family is not something one feasts on by turning their grief into spectacle.'

He leans back, unhurried, his eyes steady on mine. 'Yes, I was the one who paid off that magazine. The editor wanted to make money by tearing open her last hours for the world to consume. I couldn't let that be her memory. I wanted her to be remembered for what she gave—her vision, her brilliance—not the way she left this world.'

I keep my voice sharp, 'And were you alone in doing this?'

'Yes,' his reply comes quickly, as though the truth requires no hesitation. 'And I don't think you need to dwell on this any longer, Marigold. Your library is suffering without you. Why don't you go there regularly anymore?'

A chill runs through me, 'How do you know I work in a library?'

His smile is faint, knowing. 'I've seen you there. Twice, maybe more. I'm often at the café nearby—you must have seen me. I asked around. They said you run it all by yourself. I am proud of you, Marigold.'

Chapter 24

My brain is a maze, but not the kind built of stone. It is a shifting labyrinth of mirrors, each reflection opening into another, until I can no longer tell what is mine and what belongs to someone else. I float above myself like driftwood on the surface of an ocean, knowing that beneath me thousands of stories swim and circle—some mine, some not—but all unreachable, glimmering just out of grasp.

I don't remember when sleep claimed me, or if it ever did. When I stir in the morning, I find myself still before the mural. The first light of the sun spills across the wall, catching Cleopatra's painted face in its ascent. Half her features glow golden—alive, sensuous, defiant—while the other half drowns in shadow, like a secret withheld.

For a moment, she seems to breathe.

I touch the corner where Mom signed her name, my fingers trembling as though I could summon her through the pigment.

'Help me, Mama,' I whisper, my voice breaking.

Later, at the library, Gaius is already waiting for me. His face looks paler than ever. He confesses the seizures are growing worse, that the epilepsy is swallowing more and more of him each day. Shame burns in me—I had doubted him, and in doing so, betrayed the only person who stood beside me without question.

'Let's think again. What happened that evening, as you remember it?' His voice is steady, almost professorial—determined to guide me back through the shadows of memory.

I close my eyes, forcing myself into the old rooms of my memory. 'I was with Mom in the drawing room. I had my book open on my lap, and Dad was shut in his study with his papers. At some point, I must have drifted off on the sofa. When I woke, Dad was gone. I asked Mom if she wanted tea. She looked… unwell. Exhausted. Her face was swollen, her eyes red, as if she had been crying for hours.'

The words cling to my throat, 'I went to the kitchen, hoping the tea would soothe her, like it always did when Donna made it for her. I wanted to do better than Donna at helping her, now that she was gone. But instead…' The image of her lifeless body rises, smothering me. The words die in my throat.

Gaius leans forward; his tone is gentler now, 'What about the painting? Perhaps there's a clue there. Your mother often spoke through her work. There was always a hidden narrative, woven quietly into her strokes.'

'Yes… yes.' The thought ignites a spark in me, until suddenly something pricks.

'But—Gaius, how do you know she was painting that evening?'

He smiles, looking away as if amused by a child's question. 'Don't be silly, Mari. You told me. Yes, you did. Remember?'

His eyes fix back on mine, unblinking, pulling me under. I feel the floor tilt.

'Yes,' I whisper, more to myself, like learning a rhyme, even though I can't remember telling him. 'Yes, I did,' I say, nevertheless.

He nods, satisfied. 'Now, your father. You said he went somewhere. Where did he go?' he asks.

'To a client's office.'

'You said he never left her side. Then why did he go when she was in a state like you said… What if—'

The thought is too heavy, too dangerous to say aloud. I look away.

'The drugs don't devour you all at once,' he says quietly. 'They take their time—slow, steady, patient. After Donna left, it was only him… he was the one meant to place those pills in her hand.'

'No. No, Gaius. Don't,' my voice cracks, as if denying him could keep the possibility from becoming real.

'The driver,' he says. 'We can ask him. Perhaps he knows where your father went that night.'

I run down my memory. 'The old driver had already left. The one we had that day was new—he'd joined only two days before. He was with us for barely three nights. I don't even have his number.'

'Then Lorenzo,' Gaius suggests smoothly. 'He might know. After all, wasn't it Lorenzo who found the driver for your family?'

My heart hammers, but I nod anyway. How does Gaius know all this? I only met him months after Mom died. His words wrap around me like smoke—seeping into my lungs, clouding my reason.

Maybe I had told him, I convince myself. I want to believe him.

'Yes. Lorenzo would know,' I say, certain Lorenzo will help.

When I call the driver, he doesn't hesitate.

'Hello.'

'I'm Mari. Marigold Lall Sagg.'

'Marigold! How are you? And how is Nihal? I pray to the Lord for your family's strength every day,' he says.

'Can I ask you something?'

'Of course, love. Anything.'

'Where did you take Dad on that day?'

'Which day?'

'The day Mom died.'

Silence stretches. Then a small sigh, heavy as if memory itself hurts him. 'What happened, love?'

'I'm writing a book on my mother's life. I need to document everything, and Dad is travelling. He asked me to ask you.'

'Ah… sì…' he murmurs. 'I don't recall the name exactly. But it was a new Indian restaurant. Just opened.'

'You remember it clearly?'

'I do. Because your father came running out when he heard the news. Told me to stay and pay the bill. He took the car himself.'

'Was someone with him?'

'Yes. A woman. Beautiful… bellissima.'

My breath stops. 'Was she Italian?'

'I cannot be certain. Could be Indian like you. But her Italian…' his voice softens, almost admiring, '…smooth, elegant. Like someone raised on Dante.'

'Anything else about that night?' I ask.

He clears his throat, 'When I went to pay, they told me it was already done. Paid in advance.'

'Paid? By who?'

'Why would I ask? All I know is—flowers, champagne, a dinner for two. Somconc arranged it all.'

Gaius and I lock eyes. I thank him and disconnect.

'It sounded like a date,' Gaius says, 'far from being a client meeting.'

I want silence. I want Gaius not to speak any further. 'Marigold, do you remember the last words of Julius Caesar? Your mother had them written in one of her paintings that were displayed in Rome at her exhibition the next day.'

'How do you know so much about my mom and her art? We hadn't even met until then.'

My voice comes out sharp.

'Mari… what were the words?'

'Et tu, Brute,' I whisper.

'You too, Brutus,' Gaius repeats, his voice raw, carrying pain that cuts through me. 'It's the closest friends whose betrayal hurts the most.'

'No…' I tell him. 'No.'

My strength leaves me. I sit down.

Inside, a scream rumbles.

CHAPTER 25

'Aunt Solo, do you have anything to eat? I'm hungry.' Solo is kneeling on the rug, aligning its edges with exact symmetry, as though one crooked corner might unravel her entire world.

'I'm fasting today, but let me fix you a meal. A sandwich?' She asks.

'Yes. No tofu or lettuce.'

She rises and dusts her hands on her hips. Then looks back at me. 'And Mari. I spoke to the doctor the other day. He said you are very irregular with your visits.'

'I was occupied in my writing group.'

Her smile lingers too long, trained, professional. 'Writing is therapy too. Nihal told me about your novel. The first fiction I'll ever read. I promise.'

'It won't be fiction,' I say.

Solo sighs. 'Alright then. It will take a little while. My kitchen is on leave today… Why don't you just—'

'I'm around a bookshelf. Don't worry about me.'

Once she disappears, I check her drawers, her shelves, but find only this year's diaries. On the corner-most shelf, arranged in neat, perfect rows, are old newspapers, magazines, and more diaries. I begin to go through them one by one.

On one of the magazines, my hands stop. On the cover is Dad's picture—the same issue I had once seen him reading.

I stare at it for a long time. It feels strange to imagine him preserved here, with Solo.

'Five more minutes!' shrieked Solo from the other side of the wall, her voice crisp, precise, like she is timing a patient's exercise. She reminds me I am still on my forage.

I finally locate the diary for 2017. Each page is divided neatly into three sections: clinical appointments, notes, and personal engagements. I leaf through gently, careful not to disturb the perfect order, until I reach 24 September 2017.

The appointment section is blank.

The notes section is blank, too.

My fingers tremble slightly as I turn toward the end of the diary—and there it is, something I had not remotely expected.

7:30 p.m.—Taj Mahal restaurant.

The words seem to zoom and take shape before my eyes, circling around me like a storm I cannot escape.

Sonam—the beautiful woman at the Taj Mahal that evening—was there with Dad, drinking champagne, laughing perhaps, while my mother lay lifeless, like her unfinished canvas, on the rug in her drawing room.

It all falls into place, painfully obvious, and I feel like a fool for not seeing it sooner.

Solo had always said my father could kill for the people he truly loved. And wasn't Sonam the girl he had adored when he was young? Wasn't this the truth Mom had lived through in all her inscriptions?

I had been seeing Mom's story only through Solo's carefully filtered eyes—perhaps that is why something so glaring eluded me until now.

He left his wife, in that fragile state, a day before her exhibition, to meet his decades-old lover. He poisoned my mother with her own medicines while I slept, and then silently left so no one would doubt him. And then he convinced Lorenzo to stop the media from speculating about Mom's murder.

When Solo comes out of the kitchen, I am like a pair of socks on the floor. Teardrops spill like blood from rage and pain. She offers the plate. I shove it away. The plate shatters on the floor. The sandwich smears the walls before spreading across the room.

I must have passed out, because when I come to my senses, I am in my bed.

Dad and Solo are in the room.

He sits at the edge near my feet like a sentinel guarding broken ground. Solo perches on the couch, her knees pressed together, as though trying to hold her silence from spilling.

'You killed my mother,' My voice cracks like an eggshell dropped on stone.

The two exchange a knowing look before Solo begins, 'On the morning of September 24, Ira called me from the rehab. She sounded ecstatic. She said she had made a decision. She wanted to meet me at the Taj Mahal restaurant at 7:30 in the evening and tell me everything that was on her mind. I went. But instead of her, I found Nihal.'

She glances at Dad. 'She had also sent your father there, under the pretext of meeting a curator from France. She told him she didn't want to work with Lorenzo anymore.'

I close my eyes. A tear slides down, tracing its way to my ear like a river trying to carve an escape.

'We learned she had planned it all. She had booked the dinner, champagne, and flowers. There was a note.'

I hear the paper rustle.

'You both have been very kind to me all my life, but I am not worth any of it. I'm returning to you what I wrongfully took years ago. Please accept it.' Solo holds the note out. I turn my face away.

Dad hands me a stack of papers, 'These are the autopsy reports. Your mother died of an overdose. We didn't want to make it a spectacle. We wanted to protect her name. Her memory. That's what she would have wanted.'

'I want to sleep,' I say, and close my eyes.

~

When Dad leaves to drop Solo home, I make tea and let it cool untouched on the table. Hunger claws at my stomach, but the thought of food feels like swallowing stones. The evening bleeds into a cavernous night.

I crawl into the studio—my refuge, my one place of nourishment and comfort.

The room has cradled me like a mother holding a fevered child.

I fill my lungs with the earthy scent of old books and memories of my mother.

I close my eyes and feel the hair on my neck rise. A breath, warm as confession, grazes my ear.

I feel a presence.

Then a touch, certain, intimate.

His touch.

'Gaius…' I whisper, 'You are here.'

'Your father left the door open,' he says, gathering me into his arms. 'I saw him go out with your Aunt.'

I nod, still blind. It feels safer that way—as though our belonging exists beyond our years, beyond the frail architecture of moral boundaries.

'I don't believe what they say,' he murmurs, folding me into himself. 'May I see it—the artwork? The last painting Ira touched?'

A thought flickers again—then vanishes.

Perhaps I had told him. I pull out the easel. The hinges cry out, as if warning us. 'It's unfinished,' I say.

We stand before it in silence. Our fingers move together, following the raised veins of paint: marigolds in bloom, a rope threading through them, coiled and hesitant, like a snake unsure of its own hunger.

'What does it say to you?' he asks.

'That some truths arrive broken,' I say. 'And some never arrive at all.'

Midnight gathers us.

Sleep slips in quietly, like forgiveness.

Beside his warmth.

Under the watching mural.

For the first time in days, I am unafraid.

'Marigold.'

'Mmm?'

'Come to Paris with me.'

I don't open my eyes.

'I would follow you anywhere.'

Chapter 26

The city looks nothing like the postcards. They are too loud, too eager. They never capture the quiet—the way it arrives early, before the cafés open, before the day decides what it will demand. Mornings smell of fresh bread and rain-darkened stone. By evening, the Seine pales into silver, smooth and reflective, as though the city has laid its thoughts gently upon the water.

Somewhere in my mind drifts a line from Anna Karenina—about happiness being ordinary, and unhappiness insisting on its own shape. Paris seems built around that idea. It makes no effort to rescue you from yourself. It simply allows you to exist, fully, in whatever state you have arrived.

We live above a bookshop in the Latin Quarter, in a narrow two-room apartment that creaks softly when we move, as if aware of us. When the bells of Saint-Séverin ring, the windows shiver, and for a moment everything feels suspended. At night, the streets below fill with low voices—measured, intimate, unfinished. It sounds like a language meant not to be understood, only overheard, the way one overhears a truth not meant for them.

I have to admit—I am one of the fortunate few who are paid to do what they love. I am paid to read. My inbox is an orchard heavy with requests from debut authors, their messages polite but trembling with hope: *Will you read my book, will you speak of it to the world in your next video?*

I write reviews of bestsellers for journals. It pays enough for rent, for three simple meals, for the quiet dignity of living by words. I also publish my own theories on the classics, shaped during my hours in the library. The library, which I later discovered was Lorenzo's, was offered to me as charity disguised as kindness. For months, I believed I was guarding a secret. In reality, they had known all along. I was the secret. And I was the joke.

This afternoon, I am reading my book, again—the one that still holds my father's breath from his boyhood, *Anna Karenina*—when the bell rings. Visitors are rare in my apartment; apart from the photographer who comes once a week to stage corners of my life for Instagram, no one really knocks on my door.

'How are you doing, Marigold?' Solo looks glossy, like the crown of trees that catch the first light and keep it for themselves.

We sit together on the balcony, facing the narrow street below, where a thin run of water splits the stones like a ribbon of glass. The flower market is already alive, spilling colour into the air—marigolds, roses, tulips—crowded into metal buckets that catch the sun. Vendors call out softly, their voices threading through the ring of bicycle bells.

I tell her about my work—about the books, the reviews, the conversations I record with strangers who become, briefly, my companions. I watch amazement flicker in her eyes, like a match catching flame.

'Do you still talk to Gaius?' Solo asks, her voice careful, as if testing the strength of thin ice.

'We are married.' I watch the colour drain from her face, the way twilight bleeds the sky pale.

'We have a little boy now,' I add, softer, almost tender.

Her lips tremble. 'Can I meet him?' The words break into tears before they fully leave her.

Heat rushes to my cheeks, a furnace I can't control. Why can't she ever leave me with the small world I build for myself?

I look away. 'I'm afraid… he is—'

'Fictional.' Solo snaps.

My heart hammers. Her words reach me like shards of glass—cutting skin, sinking deeper, slicing places no one can see. '…and so is your Gaius, Marigold. He always was a fiction.'

'No!'

'You made him up, Marigold. Gaius is only a story you kept whispering to yourself. A tale you painted into flesh, stolen from your mother's canvases—that mural in her studio.'

'No,' I say, slowly, unwilling to listen to myself.

Solo's eyes cut through me. 'Tell me this,' she says quietly. 'How does every detail of him mirror Julius Caesar in that painting? How do your gestures together echo Caesar and Cleopatra—again and again?'

She doesn't wait for me to answer.

'His age. His authority. His ailments. His clothing. Even his name—*Gaius*. *Gaius* Julius Caesar.'

Her voice lowers, 'Tell me, Marigold—does your Gaius suffer from epilepsy?'

A pause. Then, softer still.

'Why does he never take your calls? Why do people stare when you speak to him in public? Why does no one ever speak *to* him?'

Her voice is relentless, a chisel striking stone, 'You created him so you wouldn't have to look at the truth you keep caging inside your head. And that truth, which you already know, is worse than this misery.'

Her words burn through me like wildfire—unstoppable, devouring, leaving behind only ash.

She does not stop.

'That evening—September 24—you know what happened. You made your mother some tea. You wanted to soothe her. To help her. And you had only ever known one way to do that. You did what you had always seen Donna do.'

I shake my head.

'You mixed the pills into her tea. Thinking it was mercy. Thinking it was love.'

Solo looks at me the way one looks at an animal still breathing but already slaughtered.

'Only…you didn't know which pill. You didn't know how many.'

'I didn't kill her!' I cry. 'I didn't kill my mother!'

My voice frays, already breaking.

'Pack your bags, Marigold.' Her tone leaves no room for negotiation.

'Enough time has passed. Your father believed handing you Lorenzo's ancestral bookshop would anchor you back in the world.'

She exhales, thin and tired. 'I always knew no one finds light by hiding in the ruins of fiction.'

A pause.

'I'll speak to Matteo. I'll come for you tomorrow.' She meets my eyes.

'No.' The word rises but never leaves me. My voice abandons me when I need it most. I watch her walk to the door. She does not look back.

The room seems to contract after her, as though it has taken her side. The air thickens; even breathing feels like an accusation. I remain where I am, unmoving, as if any motion might confirm what I am not yet ready to accept.

I am left alone, drowning in the unbearable weight of what she has named aloud—a truth that now knows my name, whether I claim it or not.

~

At night, I press my lips to Gaius's forehead—a gesture as weightless as moonlight on still water. I hold him close one last time, careful not to disturb the shape my mind has given him. His warmth lingers against me, persuasive and fading, a small, stubborn ember. Proof that love does not need a body to feel real—and that what we imagine can still learn how to leave us.

I sit at my desk and open my notebook.

It is time to write the final chapter.

The Last Painting

She stared at it like one stares at a child long birthed and long lost. It was Ira's last canvas. The oil gleamed against the easel, heavy with stories she had never dared to claim.

For two decades, she had poured herself into colour—victories and defeats, conquests and rivers, music flowing through generations. All the stories, except her own.

This time, she would paint her truth through the muse she had loved since she was a girl in New Delhi.

Cleopatra.

And her final countdown.

Cleopatra's death has always been a myth and a warning. She chose to die a queen, not a captive paraded through her own empire. The asp hidden in a basket of figs was her crown of thorns.

Ira's canvas stood unfinished. Yet it was complete in what it implied—a prophecy disguised as brushstrokes, a farewell disguised as art.

It was the end of an era. The end of an artist known only for painting history. A story the world would never fully understand, nor forget.

The snake.

The figs.

The marigolds, blooming like small suns, even after everything else was gone.

Perhaps Ira knew. Perhaps this was why she asked her daughter to make her tea. Perhaps this had always been her plan. Ever since she borrowed that book from the only man she knew she would ever love. Ever since she painted the woman with a rose on its cover.

I think of Anna Karenina. They say she chose steel and earth, but I think she chose silence. She stepped out of a world that demanded too much and gave too little.

Ira had no train, no snakes—only her canvas. Her colours were her iron wheels, her venom and her nectar.

Anna's death was a scream of metal. Ira's was the scrape of a brush stilled forever.

Like Cleopatra, Anna refused to live as a captive in her own story.

Ira wore her truth.

And the truth has always been more devastating than the emptiness that comes after.

Ira—the celebrated Indian-origin artist of Rome—died a queen.

The End.

ACKNOWLEDGEMENTS

This book was written in layers—of time, silence, and becoming—and carries more than one life within it.

I am deeply grateful to my husband, Nishant, who has listened to every story I have ever told—the ones that found their way into this novel and the many that did not. Thank you for your patience, for listening and listening again, and for holding space when words needed to be spoken aloud before they could be written down.

To my daughters, for their patience and quiet understanding, for staying with me through my restless, absorbed, sometimes chaotic days—when their mother was lost in writing or painting to decode herself. Thank you for letting me be both present and absent, and for loving me through it all.

To my parents and family, for shaping the woman I am—often without realising it—and for standing beside me through every version of myself, thank you.

I am thankful to my publisher and editor for believing in this book, for seeing possibility when it was still taking shape, and for trusting my voice. Your faith gave this novel its final courage.

To my friends, near and far, who checked in, encouraged, waited, and believed—this book carries traces of your kindness.

And finally, to the reader: thank you for choosing to step into this world. May these pages offer you not answers, but recognition.